PRAISE FOR *AS DEAD AS IT GETS*

"A frenetic and funny debut . . . Kalian milks plenty of stereotypes, but does so with panache and enough originality to be refreshing." —*Publishers Weekly*

"A thrilling whodunit with one of the most likeable heroines in modern history." —Brenda Strong, actress, aka Mary Alice Young of *Desperate Housewives*

"An intriguing whodunit with plenty of humor, mystique, and fascinating characters." —*Romantic Times BOOKreviews* (4 stars)

"I loved it. If a movie is made of it, Ulysses Grant Mars is the role for me." —Larry Hagman, actor, aka J. R. Ewing of *Dallas*

"Kalian crafts a first-rate mystery while convincingly portraying Hollywood and its shallow and neurotic denizens. An auspicious beginning to what is sure to become a popular series." —*Booklist*

"Good stuff. Very engrossing. It captured the Hollywood scene and held my interest throughout." —Henry Winkler, actor

"Plenty of humor, action, and relationship problems makes this debut mystery by a veteran screenwriter a lively, entertaining read." —*Library Journal*

"A fast-pac d me on the edge of my son, actress, exas Ranger

D1115536

Also by Cady Kalian
from Tom Doherty Associates

As Dead As It Gets
*A Few Good Murders**

*Coming August 2007

as dead as it gets

cady kalian

A TOM DOHERTY ASSOCIATES BOOK
NEW YORK

This is a work of fiction. All of the characters, organizations, and events portrayed in this novel are either products of the authors' imagination or are used fictitiously.

AS DEAD AS IT GETS

Copyright © 2006 by Naomi Gurian and Irma Kalish

A Forge Book
Published by Tom Doherty Associates, LLC
175 Fifth Avenue
New York, NY 10010

www.tor-forge.com

Forge® is a registered trademark of Tom Doherty Associates, LLC.

ISBN-13: 978-0-7653-5226-2
ISBN-10: 0-7653-5226-5

First Edition: August 2006
First Mass Market Edition: July 2007

Printed in the United States of America

0 9 8 7 6 5 4 3 2 1

Dedicated to

ROCKY aND BUrT,

for being there, always

ACKNOWLEDGMENTS

Thanks to

Arthur Alef, Esq.

Chalmers Armstrong III, M.D.

Dr. Gary S. Aumiller

Henry Denker

Ellen Geiger

Claire Eddy

Anna Genoese

West Los Angeles Police Station
Community Relations Department Officers

And special gratitude to

Nancy Biederman

Vicki Horwits-Stern

Bruce Kalish

as dead as it gets

as dead as it gets

1

What in the world was the Executive Director of the Creative Artists Union doing in a garter belt and bra?

But there he was.

And dead in the bargain.

Of course, no one except Roger Urban had the explanation for that. And since he is now the late Roger Urban, it's purely a rhetorical question. I have a passion for rhetorical questions. Probably it's because I don't have to deal with the answers. It's always the answers that throw me.

Grandmother Anna, who passed away when she was ninety-six, used to say, "If I had known I was going to live this long, I would have taken better care of myself." And if I had known Roger would die so unexpectedly and so luridly, I would have been much nicer to him.

Woulda, coulda, shoulda.

It wasn't that I treated him so badly. After all, as a Board member, I had to work with the man. I did respect him, and learned a lot from him. But I could have been on a more social footing with him. We might have gone out for a few drinks. Even though my beverage of choice is designer water. Or I could have had dinner with him at one of the trendy restaurants he was always menu-dropping. Or I might even have accepted one of his frequent invitations to drop by his condo to watch a late-night DVD from his highly prized collection of classic old movies. But that would have been the extent of it. Definitely no bedroom stuff. Not even if I'd known it was the last time I would see him alive.

Who wants to sleep with a man who wears sexier underthings than you do?

But that's hindsight. That was before I got the mind-blowing phone call from Samantha. Despite the murder investigations I had covered, Roger was the first chalk outline I knew well.

My name is Maggie Mars. No relation to the candy bar. When people ask me what I do, I tell them I'm a writer, and someone is sure to ask, "Yes, but what do you do for a living?" That's it, people. I write screenplays. At least now I do. Before that I wrote articles for magazines. And before that I was happy. It was one of those magazine articles, an investigative reporter piece for *Vanity Fair,* that led to a sale for film development, and so to Hollywood and to my present position as a Board member of the Creative Artists Union, the C.A.U., irreverently known as COW.

It also led to my breakup with Joe Camanetti.

That was one helluva piece.

Let's see. . . . How to explain Joe, considering that he defies explanation. He used to be my live-in boyfriend . . . my lover . . . my everything. . . . Strange how someone can go from everything to nothing in little more than two years. But that's what can happen when love gets outbalanced by family obligations, by careers, and, of course, by geography. The reasons, if that's what they were, are no longer important. I go whole weeks now without once thinking of Joe.

"As if, one by one, the memories you used to harbor decided to retire to the southern hemisphere of the brain, to a little fishing village where there are no phones."

Billy Collins, a former Poet Laureate of the United States, wrote that. I like that we have Poets Laureate. Much more inspiring than hip-hop stars.

Come to think of it, it was Roger who first read me those

lines. From a book of poetry he kept in the top drawer of his desk. There were at least a dozen bookmarked places in the little volume, so I imagined he used those poems as a come-on to other women.

That was of no concern to me. Roger Urban was just not my type. If I had been looking for any type of type to be mine. Which I wasn't. Life was treating me well. I liked my work, I liked being in Hollywood, and I liked being free of attachments.

And then I met Henrik. Henrik Hudson. And, no, I'm not making that up. His name is Henrik Hudson, he's a criminal defense lawyer, and he looks like Tom Cruise on growth hormones, with a face lifted from an old Roman coin.

We met at one of those Hollywood parties where people gather to dis the industry that feeds them. I was in animated conversation, which means that my hands move as fast as my lips, talking with a fellow Union member, an unrepentant director of blood-spattered horror films, when my outstretched hand holding a pizza-type hors d'oeuvre, collided with Henrik's Hugo Boss jacket.

While I was wiping tomato sauce off his lapel with the cocktail napkin in my right hand, my left hand, entirely on its own, was sending a lemon Perrier down his right sleeve. I apologized and wiped, wiped and apologized while he just looked at me. When finally I paused to take a breath, still wiping, he separated the now empty glass from my clutches. Then, with great panache, he removed his drenched jacket, took my arm, and led the way to the bar where he ordered me another Perrier. We spent the rest of the party together, and by evening's end he had offered to help me with legal details for my screenplay.

Which he did, *pro bono*. *Pro* very *bono*. I'm not sure where our relationship is going, but I'm enjoying the trip. He's divorced, I'm flying solo, what could be more adult than that?

Speaking of adult, that's where I was right now. In Henrik's bed. Which is a great place to sleep, to make love, but not to solicit professional advice. Especially about Mercedes

Pell, the heroine of my current screenplay. Which is what I was doing.

"But could she really be arrested for searching Dante's apartment?"

"Mmmmmm . . ."

"Anyway, it's not quite breaking and entering. I mean, she broke into, but she didn't really enter. She was dangling from the ceiling fan."

"Mmmmmm . . ."

"Henrik . . ."

"Maggie, I'm kind of busy."

"I know. But this is important. Truly important."

"And this isn't?"

"Of course it is. You know I love it. But if Mercedes is arrested, then I'll have to write a chase scene and put off the part where she confronts Dante at the premiere and where she—"

"Maggie?"

"What?"

"Shut up."

Which I did. Except for the heavy breathing and the barely stifled scream at the end.

Henrik reached out and drew me into his arms.

"Was it good for Mercedes Pell?"

I nodded. "And for me."

I dug out my T-shirt from under the sheets and began to pull it on.

"Except I still don't know if I'm going to have her arrested or not."

He kissed the top of my head when it emerged from the shirt and the conversation ended with no real ending, as so many others had ended whenever I tried to mix business with pleasure.

Even when I was with Joe. The same Joe I never thought of anymore.

Sex with Joe was indelibly affixed in the scrapbook we all keep of past lovemaking. Joe and I had done it too well and too often. Even more fervently as the beginning of the end turned into the final split-up.

I scrunched up higher on Henrik's shoulder, so the next kiss would meet my lips. And it did. Henrik is a good kisser, especially in bed, where kissing often takes second place to his other gold medal proclivities.

"What time is it?"

He glanced over me at the bedside clock with its green glow-in-the-dark numbers. "A little after two. You want to go back to sleep or what?"

"What," I said, reaching for him, and he was already hard in my hand by the time he got my shirt over my head.

The next morning we dressed in tandem, me hunting for my panties and finally finding them marinating in the puddle-melt left by the overturned ice bucket on the living room floor. Don't ask.

Memo to Maggie: Next time bring backup panties.

We usually end up at Henrik's place. It's very old Hollywood, having been built originally for Fatty Arbuckle, the silent screen star whose celebrity was eclipsed in the glare of a murder charge. A succession of directors and set designers owned it after that, and then along came Henrik, a non-pro as they say in *Variety* and *The Hollywood Reporter,* more intimately known as the trades.

The house was all glass and stone and old wood, with picturesquely defining touches bequeathed by the past progression of set designers. Pieces of colored glass covered all the chandeliers in the dining room, and there were five, count them, five of them lined up over the table, all glittery and all different. The bedroom ceiling was inset with hundreds of small silver stars that gleamed in the dark. Take my word for it. I've been in a position to look up at them often enough.

Best of all, Henrik lives alone.

My place is no slouch, thanks to sharing it with Lionel Fogg, who owns it, but that's the snag right there. Lionel has proprietary rights, and so do Harpo and Groucho, the felines who believe they are warriors from the Tang dynasty.

Henrik was in the middle of a trial, when wasn't he, and I had the Annual Meeting of the Creative Artists Union on my calendar that night, so we kissed good-bye, unsure when we'd be free to see each other again but promising it would be soon. I went home to the somewhat dubious pleasures of a lonely laptop computer, a screenplay that was behind sched-ule, a stack of bills to pay, and a blood glucose testing kit.

I'm a diabetic. There was a time, right after I first found out that I had type 2 diabetes, that I was depressed and scared. I spent months being angry at fate and doing the poor-me-why-me bit. Finally, when I could no longer stand myself, I said to myself, "Get a grip. Okay?"

I didn't answer that, of course. It's bad enough that I talk to myself without holding a full-blown conversation.

So I do as so many do. I live with it. I monitor my diet, I test my blood, I exercise, off and on, and I inject insulin twice a day. It's not a big deal anymore. I've learned that you can't direct the wind, but you can adjust your sails.

My blood sugar was fine, and since it was, I tried, as usual, to put off writing as long as possible, even though Mercedes Pell was clamoring for my attention. I attacked the bills first, sorting them, as I usually do, according to amounts. Little ones can be handled quickly, those with due dates have to be met right away, and a third pile comes under the heading of What Can I Do With These?

I went through the first two stacks as if my accounts were full of cash, but came to a screeching halt with the third stack. U.G. had sent me a note reminding me that the retirement home had raised its rates and I had promised to help out.

"Maggie, if you can't, I'll understand," he had written. "Just let me know and I'll find the money somehow."

There's a frightening thought.

My dad, U.G. for short, or Ulysses Grant Mars for long, lives at the Pacific Sunset Village in Manhattan Beach. There he has his independence, his harem of lonely wid-owed women, and the freedom to indulge his penchant for

scientific research. Well, he calls it research. I call it Please
God No More Chemical Experiments!

U.G. was right to remind me. I had promised to help,
back when I thought my screenplay would have long been
finished and the final payments from the studio banked by
me. Wrong on both counts. I can make this first payment,
and maybe the next one or two, but after that . . . There was
no extra money for "after that," only a great big question
mark.

That was all the incentive I needed to get back to my
screenplay. I'd left it at a stage where if I were to have a
heart attack, first I'd burn the script, and then I'd call the
paramedics. For once the work went well.

```
EXT. AIRPORT HANGAR—NIGHT

Mercedes, dressed in a tight skirt and even
tighter blouse, moves cautiously around the
outside of the hangar. As she looks around
the corner, she sees . . .

MERCEDES' POV—FRONT OF HANGAR

A LEARJET rolls to a stop. The passenger door
opens and TYLER BILLINGS, mid-fifties, steps
out with a beautiful woman, AMANDA PETERSON.

BACK TO MERCEDES

As she watches, she takes out a small
RECORDER from her pocket. She brings it to
her lips and speaks softly.

                    MERCEDES
    Interesting. Tyler Billings, CEO of En-
    cor Energy . . . he's supposedly fled
    the country . . . and Amanda Peterson,
    from the Beverly Hills I-fuck-the-
```

richest-guy-I-can-find-until-I-find-
someone-richer Petersons. . . . I wonder if—

Mercedes stops mid-sentence as a loud CLICK
is heard and a BARREL of a GUN is pressed
against her head.

                    MERCEDES
    Not in the head.
              (beat)
    I just paid Paolo two hundred and fifty
    bucks to get highlights and a
    trim. . . . I think a hole through it
    will damn well ruin it.

REVEAL DETECTIVE JACK MACKENZIE standing
behind her.

                    JACK
    How about you shut the hell up and tell
    me who you are and what you're doing here?

                    MERCEDES
    That's a little hard to do if I'm shut-
    ting the hell up . . . and speaking of
    hard . . . Do you have two guns on me?
    'Cause you're standing so close I can
    feel something poking me.

Jack backs off a little. Mercedes smiles.

                    MERCEDES (CONT'D)
    That's better.
              (pushing the gun down)
    My name's Mercedes Pell and I'm an in-
    vestigative reporter doing a story on
    small airport security.

                    JACK

    Bullshit. I'm LAPD and whoever you are,
    you're stepping on my case. So my sug-
    gestion . . . unless you want Paolo to
    be doing your hair at the morgue, I sug-
    gest you get out of here.

                    MERCEDES
    What's the case?

                    JACK
    NOW!

As Mercedes steps away from the hangar, her
skirt catches on a BOLT and rips up the
back. She walks away as if nothing has happened, her thong-covered butt in full view.

TIGHT ON MERCEDES

                    MERCEDES
          (under her breath)
    Fuck.

ON JACK
Watching her go.

                    JACK
    Fuuuck.

Mercedes was hot.

There's nothing like a night with Henrik to exorcise
writer's block.

In my screenplay, Mercedes is an investigative reporter
looking into a murder case that the police have called a suicide, and bumping heads with the establishment every way
she turns. She's audacious, brash, intrepid, outspoken—

what's on her lung is on her tongue, as my mother used to say—gutsy and totally disrespectful of authority figures.

In short—and Mercedes isn't short, she's tall and sexy, utterly and magnificently sexy—what Mercedes is, is everything I'm not.

"I still haven't decided whether to have you arrested," I told Mercedes. "I can always get in a chase scene somewhere else. Maybe near the end."

"If you ever reach it," she said.

Mercedes talks to me all the time. Of course not really. I haven't completely gone off the deep end. Mercedes Pell is my alter ego, and she and I occupy a time-share in my brain.

Before I knew it, it was time to Save and Exit and leave for the COW meeting. In light of coming events, maybe I should have chained myself to my computer.

2

The house is a *garish nightmare. There are columns and pediments and statues all looking as though they were refugees from an architectural flea sale.*

I wonder how a man who worked every day with artists and creative types could have such shitty taste. Then again, the house isn't his. But he's here, all right. I spotted his car parked around the corner, up the steep side street, its front wheels backed into the curb.

There is no sign of anyone else, of course. Still, just to make sure, when I reach the entryway, I wait a few minutes more in the shadows of the large white oleander bushes. Then I pull on a pair of surgical gloves and slide the key into the front door lock. It goes in like butter and turns easily. I step in and look around, listening.

There are no sounds. Absolute silence. The interior is dim, the heavy drapes drawn. If I didn't know better, I would think the house is empty. But I know better.

Then I hear a noise. Something is moving across the floor upstairs. The air seems to stir slightly, as though a door were closed or opened somewhere. For a heartbeat I freeze. But the noise isn't repeated. The air is still. I move through the kitchen and the laundry room, past what must be a maid's room, and find myself at the foot of the back stairs. I climb slowly up, relieved that there are no creaks from under my rubber-soled tennis shoes.

The hall is dark, no windows or skylights, but opulent, with soft, thick carpeting and unlit sconces on the walls. Paintings framed in heavy, gilt carved wood, and here and there a mirror, hang on both walls, giving the hallway the look of a set from an old British mystery movie. I see myself dimly in one of the mirrors as I pass and I don't recognize me. I am a stranger.

There is illumination enough to see that all the bedroom doors are open, except, of course, for the one at the end of the hall, which is just slightly ajar. The one where he must be. The one where I am headed. Carefully, soundlessly, I open the door just a crack more. I allow myself only the briefest of hesitations while nerves are steeled, jitters are numbed, and determination is hardened for the job that lies ahead. For what has to be done.

For what must be done, I tell myself, not for the first time. This is required. This is necessary. No negotiating, even with myself.

My heart is beginning to pound, so loudly I think he will hear it.

I edge into the bedroom and pause again, listening. I am alone. Then I hear sounds. The room off to my right with the door open and a pool of light spilling out, that's where he must be. I move over and peer in. It is a huge bathroom. Walls and floors of marble with mirrors everywhere, even on the ceiling.

I pull back a little and scan the room again. It is his mirrored reflection that I see first. His back is to me, and he is bent over, folding his clothes and placing them on a delicate satin-and-gold stool.

I could stop this while I have the chance, get out of there while I can. But I won't. He deserves this. He has it coming.

Now I have the gun out. I hold it as I have been taught,

with two hands to steady my grip. I know I must aim for the biggest target, his gut.

Do it! Do it! My head rings with the command. He straightens up and is turning towards me. Do it!

The gun goes off. I don't know how many times. Gunshots echo off the marble and bounce off the mirrors, until I hear the click of the empty chamber and it finally stops. My finger won't release the trigger. I will my hand to open and the gun falls to the floor, clattering on the marble.

I wait until the echoes fade to nothing and he hasn't moved.

He's dead. He's lying there, one arm over the edge of the tub, the marble reddening with his blood. . . .

God! Look what he's wearing!

Wrenching my gaze away from him, I pick up the gun and return to the hall to listen. Nothing. Absolute silence.

Back in the bathroom I go through the pockets of the clothing he has so neatly folded. Why the hell did he bother? Neatness doesn't count when you're dead. I find nothing but the usual stuff. No clue to where he keeps it. No matter. He can't do anything about it now.

He is staring at me, his eyes wide open. Damn him! I lift his legs. Would you believe they're shaved clean? I dump him into the tub, so he is facing away from me and I can't see his eyes. I pull shut the glass doors enclosing the tub and the last sight of my tormentor.

Got to get out of here. I run down the back stairs and I carefully open the kitchen door and look around. Nothing. Nobody. I lock the door behind me. Same key for front and back locks. How stupid of them. I make my way through the garden to the corner of the lot. Here it is a simple matter to conceal myself in the shrubbery. I wait. Patience is a virtue, and I am nothing if not virtuous.

I don't have long. She's right on schedule. Fortunately for me, and for her, she did not arrive any earlier. I watch her let herself into the house with a key, and then I walk briskly downhill to my car, peeling off the gloves and stuffing them in my pocket with the gun.

It's over. Thank God it's finally over.

3

The hotel parking lot was full. I self-parked, and found a spot on the upper level, maneuvering my RAV between a black Lincoln Navigator and a bright yellow Hummer wedged into spaces clearly marked Compact Only. In California, drivers have a tendency to underestimate their automobiles and overestimate their penises.

The lobby was crowded as well. Most of the people were lined up at the registration counter, probably a tour busload checking in or heading for a restaurant. They weren't looking for Ballroom A, like me. And, anyway, they didn't look like writers or directors.

What does a writer or director look like? Me, I guess. I was wearing the Hollywood uniform—Earl jeans, broken-in Ecco boots, and a black turtleneck sweater. Even in uniform I don't really think I look like I belong. Maybe if I was wearing a turned-backwards baseball cap. Or if I had a beard.

Showing my Union card, I signed in at the "K to O" desk. Dee Dee Russell, dressed in a long black skirt and tunic, was behind the desk and we greeted each other warmly. Dee Dee's most noticeable feature was a wide streak of gray highlighting raven-dark hair that she was always brushing out of her eyes. She is the assistant to Neville Lake, the

Union's Assistant Executive Director. Only in Hollywood does an assistant have an assistant.

After saying Hi to a few other acquaintances, I walked down the side aisle, finding an end seat halfway down. There were rows and rows of empty chairs, but people in the Biz are notorious latecomers. It isn't simply that they like to make entrances. They disregard deadlines as a matter of principle.

My stomach growled. Rooting around in my tote bag, I found an old sugar-free cookie and bit into it, noticing at the same time that, on some previous occasion, it had already been bitten into. I'm the only writer I know who carries a used cookie in her bag.

Memo to Maggie: Re-stock the bag.

It was while I was munching that I noticed the empty seat at the front table. The officers and the co-chairs of the Negotiating Committee were taking their places, shuffling their papers and adjusting their mikes, but our Executive Director, Roger Urban, was not there.

"Looks like Roger stopped off for some liquid fortification," Ian McConnell, the Union's *éminence grise,* said, coming up alongside me and squeezing my shoulder before moving on. I like to use that *éminence grise* expression even though Ian by no means exercises unofficial power. He is lean and trim and with only a sprinkling of gray hair. He is known for having directed many of the old classic comedies, and I find him to be a sardonic, funny man.

In previous years Board elections were held at the same time as contract ratifications, but that's been changed. Since writers and directors almost never like the proposed new contract, they'd veto the contract and boot out the Board of Directors. Eventually the Board wised up and scheduled the elections at a different, safer time.

Now I could see that the room was fast filling up, which was an indication that the crazies were turning out in full force. Every Union has them, COW more than most. Sometimes I think terminal derangement is a requirement for membership. Present company not excepted, or I never would have agreed to run for the Board last election. I won because the members engaged in their usual housecleaning and swept most of the previous Board out of office.

In that same election, Barclay Thomas ran against Chris Osborne, the incumbent President. At that time I didn't much care which one of them got elected. There wasn't any None of the Above category on the ballot, so I voted for Bark. He's sexier. He has a beautiful head of gray hair, like Richard Gere's, and he is tall and Montana-cowboy lean with a penetrating blue-eyed gaze. His fame as a screen-writer is such that there isn't a director in Hollywood who would dare claim "A Film by" credit on anything Written By Barclay Thomas. Even the moviegoing audiences know his name.

That is no small accolade in an industry where writers are considered only the first drafts of human beings. An old but still recurrent joke: "Did you hear about the Polish starlet who slept with the writer?"

In a land of superstars Bark is a supernova. He holds back-to-back records for the most mentions in Army Archerd's *Variety* column in any one year. He is soon to have a star on Hollywood's Walk of Fame, with all the attendant celebrations, and he didn't have to pay for it. No film festival, no Hollywood party or "preem" is considered a success unless Bark and his wife attend, she in her own Harry Winston diamonds and a to-be-worn-only-once designer gown, and get their pictures splashed all over the papers and *People* magazine. Golden Globe, National Board of Review, Oscar . . . You name the award and it sits on a shelf in the Thomas den.

In the past, it was accepted that the President of COW had kind of a titular position. Someone who chaired the Board meetings and ate the various disguises of chicken at industry luncheons and wrote letters to the membership that had been authored by Roger. All that was before Bark Thomas was elected. From the beginning of his term as President, he proceeded to take the office seriously. He made decisions on his own and relegated Roger from a manipulator to at best a co-

conspirator. The two of them never came to argumentative blows in public, but there was much juicy speculation as to what must go on behind the scenes.

After the last Board meeting, Bark asked me to join him for a cappuccino (I settled for Diet Coke) and enlisted my support for the recently negotiated contract. I thought it was a serviceable contract with improvements in the important areas of minimums, residuals, and creative rights for directors and writers. Besides, I respected Bark's knowledge and experience, so I readily agreed to vote for it and I enjoyed his company. Not that I entertained any expectations that it would go any further than that. He's very much married to Althea Thomas, who is known, industry-wide, as the quintessential Hollywood wife. Still.

By now the stage had its full complement of Union leaders. Bark was there, along with Adam Tyler, the Vice President; Evan Lantzy, Treasurer and co-chair of the Negotiating Committee; and Clark Newman, the other co-chair. Neville Lake and Royal Underhill, the Director of Strategic Analysis, wearing his trademark sweater-vest and bow tie, were just joining them.

As for Roger, his chair was still empty, but I was certain he'd be there. COW's Annual Meeting was always a circus and he owned the lion tamer's whip and chair. Besides, he had been the Chief Negotiator of the contract.

Members still recalled the time that the Union was holding a meeting to ratify a particularly controversial contract that Roger had negotiated. The opposition was gaining ground when the proceedings were halted and everyone evacuated because someone had called in a bomb threat. There was a rumor that Roger had arranged for the phone call so that the meeting could be postponed and cooler heads prevail.

Now that's leadership.

I was bombed once. It was at one of those school carnivals with pre-fabricated rides and crepe paper-festooned game booths, and a kid atop the Ferris wheel threw down a film canister filled with explosive powder and nails and BB ammo, and I was standing in the drop zone. Other people won stuffed animals and goldfish in little jars. I went home with three stitches in my leg. I still have the scar. Joe used to love to kiss it—

Hold it, Maggie. Don't go there.

"Mag . . ."

I turned. It was Dana Salinger, another Board member, a television sitcom director. She always called me Mag, her tone implying that it was short for Maggot. I smiled a small smile, hoping she wouldn't stop.

She said, "Can't talk. I want to line up at a mike."

Good. I didn't intend to point out to her that the meeting hadn't even begun yet. Dana was a chronic protestor. She opposed everything. Right now her current bane was Roger and his contract, and she made no secret of it.

She parked herself in line at an aisle mike near my seat and stood there, jiggling her capacious butt, impatient for things to get started. I studied her as she jiggled.

"Why don't you get behind her and push her," said Mercedes.

"No, this is a public place. I'll be nice."

Actually, the thought occurred to me that seeing Dana fall flat on her face would be very nice.

In her youth Dana might have had a figure that wouldn't quit, but now it has. Her skin sags, her stomach pouches out, and she uses Scotch tape to pull up her wrinkles, up in the hairline where she thinks it doesn't show. Her voice is deep, husky from years of smoking. She should have been Empress of Transylvania, but had to settle for being the bug up everyone's ass.

Her car has a bumper sticker that reads: "I have PMS and ESP. I'm a bitch who knows everything." Perfect.

On the plus side, she's fluent in four languages, having made it a practice to take a lover in whatever foreign country she happened to be visiting, and then dump him once a decent conversational vocabulary had been consummated. It's what's known as a been-there, done-him philosophy.

A delicious comment about Dana once made the rounds,

and somehow she attributed it to me. Now would I have said that Dana Salinger hasn't had a period in so long, she doesn't even put them at the ends of sentences anymore?

No matter. Now she barely condescends to speak to me. Good. There is nothing quite so satisfying as requited animosity.

"Tes . . . tes . . . testing . . . one, two, three . . ."

That was the hotel technician doing his thing. We were getting close.

Tad Reston slid into the seat next to me. Tad's directing career ended years ago and only he is ignorant of this. Back in the McCarthy era he was blacklisted, and now I've heard it said that he won't be satisfied until he's ostracized by both sides of the political aisle. I think he has a dedicated line to the Labor Department just so he can register his frequent complaints against the leadership, but he can't seem to generate any interest in his real complaint, which is that he can't get a job. He spends his days drinking, and, judging by his 100-proof breath, his nights, too.

"So what's your guess about our dear Roger, Maggie? Has he forgotten about us in the heat of passion, or is he afraid he'll be stoned for bringing in this contract?"

I noticed, even in my brief connection with COW, that those members who were no longer active in the Biz came up with the most criticism and the most grievances. Looking around the room, I recognized many of them, members who probably hadn't crawled in since the last Annual Meeting. It was another Night of the Living Dead.

I didn't bother to answer Tad because Bark was speaking into the mike.

"Okay, people, let's come to a semblance of order."

The room quieted quickly and I wondered, not for the first time, how Bark did it. I think it's his voice, that wonderful, deep, honey-and-spice voice, and, of course, those eyes.

The meeting began, as always, with a not-to-be-heeded plea to turn off the cell phones, please. Also the beepers, the pagers, and the heart monitors, the last being Bark's stab at lightening things up.

I went to turn off my cell phone and saw the message thing flickering. I must have missed a call. I knew it couldn't be my producer because no writer in her right mind would ever give her producer her cell phone number. Well, I'd have to pick it up during the break.

After the shuffling and noise subsided, there was the roll call of licenses of cars whose lights had been left on, and then the list of cars illegally parked.

The meeting was beginning. Without Roger.

Bark then introduced Adam, who gave the particulars of the voting procedure that would take place following the meeting. Adam droned on. Bark holds audiences in the palm of his hand, and Adam puts them into a deep coma, instantaneously. I had already voted by mail, so I paid scant attention until I saw Samantha Winger come up to Bark and whisper something in his ear.

Samantha was Roger's executive assistant, his right-hand person, very loyal to him, and a bulldozer when it came to getting things done. Any woman within a few feet of Roger was invariably linked to him romantically, and since Samantha had come to the Union with Roger, the chances were fairly good that there might have been something going on between them.

She was short, very striking looking, with ash-blond hair that she wore pulled back into an impeccable bun. Tonight she was wearing a black leather skirt with a lime green sweater, which showed off a bustline I could have used a picture of to show God what I meant Him to give me in the first place. I guess anatomy just looks better on some people than on others.

Samantha walked off, and all eyes followed. Bark banged his gavel for attention.

"Ladies and gentlemen, it appears that Roger Urban has been unavoidably detained. . . ."

There were murmurs of surprise, but they were soon drowned out by derisive shouts from all sides.

"He's probably sleeping off a doubleheader!"

"What happened? Did it get caught in his zipper?"

"He can't come out of his coffin until it's dark."

"Who's he Rogering now?"

"He can't be screwing anyone. The screwees are all here!"

You get the drift. Writers and directors consider listening to be an interactive sport.

Bark banged again. "He'll be here presently, and in the meantime I suggest we get on with the meeting."

It was a good suggestion. The natives had been getting restless, but now something resembling a respectful silence settled in. I wondered if Samantha had given him any particulars attached to the "unavoidably detained."

"You received handouts when you came in, outlining the salient points of the contract and the gains we've made. The white sheet covers material applicable to all. The yellow sheet is for writers, the blue sheet for directors. If you find yourself with a brown sheet, you're full of shit and can't vote."

Laughter erupted, and even before it had died down, Bark was moving on.

"Until Roger gets here, those of us at the front table will attempt to answer your questions about the contract. There are floor mikes in the aisles, so if you'll just line up and state your name when called on, we'll alternate from one aisle to the other."

The announcement was unnecessary. There were already long lines at both floor mikes.

The first few speakers were articulately, and briefly, in favor of the contract. Then it was Dana's turn.

"Okay, someone has to stop the cheerleading," she said, without preamble, "and it's going to be me."

More hoots, in tribute to Dana's reputation for dissent. Having delivered that shot across the bow, she was off on a litany of opposition to every point in the contract.

When she stopped to draw a breath, Royal Underhill, on

the dais, primed with his statistics and his pie charts and analyses, reached for his mike and attempted to answer her. But Dana wasn't looking for answers.

"Roger doesn't have the guts to face us after signing off on this contract," she said. "That's the real reason he isn't here!"

"He'll be here. You know Roger," Tad said to me. "He likes to come in like the cavalry, leading the charge in a last-minute rush to save the day. Makes him feel important."

"He's over half an hour late already," I said.

"What's thirty minutes in his parallel universe?"

I mumbled an "Excuse me" and left my seat, ducking out a side door to a small patio area where the lepers of today's society, the smokers, had congregated. I checked my voice mail and the message was from U.G. I called him. He wasn't in his room, so I had him paged, and he answered all out of breath.

"Hi, honey."

"What are you up to, Dad?"

"Now what kind of a greeting is that?"

"Sorry. I expected to catch you in your room."

"I was just visiting a lady friend. Being sociable."

Right. I smiled to myself.

"Listen," he said. "I'm working on a new gas detection device, and I think this time I may have something. Really, Maggie, this one is a winner."

I'd lived through many of my dad's "winning inventions," all of which were going to make us rich, and somehow, I was still working for a living.

"Dad, you are taking care, aren't you? We can't afford any more—mishaps."

Shorthand for reminding him that, outside of Medicare, he was uninsured and uninsurable, and any damages suffered by anyone due to his tinkering would have to be paid for by me.

At any rate, he got my drift and spent the next few minutes alternating between reassuring me and thanking me for the check I told him was in the mail.

As I ended the call, Chris Osborne and Dennis Bird, another Board member, joined me, and we stood off to the side, keeping our distance from those puffing away.

Chris, a rabid anti-smoking spokesman, said, "I'd rather die of second-hand smoke than of first-hand boredom."

"I fantasize about breaking Dana's jaw," Dennis said. Dennis was an animation writer, so I guess he was more attuned to violence than most of us.

Another member came over. "Hey, isn't it weird about Roger? What do you think kept him?"

"The usual," Dennis said.

"Must be someone unusual to make him late for an Annual Meeting."

I said, "Isn't this odd behavior, even for Roger?"

There was a group shrug. It was accepted that Roger had his quirks and peccadilloes, but he had style, and he was a crafty negotiator, in that he could argue about anything for five minutes and nothing for six. When I first became a member of COW, Roger had taken me under his wing and shown me the ropes. He became my spiritual advisor in the doctrine of Union politics.

Okay, enough with the euphemisms. There was nothing spiritual about it at all. What Roger did was hit on me.

But I wasn't a native New Yorker for nothing. I put him off in such a manner that he was convinced he was the rejecter and not the rejectee. We remained friendly and he took on the role of a genuine mentor, and I was fond of him. Unemotionally so. Still, there's something to be said for sentiment without sex.

"But not much," Mercedes said.

More people escaped the meeting and joined our little group. Dee Dee Russell came up to us, looking anxious.

"Neville is fit to be tied," she said. "Roger didn't say anything to him about not showing up."

Chris said, "Great. If this isn't typical of COW. We book a ballroom, the place is jammed, we're waiting to hear the Chief Negotiator tell us the virtues of the contract—and he's not here."

"How does the joke go?" Dennis said. "Who do I have to fuck to get out of this Union?"

The conversation grew more lively and engrossing, soon leaving the subject of Roger behind.

This is pleasant, I thought. Maybe I would just stay out here until the meeting was over. Maybe I would even take up smoking. But more and more people were collecting on the patio, and if their fumes didn't get to me, their coughing would.

I went back inside to find that Dana was in her seat and Ian McConnell was at the floor mike.

"This is a good contract. Notice I said good, not great. It will buy us peace for another four years."

Mike or no mike, Dana was still bent on making herself heard.

"It's a lousy contract! That's why Roger isn't here. Let's hope he's committed hara-kiri! It would be the first honorable thing he's ever done!"

During the predictable pros and cons that followed, I was surprised to spot Noelle Sears down front, in a Chanel suit and chic Bakelite pin.

"Hey, I'd look great in something like that," said Mercedes.

And she probably would, if she weren't so limited by her undercover work. And her income.

Noelle was the Branch Manager of the New York office of COW, short and not too unpleasantly plump, with an intelligence that was camouflaged with short, curly reddish hair and an exquisite face, a face out of a Titian painting.

I met her when she guested at one of our Board meetings, and learning that I was a refugee from the east, she filled me in on the New York scene. And so when she got up to take her place at the mike, I waved to her. She waved back but I'm sure she didn't remember me. It was that kind of a wave. She made a reasoned, articulate speech in favor of the contract, and that seemed to quiet things down a bit.

Me, I couldn't have been so reasoned. This was not a six-page double-spaced paper we were talking about. This was a book, a document of several hundred pages covering years of negotiations, all in legalese. I've tried to read it, but a few pages in and my head hits the desk.

Roger once told me that the length of the contract coupled with the legalese combined to confuse everyone, and that left him the last man standing, The Expert. I was looking forward to his advocacy of the deal at tonight's meeting. Only, where was our guru when we needed him?

Bark managed to get through the rest of the agenda, and, finally, mercifully, the meeting was over. People dispersed to fill out their ballots at the voting stations. The votes would be counted late into the night, and tomorrow the results would be announced, so members would be clogging COW's Web site.

I was crossing the lobby, heading for the ladies' room, when I ran into Royal Underhill. He was carrying not one but two attaché cases filled with documents. Or tissue paper, for all I knew. Like my adolescent bras.

"How do you think it went?" he said.

"I'm sure the contract will be approved," I said. "No one wants a strike."

I wasn't sure at all, but I knew Royal had worked very hard on his database during the negotiations. We can all use a little encouragement now and then, bogus though it may be.

Royal and I veered off in different directions. I entered the restroom to find a small congregation of waiting women.

"Is there an express line?" I asked.

A dozen women turned to stare at me, confirming my long-held belief that people with full bladders have no sense of humor.

"If you have to pee that badly, why don't you use the men's room?" said Mercedes.

I considered it. And I would have, but I didn't have anyone to stand guard.

Once more out in the lobby, I was on my way to the exit and my car when I heard footsteps behind me.

"Hey! Maggie! Wait up!"

I turned to see Bark.

"Running out on us?"

"Well, it is kind of late and I've got work—"

"Come along to the bar. A bunch of us are having a post-mortem, and I need to look at a face without fangs."

I thought about it. On the one hand, industry chatter has always intrigued me. On the other hand, I *did* have to get home—and on the other, other hand, the guy asking me was still Barclay Thomas. I met them in the bar.

I should have known what it would be like. Several big-name writers and directors were in a group talking shop talk about film festivals, their experiences on location, and the Care and Feeding of Agents. Another gathering was trading opinions on a picture that had just been released, a sequel to a film that had done eight hundred and twenty million dollars worldwide. So much was riding on it, there were such high expectations, that the producers canned the original star and the lead bad guy and made the sequel with a new, more bankable cast.

This bunch was having a field day with the film. It seemed to be a game of Who Can Top This with one-line reviews that were ambiguously scathing.

"It was interesting," one of them said.

"Peter's done it again," said another.

"Where does he get his ideas?"

And the acclaimed winner: "Terrific isn't the word for it." And so the conversation ebbed and flowed and eddied around me, while everyone ignored the elephant in the bar—Roger's no-show.

Moving up to the counter to order designer water, I found myself next to Bark. Unabashedly political, I was complimenting him on the way he had run a difficult meeting, when a woman came up to him and placed a proprietary arm on his sleeve. The first thing I noticed about her was her hair, a natural silver-blond, cut very short. A second look showed me she was tall and slender with an athletic build. She had on a slim black pantsuit, a simple white shirt open at the neck, and no jewelry.

This was the fabled Althea. Take my word for it, she was a knockout.

I could swear there was a visible aura encasing her. The gilt-edged aura of success. Bark's wife was the chairperson or on the Board of several foundations. At least half a dozen charity organizations had, at some fantasy-themed gala event, made her their honoree for outstanding achievement. She was a legendary hostess, and invitations to her soirees—other people had parties, Althea had soirees—were as treasured as a winning Powerball ticket.

Bark gave her a welcoming kiss. "Glad you could make it, honey." He turned back to me. "Maggie, I think you know my wife, Althea."

Actually, I didn't. Still, we did the nice-to-see-you bit, and, even as we exchanged the expected pleasantries, her gaze was already traveling the room, seeking out more worthwhile prospects. "Excuse me," she said, evidently finding one. "I think I see someone . . ."

She moved away. Bark scooped up a handful of peanuts from the bar and offered me some.

I shook my head.

"Bark, what are you going to do if he doesn't show?"

"Roger? God, I wish you hadn't asked me that. Samantha's tried his house and his cell phone and he's not answering. I don't know what else I can do. Anyway, it's probably too soon to get all wound up about it."

"Well, tomorrow morning, if he hasn't surfaced, Samantha should call his family and friends, and then the hospitals, and, sorry, the morgue."

A few nearby members had overheard.

"What about the police?" one of them said.

I said, "Well, if L.A. is anything like New York, they won't do anything yet. Not enough time has passed."

"A celeb like Roger? They ought to jump on it right away."

"Only if it's a child that's missing. And despite opinion to the contrary, Roger's an adult."

Bark was plainly intrigued. "How do you know so much?"

"I used to . . . go with a homicide detective."

That was a conversation stopper. I turned away so no one would notice my discomfort. Several of the group soon drifted off, and I was preparing to do the same when Bark said, "That's an interesting background you have, Maggie. I just realized, I really don't know much about you."

I shrugged. "There's not that much to know."

"Tell you what. We'll have dinner soon," he said. "The four of us."

"Four?"

"Althea, me, you. And your Significant Other. There is one, isn't there?"

I took the con side in a debate with myself, lost, and nodded yes.

"You see?" he said. "I'm already learning more about you. Dinner it is. Althea will call you."

I didn't think she would. But Bark seemed gratified with his role in whatever social byplay had just gone down. I suppose it was all part of the choreography of the evening and Bark feeling good that the meeting was over.

He signaled the bartender. "How about letting me buy you a real drink?"

"Thank you, this is fine."

Bark was already distracted. His pocket was ringing. In Hollywood, status is achieved in inverse proportion to the size of your cell phone. The smaller it is, the more important you are. Bark pulled his minuscule version out of his pocket and turned away.

"No, I have to hang around a little while longer," I heard him say. And then: "No, sweet, don't wait up. I won't be long."

I looked over to the other side of the room. Althea was by the door, on a matching phone. The two of them, husband and wife, were in the same bar, talking to each other on their his-and-her cell phones. It's a Hollywood kind of thing.

A gaggle of comedy writers was gathered in the corner and I joined them. They were bemoaning the dearth of good comedy on television these days, comparing the new shows to the classic episodes of what was still known as The Golden Age. I did my best to laugh at their inside jokes and nod knowingly at their more serious perspectives on the situation.

"Don't stand there like a dummy," said Mercedes. *"Jump right in."*

"A television show used to have a beginning, a middle, and an end," I heard myself say. "Nowadays it's more like a beginning, a muddle, and no end."

One or two of them laughed. Then the conversation got switched to their weekly poker game and I wandered away.

Bark was still on the phone with Althea, so I decided I wouldn't wait up either. I went home.

4

Vivaldi was playing on the living room speakers, but Lionel's door was closed, which meant I didn't have to report any gossip to him, the price I pay along with the pittance of rent he asks from me. His two acolytes, Harpo and Groucho, jumped up from the couch, and headed straight for my pants leg, checking to see if I had been unfaithful with any other of their feline persuasion. Nope. Not tonight, fellows. They hopped back on the couch, and let me continue on into the bathroom so I could test my glucose level and take my shot. I recorded the results in my personal logbook and put away my kit.

As I undressed for the shower, I wondered if Roger had surfaced. He never should have missed that meeting. But he had. So where was he? It was all very peculiar. I tried to think what Mercedes would do in a situation like this. I had a feeling I knew. She would grab her coat and bag, jump in her car, and scour the streets and late-night haunts of the city.

Me? I wrapped myself in a towel and looked up Samantha's home number.

She answered on the first ring, so I knew she was awake.

"Oh," she said. "I thought you might be Roger."

"You still haven't heard from him?"

"I've been trying his number every ten minutes. Bark is sure he'll turn up in the morning."

What more could I suggest? Bark was sure he'd turn up in the morning, so we might as well wait to see what happened in the morning, right?

In bed, sleep eluded me. Lionel was a disciple of the principles of Feng Shui, believing that one could manipulate one's physical surroundings for the purpose of nudging fate in a favorable direction. The usual soft murmur of the fountain he had placed on a bookshelf just outside my door seemed like the roar of Victoria Falls.

"Water, when properly placed, can increase the flow of money," Lionel said. "Think of it as a harmonious movement of energy."

Right now I could only think about Roger and all the worst-case scenarios behind his non-appearance. Maybe his car had plunged off a cliff, maybe he had suffered a stroke, maybe he had gone to the beach and drowned—

No, not drowned. That was because I was listening to the Feng Shui fountain.

I tried rewriting those worst-case scripts and telling myself it was most likely something very ordinary, very unavoidable, but it didn't help. Probably it was because my pillow pointed in the wrong direction. Lionel's best direction was the northeast, he said, and that's the way his pillow pointed in order for him to get restful sleep.

I envied him his restful sleep, and I turned my pillow around. Still wide awake, I gave up, glanced at the clock, and thought it didn't matter what time it was. I turned on the light and called Henrik. He seldom goes to sleep early, especially when he's in trial.

Not only wasn't he asleep, he wasn't at home. I should have remembered. He and his staff were at the office, coming up with inventive new ways to put another lowlife back on the street.

"Hi, honey," I said to his machine. "Up working hard for that deviant you're representing? Did the Judge ask you to brief that obscure law you quoted from the Napoleonic

Code? Speaking of briefs, I don't have any on and I miss you. Now you're missing briefless me. Call me."

Henrik was fun to tease and great company. Our relationship-lite hadn't reached the point where either of us was trying to move it to the next level. I was fine with it the way it was, but there were times I wondered why Henrik seemed so fine with it. Was he having doubts? Were the doubts about me?

One major failed relationship and here I was, afraid to move further with a truly great guy.

Well, except for his work. I know, I know. Everyone deserves the best defense possible, but, still, some of the sleaze-oids he reps are just too scummy for the good lawyering that gets them off.

I turned off the light, swiveled the pillow around again, lay back, and closed my eyes.

"Why not call Joe?" Mercedes said.

"Who asked you?" I said. "I thought you'd be out scouring the city for Roger."

"I didn't find him and I looked for him high and low. Mostly low."

"I bet."

"Call him," she said.

No. The last time I called, the *only* time I called, a woman answered. I would not call Joe. I would not write checks that my ass couldn't cash.

But when it came to willpower, resolution was not my middle name. I knew I would give in. Again the light came on, and I dialed, furious at myself for giving in, and humiliated that I knew his number by heart.

"Hello." The familiar middle-of-the night rasp.

"Joe, it's Maggie."

Silence.

"Joe?"

"What's wrong?"

"Nothing's wrong."

"You're not dead? You're not hurt? Not in jail?"

"Nope." But thanks for caring, Joe.

"Then why in hell are you calling me at"—A pause while he must have checked his bedside clock—"one forty-three in the morning?"

A good question. Why in hell *was* I calling him? Because he was a detective, of course. Sure, Maggie, if that's what you want to believe.

"Where are you?" he said.

"Here. I mean here in L.A."

"I know that." He *knew* that? "Maggie, what is it? What's wrong?"

"Roger has disappeared."

"Who the fuck is Roger?"

"Roger Urban, you know, our Executive Director."

"No, I don't know. Give me a clue."

"COW! The Creative Artists Union!"

"Oh, yeah. That." Another silence. "What do you mean disappeared?"

"He never showed up at our meeting tonight."

A grunt.

"Joe?"

More silence. That man was so aggravating, so infuriating, even now, that we might as well have stayed together.

"You call me for the first time in two years, at one forty in the morning, and then it's about another guy?"

"Roger's not 'another guy.' He's a friend."

"I still don't like being woken up unless it's a goddamn emergency. And this doesn't come close to smelling like one."

"You always used to stay up late."

"Yeah, I used to do a lot of things."

After a meaningful silence, I said, "Okay, Joe, I know it's probably nothing, but you being a detective, I thought you could . . ." I trailed off, unsure of how to finish the thought.

"What? You thought I could what?" Henrik would have known what to do. I wouldn't have had to spell out everything for him.

"Look, just pretend this is a wrong number! I'm sorry I woke you and I'm sorry this isn't a goddamn emergency!"

Grudgingly: "You didn't wake me." No? Why not? Was someone else there with him? "Maggie, get some sleep. I'm sure the guy's okay. He'll turn up. They usually do."

"But he should have been at the meeting. Why wasn't he at the meeting?"

"How should I know? He probably had his own reasons for skipping it. That's all you do in that fucking business, have meetings. Well, meetings suck. He probably couldn't face another one."

"I see. You've got it all figured out."

I was about to hang up when he said, "In the morning, if you still haven't heard from him, you know the drill. Make the calls, family, friends, hospitals, the morgue. If he stays missing, let me know and we'll look into it."

"Right. Well . . . thanks, Joe."

"Any time. Listen, how've you been?"

"Oh, fine. You know, same old same old."

"Run into Jack Nicholson yet?"

He remembered my obsession.

It started years ago when I read in an article a line Jack had said: "You only lie to two people in your life: your girl-friend and the police." I admire a man who says out loud what we all know and don't say. I like his movies, his dev-ilish smile, and his dark glasses at the Laker games. He lives the life the rest of us only dream of.

"No," I said. "But as soon as I figure out which of his houses he's staying in, I'll probably stalk him."

"Have you been to the Staples Center? He hangs out at Laker games."

"I know. I'm thinking of trying out as a Laker girl."

"Sounds like a plan. Well, 'night."

"'Night, Joe." I broke the connection. A tenuous one at best.

5

I slept only fitfully, willing myself not to think any more about Roger. Instead I concentrated on thoughts of Henrik, focusing on what a healthy dose of reality he was, compared to Joe. Joe was the past, yesterday's news. So why were my emotions in a tailspin, and this over a five-minute telephone call?

I was awakened by an early morning phone call from Henrik. He sounded dead tired.

"We pulled an all-nighter at the office and I just have time for an hour nap before I have to be in court."

"Poor baby," I said. "It's a lucrative job but someone's got to do it."

"You sounded funny on the message you left. Horny, which is good, but odd. Is everything okay? Other than having lost your panties again?"

"Roger Urban's missing."

"What do you mean missing?"

"He was a no-show last night."

"You're kidding! The big contract meeting and he wasn't there?"

"You got it and that's not like him."

"That's for sure. Give Roger a microphone and a captive

audience, and he's in heaven. Strange he would miss it. Well, listen, don't worry about him. He's probably got a real Roger reason for not showing up."

"I suppose."

"You talk about my deviants? You've got some of your own weirdos to deal with."

"Small comfort," I said.

And he was gone. I put the phone down.

Immediately it rang again. A call from one of the COW staff. Bark had called an emergency meeting of the Board for nine thirty. No particulars. Just be there. It didn't sound good, but nothing ever does that early in the morning.

Still somewhat groggy, I stumbled into the bathroom and had the misfortune to look in the mirror. God, I looked awful. I keep myself thin because of the diabetes so I always have prominent cheekbones, but this morning my cheeks were so sunken I couldn't find them. My brown hair hung round my face like string, and my green eyes, undoubtedly my best feature, were rimmed in red, which made for a kind of premature holiday look.

I gave me up as a hopeless case and went into the kitchen where Lionel was putting dishes of homemade cat food on the floor. He stared at me.

I stared back. "What?"

"You look like hell."

I gave him a look and he knew me well enough to drop it.

"Your father called last night," he said. "I told him to try your cell phone."

"He did. And what else?"

"What else what?"

"What else did he have to say?"

"You mean, outside of greeting me with 'Hello, Tinkerbell, what are you doing home?' "

"Never mind."

We sat down to breakfast, which for me was my usual English muffin with sugar-free jam. Lionel wanted to know all about the meeting. He didn't care anything about the contract, he just relished finding out who wore what and who was doing whom.

But he showed more than an offhand spark of interest when I told him that I had actually met Althea Thomas. The news sent him off and running.

"She's his first and only wife," he told me, "which, of course, is very unusual by Hollywood standards, certainly by mine."

"Why, Lionel," I said. "How refreshing to know that you do have standards."

"I'll ignore that," he said, "but retribution shall follow. Tell me, was she very suntanned?"

"Not that I noticed. Why?"

"I just thought she might have some color in her face, being that she loves to bask in her husband's reflected glory."

He went on to tell me it was industry gospel, not gossip, that Althea was Bark's best career asset. "But she's not simply your conventional woman behind the man, oh no. She's the manipulator behind the puppet. It's just that the strings are invisible."

I said, "I don't believe it."

"Believe it," Lionel said. "Consider the source."

As well I might. Lionel Fogg and I were born on the same day in the same New York hospital. Our parents were best friends, and we grew up together until his family migrated to sunny Southern California. God's country, as his mother said; the back of beyond, as my mother said. She needed the big city with its hordes of people and its noise and energy. Lionel's mother needed not to have to put a snowsuit on her child one more time.

Thoughts of my mother always brought a smile to my face. She and her sister, Aunt Gladys, were concert pianists who toured all over playing their twin grand pianos. Then came my mother's sudden, fatal illness. Followed within six months by Aunt Gladys' death. The sound of music was no more.

My dad and I were knocked for a loop but eventually we recovered. About then, I received an offer to write a screenplay based on a series of articles I had written for *Vanity Fair.*

Dad and I headed out to Los Angeles. He opted for the Pacific Sunset Village and I was taken in by Lionel, who volunteered the empty bedroom in his West Hollywood condo. I stayed on through my next screenplay, and now this one. I still regard it as temporary, of course. Just until I decide whether I'm going to stay on the left coast and write movies, or return to the right coast and go back to magazine work, or starve. Whichever comes first.

The reality is that I'll have to put down roots here. My father's bills have to be paid, and someone has to be around to keep an eye on him. That's not me volunteering. That's me facing the facts of daughterhood.

It's worked out pretty well. I would trust Lionel with my life, he gets on my nerves no more than twice a day, and we never ever date the same men. He's a born-again Truman Capote, short, no more than five-seven, with very pale skin, fair, thinning hair, and almost no eyebrows. His pale blue eyes are slightly protruding and hooded, so you're never quite sure what thoughts are churning in his mind, except that you know they're devious ones. He's one of the most popular party guests in the city because he always knows everything about everyone, and imparts his gossip with delicious verve.

When I first moved in with Lionel, I used to wonder how he learned the things he knew about the Hollywood scene. Before long I came to realize that his shop—Record Requiem—where he sells very expensive and rare classical records, was a hangout for lots of TV and film people, music notables, and gays. He's developed a sizable network of informants, and, being in the company of writers and directors, I, of course, have an honored place among them.

Lionel seemed very casual about the news of Roger's no-show.

"Probably having one of his little flings," he said. "You wouldn't believe where he's been planting his Willie. I could tell you any number of amusing little tidbits."

It was an invitation for me to RSVP with "Please do," but I resisted the bait.

I said, "Save it, Lionel. I'm running late," and got up from the table.

"Me, too. I have to put some air in my front tire."

That front tire was attached to a bicycle. Lionel didn't own a car. He pedaled his way to work and everywhere, with baskets fore and aft to carry the day's necessities.

I blew him a kiss good-bye, but he was already reaching down to tuck his pants into his socks. Lionel disdained the use of bicycle clips, at least until some discriminating designer would come out with some jeweled ones.

Driving to the COW offices, I was behind a motorcycle whose driver wore a T-shirt reading: IF YOU CAN READ THIS, THE BITCH FELL OFF. What is it with this town?

"Follow that hog," said Mercedes.

I would have liked to, but I was anxious to get to the meeting and see if there was anything new.

In the main lobby of the Union building, there was an eerie silence. It was a little after nine, so they were open for business, but the usual clamor was absent.

Climbing the stairs to the second-floor Boardroom, and counting that as my aerobic exercise for the day, I found Bark in a huddle with Samantha and Neville. Board members and staff personnel were standing around, talking in small groups, contributing to a discordant hum of agitated conversation, while eating their bagels and cream cheese and drinking their coffee.

I was surprised to see Noelle Sears among them, talking to Royal Underhill. He looked even more worried than usual. I always attributed his stressed expression to the fact that he works with decimals and percentages all the time. I know math always did that to me.

The emergency meeting had been called, I soon learned, because there was still no sign of Roger.

Bark banged his gavel for attention, but it was Neville who called for everyone to take a seat. Neville is young, early thirties at most. He is a Study in Brown—brown hair, brown eyes, a small brown mustache, and a little brown Fu Manchu beard grown to make him look older, I suppose, but it doesn't. He wears suits and ties and wire-rimmed glasses, and you get the feeling that's how he dresses to take a shower. The most mild-mannered of men, he simply never gets excited, so when he raised his voice, as he did now, it had the desired effect.

Bark took over and got right to the point. "If anyone is interested, the contract was approved by a slim majority."

There was a moderate amount of applause, sustained only briefly. We were waiting for some further revelation.

"And so, in Roger's absence—" he said.

"Where is he?"

"What have you heard?"

"Has he called?"

The questions lapped over each other from all around the table, inundating Bark, who had to use the gavel again.

"There's nothing to report," he said. "We don't know anything about Roger. He's not here. He's not home."

"How do we know?" I said. "He could have had an accident."

"Samantha went to his condo and the manager let her in. No sign of him."

"I move we fire him," Dana said.

"We're not firing him," Bark said, ignoring all the hands that shot up.

"We don't know that he isn't gone for good. His car hasn't been found, has it?" This from Clark Newman, who always came armed to the meetings. At least that's what I heard, though I looked for telltale bulges in vain.

Well, not always in vain.

"There's a motion on the floor," Dana said.

"The motion's out of order," Bark said.

"Then I move we take an ad in the trades and offer a reward."

"Are you serious?" Evan Lantzy, the Treasurer, said, and then, his eyes narrowing, "How much?"

"Five thousand dollars," Dana said. "To anyone who finds him and doesn't return him."

No one laughed.

Bark said, "We have a guest this morning. Noelle Sears has asked to speak to the Board before she returns to the east. She has a noon flight, which assures us she'll be brief."

Noelle rose from her seat at the end of the table. Today she was wearing a black-and-white checked mini-skirt, a black Armani jacket with a white silk flower in the lapel, and high-heeled black patent pumps.

I fly in sweats.

"I know that your overriding concern is for Roger," she said, "and I'm concerned, too. But there are matters that can't be left to drift any longer. I met with Roger yesterday morning, and we discussed setting up a joint committee, Los Angeles and New York. The committee's mandate would be to make recommendations on the restructuring of the Union. Right now, the main office is here in L.A., and the rest of the branches—New York, Chicago, Dallas—have much less authority."

Bark said, "Noelle, we're not about to discuss this now, with Roger missing. If you'd told me the subject matter, I could have saved you the time and trouble." He was visibly angry, which was rare.

Any normal person would have immediately deflated, but Noelle remained standing. "I appreciate the invitation to be here this morning," she said. "Just remember—New York needs things to be different."

Then she picked up her bag and left.

"Whoa, sounds like a threat," said Neville.

"She never stops beating that drum," Dana said. "She's like a grizzly bear with her teeth in your calf. She doesn't let go."

"Mixed metaphor, mixed metaphor," chanted Dennis.

Tad Reston waved his hand. "Mister Chairman . . ."

"Tad?"

"I suggest we appoint an interim Executive Director."

This was the Board members' cue to turn what should

have been a ten-minute discussion into forty minutes of pure drivel. Joe was right. Meetings suck.

Finally, the consensus was that there was no need—yet—for an interim Director.

"I will entertain a motion to adjourn," Bark said. And that was it. So long, folks.

As we were gathering up our belongings, Evan Lantzy passed by Clark Newman, who was sitting next to me, and murmured, "I'd give the whole treasury for just one of Noelle's brass balls."

"Why not both of them," Clark said. "You could always sell the other one on E-bay."

"What do you think she's really after?" I said.

It was a tactic of innocence, my favorite kind when I want to hear someone else's version of what I already assume.

"Nothing much. She wants to elevate the New York branch to the main office, gather all the branches under her wing, and boot Roger out, that's all," said Clark.

"Never gonna happen, not ever," said Evan. "But she keeps pushing."

I nodded sagely, my second-favorite tactic, then said good-bye and headed down the hall towards Samantha's office. Bark caught up with me en route.

"Maggie, how about tomorrow night?"

I must have looked blank.

"Remember? You said we'd have dinner soon. Althea said to ask about tomorrow night. She would have called but she knew you'd be at the meeting. What do you say? We'll do Spago's."

I heard myself telling him I'd let him know, at the same time thinking I'd have to call Henrik, and he'd use the trial as an excuse, and that would let me off the hook.

After exchanging a few anxieties about Roger, I continued on to Samantha's office.

She was on the phone. "Thanks, anyway," she was saying wearily, as though she had been saying it so often, it was rote. She hung up, shaking her head.

"No news?"

"Nothing."

"Let me help," I said. "I know all the right calls to make."

"Bark told me. I've already called the hospital and the morgue. Negative, thank goodness."

"What about the police?"

"I did that," she said. "Maybe even spoke to your . . . what was he anyway?"

"My friend."

"Right. Your 'friend.' " Her tone was disbelieving, but I remained silent. I wasn't about to enlighten her by discussing my love affair with Joe.

She gave up. "They told me to file a Missing Persons report."

"Do it. What about Roger's friends? Family?"

"I'm making my way through his address file right now. Dee Dee's helping and a few others. So far, nothing."

"Okay, give me a couple of names, too."

The trouble, I knew, was that the more people we called and spoke to, the more the word would spread that Roger was missing. Well, it couldn't be helped.

Samantha gave me the number of Roger's aunt who lived in Pasadena, and of a woman he'd been dating, Karen Thorstensen, who owned and ran a janitorial service.

"Really? A janitorial service?" I hadn't meant to sound so surprised.

"Okay, Building Maintenance, if you want to be PC about it."

"It does paint a prettier picture."

"Hey, I'm not responsible for his love life." But she didn't sound quite as offhand as her words.

I took the numbers and went into Roger's office to make the calls. Mrs. Theodosia Urban, who was Roger's aunt, wasn't home, or maybe chose not to answer. Whenever I have the choice of two scenarios, I invariably go for the one that's the more damaging to my esteem. A voice informed me, in a recorded message, to leave a phone number and a brief message, and I would be called back as soon as possible. I left the Union number, and hung up, a little shaken. The recorded voice was Roger Urban's.

Next I tried calling Karen Thorstensen.

"Maids-To-Order Housecleaning Service," a woman said. "This is Edra. How can I help you?"

"I'm trying to reach Karen Thorstensen. May I speak to her?"

"Ms. Thorstensen is busy, but I will help you." Did you ever have the feeling the person on the other end of the line was chewing gum? Edra must have had a whole pack in her mouth. "Are you a new customer?"

"No. I'd really like to—"

"Please give me your name, address, and phone number and the number of rooms in your home. Is it more than one story?"

"It has no stories. Could I please—"

"May I make an appointment for one of our Maids-To-Order Maids to give your home a clean sweep?"

I refrained from telling her that Maid Lionel already had that job. I said, quickly, so as to avoid another onrush, "I need to speak to Ms. Thorstensen. It's very important."

"We have a special this month. If you let us do your windows, we will go up on the roof and clean out your eaves."

"My eaves?"

"Could they use a good cleaning out?"

"I'm afraid to look. Please tell Karen Thorstensen I need to speak to her right now!"

"She can't come to the phone. She's not here. She's out in the field."

"The field? What in hell is that?"

"I don't know. That's what I'm supposed to say. She is out in the field."

"Does the field have an address?"

"I'm sorry. That's private information."

"Listen, Edra, this is also private information. I'm a writer. I write for the movies. I need to speak to Ms. Thorstensen about a movie we're doing."

"Oh my God! Is she going to be in a movie? Who else is in it? Antonio Banderas? Nicolas Cage? Leonardo DiCaprio?"

"Adam Sandler."

"Oh." There was a pause, while, apparently, she either swallowed her gum or shifted it to the other side of her mouth. "Well, what part will she play?"

"First, you tell me where she is!"

Finally I got an address on Capri Drive in Pacific Palisades. I sat there for a while, thinking. The office was quiet with the door closed, and Roger's computer monitor was staring at me. I could see from the light on the phone that Samantha was making her calls, and I thought, why not. It would be stepping over the edge, I knew that. Joe always said that was one of my character deficiencies but Joe wasn't here. Which was one of *his* character deficiencies.

"What are you waiting for?" Mercedes said. "She who hesitates is road kill."

I turned on the monitor, but when I tried to open Roger's files, it turned out to be password protected. Now hacking is not a regular pastime of mine but I'm not bad for a hack hacker. I tried Roger's birthday, which the Board had celebrated a few weeks ago, his middle name that he had told me was Stanley, and then pondered the situation. R.S.U., his initials. Sounds like the morning-after pill. I pondered some more. Some machines will close down after the third wrong password, so the next one had to be right.

The light on the phone went off. I buzzed Samantha.

"Do you know Roger's password for his computer?"

"No." Disapproving pause. "What would be the purpose of the password if anyone else has it?"

"Good point."

"Maggie, what are you doing in there anyway?"

"Making calls. I just wondered."

"Take the phone off the hook, dumb ass," Mercedes said.

I did. Samantha went back to her phone and I turned back to the monitor and thought again about using some component of Roger's name. Not Roger or Urban, of course, that was too easy. Then I got to thinking some more about the name Roger, and, for some reason, that brought to mind the breakthrough movie *Who Framed Roger Rabbit?*

The reason was right in front of my eyes. There, on the opposite wall, was a framed poster from the movie, signed by Bob Hoskins. Could Rabbit be the password? It was certainly in keeping with his rumored sexual prowess.

The trouble with stepping over the edge is there's no turning back. I tried Rabbit—and it worked. Finding an empty Zip disc in his desk, I downloaded his files. It briefly crossed my mind that I could e-mail them to myself, but that would leave a trail leading right back to me. I shut the computer down and left for the address on Capri Drive.

6

There was some sort of tie-up at the Santa Monica–Wilshire intersection and it took forever to get across. It looked like the cops were working a drug bust on the corner next to the fountain, and the lookie-loos had snarled traffic on both streets.

The house proved to be a mini-estate, Georgian style, set back from the street by a generous expanse of lawn and a rosebush-bordered brick walkway. I rang the bell and was rewarded with a melodious orchestration of chimes.

From somewhere inside I could hear the drone of a vacuum cleaner, but no one came to the door. I peered through a beveled glass inset, and could make out the figure of a woman maneuvering the vacuum. I rang again. Then I knocked. Finally I banged. That got the woman's attention, and she came to the door, still vacuuming, and opened it a cautionary, unwelcoming gap.

From the narrow slice of a view I had, she was tall and quite pretty. Large bones, long arms, long legs. A scarf sprinkled in sequins bound up her hair, with a few tendrils of streaked-blondness peeking out. She wore dark green farmer's overalls and a tight T-shirt, and had tied the strings of a smudged apron twice around her middle. The apron bore the lettering: "Maids-To-Order." One hand rested on the handle of a vacuum cleaner that was still in full-throated operation.

"Yes?" The word rankled with impatience.

"I'm really sorry to bother you. I'm looking for Karen Thorstensen."

She rewarded me with a dubious look.

I raised my voice to be heard above the din of the vacuum. "Thorstensen! Karen Thorstensen! May I come in?"

She turned off the infernal machine and stepped back from the door, opening it wider. I moved into the hallway.

"Did you wipe your shoes?" she said. "I just cleaned the rugs."

"If you'll please tell Ms. Thorstensen I'm here, I promise not to step on anything."

"I'm Karen Thorstensen," she said. "Now what do you want? I'm very busy."

"Oh. I thought—" Well, it was obvious what I thought. Wasn't she supposed to be the owner of the business? "It's about Roger Urban."

"What about him?"

I explained briefly. "He seems to have disappeared. He didn't show up for our Union meeting last night, he didn't show up today, and no one's been able to reach him. I thought you might know where he is."

"I haven't seen him," she said.

"Well, when was the last time you were with him?"

"That's none of your business, Miss Whoever You Are, and like I said, I'm busy."

"Maggie Mars. I'm a writer."

"Condolences. I'm still busy. I should be at the office, only I'm trying to finish a job here because we're short-handed today, so unless you'd like to grab a mop and bucket and tackle the kitchen floor, please leave."

Reluctantly I headed out, but then paused on the threshold. I remembered what Lionel had said about Roger's "little flings," and I should have known better, but, hell, when did insensitivity ever deter an investigative reporter.

"I wonder . . ." I said. "Would you know of any other women he was dating?"

For answer, she turned the vacuum cleaner on again, full blast.

A glorious sunset was turning the sky red and pink and violet in my rearview mirror. Someone once told me that the sunsets are so beautiful here because of the smog. Something about the particles in the air and the refraction of light, which still mystifies me. The colors made a halo around the tops of the palm trees, as I left the Palisades and headed east, intending to make my way home.

My cell phone rang, but of course it was in my pocket and the seat belt prevented me from getting to it in time. It never fails. I hate carrying the phone in my hand. My pocket or tote bag is perfect, except in the car when I'm buckled up.

I pulled over, unbuckled, and looked at the readout. It was U.G. He had a knack for calling me at all the wrong times. A parental attribute, I guess.

"Hi, Dad, I couldn't get to my phone in time. How are you?"

"I'm great. Are you free tonight?"

"Uh-huh. What's up?"

"Why does something have to be up? I just want to see you. Let's have dinner out. Your treat."

I laughed. "Okay, meet me at my place."

"Oh. No. Is what's-his-face gonna be there?"

"Dad, for heaven's sake. You've known Lionel as long as I have."

"That's nothing to brag about. I'll be there at six thirty. Bye."

I buckled up again, and was continuing on my way home, when, instead, I took a detour south. Disregarding all the little stoplights blinking away in the traffic patterns of my head, I drove to the West L.A. Police Station. I won't even pretend I just happened to be passing by. It was as deliberate a dumb move as I've ever managed to conceive.

However, maybe he wouldn't be there. Plan A—I could just leave a token message and go. I would just say Roger hadn't shown up, which he must have already known. Plan B—I could ask if they needed a description of Roger—or—

Plan C—I could just run into Joe as I was walking into the station and he was coming out. He was with another man, deep in energetic conversation.

It was the first time I had seen Joe Camanetti in two years. I had almost forgotten how just the sight of his muscular, not-quite-good looks could do indecent things to my resolve not to feel anything for him, could trigger all the wanton memories I thought I had left behind.

I weathered the breakup with Joe fairly well, I thought. We met, unromantically sounding enough, at the John Jay College of Criminal Justice. He was a detective, on leave from the NYPD, teaching courses on Advanced Criminalistics, and I was in the library doing research on an investigative piece. The rest, as they say, is history. Ancient history.

I moved into his place, and for two years it was good, amazingly, incredibly good. But happily ever after doesn't last as long as it used to. LAPD offered Joe a promotion in rank, with benefits and a pay raise to match, and who wouldn't want to move out to the land of sunshine, palm trees, and movie stars?

Me, that's who. I wanted to remain in Manhattan, near my parents and my work. So, he went and I stayed. For a while we racked up the Frequent Flyer miles and I figured our love could survive the separation, but I figured wrong. The bi-coastal thing just didn't work out. The distance and the disconnection killed it. Or maybe it was the babe he began to date, after I had suggested, in a fit of magnanimity, that we both see other people.

"No good deed goes unpunished," Mercedes said.

Even though we both lived on the same coast for the last two years, in the same city, you can't keep patching a tire that's been punctured too many times. Sooner or later you were headed for a blowout. Some things were best left alone, and that's how we left them.

Now, seeing him, my hands began to tingle and sweat.

"Hello, Joe."

I'm not sure what I would have done if he hadn't stopped. But he did. He even offered a long-time-no-see smile.

"Hey, Maggie. What are you doing here?"

"You're busy," I said. "Is there someone inside I should talk to?"

"It's okay, you can talk to me. This is my partner, Martin Wu. Martin, this is Maggie."

The other man beamed at me. "Maggie, yes. I think you've mentioned her once or twice."

"Don't believe everything he says. Hi, nice to meet you."

I shook hands with Martin, noticing that he was a pleasant-looking Asian man, dark-haired, short, probably just making the height requirement for the Force. And he had dimples. When had I last seen a man with dimples?

"Any luck with Jack Nicholson yet?" he asked with a straight face.

I shot a murderous look at Joe. It was one thing to remember my obsession, but he had no business sharing it with anyone else!

I put on what I hoped was a pleasant expression.

"No Jack," I said. "No Roger either. Do you think it's a conspiracy?"

Joe said, "Could be. Were you close to this Urban guy?"

"No, not really."

"Then why are you involved?"

"I'm not *involved* involved. I'm concerned, that's all."

"Just concerned, huh?" He winked at Martin. I could have killed him. Right there in front of the police station.

"I'm on the Board," I managed to say without gritting my teeth. "I'd just like to make sure he's okay."

"We've got the Missing Persons report. We're investigating all possible leads," he said. "We're on top of it."

"Sounds like a press release."

He looked as though he had a more acerbic comeback, but what he said was, "You should know the routine."

"Then I'll hear from you?" I didn't mean to make it sound like a question.

"You'll hear from someone," Joe said.

Touché.

Martin excused himself. "I'll wait in the car."

"I'll drive!" Joe called after him.

For a moment, the silence enveloped us like a shroud.

"Well," I said, and didn't know where to go from there.

"If it hadn't been for this Roger thing," he said, "would you have ever called me?"

Would I have ever called him? Of course I would have. I was a glutton for punishment. "I called you before," I said. "When I first arrived in town. A woman answered and I hung up."

He nodded.

"It was early on a Sunday morning."

"Would you believe we were going to church?" There was the trace of a smile.

"I would believe she had spent the night."

"Yeah, well, you know how it is."

"I know how it was."

Just then Martin pulled up at the curb in an unmarked car.

"Goddamn it!" Joe yelled. "I told you *I'd* drive!" He hurried over to the car and didn't bother looking back.

"That's why you can't go home again," said Mercedes. "Nobody's there."

7

Lionel was looking upset as he prepared dinner for one.

"Why does Ugh insist on eating out all the time? Is it my cooking or *moi*?"

"His name is not Ugh, it's U.G., and you'd better not call him that to his face. He just wants to talk to me, I don't know about what."

U.G. arrived, right on time for a change, and looking rather dapper. He had on freshly pressed Dockers and deck shoes and blue paint on his right hand.

As he hugged me, he glanced over at Lionel.

"Hello to you, too, Twinkletoes."

"Back atcha, Reverend Falwell."

I said, "Okay. That's enough, guys."

"Sorry, Maggie," U.G. said, only I knew he wasn't. He turned to Lionel. "So, Lionel, who do you like in the World Series?"

"Well, of the two teams—"

"Oh, I don't mean the teams," U.G. said. "I mean any particular first baseman?"

He was hopeless. Lionel retreated to the kitchen before the bell rang for another round.

U.G. and I went to the Cheesecake Factory in Brentwood, and over his Kamikaze and my Diet Coke, I checked him out. He had my eyes—or, to put things in the proper sequence, I had his eyes—and they were clear and unclouded. He had always been a fitness nut, and, even though he was short, he had the form of a guy still in really good shape.

During dinner, he opened up. "Maggie, I'm real sorry to be costing you so much extra money."

"I told you, Dad, stop worrying about it."

"But I do. You know, honey, I can always move to another retirement place. They're popping up all over. Maybe there's one even closer to you."

I groaned inwardly. That's all I needed.

"I can find one that's a little cheaper," he said. "Maybe get some sort of a part-time job. The last thing I want to be is a burden on you."

"You aren't a burden. The extra cost is minimal, and my screenplay money will more than cover it."

"Yeah, but I keep thinking that if I saved you cash, you could afford to move out of Peter Pan's home and into one of your own."

"I don't want to move from Lionel's and stop insulting him. He's my best friend. And his parents were Mom's and your best friends. What ever happened to compassion for your fellow man?"

"I don't think Lionel qualifies under that heading."

What was the use?

U.G. buttered his roll. "By the way," he said, "I understand you saw Joe."

So he had talked to him. I wasn't surprised. My dad always liked Joe and they kept in touch after the breakup. U.G. was sort of a shared custody thing.

"It was just about Roger Urban's disappearance, that's all."

"It's a move in the right direction."

I changed the subject and inquired about the blue paint. That was enough to start U.G. happily off on a prolonged discussion of his latest invention, some kind of portable device to detect explosive gasses.

"Great for industry and for the home," he said. "This one is going to put us on Millionaires Row, Maggie."

"Just as long as you don't blow up something. The budget will never stretch to cover those costs."

"I swear, Maggie, a man blows up one high school chem lab, and you act as though he's Public Menace Number One."

I let it go. Why ruin a perfectly good dinner that I was paying for.

U.G. was a chemist slash inventor and was always messing around with things that go boom in the night. The last thing that went boom in the night was the lab at the high school where he taught chemistry. It wasn't entirely his fault, but go tell that to the Board of Education. So long, lab. Hello, mandatory retirement.

The rest of the meal was pleasant. We talked about relatives back east and ended up companionably sharing a fresh fruit plate.

I dropped him at his parking place, and as he fumbled with his key, I stared at the car. It was a maroon Jaguar, so old I couldn't remember him in any other car. It must have at least two hundred thousand miles on it. How in hell was it still running? Better I not think about it. A new car is definitely not in the budget, not even a new, old car.

The next day, I sat down at my laptop. I was screening my calls. My producer, the famous-in-his-own-mind Fowler Mohr, was the kind of producer who wants to be consulted over every comma, and I need to be left alone in order to write. We were like oil and water, but I needed this job, so I didn't want to blow him off, I just wanted to dodge him as much as possible. I was trying to keep thoughts of Henrik and Joe from scrambling my brain. Not to mention Roger.

There was nothing I could do about Roger. Joe and Henrik were not so easily put aside. Henrik was everyone's idea of Mr. Right. Funny, successful, popular, easy to get along with. Joe was stubborn, taciturn, a loner, and most of all no longer in my life. So, how come I was brooding about him? Why was I giving him the same amount of air-time as Henrik?

"You left out how great he was in bed," said Mercedes.

I ignored her. That's it! No more distractions! I went back to work.

INT. PENTHOUSE CONDO—NIGHT

Detective Jack Mackenzie huddles with two uniformed officers and a few plainclothes detectives. They turn as a BING! signals the arrival of the interior elevator. As the door opens, CAMERA PANS UP the attractive nylon-covered legs, shapely body, and beautiful face of Mercedes Pell as she steps out into the living room.

ON JACK

As he grimaces and turns to the officers and whispers to them. They nod as Jack heads for the bedroom with the other detectives. As Mercedes starts to follow them, the two officers step in her path.

                    OFFICER #1
   Sorry, Ma'am. This is a police investigation.

Mercedes moves right into his face and smiles. She speaks in a calm voice.

                    MERCEDES
   Officer, I understand you were given a job to do by the detective. And right now you're trying to do that job. But my dad is the Chief of Police, and Detective Mackenzie, the one who just whis-

pered to you to stop me, I just found
out he knocked me up. . . . And if you
don't let me go into that room right
now . . . I will get both your badges,
turn them sideways, and SHOVE THEM UP
YOUR TIGHT BLUE ASSES!

The officers look to each other, then back to
Mercedes, who just smiles. They step aside
as she passes.

INT. CONDO BEDROOM—CONTINUOUS

The detectives are standing over the bed.
Lying on the rumpled sheets is the dead body
of a beautiful naked woman. On the bed next
to her is an empty pill bottle. Jack turns
as Mercedes enters the room.

> JACK
> I didn't think they could keep you out
> of here. I just thought I'd give it a
> try. What did you tell them this time,
> Mercedes?

> MERCEDES
> That you knocked me up and my dad was
> the Chief of Police.

> JACK
> Knock you up? No chance of that. And by
> the way, about being the Police Chief's
> daughter . . . he's black.

> MERCEDES
> They're your officers, not mine.
>   (looking at body)
> Amanda Peterson? . . .

Belatedly I remembered I hadn't called Bark to beg off this evening's dinner, so I logged off and tried reaching Henrik first. At least my conscience would have an alibi.

Surprisingly, he said he could make it. They weren't in session on weekends and he was caught up on his trial preparations. He also spoke of after-dinner pleasures, and I remembered why I loved him. Or at least was on the verge of loving him.

Maybe it would be easier if he had some flaws. If he wasn't so absolutely terrific. A picture came into my mind, of Henrik on Court TV a month ago. He was a guest analyst on the case under review, not his of course, and he was in his element, talking about the problems the prosecution was having in the case. The two women hostesses were fawning over him. It was quite apparent he liked it. If Henrik had a shortcoming, it wasn't his good profile, it was his high profile.

Pulling myself together I called Bark at his office, and we set the time for eight.

When Lionel heard we were going to Spago's, he was beside himself with ecstasy.

"Take notes! All the name noshers will be there!"

I promised to bring back any titillating nuggets of gossip, and that evening Henrik and I joined Bark and Althea.

She was resplendent in a white silk dinner suit, and, along with Bark's recognizable face and his sinewy good looks, they turned all heads as we were ushered to our table. Henrik was grinning, obviously relishing being in the limelight. He was used to having people stare at him, but most often it was juries. Tonight he could relax and not have to make a closing argument.

I, on the other hand, was used to people not looking at me. Once, when I was invited to a red-carpet movie premiere, a young teenager, autograph album in hand, called out from the edge of the surrounding crowd of fans, "Are you anybody?"

Nope. I wasn't. So I was glad when we were finally seated, smack in the center of the patio, which was the Thomases' regular table.

The table was primo if you like to be noticed, and also if it turns you on to be asphyxiated by cigar smoke. For me, its main advantage was that it was the most favored spot in the place to catch a glimpse of Jack Nicholson if he should by any chance come in. Maybe even be seated nearby!

I could see the bar and the gorgeous females draped around it. No one weighed more than a hundred pounds. I felt like Gulliver in Lilliput. They all had perfect breasts, perfect hair and makeup, and they all wore thin, wispy dresses with tiny spaghetti straps. Lionel would particularly want to know that. I particularly wanted to know how they kept from freezing in the restaurant's air conditioning.

Bark said, almost immediately, "There's no news, Maggie. Roger still hasn't surfaced."

"Bark, you promised we wouldn't talk about it tonight," Althea said.

"Done," he said. "Let's order drinks."

After that, it was Henrik who proved to be the conversational *pièce de résistance.* It fed right into his love of attention. Althea and Bark appeared to be fascinated by his stories of murder cases he had successfully defended. For me, that was the dark side of Henrik, the fact that he doesn't seem to suffer from regrets about freeing some of these creeps.

To her credit, Althea brought up the same objection.

"Better that a scuzzbag walks free than an innocent person go to jail," Henrik told her. "That's the whole basis of our justice system. The effort is on protecting the innocent and if a few errors are made, it's better to err this way."

Bark said, "I once wrote a movie about a lawyer who felt as you do. Honey, what was the name of it again?"

"For the People," Althea said promptly. "And, if you remember, the lawyer was killed in the end."

"Henrik, take that as a warning," I said.

"To stop defending my clients?"

"To watch your ass."

They laughed.

"Now, if the prosecutor and the jury did their jobs," Henrik said over his sour apple martini, "they wouldn't go free."

It was his standard defense of himself, and it did have a slight tinge of truth to it, especially since Althea now echoed the sentiment.

"I suppose you're just doing what you get paid for," she said, "and obviously you do it very well."

How sweet.

Henrik's foot pressed against mine with just the slightest of touches. Bless him.

While the waiter was hovering, waiting to take our orders, Althea looked over at me from behind her menu.

"Maggie, I presume you like fashion shows?"

I could hear the hesitation in her voice, and realized she must have a very poor impression of my fashion sense, that is, if I had any at all. We first met after the general meeting when I wore my "writer's outfit," jeans and boots. Tonight I was wearing my only skirt, a tight camel-colored lightweight wool, and I had paired it with a gray, short-sleeved T-shirt, also tight. The only concession I made to the present company was to put on my prized pair of Manolo's beige slides.

But Althea had asked me a question, and I needed a courteous answer. She was dressed this evening by Armani, and I was dressed by the Gap. What kind of fashion show would appeal to the both of us? The only one I had ever been to featured the latest styles from Sears. I remember not particularly enjoying myself, because who wants to be at a fashion show where you can afford the clothes?

"I adore them," said hypocritical me.

"Good. Then consider this a Save the Date card for December the twelfth. The Women's Hospital Auxiliary is having our annual Christmas Luncheon and Fashion Show. The trendiest designers will be showing off their wares. I'd love you to be there."

I mumbled something that I hoped would pass for a "thank you."

"I must get something fabulous for the Walk of Fame Gala." Even as she spoke, her eyes were checking out my T-shirt. "Of course, even if the clothes don't interest you, you'll be doing a good deed because it is a charity fundraiser."

A clever way of telling me to bring my credit card.

After the waiter had taken our orders and removed the menus, I went into a conversational shift.

"I hope Althea will excuse me for bringing up shop talk again, Bark, but if Roger doesn't show, what's your next move?"

"He's going to appoint an interim Executive Director," Althea said.

"The Board will make that decision," Bark said evenly.

"Of course, darling." Althea smiled, but there was steel there.

She turned to me. "I'm just there for moral support," she said.

Bark was spared whatever his opinion of that might have been, because just then a man passing by our table abruptly stopped.

"Henrik, what are you doing here?" he said. "Is your jury out already?"

"Hello, Dewey. I hope not." He rose and shook the other man's hand. "We're just off for the weekend."

"Dewey" turned out to be one Dewey P. Forrestal. Henrik introduced him, complete with middle initial. He was tall, solidly built, with sparse blond hair and puffy red cheeks. I wondered if he had spent too much time either in the sun or on the sauce.

At any rate he lingered only long enough to brown-nose Bark a little—I wouldn't have been surprised if he had a screenplay in the pocket of his Ermenigildo jacket—and to tell Henrik they must do lunch some time soon. He then proceeded to pass business cards all around and move on.

I looked at his card. "Dewey P. Forrestal. The Committee on Moral Decency? What's that?"

"A political plum. He's a friend of the Mayor," Henrik said.

Bark seemed interested. "Isn't that the committee the Producers Association set up in order to derail Congress's efforts to clean up movies and television?"

"It's much better if we keep that type of thing in the family, so to speak, don't you agree, Henrik?" Althea said.

"With Dewey P. leading the way," said Henrik.

"You got it," said Bark. "Where's the First Amendment when you really need it."

I couldn't help thinking that if Joe had been sitting here with me instead of Henrik, Bark would have gotten an earful about the First Amendment, and Bark wouldn't have been so friendly and the conversation wouldn't have flowed like wine, or, in my case, water, and why, oh why, was I thinking about Joe again.

I think it was over dessert—tiramisu, which has replaced Apple Pie as the All-American dessert—and raspberry sorbet for me—that Tom Cruise came in with a party, all of whom were taller than he. I thought I spotted Steven Spielberg among them, but all beards look alike to me. No Jack Nicholson.

By unspoken mutual consent—I told you it was an adult relationship—Henrik and I didn't end up at his place, after all. It was late and he was tired. He drove me home and gave me a promissory kiss for next time.

8

I let myself in and found Lionel and Troy Merino parading around in harem girl outfits, with pink sequined bras and filmy pants and lots of gauzy veils and makeup. I would have even sworn they had incense burning.

Troy is Lionel's best friend, an adjunct to his life long before I arrived. He is small and wiry, his hair and his eyebrows and long lashes bleached an impossible shade of strawberry blond. Since he works for a studio wardrobe department, I imagined that was the source of the harem girl costumes. Probably they derived from some years-gone-by desert epic, and, if you shook them, sand might still fall out. The few visible stains on the apparel might or might not be camel dung.

I said, "Isn't this a bit much, even for you guys?"

Lionel said, "We're considering these as our outfits for the Halloween Gay Pride parade. Do you like them?"

"You look like you're wearing the Victoria's Secret catalogue."

"Good. I'm supposed to be Salome, and Troy is Scheherazade, or maybe his vice is my versa. I can't make up my mind which."

Troy was looking unhappy. "I told Lionel it'll be too cold

to run around in veils at night. You know how susceptible I am to the cold weather." He plopped down on the couch, veils fluttering. "Maggie, tell him we need something warmer and with more pizzazz."

"Why not go as the Team Canada hockey team?"

They looked at me blankly.

Lionel said, "Ignore her, Troy. What would the ex-inamorata of a homicide cop know about pizzazz?"

What, indeed? I kicked off my shoes and retreated to my bedroom for a robe and slippers.

When I came out again, Lionel was opening a bottle of wine, Shiraz, this month's favorite, and he had thoughtfully brewed a cup of mango tea for me. I made myself comfortable and prepared to face a barrage of questions about Spago's.

How was the food prepared? Who was there? What was everyone wearing? How did Tom Cruise look from the rear?

"Oh, by the way," Lionel said, his veils aquiver in my face. "I have messages for you."

"Who from?"

"I have it here somewhere." He looked around in vague perplexity, then brightened, and reached into the sparkling bra, pulling out a piece of paper.

"Here it is," he said. "The Fowl called—"

"If you mean Fowler Mohr . . ."

"That's what I said."

"He'll keep till tomorrow."

"And, oh yes, Joe called."

"Joe? Why didn't you tell me?"

"I just did."

"Be glad he kept the message in a safe place," Troy said.

It seems Joe had left word that there was nothing new. Roger Urban was still very much a Missing Person. Missing or worse, I worried, and kissed Lionel and Troy on their painted cheeks, did the glucose check, and went to bed.

To bed but not to sleep. Mercedes kept nudging.

"Why aren't we out looking for him?" she said.

"Looking for whom? Roger Urban?"

"No. Mr. Goodbar. Of course, Roger Urban. Pull on your sweats and let's go. We'll make the rounds."

"Make the rounds of what?"

"It doesn't matter. The thing is, we'll be doing something."

"But why do I have to be doing anything? It's a police matter."

"Asked and answered," said Mercedes.

I buried my face in the pillow.

The next day, the *Times* and the trades carried big articles on Roger's disappearance. *Variety* even had it in a black-bordered box on the upper right of the front page, and mentioned that fourteen writers had registered the idea for a movie. There was no conjecture about what might have happened to him, although Tom Vincent's column in the *Reporter* quoted an unidentified source as saying that several women were being questioned.

Bark did appoint an interim Executive Director—Neville Lake—and Board members were asked to approve this by a telephone vote. I approved it.

I didn't think Joe would call, of course he wouldn't call, why should he call? But after I opened my laptop, I got up again, fetched the portable phone, and planted it alongside. Immediately it rang, and I answered on the first ring, to find it was Fowler.

He was pleasant as always, and seemed to be satisfied when I said that yes, the work was going well, and no, I didn't need his help, and yes, I would soon be done, and no, he couldn't see any pages yet, and yes, I was working on it this very minute and would get back to it just as soon as he hung up. . . .

He hung up.

                    JACK
     Let's go, Mercedes.
          (escorting her out)

And just to get your investigative butt
out of here . . . she's a suicide.
Probably got dumped and O.D.'d on Perco-
dan. No story here.

MERCEDES

Suicide?! Buzzzzzzzzzzz. Wrong answer.
It's a definite homicide.

JACK

So when there's no story, you just make
one up. Is that it?

Mercedes breaks free of Jack's grasp and
heads back towards the bed.

MERCEDES

Women like Amanda Peterson don't kill
themselves over a man. Look at those
tits, they're not your Wal-Mart five-grand
jobs. . . . Those babies are twenty-five-
grand Park Avenue, New York, New York
specials. And her face, guys . . .
        (looks at Detectives)
Guys, you're still looking at her tits.
LOOK AT HER FACE! That's better. There's
enough *Restylane* in there to fill the
Grand Canyon. And I'm sure those ass
cheeks aren't hers either. Her body
costs more than all of you make in a
year. If women like that get dumped,
they just find another rich guy and do
him. Why do men always think it's about
feelings to women?

JACK

Thanks for the better living through
plastics lecture, Mercedes. Now if you

will kindly take your butt out of here,
we can finish up this suicide investigation.

                    MERCEDES
Murder. It's murder. She was killed.
Give me a few days . . . I'll prove it!

9

"I think you'll be interested in this one," *Pat Draper was saying, as she undid the realtor's lock on the front door of the classic Mediterranean house. "It belongs to a very famous producer."*

"Would I know him?" asked the woman.

"I'm not free to reveal his name, but his last movie earned titanic grosses."

"Really? He produced Titanic? *The one who said he felt like the king of the world?"*

"You're thinking of the director, and, anyway, I didn't mean the movie, I meant it was big. Very big. I think he got an Oscar or something for it."

Pat opened the door and they went in.

The entry was of stone flooring, flanked by glazed terra cotta urns, and ahead of them rose a main staircase with a balustrade of iron spindles, tipped with gilt. Leaded glass windows ascended along with the stairs. The living room was furnished in the kind of antiques that were all circa some long-gone bygone year.

The woman wrinkled her nose in a delicate sniff as she looked around, approvingly, Pat thought.

"The chandelier is nice," the woman said. "Are those real flowers hanging down from it?"

"A very desirable decorative feature. Doesn't it just reek of Italy?"

"It reeks of something," the woman said. Again that little sniff.

"The producer is shooting a new picture in New York and London, and the house has been empty for a while," Pat added, hastily. "Not that it isn't desirable. You know what they say. It just takes the right buyer." She forged on in her sales spiel, all too conscious herself of an unpleasant aroma. "You'll love the kitchen. It has dark beams, wood cabinets, a Louis XIV–style stone fireplace, and it opens onto a glorious terrace."

"Let's go upstairs first," the woman said. "I want to see the bedrooms."

"I can't wait to show them. The view up there is to die for," Pat said.

They went up the curving staircase, Pat keeping up the prescribed patter.

"You'll adore the dhurrie rug in the master bedroom. I'm sure it can be included. And wait till you see the luxury baths and dressing rooms. His and hers, of course."

"Of course," the woman said. They entered the spacious master bedroom.

"Notice the French doors," Pat said. "They open to a private balcony."

The woman sniffed again. "That smell is even stronger up here."

"Really? I hadn't noticed," Pat said.

But, of course, she had. It was definitely something pungent, something disagreeable.

The woman pointed. "It seems to be coming from that bathroom," she said. "You're sure nobody's been staying here?"

"I'll have a look," Pat said. "Why don't you go out on the balcony and take in the view."

The bathroom door was open. She went in, trying not to

breathe in too deeply, because the smell was now unques-
tionably strong, sweetish and awful and smelling of iron.
With her hand already half pinching her nose, she checked
the toilet cubicle. Nothing. Then she noticed that the etched
glass doors enclosing the spa-tub were closed. She would
want her client to see the elegant marble step-down bath.
That would take her mind off whatever that odor was. Unless, of course, and please don't let it be, that was the source.

Before she could reach the bath, she saw it. A pool of dark
blackish-red stuff on the marble floor leading up to the tub
and over the side.

She hesitated before the glass doors. Should she see what
was behind them? But she knew she would have to. She
opened them.

And screamed. And screamed. And screamed.

Turning to run, she bumped into her client, who had come
up behind her.

"What?" the woman said. And then she saw it, too. "Oh
my God! There's a body in there!"

She clutched at Pat, who stopped screaming and began to
hyperventilate. The client sank to the floor, covered her face,
and began to howl.

Pat said, "I know there's a body in there. There's not supposed to be a body in the house. It's supposed to be ready to
show. It's not supposed to have a body."

Much less a body in a garter belt and red satin bra. . . .

10

I had finished the scene in Dante's apartment, and now it was decision time. To be in jail or not to be. That was the question. I stared and stared at my Windows desktop until the gurgling fish came out to play. No help there. I decided to get busy with other things until I was in a more creative mood. Translation: Mercedes would have to wait until I could stop thinking about Joe, Henrik, Roger, Joe, Henrik. They were now taking turns obsessing me.

So I busied myself cleaning the cat hairs off my black sweats, washing my hairbrushes, sorting and labeling discs, and rearranging my underwear drawer. The underwear drawer was always my last resort. How many times can you assort bras and panties by color? Especially when they had all started out white?

Finally, I sat down at the laptop again. But only to play three games of Free Cell. Then my thoughts strayed to the next month's check for my father, and all the checks to come, and only then was I ready to focus on what I should be doing.

INT. JAIL CELL—MORNING

Mercedes lies on a cot, her eyes closed. Suddenly a large shadow creeps over her face. She opens her eyes to find . . .

DOT (a BEEFY BLACK WOMAN), a CHICANA, and a smaller BLACK WOMAN standing over her. They're obviously gang members.

                    DOT
  You laying on Dot's cot.

                  MERCEDES
  Dot said I could lie here.

                    DOT
  I'm Dot.

Dot reaches down, picks Mercedes up by the collar, lifts her to her feet like a feather, and pulls her to within inches of her face.

                DOT (CONT'D)
  And I didn't say nothing to you.

                  MERCEDES
  Must have been another Dot.

Dot flings Mercedes across the cell. Mercedes winces away the pain and slowly gets to her feet.

              MERCEDES (CONT'D)
  You're going to jump me, aren't you.

Dot and the other girls nod. . . .

When I glanced at my watch I saw it was almost one. I shoved back my chair and was immediately rewarded with a screech from Harpo.

"How many times have I told you to be careful where you sit to lick yourself?"

I felt a little shaky, like low blood sugar shaky, so I went into the kitchen and prepared a sandwich of thin slices of turkey on a hard roll. That was a mistake. Not the turkey or the roll, but being in the kitchen where I could glance at the wall calendar's October page, which showed the brilliant turning of the leaves in New England.

My mind flew back to those autumn Sunday mornings when Joe and I would wake up slowly, somehow, amazingly, at the same moment, reach for each other with our eyes still closed, and move slowly into our lovemaking rhythm. Sunday morning slow, the two of us in a universe of our own, until the rhythm took on a new urgency and exploded into blazing stars and flame-tailed comets circling his body as it curved over mine, his hands on my breasts and his mouth moving down from my throat, down, down, down . . .

The shakiness was worse now. The memories were ricocheting in my brain, and I didn't know whether they were tinged with regret at what might have been or anger at what had happened between us . . . or whether it was just my sugar bouncing around. To be on the safe side, I helped myself to a cut-up orange and ate half the sandwich.

Then I went back to my screenplay. . . .

                    MERCEDES
        Okay, but before you do, I need to say
        something. The last twenty-four hours
        have been the longest in my life. I have
        been chased, shot at, run off the
        road . . .
                (she starts approaching)
        Shot at again.

The smaller black girl gets in front of Mercedes and is met with a fist to the abdomen, knocking her breath out. She crumbles to her knees.

> MERCEDES (CONT'D)
> Lay on the floor, raise your hips, and your breath will come back to you. Where was I?

> DOT
> Your second shot at.

> MERCEDES
> (resumes approaching)
> Thank you. My fiancé called the wedding off, I've got ants in my kitchen again. . . . The cable company won't come out and fix the fucking teevee. . . .

The Chicana comes up from behind and Mercedes meets her with a chop to her windpipe. She crumbles beside the black girl.

> MERCEDES
> You better lay down, too. Put your head back and try to breathe slowly.

She looks back to Dot.

> DOT
> (reminding her)
> The cable company won't come out and fix the fucking teevee.

> MERCEDES
> Right. My vibrator burned out. I'VE GOT

```
THIS  DICKHEAD  DETECTIVE  TORN  BETWEEN
TRYING  TO  GET  IN  MY  PANTS  AND  ARRESTING
ME . . . I'VE  GOT  PMS . . . AND  MY  BEST
FRIEND  WAS  JUST  MURDERED . . . SO  IF
YOU  WANT  TO  JUMP  ME,  NOW'S  NOT  A  GOOD
DAY!!!!!!!
```

```
                    DOT
Okay, got it. You cool. Take the cot.
I'd rather stand.
```

```
Mercedes  returns  to  the  cot  and  lies
down. . . .
```

When I later remembered to check my glucose level, whatever it had been, it was now normal.

It was some time in the middle of the afternoon that Samantha called. I lose track of time when I write.

"Maggie? Are you sitting down?"

I hate telephone calls that start like that. Someday I'm going to put a phone in my bathroom, so that when someone says, "Are you sitting down?" I'll already have assumed the position.

"What is it, Samantha?"

Silence. I hate that, too. But I persisted.

"Has Roger turned up?"

"They found his body."

11

It took me a second to register the full import of her words. "He's dead?"

Real brainy, Maggie. Of course he's dead. They don't go around finding your body unless you're not in it anymore.

"What happened? Was it an accident?" I said.

"The police said he was murdered."

I'm a writer and I couldn't think of a damn thing to say. Maybe because the other thing that hit me was that Joe hadn't been the one to call. Why hadn't he called? You'd think he'd have called, especially since I was the one who first reported that Roger was missing. I pushed the thought away. Roger was dead. That was what I should be centering on.

"How did it happen?"

"I don't know. They haven't released any details. The rumor is they found his body in the bathtub."

"Drowned? In his bathtub?"

"Someone else's bathtub. And I don't think he was drowned."

My mind was reeling, trying to take it all in.

"I just can't believe it."

Samantha said, "I don't want to believe it."

She was trying to keep from crying. I listened to the telltale sounds, a little embarrassed, feeling as though I were peeking in on someone who wasn't wearing any clothes.

"Bark . . . Bark's called a special meeting," she said. "Tomorrow at four."

"I'll be there. Sam, I'm so sorry. Is there anything I can do?"

"Thanks, but the police are here now, sealing up his . . . his office. They're talking to me, they're talking to the staff, asking all kinds of questions."

"That's to be expected," I said. "Standard operating procedure."

The police were at the COW offices. Did that mean Joe?

"Samantha, listen, is there a Detective Camanetti there? Joe Camanetti?"

But I was talking to dead air.

I hung up, feeling somewhat guilty, because I was focusing on Joe, when I should have been absorbed with sorrow-laden feelings about Roger. He had been a friend. A good friend. I knew I would miss him, probably more than I suspected right now. Maybe, in time, I would even allow myself to cry for him. But at this moment I was dry-eyed and rational, almost clinically detached from any thoughts other than speculations about his murder.

I did like Roger. Above all else, he was out-front. True, he was sort of what you might call a loose cannon, but that was part of his charm. Nothing predictable about Roger Urban. Least of all that he would be murdered.

But how, and why, and by whom were the questions that were already riveting me. I guess it must have been my investigative reporter past kicking in. And, of course, Mercedes was already on my case.

"Girl, we've got ourselves a real, kick-ass murder case."

"We'll see."

"Fuck we'll see! Aren't you curious about who did him?"

Well, obviously I was. And I was going to do something about it.

I called Henrik's cell phone and left the brief message: "Call me."

Ten minutes later, he called. "Maggie, what's wrong? You sound like death."

"Funny you should say that. They've found Roger. He's dead. Murdered."

Even hearing myself say those words, I didn't accept them as true. I was making up the whole thing because that's what a writer does.

"How in hell—What happened?"

"I don't know. They found him dead in a bathtub somewhere."

"Thank God I'm a shower man myself."

"What?"

"Just a little joke. Very little, I guess."

"Henrik, they think he's been murdered!"

"Sorry. Are you okay?"

"I'm fine," I said, which was just a little off-white lie. "It's just a shock when it hits so close."

"I'll see what details I can pick up and call you back, okay?"

"Okay. Thanks." I felt better after that much-needed dose of Henrik's matter-of-factness.

When Lionel came home and heard the news, he put down his load of grocery bags, and gave me a big warm hug.

"Oh, my poor sweet darling. I know how dreadful you must feel."

I nodded and tried to look suitably distressed.

"It hasn't sunk in yet, but I'm sure it will. Poor Roger."

"Roger!" Lionel unhanded me. "Who's talking about Roger! It's that schmuck Dick Tracy! How come he didn't break the news?"

"Who knows," I said stiffly. "And, anyway, the thought never crossed my mind."

"Liar." Lionel picked up Groucho and stroked him, while Harpo rubbed against his leg. "And now for the steamy particulars. Give!"

"I don't know the steamy particulars. I don't know any particulars."

"Maggie, you have got to get the dirt on this. Why would anyone want to kill him? Was he doing some other guy's wife? I bet that's it! You've got to find out everything you can and tell me immediately. I can dine out on this for weeks."

"Why are you assuming Roger must have been involved in something sordid?"

"Honey, here in La-La Land, being in the wrong tub with the wrong person will get you offed nine times out of ten."

"Who said anyone was in the bathtub with him?"

"Even if he wasn't drowned, I bet he must have gone down for the third time."

"Lionel!"

He shrugged. "Well, it does make a more succulent story."

Afterward, I sat in the kitchen while Lionel put the groceries away and began to prepare lime-marinated Chilean sea bass and green noodles for dinner. Thank God one of us likes to cook.

"Lionel," I said, "maybe I need a little filling in. Do you know anything about Roger's background?"

"Quiz me."

"Well . . . How did he get to COW?"

"He was just a dime-a-dozen entertainment lawyer working for a small firm in Beverly Hills, doing what they all do, screwing up contracts for above-the-line people. When the last Executive Director retired, the Union did some interviewing through a headhunter and they chose him."

Lionel was uncorking the Chardonnay to go into the marinade. He poured two glasses and held one out to me with a questioning look. Ordinarily I would refuse. In general, alcohol does not mix well with diabetes. But I knew a few sips tonight might be of more help than harm.

"It was all over town at the time. Two others were offered the job, but they turned it down because the Union was so stingy with their salary package. Roger was their third choice. And he worked cheap. Then."

"You amaze me. I didn't know that."

"You weren't in town then. You were in New York."

I reflected on what he had told me. "Could he have been killed because someone wanted his job?"

Lionel gave me a disdainful look, which was answer enough. No one in this town, even as a figure of speech, would harbor the thought: "I would just kill to be the Executive Director of the Creative Artists Union."

"Then you think it was a jealous lover? Or husband?"

"That's for me to relish and you to find out," Lionel said.

The next day's Board meeting had been called for four sharp, but I wanted to arrive early.

Many of the other Board members had the same idea. They were milling around the Boardroom and clustering in animated groups, their buzz of conversation punctuated with incongruous eruptions of laughter. A stranger could have entered the room and never been aware that the talk was about someone who had died. What I did learn, from Evan Lantzy, was that the police were there and would be asking questions.

I left and walked down the hall, with the vague idea of stopping in at Samantha's office, which was, of course, just a delaying tactic. In reality I was bracing myself for the possibility of running into Joe.

When I stopped by the station to see him, he asked me what I was doing there. Well, I would return the favor. Of course, I knew what he was doing here, so there went that opening line. But I might ask him anyway.

I had just turned the corner in the direction of Samantha's office when suddenly there he was. Not Joe. Martin Wu.

"Hello, Maggie." And, with a grin, "What are you doing here?"

Damn him.

I managed to return a cool smile. "Martin, how very nice to see a familiar face. I was afraid we were going to be swamped with a bunch of hard-nosed cops."

"Hey, what kind of way is that to refer to us responsible public servants?"

"Sorry. Hard-nosed dicks."

He grinned again, and all the while I was trying to peer around him, to see if Joe was anywhere in the vicinity.

"He's in Neville Lake's office," Martin said.

Double damn him. Just then I heard the William Tell Overture of my cell phone ring.

I said, "I wasn't looking for Joe, if that's what you're thinking."

"Well, he'll be looking for you."

No telling what that meant. My phone rang again.

"Shouldn't you answer that?"

"I'm going to," I said. He took the hint and moved away.

It was Henrik. "You were right, Maggie. He was found dead in a bathtub. Somebody shot him."

"Do they know who?"

"The cops don't have a clue. But get this. He was wearing something weird."

"Weird . . . like what?"

He hesitated. "Like women's underwear."

"I never would have made that my first guess."

"Where are you now?"

"At the COW. There are detectives here. I heard they'll be questioning us."

"Will you be confessing?"

"Only if you know a good lawyer."

"Listen, I've got to run. Talk to you later."

And he was gone.

I took the long way around the hall, back to the meeting room, surveying the territory as I went. Neville's door was closed, Roger's office was behind yellow crime scene tape, and in Samantha's office the phones were ringing off the hook. Staff members I passed were talking in whispers, breaking off into silence as I went by.

Passing by the computer room and the adjacent supply area, I thought I heard the sound of someone crying. The door was partly ajar. That was as good as an invitation. I stuck my head in and saw Wendy Bassett, the Union's computer maven, checking off supplies on an inventory list. Tears were coursing down her cheeks, and, between cigarette puffs, she was wiping them away with a well-used tissue. Smoking wasn't allowed in the building, let alone in the computer center, something Roger was adamant about.

But, of course, Roger doesn't live here anymore.

I came all the way in. "Wendy, I'm so sorry to intrude."

I wasn't, but even in the most awkward of circumstances, I'm a stickler for good manners.

"Oh, God!" Wendy looked wildly around for a place to stub out her cigarette, and then, glancing back at me, took a paper clip box out from behind some supplies on a shelf and stubbed out the butt amongst several other butts.

"Please don't rat me out," she said. "I'm just so upset. I gave it up three weeks ago. But all this commotion is driving me batty."

If she gave it up three weeks ago, then those old butts were really rotting away.

"I'm not going to tell anyone." I patted her on the shoulder, rather clumsily, because this woman was so off-kilter and so vulnerable, I never was comfortable around her. "Can I help?"

"Nobody can help. Roger's been murdered!"

"I know. It's horrible, but somehow we have to get past this."

"You don't understand. Maybe the next Director won't let me keep my job and I'll be out of work and I spent everything to move out here! My mother told me not to leave New York!"

I remembered Roger announcing Wendy's transfer from the New York branch a few months ago. She's a computer whiz, he told the Board. But the fact is she was an absolute disaster in every other part of her life. When she applied for the job on our staff, we were in desperate need of her expertise, but everyone in New York, including Noelle, advised against our taking her on. She required so much stroking, we heard, that she couldn't get along with the rest of the staff.

"She's a nutcase," Roger had said frankly. "But what's one more nut among you artists?"

She was needed to run our Information Technology systems, and Royal depended on her. I think Roger and Neville felt that the staff problem in the east was Noelle's fault anyway, and they could handle her.

Wendy's nose was running and her tissue was in shreds on the floor. I took a tissue out of my bag and handed it to her.

"Thanks." She blew her nose. "I'm sorry about carrying on this way. It's just that I left New York because working for Noelle was the pits."

"Why? What was so bad about it?"

She stared at me through red, puffy eyes. "Noelle's the worst," she said. "Always plotting. She dreams of being queen of the universe and wakes up to realize she's only head of a branch office. She'd love to overthrow Roger and . . . Oh, God! He's gone! She'll want to come out here and take over! Oh, God!"

The wailing started in earnest then.

I said, lamely, "Wendy, don't worry. We're a long way from replacing Roger."

"Oh, please don't let it be Noelle. She made my life so miserable I tried for months for a transfer out here. Noelle wouldn't even sign off on it just to spite me. And now this happens. Roger had to go and get dead!"

I sensibly refrained from telling her that the man didn't do it on purpose.

"I'm sure your job will be okay," I said, not really sure at all. "Royal and Neville depend on you, and so do the rest of us."

She sniffled. "Then would you do me a favor and speak to Neville about it?"

"Uh . . . sure. . . . I'll be glad to," I heard myself saying.

"Oh, thank you, thank you," she said, and handed me back my soggy Kleenex.

In the Boardroom I took my usual seat and waited for the four o'clock sharp meeting to start. At twenty past four, Bark called the meeting to order.

"Please be aware," he began, "that this meeting comes under the rules of confidentiality."

It was at that moment that Joe and Martin walked in and stood at the end of the table nearest the door. You know how the Wave runs around a baseball stadium? That's how the silence made its way around the room, as everyone looked over in their direction.

12

"Ladies and gentlemen," Bark said, "we have with us two detectives from the West Los Angeles police. Please give them your attention, and then we will resume our meeting."

Joe fixed everyone with a piercing stare, as though he could see right into our innermost beings and know we were all guilty of something.

Or was it only directed at me?

"I'm Detective Joe Camanetti, and this is my partner, Detective Martin Wu," he said. "By now you've heard that Roger Urban is dead. His body was found yesterday and it does not appear that he died of natural causes." There was a ripple of laughter which ceased as abruptly as it had begun. "For now, we are treating it as a homicide by person or persons unknown."

Again his circling gaze fixed on each one of us, and, again, the room was so quiet you could hear an accusation drop.

Now it was Martin's turn. "We want to know everything you can recall about any dealings you may have had with Mr. Urban during the past three days, particularly the forty-eight hours preceding his disappearance. Mr. Lake has allowed us the use of your library and we will call each of you in there."

"We appreciate your cooperation," Joe picked up on their routine, "and I promise you we will take up as little of your valuable time as possible. Please don't look at this as an interrogation, but, rather, as a friendly, informal chat."

A hoot of derision greeted this. Bark rapped for order.

"My partner will organize the questioning," Joe said, "and then we'll be out of your hair."

I was staring at Joe throughout, but he was all business and didn't appear to give me any more attention than any of the others. Fine. When he turned and left the room, I couldn't help but notice that he still had a great ass, even under the drape of his pale gray suit jacket.

Isolated at the end of the table, Martin exuded quiet strength. He was like a coiled spring, tense and ready for action.

"Your Vice President has given me a list of Board members," he said, "including those who aren't here today." He consulted a pocket notebook. "Let's see. . . . Cody Cooper, how about we lead off with you?"

"Like I have a choice," Cody said, but he followed Martin out. Cody was a staff writer on a top-rated reality show.

As soon as they left, Bark proceeded to deal with a few agenda items, mostly the usual housekeeping matters. Then he dropped the bomb.

"I think you're all familiar with Tom Vincent, the *Hollywood Reporter* columnist?"

Dana squirmed a little in her seat. Once or twice there had been leaks to the trade papers of confidential Board matters, and the general suspicion was that it was Dana.

Bark went on. "He called me this morning. It seems that the *Reporter* is going with the story that Roger was found in a bathtub, which we're all now aware of, of course, but what we didn't know was—he was wearing only a garter belt and red bra."

The meeting exploded.

"He was a cross-dresser?"

"You mean Roger was really Roxanne!"

"Did he buy them at Frederick's of Hollywood?"

"Does that place still exist?"

"Roger Urban sure doesn't."

"I've heard of a closet red, but never a bathtub red!"

This confirmed what Henrik had told me. I was trying to make sense of this latest development, but the suggestive remarks and comments were coming way too fast and furious for clearheaded comprehension.

Dana's voice rose above the rest.

"How could we have hired a degenerate like that in the first place? Who was on the Executive Search Committee?"

"Jeez, Dana," Dennis said, "what would you like us to do? Have an underwear check on all potential staff members?"

This elicited more laughter. Trust Dennis to heap deserved derision on Dana.

Once more Bark had to resort to the gavel.

"Okay, back to business. Vincent asked me for a comment on the garter belt and bra item which will run on their front page tomorrow. I took the high road, guys. I said no comment."

Hands shot up.

Bark ignored the barrage. "And I advise you to do the same. Anyone talking to Tom Vincent—or to anyone else in the press—about Roger Urban will be subject to disciplinary proceedings. Are there any questions?"

The hands all went down except for Dennis'.

Bark nodded to him. "Dennis?"

"Can I at least tell Cody when he comes back from his grilling?"

Bark went on with the meeting. Cody returned from his stint in the interrogation room and Dana was called in next. I wondered how soon it would be my turn, especially since Dana could filibuster for hours.

Maybe my turn wouldn't come until tomorrow.

"The Union has to move forward," Bark was saying, "which means that priority has to be given to finding a new Executive Director. An Executive Search Committee will be appointed, and Neville Lake will serve as our interim Director until someone is in place."

"So soon?" Clark Newman said.

"Yeah," Cody said. "Roger isn't even cold yet."

"He soon will be, wearing just a garter belt and bra," Dennis said.

Even Bark had to smile at that.

"We're aware this may seem a little rushed," Neville said, "but Samantha is already getting calls and faxes from people interested in the position."

"Ghouls," Clark said.

"Perverts," Tad said.

"We have met the perverts and they are us!" That was, surprisingly, Treasurer Evan Lantzy, who usually never spoke up unless it had to do with money.

Bark said, "You might be interested in knowing that Noelle Sears has also called. She was shocked to hear about Roger."

"And wanted to be considered for his job?" Cody said.

Bark shrugged. I imagined that Noelle had expressed only the most obligatory sadness over Roger's death. We were all aware that there was neither love nor respect lost between them.

"To get back to the Search Committee," Bark said. "Just before we convened, I had a brief meeting with the other officers, and we are asking the following members to serve: Clark Newman, Dana Salinger, our former President Chris Osborne, Ian McConnell, Maggie Mars, and myself."

I was surprised to hear my name included in that somewhat exalted company, and the thought of working with Dana tied knots in my large intestine. Still, I didn't see how I could tactfully get out of it.

There then ensued endless discussion about planning a tribute to Roger. Of course, there was the requisite suggestion to hold the event at Victoria's Secret. Cody Cooper proposed that we put up a large sum of money for information leading to the arrest of the killer.

"How much?" Evan Lantzy said, visions of dollar signs dancing before his eyes.

"If you throw in his little black book, you won't need to give cash," Adam offered.

At one point during the endless talk, I left my seat and went into the kitchen area to get some tea. Dennis was there, popping a soda can.

"Can you believe that Noelle?" he said. "What *chutzpah*!"

I picked my words carefully. In the Union you never know whether you're talking to a buddy or a blabbermouth. "She certainly doesn't waste any time."

"Her expressing any sorrow over Roger's death makes me want to puke."

"Why?"

"You didn't hear about their having this big argument, then?"

I shook my head no. "Nobody ever tells me anything interesting."

"Well, your luck has changed." Dennis looked around to make sure no one else was in earshot. "I happened to drop in here the morning of the big meeting, and as I passed Roger's office, I overheard him and Noelle screaming at each other. I've heard Roger get angry before, but I've never heard him explode like that. He called her the 'c' word."

Roger's language didn't really shock me, but I wondered what triggered their argument. "What were they fighting about?"

"I bailed. Arguments like that are personal."

Sure, I thought, and you didn't want to get caught eavesdropping. "Probably the usual," I said. "Noelle never changes her tune."

"Right," Dennis said. "Roger has too much on his plate. So let Noelle run the east coast and the Canadian branches out of New York. The same old trite song."

"Are you going to tell that to the police?"

Adam Tyler came in just then, looking for a piece of fruit.

Dennis just gave me an enigmatic look and headed back to his seat. So did I.

I saw that Dana had returned from her session with Joe and Martin and was looking curiously subdued. I wondered what could have gone on in her questioning to account for The Taming of that particular Shrew.

Periodically, either Martin would appear at the door to summon one of us to the library or the last person called in would return with the name of the next one. I knew my time was getting close and I could concentrate only fitfully on the Board business at hand. However, I did come to life when Tad made a motion that we should organize an ad hoc committee to work with the police.

"Joe would throw you out on your ad hoc asses," I said, and when Bark turned to look at me, I realized that he had made the connection, and before long everyone else would, too. I had talked about a "friend" who was a homicide detective and now the "friend" had taken form and substance.

Fortunately, the ensuing debate covered up my chagrin. The motion didn't get anywhere, nor did Dana's motion to put an ad in the trades.

"Isn't Tom Vincent's article advertisement enough?" Dennis said.

No wonder our Board meetings never ended till midnight.

13

Ten minutes later, Adam returned from the library and beckoned to me and I left to be interviewed by Joe and Martin. I knew I was the last one to be called, and as I pushed the elevator button to go down the one floor, I couldn't help but wonder what it was going to be like to be interviewed in connection with a crime. Not that I had anything to hide, but the interrogator was going to be my ex-lover! If he were to give me a lie detector test, I'd be toast.

Be more like Mercedes, I told myself. She wouldn't get panicky over a few questions if she had nothing to hide.

"Or even if I did," said Mercedes.

"However, being grilled by your ex . . . Even you, Mercedes, might find that a little difficult."

"Difficult, maybe, but not friggin' impossible."

The thought crossed my mind as I entered the library and took a chair facing Joe and Martin that I could do a Sharon Stone bit. But what was the use. I was wearing jeans and the view would be all denim seams.

"Look, Maggie," Joe said. "I know this is uncomfortable for you and it is for me, too. Let's just try to get through it."

I flashed a sugared smile. "Thank you, Joe. I appreciate that, but before we start, I have something to ask you."

"Yeah?" He looked wary.

"Why didn't you call me when you learned about Roger? You knew I was involved in looking for him."

"A lot of people were looking for him. I can't treat you any differently than anyone else."

"There are good reasons for you to treat me differently than the others and you know it."

The silence grew heavy. Martin shifted uneasily in his chair. "If you like, I'll excuse myself."

"Sorry, Martin," I said. "We didn't mean for our backstory to be a spectator sport."

Joe kept his gaze fixed on me, but his words were for Martin.

"Maggie knows we have a homicide on our hands and we have to clear it. She's just another member of this Union, and that's how she's going to be treated."

"Shall I kick him in the balls or will you?" said Mercedes.

Martin threw a reproving glance at Joe. "Look, Maggie. We could use your cooperation. Joe and I aren't on the inside. You are. We'd be most appreciative of any help you can give us."

Joe stood up and started to say something, but Martin silenced him with another sideways glance and he sat down again, settling back with his notepad.

"Let's start with the day of the Annual Meeting," Martin said. "What can you tell us about your activities?"

"Well, let's see. I guess I was at home that day. I was working on my screenplay."

"Did you talk to anyone?"

I shook my head. "Nope." Then I remembered. "Unless you count the telephone tree."

"Telephone tree?"

"Yes, the proposed contract was up for a vote, so someone called me to remind me to attend the meeting, and then I had to call five other people."

"Were they all at home, the ones you called?"

"No. Mostly I got their machines and then left messages."

Joe said, "We'll need a list of names."

"I'll get it to you." That's me. Nothing if not cooperative.

"What time did you arrive at the hotel?" Martin again.

"It must have been around six thirty. The meeting was called for seven and I got there early. For a change I wasn't delayed by construction. Have you noticed there's not a major road or freeway in Los Angeles that doesn't seem to have some kind of construction going on?"

"Not my job." Martin smiled.

Joe took over the questioning. Obviously, he wasn't in the mood for small talk. "Who did you see and talk to at the meeting? Did you notice anything out of the ordinary?"

"Yes. Roger wasn't there."

"Besides that."

As both Joe and Martin led me through that evening, practically minute by minute and speech by speech, I gradually lost my feelings of tension and became more relaxed.

Finally, Martin stood. "Well, that seems to cover it. Thanks, Maggie."

"That's it?" I tried not to sound disappointed.

I guess I didn't succeed too well, because Joe took that as a cue. "Why? You have something more to tell us?"

"Well, no, but I do have some questions of my own."

"And I'm sure they're important," Joe said, the sarcastic prick. "Save them."

Well, screw him. "I was just wondering about this bathtub where they found Roger. Where was it?"

Martin said, "In one of those large fancy Brentwood homes, north of Sunset. Belongs to a wealthy producer who moved back to New York, so it's up for sale."

"What was Roger doing there?"

"He was getting himself killed," Joe said. "Give us a call if you think of anything else."

As Martin walked me to the door, I tried again, quite conversationally, "How was he killed?"

Martin hesitated, looking back at Joe, who was engrossed with his notes.

"He was shot," he said.

"Was he robbed?"

"No comment."

"What about the clothes he was wearing?"

"No comment."

He opened the door, just as Joe came over.

"Maggie, Martin's right," he said. "We would like your cooperation. Especially because you're on the inside. You can help us learn everything about the Union, the people, Roger . . . We can handle the rest."

Was I wrong? Was Joe trying to be Mr. Congeniality? He certainly seemed to have thawed a bit.

"What we can't handle," Joe said, "is you butting in all over the place."

I wasn't wrong.

Upstairs the meeting had broken up, and only Bark, Dana, and Clark were still hanging in there.

"Maggie, get out your Blackberry," Bark said. "We're setting up some dates for the Search Committee to meet."

"What about Ian and Chris? Have they agreed to serve?"

"They're already signed on," Clark said. "Bark called them before the meeting."

"Be right with you."

I detoured to the adjoining kitchen and foraged in the cupboard, coming up with a can of non-diet soda and a handful of pretzels. I was feeling a little hungry and headachy and didn't want to risk passing out.

We had a brief meeting. Bark told us that COW would be using the services of a professional Human Resources Management consultant to assist us in our search. Meanwhile, we were to be thinking of the information that would go into a job description. We were all tired and out of gas, so we quickly decided to set an interview agenda later, after we had some idea of the candidates who were surfacing.

I wasn't aware if Joe and Martin were still in the building. Anyway, if they were or if they weren't, what difference did it make to me? Yeah. Right. It was starting to make a difference. That meant trouble ahead. The storm warnings were up.

The four of us said good night in the garage, and dog tired, I went home to Lionel and the Marx brothers.

14

The population at home had increased. Troy was in the kitchen having coffee and Key Lime pie with Lionel. I don't think Lionel and Troy have ever been lovers, but friendship has its plusses, too. Whenever Troy suffers the breakup of another affair, he comes to Lionel for solace and understanding and a shoulder to blubber on.

There are times I envy them.

They were doing the Halloween thing again. Troy had brought more offerings from the wardrobe department. He was dressed as a very good Sonny Bono, complete with bell-bottoms, and Lionel was a not-so-good Cher, lacking the wraith-like shape to support the typical Cher non-dress.

"What do you think?" Troy asked. "I wanted to be Cher, but Lionel saw the wig first."

"Back to the drawing board," I advised. "I arrive bearing tidings of great scandal and joy."

I then spent the rest of the evening, late as it was, bringing them up to date on everything I had learned, including the red underwear. I had no choice. I knew they wouldn't let me sleep until I did.

Both of them, of course, knew more about that kind of thing than I did. As a reward, and knowing that I couldn't indulge in the pie, Lionel brewed me a pot of decaf green tea and he and Troy talked in itemized and intimate detail about the cross-dressing scene in town.

"Does this mean that Roger was gay?" I said.

They shared a knowing laugh at my ignorance.

"Not all cross-dressers are," Troy said. "Some are regular guys who get it on by wearing silk and lace undies."

"You never know," Lionel said. "When you go in for your next studio pitch meeting and sit across the desk from some suit, he very well could be wearing a frilly flowered ensemble underneath his Armani."

"Or a teddy! A buttoned-at-the-crotch satin teddy," Troy offered with a shiver of delight.

I shook my head in amazement at my own innocence.

"But why does a man feel the need to wear women's clothes?"

"It could be for sexual satisfaction," Lionel said. "But there are also psychological urges. Like, with some men, cross-dressing is a way of offering a challenge to society's preconceptions about gender."

"Hold it," I said. "The hour's too late to go Freudian on me."

"It doesn't happen to be my style," Lionel said, "but I do admire Roger's panache."

"If ever I had seen him in his garter belt, I would have admired more than that," Troy said.

They laughed again. I then heard more than I ever cared to know about the major clubs and the parties, and the very prominent box office star who was known for answering the door in his wife's bra and panties, and his wife merely laughed it off at their dinner parties, calling her husband "amusing." There was even a beauty salon in town where they sell clothes, shoes, wigs, nails, jewelry, and makeup to men to help them be more feminine.

When my eyes refused to stay open, I went to bed, leaving Lionel and Troy exchanging fashion nuggets about silk underwear by Fernandez. I can't say Harpo and Groucho weren't fascinated.

The next morning I woke early, threw on some sweats, and went out. At the corner newsstand I picked up both *Variety* and *The Hollywood Reporter,* then stopped at the Coffee Bean for a cup of decaf and a low-fat, sugar-free muffin. I spread out the trades, starting with the *Reporter.*

The front page headlined Roger's murder, and the byline was Tom Vincent's. He wrote in that tone that reporters adopt when they want you to think they are objectively reporting the facts, but are actually filling space with innuendo and insinuation from unnamed sources.

And there it was. The red bra and garter belt in black-and-white. There were all kinds of muted hints and speculations about what Roger was doing in that bathtub and in that bizarre attire, and about what might have been the motive for the killing. Vincent even referred to the recent vote on the contract, but was careful not to make any explicit connection.

The article in *Variety* was also rife with conjecture, but for the most part the writer stuck to the facts, probably because he didn't have the scoop on the underwear.

Walking home, I remembered that Martin hadn't answered my question about what Roger was wearing when his body was found, and Joe hadn't said anything about it either. They clearly were playing it very tight-mouthed, not giving too much information out. Maybe Martin preferred it that way, but he hadn't shared my bed. Joe could have confided in me. And he could trust me, surely he knew that.

Wait a minute! Suddenly it hit me. Joe wanted the names of all the people I had spoken with or seen the day of the murder. Of course! He wanted to be sure I was where I said I was and not out shooting Roger. Damn Joe anyway! Was he really thinking I needed an alibi? How could he believe for one minute that I was involved in Roger's murder!

I didn't know Joe anymore, that was clear. You're deeply in love with a man, you sleep with him, you welcome him into your body, and then you're not an ex-lover anymore. You're not even a former anything anymore. You're a suspect. A fucking suspect!

But no matter. He had thrown me a crumb. He needed my

help. He expected me to report to him. Ha! Probably that was so he could keep an eye on me.

Thoroughly unsettled, I went home, to be greeted with more troubling news.

The phone rang and it was U.G.

"Don't worry about the evacuation," he said.

"What evacuation? What are you talking about?"

"Oh. Then the Manager hasn't called you."

"No, the Manager hasn't called me. What did you do, U.G.?"

"Nothing. The odor wasn't that bad. And we only had to get out of the building for half an hour. The ocean air is very invigorating."

"U.G.! What happened!"

"I was working on my invention, you know, the one I told you about, and somehow one of the noxious gasses escaped. So, of course, it made a bad smell."

"I know what noxious means! Dad, I warned you!"

"Look, it wasn't anything. A little smell, that's all. Believe me, there are worse things you can smell when you live in a retirement home."

"Okay, okay, Dad. Please be more careful next time."

"I will. That's what I promised the Fire Department."

"The Fire Department!"

But I was speaking to a dial tone.

After that, and two aspirin, I sat down at my laptop but I never got to work, because, suddenly, this great idea came. Monumental, even for me. I telephoned *Vanity Fair* magazine in New York and left a message for Griffin Grace, the Senior Articles Editor.

Gracie is the world's best editor, and I've worked with him on several major pieces. At first, he tried to micromanage me, same as my producer, Fowler Mohr, is doing now. But I can't work that way. I need to follow my gut feelings, my intuition, without someone breathing over my shoulder. After several minor skirmishes, Gracie and I had one major blowout. It took place in his office, and to this day, the staff still talk about how they had to take cover. When it was over, Gracie drew a deep breath and let me do my thing, and we've had a great professional friendship ever since.

The man is cosmopolitan, wickedly funny, and smart. So smart, in fact, that when he called back a half hour later, he immediately knew what I was going to ask. When I picked up the phone, he didn't say hello, he said yes.

"Let's make sure we're on the same page here, Gracie. I want to do the investigative piece on the murder of Roger Urban. I think it's going to be a series of several articles. If and when they catch whoever did him, I want to cover the arrest and trial as well. Do we have a deal?"

We did. Ten minutes later I hung up, feeling inordinately pleased with myself. Both the name of Griffin Grace and the mantle of the magazine were going to open a lot of doors for me, doors which even Joe couldn't close.

I had received the usual caveats from Gracie. "Don't accuse anyone without plenty of proof, kid. And don't piss off the cops. In New Jersey they still hold up a cross when they hear your name."

Wouldn't anyone ever forget about me and the New Jersey State Police?

To me, the one thing that mattered was that I would be doing what I do best, investigative work. Those articles would give me enough to cover my expenses and also, not insignificantly, the extra cash I needed to tide me over until I finish the screenplay.

"We might also be helping to solve Roger's murder," Mercedes said. *"After all, Joe has invited you to be second lead on the case."*

"That's ridiculous. He has not."

"Oh, chill out. You'd like to be working under him, wouldn't you?"

I was torn between yes, it would be productive to work with Joe, because it would help me with my articles, and positively not, why should I want to get that close to him again? And then there was Henrik, with whom I was already close and more than content to be so.

Which reminded me. What I should do now was call Henrik, and share the news about my new assignment. I reached him on his cell phone.

"Henrik. I'm back in the investigative business. *Vanity Fair* wants me to do the story on Roger's murder."

"Uh-oh."

I was thrown. "What's that supposed to mean? Uh-oh?"

He said, "For one thing, I'll see less of you than I do now."

He was sweet. "And for another?"

"It means I'll miss you."

"We'll just have to make sure we have quality time," I said. "How about tonight? I'll bring the quality."

"Can't. I'll be working late. I'm on my way to the courthouse now."

We signed off with mutual regrets and suggestive promises for the next time we were together. Then I called Bark to tell him that I was doing the story for *Vanity Fair.* I needed certain doors opened for me at the Union and in the industry as well, and Bark was the man for that.

I caught him at a busy moment when he was just leaving to do a Larry King interview. He didn't have too much time to talk, but he was agreeably enthusiastic.

"Go to it," he said. "If anyone's going to write it, I'd just as soon it was you."

"Thanks, Bark."

"What about the Search Committee? Will you still have time to serve?"

"I'll make time," I assured him, not really knowing if I could or not.

"Good. Let me know if there's anything I can do to help."

Great. That was the Open Sesame I was looking for.

After I hung up, I debated briefly about whether I should call Fowler and ask for more time on the screenplay. No. What the hell. Ms. Superscribe could do both.

Opening a fresh five-by-eight spiral notebook, my usual

working prop, I entered a list of Things-To-Do. First entry was to find out the name of the real estate agency holding the listing for the house where Roger's body had been discovered. This was cheating a little, because Tom Vincent had mentioned it in his article. That's probably where he got the scoop on the underwear. I clipped the story and put it into the back pocket of the notebook. The old routine was very reassuring.

I called the real estate office and left a voice mail message for the listing agent, a Ms. Pat Draper, along with my home phone number, my fax number, my cell phone number, and my e-mail address.

Not for the first time I reflected on how we are all defined by numbers these days, and how much simpler life would be if we had just one Universal number for all our phones. Of course, that would mean that all of them would ring at the same time. But someone could work on that minor difficulty.

My message told Ms. Draper that I was interested in the Baroda Drive property, which didn't make me a liar at all.

By the time I had changed out of the sweats, showered, and put on charcoal pants and a thin lavender cotton shirt, I was ready for her callback, and it came promptly. She didn't hesitate to give me a rundown of other listings in the vicinity that might be in my price range, which was too pitiful for me to disclose to her. I quickly had to confess that I wasn't a potential buyer and prepared myself for the disconnect. But she hung on long enough for me to mention I was an investigative reporter and drop the *Vanity Fair* name and then she became my very best friend.

She gave me the number on Baroda. "I'll meet you there in twenty minutes."

15

I took Sunset across and made fair time. It would have been great time except that the stoplights were out where Beverly Glen intersects with Sunset, and it was a mess trying to get through. Finally, a tanker truck pulled into the intersection, and I rode his side across, waved my thanks, and went ahead.

There was yellow crime scene tape still encircling the house. When I pulled into the driveway, Pat was leaning against her car, smoking. She was liposuction thin with long, straight, bleached blond hair, fashionable granny sunglasses, a short tight skirt, short enough for the world to be her gynecologist, and Jimmy Choo stiletto heels.

"What about the tape?" I said.

"What are you, a wuss? Sneak under," said Mercedes.

"Sneak under," said Pat. "That's what all the reporters do, right?"

Right. The power of the press.

As she let me into the house, she bombarded me with questions. "What's your article going to say? Are you going to mention me? Do you need a picture of me? I can't give you a picture of the house, unless you want me to call the owners in New York and get their permission. And are they ever pissed right now. They'll never give me permission. Can you imagine, they're blaming me and my office for this crazy murder? What a mess!"

"I'm just beginning my investigation," I told her. "Yes, I'll be using your name, but it's too early to decide about pictures, and would you mind putting out your cigarette?"

We were in the house by then and she looked around, apparently mystified as to where there might be an ashtray. She spied a terra cotta urn, one of a pair near the doorway, and that's where she deposited her butt.

Moving through the first floor, I was content merely to focus on the layout. It wasn't until we climbed up the curved staircase to the second level that I took out my notebook and paid attention to details. There was nothing to be gleaned from the master bedroom. It had an emperor-size bed covered with a velvet throw edged in sable. Doesn't everyone?

There was a pair of ornate night tables topped by huge lamps and a large built-in console at the foot of the bed, which Pat told me housed a stereo, a DVD player, and a television set that could be raised up for viewing by remote control. I noticed there were alarm panels on the walls on both sides of the bed, but no lights were blinking. I wondered if it had been put out of commission when the owners moved.

My eyes turned to the prize: the celebrated scene of the crime, the "his" bathroom.

I entered the bathroom, but Pat remained in the bedroom. She went into autopilot mode and began her practiced spiel just as though I were a legitimate client.

"I'm sure you can recognize the old-world workmanship in the marble and limestone and tile detail. Very few baths in this town, even in your Beverly Hills estates, have both a chandelier and a fireplace."

Mine had a ceiling light fixture and a space heater. Close.

Pat kept talking but she never followed me into the room. I figured that the cops had already completed their investigation here. All that remained was some powdery stuff that hadn't been cleaned up. I prowled and took in what I could while Pat remained outside in the bedroom and rambled on.

"The bathtub is sized for two and the railings are twenty-four-carat gold leaf. The doors were etched in Venice by master glassworkers."

My thoughts were straggling all over the place. What was Roger doing here? Was there any connection between him and the owners? Nothing jumped out of the walls or even the tub that hinted at anything about the murder.

By now Pat was impatient. "What are you doing in there so long?"

"Just looking."

"I hope you're not touching anything. The police told me not to show the place. I'm really doing you a favor."

"And I appreciate it." I came back into the bedroom. "Okay, Pat, we need to talk."

"Fine, but not up here," she said. "The place gives me the creeps."

She punctuated her words by lighting a fresh cigarette.

"I gave up smoking again last month," she said, noting my frown, "but, honestly, could anyone expect me to stay off cigarettes when I live the life I live?"

What? Did she find a body in every house she listed for sale?

On the way downstairs, her heels clicking rapidly on the marble, she went back to talking about the virtues of the house. Monologues were obviously her specialty. When we reached the large kitchen Lionel would have given his right testicle for, we plunked ourselves down on two stools at the limestone breakfast bar and she went right on with her tale of woe.

"The client was really, really interested and would have paid the asking price, I just know, and then we found the body. I tell you this is not good for business. I had to take her and the rest of her family out to Valentino's for dinner and commiserate with her the whole evening just to keep her with me. If she deserts me and goes to another agency, I'll lose a really good commission, which I've already spent. The work I put into her! And this was the perfect house for her."

I tried to stop the free association flow. "Did the owners know Roger Urban?"

"They claim they only knew his name from *Variety* and *The Hollywood Reporter.* Which reminds me—do you think I should advertise the property in the trades?"

"The entertainment trades or the funeral home trades?"

"Whatever," she said.

She made a brief note on a Shopping List pad that was on the counter and tore off the page.

"Their kids are in college here at UCLA, but, like I said, they're in New York. And then I think they're going to Europe on another movie. Anyway, they no longer need the house. I'd look for a pied-à-terre for them, but I doubt if they'll even talk to me now. Still, if you hear of one . . ."

"How about you? Did you know Roger?"

"Who? Oh, yeah, the corpus. I never saw him before that day. I mean when he was alive. Do you think this will affect the selling price?"

"Nope. I think you ought to raise it. Listen, do you have an exclusive listing? How does that work? Who has keys to the house?"

"Of course it's an exclusive. No one lists any other way now. You have no idea how hard I worked with the client. I wonder how I can cover this up."

"Pat! The keys!" I was losing my patience.

"The police asked me that already." There was a disapproving tone to her voice. Clearly she wasn't giving me a passing grade for originality.

"Well, I'm asking now."

"Okay, we have two sets of keys at the office. If I'm not available for a showing, one of the other brokers will cover for me. But, honestly, why don't you talk to the police? They asked the same questions you're asking."

I leveled my best reportorial stare at her.

"My editor is looking for all sorts of detail, trivia even, that the police would never be interested in. That's what makes us different. And, of course, that's what's going to make my articles a real prospect for a screenplay."

"Screenplay? You mean, a movie? Would you put me in it? I've always believed I could be a great actress. You have to be to push real estate in this town. The competition is incredible. Do you know that half the real estate agents in town are the first wives of doctors who married their nurses?"

"Is that right?"

"In my case he was a dentist who left me for his hygienist."

"The keys?"

"They're kept in a key safe in the office, but all the brokers have access. The cops have been questioning everyone. Even the cleaning crew."

At first it didn't register, but then it hit me. "The ones who clean your office? What's their name?"

"Let me see now. . . ." Pat was one of those to whom thinking came with great difficulty. She pursed her lips, scrunched her forehead, and took in great, deep breaths.

It was so painful to watch, I had to speak up.

"Was it Maids-To-Order?"

And now a breath of relief.

"Uh-huh. They also do this house."

I'm not one to believe in coincidences, but this one was too serendipitous to disown.

"Is Karen Thorstensen—"

I got no further.

"Maggie!" a voice boomed, and I swiveled so fast on the stool that I fell off. Honestly. Would I lie about falling on my ass? I looked up and there, looming over me, was Joe.

16

"What do you think you're doing?"

"Are you yelling at me?"

That was really asinine, but it was all I could think of while I pulled myself up, trying to gather some shred of dignity about me. The effect was spoiled, I'm sure, by the fact that I was vigorously rubbing my ass.

"Oh, hi, Martin." I noticed him standing in the doorway. He nodded to me politely, and I just knew he was doing his best not to laugh. I stopped rubbing.

Joe's eyes were flinty. "Maggie, you did see the yellow crime scene tape, didn't you?"

"Yes, and I think it's so smart of you to put it up. I mean, you don't want to let in all the ghouls, do you?"

A smile flickered across his lips, and then he was all sternness again. "Did you ever think that might mean you?"

My ass really pained me, but I wasn't going to give him the satisfaction of knowing.

"No. I'm here for a reason. I'm on assignment for *Vanity Fair.*"

"Yeah?" said Martin. "My wife reads that."

Joe glowered at him. "Her assignment doesn't mean jack shit to us. If she thinks that gives her a license to play armchair detective, she's mucho mistaken. All she's gonna do is screw up our investigation."

Great. Now I was relegated to the third person.

Joe was back to staring at me, and I noticed out of the corner of my eye that Pat had straightened up and was smiling at Joe, showing all of her perfect whiter-than-white teeth, left over from her marriage, no doubt.

"You got something to say for yourself?"

I was too angry to reply. The words "Fuck you" formed on my lips but stayed there.

"I figured not."

He next turned his attention to Pat, who, still perched on her stool, was now leaning very sexily and languorously against the breakfast bar with her stomach sucked in tight, smoke drifting out of her nostrils, utterly absorbed in him.

"Ms. Draper, you were specifically told not to let anyone into this house. You are to give no further information to this woman."

Well, that was a bump up. From the third person to "this woman."

"Whatever you say, Detective."

Whatever you say, Detective . . . I mimicked her fawning words to myself. Joe does have a certain charm about him.

"Thank you." He flashed her a smile.

"I am so very sorry. She led me to believe she had some kind of official standing."

It's a wonder her nose didn't grow longer on the spot.

"Well, she doesn't and please don't let it happen again." His smile got wider. Are all men such dimwits?

At any rate, that was definitely my cue to exit.

"Okay, I'm leaving now. Thanks, Pat. I'll be in touch."

I walked away, glad to be turning my back on them, not to mention my backside, which hurt like hell.

"Hold it," said Joe.

I stopped. Joe came up behind me, close.

"Maggie, maybe I was a little rough on you."

His breath was on my neck, sending shivers down my

spine. I waited to see if he was going to add "I'm sorry." No, not Joe.

"Actually," he said, "you can still be of help to us."

"You mean I *do* have a license to play armchair detective?"

"Come on, Maggie, I said I was sorry." No you didn't. "But you have to leave the heavy lifting to us. That's our job and we're good at it."

"So, where do I come in?"

"You knew this Urban guy better than most."

I turned around and backed away a little.

"Not better than most," I said. "I knew him, that's all." What was it with Joe, anyway? He insisted on connecting me with Roger.

"Okay, but it would help if you would focus on him. Maybe you'll come up with something we missed."

I already had come up with something. I knew that Roger was dating Karen Thorstensen, and perhaps the police had that information, and perhaps they didn't. For a moment I was tempted to offer it to him.

"Don't ask. Don't tell," said Mercedes.

I shrugged. "Maybe. I'll poke around."

"Watch whom you're poking," said Joe.

Whatever that meant.

He put his hand on my shoulder and squeezed. The touch ignited a part of my body I'd just as soon not identify.

As soon as I pulled out of the driveway, I called Karen Thorstensen, got her machine, and left a message with my phone number. Then, on impulse, I stopped by Pat Draper's real estate office on Canon Drive. The receptionist bought my story that Pat had given me permission, and she willingly showed me the key safe, which wasn't a safe at all, but an unlocked drawer with a mess of keys, all tagged.

No security here. The key was available to anyone who wanted to get into that house.

As this was the kind of plodding drudgework the police

did so well, I decided **to leave** tracking down the access to the keys to them. Joe would certainly appreciate that, and I could concentrate on Karen Thorstensen. After all, Roger had been dating her, so I was focusing on Roger. In my way.

Back home, I wrote up my notes and realized that I was lacking background information on Roger. Here I was, all set to investigate his murder, and, except for the little Lionel had told me, and my own relationship with him at COW, I had not a bit of knowledge as to the man's yesterdays.

A series of phone calls to several staff members gave me some leads and I settled down to follow up on them. First, I contacted his old law firm and had a short, astringent chat with a junior partner who informed me that the police had instructed them not to give out any information. Under no circumstances. And have a nice day.

Next, I looked up Monty Cane's number in the COW directory and called him. Monty was a has-been director who had never really been a *been*. One of the staff had told me, however, that he knew everything there was to know about the Union, having been a charter member, and it might be a good idea to tap his recollections.

Monty didn't want to talk "on the horn," as he put it.

"Of course I don't think my line is tapped or anything like that, but one never knows."

I invited him to meet me at the Coffee Bean on South Beverly Drive. It was near his apartment, and from what my informant had indicated, Monty liked a reason to get out, even for a walk of a few blocks.

He looked like a classic Hollywood director, scrawny build, gray-bearded ascetic face, and bald head covered by a jaunty beret. After treating him, over his feeble protests, to a Café Caramel and an orange-cranberry muffin, I took out my notebook and prepared to take copious notes, first, because Monty liked to talk, and second, because everything would have to be double-checked.

He made me promise not to use his name in my articles, but he would be willing to serve as "deep throat" background. I felt I had struck pay dirt when it turned out that he had been on the Search Committee that had selected Roger for the position.

"Roger was a great one for gourmet food and fine wines," he told me, "but, actually, he came from very poor parents and was raised in the Sunland area of the Valley. You know, Poverty Gulch? Sometimes called the armpit of Southern California?"

He was staring over my head out at the street, as though he were visualizing the camera angles of the script.

"When Roger was eighteen, he met the head of a federally funded agency that gave small scholarships to worthy high school students, and he snagged a scholarship to UCLA. From there, his good looks, charisma, and brains carried him through, along with some after-school jobs that he wangled from relatives of classmates."

"You don't seem to have a terrific opinion of him," I said.

"That doesn't make me a suspect, does it?"

"Just tell me why you didn't like him."

"No names, you promised."

"No names."

"Well, after the first round of interviews, I vetoed him. It seemed to me that he was a little too slick and far too ambitious for us. It was apparent, at least to me, his agenda was to take care of Number One first, and that sure wouldn't be the membership. I thought that if the chance came along, he'd dump us for a job with management, and that made me wonder how he would do in contract negotiations. But no one else felt the way I did, so we hired him. Would you mind?"

He held out his empty cup. I got up to get him another and then we talked some more, for the better part of an hour, filling my notebook and my head with ideas that I would have to explore later.

Before we separated, I pointedly asked him if he had heard anything concrete about Roger leaving the Union.

"Well, someone said they heard he had an offer to run a production company. Or maybe it was one of the networks, I can't remember which."

We walked out together, Monty eyeing the stunning young

girls, or "chicks," as he called them, parading on Beverly Drive.

"So, listen," he said. "Keep my info quiet, okay? Deep intel, you know?"

Monty was watching CNN too often.

"Thanks, Monty. You've been a tremendous help."

Not really, but it was a start.

17

The next day dawned hot and humid, promising to set off a typically unseasonable October heat wave. Roger's funeral was set for eleven A.M. at Forest Lawn Memorial Park in the Hollywood Hills off the Ventura Freeway. The chapel would be jammed, and I didn't want to have to stand outside in the heat with the latecomers, so Lionel and I left early.

I was just glad he was willing to ride with me in the car and not insist on his bicycle.

Lionel had put on a wine-velvet jacket and a cashmere scarf and the heat was supposed to top ninety-five today. The man has no sense and my car has no air conditioning. When I first arrived in Los Angeles, I quickly realized that I would have to arrange for transportation. A friend of Lionel's was getting rid of his four-year-old Toyota RAV, so I bought it. It wasn't the safest vehicle on the road, and it was a very peculiar shade of blue, but it got good mileage and it was cheap.

The Hollywood Freeway was backed up at Barham, and by the time we arrived at the chapel I was sweating inside my panty hose and Lionel had relented enough to remove his scarf. One of the cardinal bits of information I had gleaned from life with Joe was that police always attend the funeral of a murder victim and stand outside and survey everyone, hoping that the killer will show up and give himself away. I decided I could sit inside and achieve the same result, so Lionel and I took seats in the last row where we could watch all the arrivals without twisting our necks.

Everyone who was anyone in the Biz showed up. Heads of studios, network executives, managers, agents . . . It was my guess that they all came just to make sure Roger was really dead. Lionel did a running narration on the fashion scene.

"Look at that man! Good God! A William Morris agent and he's wearing a Zegna shirt with those tatty jeans!" Dana arrived resplendent in a black-veiled hat. "Probably from some prop room somewhere."

Noelle Sears came in, and I realized that I hadn't known she was still in town. Or had she returned to New York and come back again for the funeral? After all, I now knew she was very anxious for Roger's job and she was one ambitious lady.

I pointed her out to Lionel. "Do you think murder would be her style?"

He surveyed her briefly. "Definitely."

That meant I would have to check her out. I was carrying a small purse and didn't have my notebook with me, so I made a few notes on the back sheet of the small prayer book the chapel provided and prayed that God would forgive me.

Samantha and most of the staff, including Wendy, were there. Samantha held a Kleenex box in her lap and was pulling out one sheet after another, constantly dabbing at her eyes and occasionally letting out an audible sob.

"Is she a good actress," Lionel said, "or was she very, very, very close to him?"

That made me think. Had she been more to Roger than just a capable assistant? Another note on the prayer book.

Wendy was sharing Samantha's Kleenex box and joining her in a Duet for Dueling Weepers.

Dee Dee came in with Neville Lake. As the new Executive Director, albeit interim, he proceeded with her to the front, where they found two seats on the aisle. Royal Underhill followed them through the door, but he situated himself in the last row, on the other side of the aisle. I noticed his regular sweater-vest had been replaced with a conventional suit, but he still had the bow tie.

The chapel was filling up rapidly, with the Ravens staking out choice seats. These are the little old ladies who dress entirely in lugubrious black and who spend their days going to funerals and the receptions after the services. For them it's the most enjoyable of pastimes. They rarely know the deceased, but they always manage to find their way to the family gathering afterward so they can feast for free at the buffet.

To my surprise I spotted Dewey P. Forrestal and wondered what in the world he was doing there. COW must have had some connection with his Committee on Moral Decency.

I saw Monty Cane come in, along with Ian McConnell, who looked as somber as a Supreme Court judge. Tom Vincent from the *Reporter* was standing in the aisle, talking to a woman I didn't recognize. She was dressed all in black, with a small hat and short veil perched on her head. Tom kept patting her hand.

Then I spotted Joe and Martin standing at the back of the chapel. They were having a conversation with Karen Thorstensen. I doubted that they were asking her how much she would charge to clean their police station. I scribbled another note.

Lionel peered over at what I was writing. "Joe?" he said. "Your Joe?"

"Not mine, but, yes, that's Joe."

He swiveled in his seat to appraise him more carefully.

"Nice," he said. "Very, very nice."

I gave him the eye roll, and he faced forward again.

The woman Tom Vincent had been talking to walked down the aisle to sit in the very first row, usually reserved for family.

"She must be a relative," Lionel said, fussing with the front of his shirt, which was clinging to his chest in the heat.

"Maybe it's Aunt Theodosia," I said.

"You made that up."

"Remember? The one from Pasadena?"

I reminded myself that she hadn't called me back. The back sheet in the back of the prayer book was used up. I tore it out, took Lionel's, and started on his.

There was a short non-denominational service, and then Bark rose to give the eulogy.

After a brief and eloquent reprise of Roger's value as a friend and colleague and his great worth to the Union, and how sorely he would be missed, Bark started, regrettably, on a more personal portrait of the deceased.

"Roger Urban was your classic Renaissance man," he said. "He loved fine wine, fine art, and fine clothes."

Lionel's hand grabbed for mine and squeezed hard as I held my breath. I could sense that most of the audience were doing the same, trying to restrain their laughter. Several people deliberately coughed to hide displays of amusement. Bark realized his gaffe, too late, but he soldiered on, speaking of Roger's "devotion to the Union" and his "love of writers."

He ended with that wonderful quotation from John Donne's *Devotions*: "No man is an *island,* entire of itself . . . Any man's *death* diminishes me, because I am involved in *mankind;* and therefore never send to know for whom the *bell* tolls; it tolls for *thee.*"

I noticed that the Ravens were enthralled by his words. One of them even applauded.

What followed was even more moving. Roger's aunt rose to face the rest of us, raised her veil over her face, and in low, throaty tones began to sing "Amazing Grace." I was mesmerized. I had read somewhere that a former slave trader had written it. As often as I had heard the hymn, I had never heard it sung so beautifully before. Her voice filled the chapel with utter sweetness and sorrow, and for the first time since learning of Roger's death, I felt the tears come to my eyes.

In the silence that followed, I could swear I heard Lionel sniffle.

As Roger was to be cremated, the service ended with an announcement by the funeral director to please drive carefully because of the ongoing construction on the Ventura Freeway. The Ravens exchanged appalled glances. No food? I watched them scuttle out of the chapel, one of them pulling a folded newspaper out of her capacious handbag, obviously to peruse the obituary columns for another funeral service.

I thought I might be able to talk to Roger's aunt, but as we poured out of the chapel into the blasting heat, I lost sight of her.

Lionel and I made our way through the crowd, stopping here and there to exchange post-funeral sentiments with people we knew, and I had no further sighting of Theodosia. Lionel was in his element, buzzing around and gathering enough gossip and rumors to fuel him for the rest of the week.

Almost all of the Board members were there, standing around, looking uncomfortable, wondering how soon they could extract their cars from the packed parking area. I overheard Dana complain to Adam, "Leave it to Roger to have a funeral on the hottest damn day of the year."

Right. You'd think he might have listened to the weather report before deciding to be dead.

Monty Cane was in deep conversation with Tad Reston. I walked over to them, my heels sticking in the sod, trying not to step on anyone's grave. Don't you feel funny about that, too?

I said hello, and we exchanged the usual cheerless sentiments you come up with at funerals.

"So, Maggie," Tad said, "Monty's been telling me that *Vanity Fair* has you investigating Roger's murder."

"And I've been helping her," Monty said. Deep intel my ass. Nobody's anonymous when there's a credit to be had. "Do we have any leads so far?"

You can imagine how delighted I was to hear that I now had a partner.

I shook my head. "His murder makes absolutely no sense at all."

"What murder ever does?" Monty said.

"We're going to hit the nearest pub," Tad said. "Join us?"

I thanked them, but no, and just then Karen Thorstensen walked determinedly past us, towards the parking lot. I hurriedly excused myself so I could catch up with her. But it was Martin who got to her first. I watched him take her arm and escort her to a car where Joe was waiting behind the wheel.

There went that opportunity to talk to her again, and there was not a chance in the world Joe would ever tell me what she had to say.

"Might she be the paramour?" That was Lionel, coming up behind me and following my gaze.

"Nobody uses that expression anymore," I said.

"We classic Renaissance men do."

As Joe and Martin drove off, Lionel and I headed for the parking lot, which by now had thinned out somewhat. We ran into Bark and Althea on their way to the same destination, and I introduced them to Lionel. Wouldn't you know he all but twittered.

"That was a very nice eulogy," I said to Bark. "Eloquent. A real class act."

Bark shook his head ruefully. "Thanks. If I could just take back that unfortunate remark about clothes."

"Not your usual style, darling," Althea said. "Definitely a lapse of taste."

"Well, I thought it was delicious," Lionel said. "One must never speak ill of the dead, but one can always trot out a little foible or two, don't you agree?"

Althea stared at him as though he were some rare specimen under glass. It was evident she didn't agree.

"I suppose Tom Vincent will have it in his column tomorrow," Bark said.

"Not to worry," I said. "He'll be too busy trying to look up John Donne's screen credits."

Bark rewarded me with a grateful smile.

"Darling, why don't we talk to Tom," Althea said. "We can find out what the *Reporter* has planned in the way of ads for the tribute issue." Then, turning to Lionel and me, "You know, for Bark's star on the Walk of Fame."

Good-byes were traded and they moved off in Tom Vincent's direction.

"Silly me," said Lionel. "I had the idea that tributes were given spontaneously."

"You must understand, Lionel, in Hollywood, spontaneity is very carefully planned."

"Okay, we can go now," he said. "I've seen everybody who's worth seeing, and the inside of this jacket feels like a wet Speedo."

As soon as we got home, I pulled out my notebook and transcribed my notes from the prayer pamphlets. As often happens with me, somehow my observations seemed more meaningful when I was writing them than now when I was reading them. To buoy my spirits, I added a few more thoughts on the cast of characters.

I underlined Noelle Sears' name, because Lionel's verdict was that she could be capable of murder. While that was hardly compelling evidence, I decided I could call in some favors from friends in New York and see what they could find out. Also, Samantha interested me now. Very much so. Either she lived on the edge of a breakdown, or, for some reason, she was unusually distraught by Roger's death. I would have to get to the root of that distress. Last but not least was Aunt Theodosia. More than ever she figured as an invaluable resource in checking out Roger's background.

The next morning, feeling the need for some physical activity, I drove out to Santa Monica. The traffic was light, the air clear, and the weather sunny. According to the travel brochures, it's what Los Angeles is supposed to be all the time.

I went down to the beach bike path and took a three-mile run while the ocean breezes were still cooling. The heat would soon be oppressive, but right now it was glorious, and I lost myself in the joy of the run. I had my candy with me, and my bracelet identification that says I have diabetes, and all was right in my Joeless, Rogerless, world.

Of course, feelings are going to get roiled up again when an old lover resurfaces. It's only normal. There. The storm warnings are down. I can stop worrying about my thoughts of Joe. They're normal and will fade away as soon as Roger's murder is solved and Joe disappears from the scene. Come to think of it, Roger will disappear from my life then also. Good-bye, obsessions, hello, happiness.

Happiness in the person of Henrik, my handsome, utterly fabulous thousand-dollar-an-hour lawyer.

I was singing as I came in the front door. I heard the phone ringing, and the answering machine kicked in. It wasn't Fowler, so I picked up.

"Hang on," I said. "I'm here."

"Is this Maggie Mars?"

I almost didn't recognize her voice.

"Karen?"

"You said I could call."

"I'm glad you did. When I last saw you yesterday, the police were hauling you away."

"They questioned me for a long time, but I had nothing to tell them. Look, Ms. Mars—"

"Maggie."

"I know I didn't make too good a first impression, but I need to talk to you. Could we meet? In about an hour? I have to do some things in the office first."

You see, that's the beauty of exercise. After a good workout, everything goes right.

I suggested the Coffee Bean or Stanley's, but Karen preferred we meet at her apartment, which was near her office in the Valley. I showered, changed out of my sweats, and spent an extra few minutes consoling Lionel, who was miffed, that's what he called it, because he had to go to work. He didn't say so, but I had the feeling that he would have liked nothing better than to tag along and hear what Karen had to say.

An hour later I pulled up in front of the address given me by Karen. There had been a fender-bender at the interchange of the 101 and the 405 blocking one lane, but, miraculously, I managed to be in the right lane at the right time.

She lived on one of those streets off Ventura Boulevard that look like a narrow canyon with apartment buildings for walls. Both sides of the street were lined with cars, and I had to drive around the block three times before I spied an SUV pulling out. I backed in, a feat for me, and only then did I discover it was a Handicapped spot. I shifted gears to pull out.

"Why are you wimping out?" said Mercedes. "You'll never find another space as good as this one."

I left the RAV there and limped down the street.

When I got to Karen's apartment, you're not going to believe this, but I found her cleaning. You'd think a woman who ran a successful housecleaning service would make enough money to hire her own housecleaning service, but no, there she was, dressed in the apron and scarf outfit, a dust mop in her hand.

It was a nice layout, kind of a country-Ikea look, two bedrooms, I think, but she didn't invite me in any farther than the living room. The room was small and sparsely furnished. There were several prints on the wall that, to my untutored eyes, looked very expensive.

I took the initiative to make myself comfortable on the teal blue chenille sofa.

"I'm sorry," Karen said.

"Oh, please don't apologize. I got here a little early. Go right ahead and finish whatever it is you're doing."

"No, it's something else."

"You mean that other time? With the vacuum? Well, how were you to know who I was? I show up interrupting your work and grilling you about Roger . . ." She shook her head. "Not that either?"

"I'm sorry," she said again. "About you coming all the way out here. I've changed my mind about talking to you."

"What?"

"I was just scared, the police treating me like a criminal,

asking all those questions about Roger. I didn't know what to do."

"You made me come all the way out here, to the Valley, for God's sake, to tell me you had nothing to tell me?"

"There's nothing to tell. Roger and I had a thing for a while. That's all."

"Did he have other girlfriends?"

"I don't know. Maybe."

"No other women in his life?"

"Stop it. You're as bad as the police."

That triggered an idea. Maybe there was another way to loosen her tongue.

I said, "Probably that's because I lived with one of them."

She sparked to that, "Really?" At last she closed the door and moved into the room.

"That detective who dragged you away."

"You were in love with that Chinese cop?"

"Asian. And, no, it wasn't him. It was the other one. The white devil."

She looked confused. I had the feeling that she looked confused a lot.

"Never mind that right now," I said. "The important thing is that I'm familiar with police procedure. They'll try to squeeze all the information they can out of you, but if you didn't murder Roger then you have nothing to worry about."

"I didn't!"

"Okay, let's start with that. I told you I was a writer, but I'm also an investigative reporter, and I'm working on a piece for *Vanity Fair*. If you tell me what you know, then maybe I can help you."

She shook her head. "I think you'd better go."

"If you need legal advice, this man I'm dating is a criminal lawyer—"

"I don't need a lawyer," she said. "I didn't kill him."

"I know that," I said. I didn't know that for a fact, but what the hell.

She said, "You went with a detective and now you're dating a lawyer?"

"I'm making my way down the food chain."

She sat down on the couch next to me. "I wish I could be sure I could trust you."

"You can. If Roger were here today, he would vouch for me."

Real sharp, Maggie. If Roger were here today, you wouldn't be here today talking to his . . . okay, Lionel, his paramour.

Tears fell down her cheeks and she swiped at them with the back of her hand. I looked for Kleenex, found a box on the kitchen counter, and gave her a handful.

I said, "Tell me how you and Roger met."

She dabbed at her eyes, and then gave an unladylike blow into the Kleenex.

"We met right after he purchased his condo. The previous owners gave him my name and number because my company cleaned the units in their complex. And when we met, we just clicked. He was a very personable guy, and he didn't mind spending money on a date. We liked the same music, the same movies, the same foods . . . Why am I telling you this?"

I ignored that.

"Was there any talk of a future together?"

"Well, we became lovers very quickly, if that's what you mean."

That wasn't necessarily what I meant, but it was promising. She dabbed at her eyes some more. "Roger made it clear he wasn't ready for marriage, and to tell you the truth, I wasn't either. There's too much divorce in this town."

In any town, I thought.

I said, "Did he have other, well, girlfriends?"

"I didn't think so. None that I knew about."

"Was he a good lover?"

She was quiet for a while, not looking at me, and I wondered if the police had asked her that. I wondered if Joe had asked her that.

"Karen? Am I getting too personal?"

"He was wonderful," she said. "A very caring lover."

"No kinks?"

She didn't grasp it at first. I waited while the thinking process played over her face.

"You mean, because of how he was found, right?" she said. "In ladies' underwear?"

"Didn't that strike you as a little unusual?"

"Oh, no," she said. "Roger always put on silk undies when we made love."

It was said in so matter-of-fact a tone, I wouldn't have been too surprised if she had added, "Doesn't every guy?"

She said, "He wasn't gay, if that's what you're thinking."

"I wasn't."

"Wearing ladies' undies turned him on. He said men's stuff was so boring, but women had wonderful, sensuous fabrics like silk and satin and lace. He said it put him in touch with his feminine side, and that got him very excited."

The remembrance shone in her eyes.

I nodded. "He got off on women's underwear."

"Uh-huh. He liked knowing that he had them on and that no one else knew. He loved having that secret. If he thought we were going to make love, he just wore them under his regular clothes, and then he took them off."

"Let the games begin," I said.

"The feel of the silk, he said, that was all the foreplay he needed. Of course, I always needed a little more."

"But you were already wearing undies."

"Sometimes," she said, completely missing the point.

And then it occurred to me. "Karen, if Roger was wearing . . . what he was wearing, then he must have been expecting to have sex, don't you think?"

"Well, yes, I guess so."

Okay, kid, here comes the million-dollar question. . . .

"Karen, were you supposed to meet him in that house?"

"No," she said, much too quickly. "Why do you ask that?"

"Because, dressed the way he was, he must have been

waiting for a woman. You told me you didn't know of any other woman he was seeing."

She looked away from me. "Just because I didn't know, doesn't mean she doesn't exist."

"She obviously must. He was waiting for someone there."

"I don't know," she said, cradling her head in her arms. "I don't know anything anymore. Please go away."

I had other questions, but I didn't think she had other answers. At least any she was willing to offer. I patted her shoulder and let myself out.

My car was still sitting in the Handicapped parking spot, unticketed. This time I didn't limp. I figured if anyone challenged me, I had a very serious heart condition and what business was it of theirs anyway.

As I got behind the wheel, my cell phone rang and it was Henrik.

"Hey, Maggie, where are you?"

"Just leaving the Valley."

"Do you have time for a quick lunch? I could use a Maggie fix."

He gave me directions to his office, which was downtown near the courthouse. I had not been there before and I didn't get to see it this time either. Parking was a bear, Henrik told me, and he met me at the curb.

We went to Chinatown for Dim Sum. Henrik was resplendent in his court suit of bankers gray, with a faint red pinstripe, pale gray shirt, and red power tie.

"How's the investigation going?" he said.

"Slow, but I'm a fast finisher."

"Don't I know that?"

I leaned across the table and kissed him.

Mid-kiss, two of his partners walked up and joined us. I was flustered but Henrik's introductions were smooth. While I concentrated on my Buddha's Feast of mixed vegetables and they dove into every tray of Dim Sum that wheeled by, they entertained me with stories of Henrik's courtroom prowess, and of the clients he got off.

My fortune cookie said: "You will be given the chance to take part in an exciting adventure."

Great! I hoped I wouldn't run into any of those "clients" in a dark alley.

Soon they were shoving away from the table. They would take Henrik back to the office and I headed west.

On the way home with lots of time to think, I tried to sort out the few pieces of information I had gleaned from Karen. There was no doubt that the red bra and garter belt were significant. Was Roger planning a tryst with Karen, even though she had denied it, or perhaps with another woman? Someone from COW? Samantha maybe?

And, above all, why did I have the feeling that sweet, heartbroken Karen, with all her tears and her dim-blonde confusion, was still hiding something?

18

Of course I had to report all this to Lionel, who was enraptured to hear of Roger's predilection for unconventional sex. "So I guess he wasn't a cross-dresser, after all," I said. "He was just your average, everyday nutcase."

He was making grilled lamb chops for dinner and was in the act of tasting his already prepared marinade of lemon slices, garlic, olive oil, and Niçoise olives. He looked at me over the outstretched spoonful.

"Honestly, Maggie, you can be such an ingénue at times." He tasted the marinade, then deliberated a moment. "All right if I add just a *soupçon* of Courvoisier?"

I nodded and he added the cognac.

"Of course he was a cross-dresser," he said. "He probably started when he was just a gosling, trying on his mother's or sister's clothing for the kicks of it, and realizing it gave him a special kind of thrill. Then, later, when he discovered that this kind of behavior is not accepted, that it's actually frowned upon in what is called polite society, he had to learn how to hide it."

I set out the plates and utensils for dinner.

"You once told me," I said, "that there are clubs that cater to cross-dressers."

"Uh-huh. What about them?"

"Maybe Roger wanted some company, others of the same persuasion, who keep the lingerie designers in business. Where do you think Roger would have gone?"

Lionel stopped basting the chops with the marinade long enough to start thinking. "He probably frequented the clubs around Santa Monica Boulevard, or, if he was really worried about being found out and wanted to keep it quiet, the ones in the Valley on Lankershim."

"Take off your apron and let's go," I said.

"What?"

"Now. Right now. I want to see if we can find someone who knew Roger in his hidden life."

"And what about dinner?"

"I'll take a snack along." I know that eating right helps me balance my blood sugar level, so I quickly brown-bagged a hard-boiled egg, half a banana, and a small bag of pretzels.

You could see Lionel was in a quandary. He was eagerly awaiting my sampling of his latest culinary creation, but on the other hand he would relish the delights of initiating a novice into *terra incognita*. The cross-dressing tour won out.

I had no idea what the appropriate dress was for club-crawling, but in the end I settled on a pale yellow linen pantsuit, with a one-button jacket and no blouse, and opted to be more statuesque and less comfortable in my Manolo Blahnik slides. Lionel, looking bikerish in black jeans and black polo, eyed my décolletage appraisingly.

"Keep that button buttoned at all times and don't lean over," he said.

We got in the RAV and, with me at the wheel and Lionel navigating, headed for south Beverly Drive near Olympic. There, crammed in between a nail salon and a Subway Sandwich Shop, was a nondescript door leading to a weathered flight of stairs.

At the top of the stairs, barring still another door, was a refugee from Gold's Gym, built like a refrigerator and just as sub-zero in attitude. Lionel flashed some sort of card, black plastic, and we were in. As I passed by the behemoth, he gave me the thumbs-up sign.

"Great shoes," he said.

Once inside, I found myself in a long, low-ceilinged room. Blue lights washed over a small stage at the back. Along the left side of the room was an immense bar with an old-fashioned brass railing for a footrest. Bottles upon bottles lined the glass shelves along the mirrored back. At each end of the left wall was a door. A busboy was entering the far door with a tray load of dirty glasses and dishes. Off to my right were tables, each with its own candle lamp throwing a soft glow on the table and leaving the surrounding area dark. Way in the back, through an archway left of the stage, I saw four pool tables.

People were standing three deep around the bar, smoking, talking, laughing.

"They look normal to me," I said to Lionel.

"As you must to them," he said.

We pushed through, trying to get to the bar. Lionel stopped to talk to someone, and after being jostled a few times, I moved on without him.

Finally I was able to commandeer a stool just in front of an Argus-eyed, burly bartender. Grateful for the safe harbor, I ordered a virgin Collins, tall and unsweetened. It's my beverage of choice when I want to appear part of the drinking crowd. I sat there with one Manolo on the brass rail and tried to look nonchalant while I surveyed the room.

Suddenly I felt a hand on my arm. I turned and found myself looking up into the blue-mascaraed eyes of a tall, attractive redheaded woman, wearing a green summery sheath and iridescent high heels.

"Honey, where did you get that suit?" she said. "It's so mouthwatering I can taste it! And who did the hair, or are you wigging it?"

I glanced at the hand holding my arm and realized that even though it was flawlessly manicured, the long nails were fake. It was the hand of a man. For some reason that unnerved me.

"The suit's old, I got it in New York," I said, "and, thank you, the hair is mine."

The hand jumped away from my arm and the blued eyes opened wide.

"Sorry, hon. I didn't know you were straight."

The sheath moved away, wiggling insolently.

I was kicking myself for not having used the encounter to ask questions about Roger when the bartender placed my drink in front of me. Flashing him what I hoped was a dazzling smile, I reached into my bag for the picture of Roger I had brought along. It was one of the recent ones that had run in *Variety*.

"Would you happen to know this man in the photo?" I said, showing it to him.

He never even glanced at it.

"Nope."

"Why don't you try looking at it?"

"Look, lady. This isn't your kind of place and you're making my regular customers uncomfortable. What say your drink is on the house and you leave now, real quiet."

"I didn't know this place was restricted," I said. "I must have missed the sign at the entrance."

I slid off my stool with as much aplomb as I could muster, and deposited a ten-dollar bill on the bar.

"Here. Buy yourself a larger sign."

Still clutching the photo, I moved back through the crowd and over to the pool tables. There were several men dressed as women playing at three of the tables, along with one or two women who may have been dressed as men, a surmise I reached from the way they fondled the cue sticks.

I walked around showing Roger's picture, asking if anyone knew him. No one responded, and as I was approaching the last table, Sub-Zero Man from the front door grabbed my arm in an iron fist, lifted me off the floor, and propelled me through the crowd and towards the exit.

As we reached the door, I heard Lionel's voice.

"Sorry, Jason. She's with me. I'll get her out of here."

Iron Fist opened up and put my feet on the floor. I turned and started back into the room. This time Lionel grabbed me.

"For God's sake, Mag. Behave!"

He maneuvered me down the stairs and out on the street, with me grumbling all the way, and Lionel paying absolutely no attention.

"Why do we have to leave? What did I do? What's wrong with those people?"

It wasn't until we were in the car, with Lionel driving, heading north on Beverly Drive, that he opened up on me.

"What's wrong with those people was you! What were you thinking? Flashing a photo of Roger in there? Do you think those people want to identify anyone? Or be identified? You screwed up but good."

"Sorry," I said, genuinely penitent. "Were you able to learn anything about Roger?"

His answer was a simmering glance.

"Lionel, I really am sorry. Don't forget, it was my first time."

"Yeah, well, that's true, I guess. I did feel a little embarrassed for you."

"Thank you."

"I mean, I should have prepped you better. *Mea culpa*."

"No, no, Lionel. Don't blame yourself. I could have been a little more circumspect, I could have been more careful with my questions—"

"And you certainly could have worn something under your jacket."

"What?"

"It was when Jason lifted you up and hauled you out of there. Quite a treat, I must say, though I doubt if anyone there really appreciated it."

I clutched my lapels closed.

"Too late but not too little," he said.

After a few blocks of silence between us, I relented and stole a look at Lionel. He smiled back.

"Listen," he said. "I asked a few questions myself. But no

one I spoke to remembered Roger there. He must have hit some other places."

I saw we were heading east on Melrose. "So where to now?"

"We're going to a place called the Junction. It's too early for the Pleasure Palace and a lot of Hollywood types prefer the Junction. Think you can mind your manners here?"

"Yes, Ma'am."

"You don't show any pictures. You don't ask questions. Just leave it all to me."

We drove down the boulevard, towards Fairfax, leaving behind all the chic restaurants and hip clothing stores, and pulled over in front of the Junction, which was fronted by a big blue door and another beefy guard, this one with a bushy mustache. Lionel was asked for I.D. and again he presented a card that got us inside.

The lights were dim, the joint was jammed, and with a sense of *déjà vu*, I could feel people staring at me.

"You go to the bar and be inconspicuous," Lionel said. "I'll see what I can find out."

I nodded.

"And keep your jacket closed."

He slipped away towards the rear of the room, and I dutifully headed for the bar. The bartender, a handsome young guy with pink hair and not one but two earrings in one ear, smiled at me and asked for my order. I briefly considered deepening my voice but I knew I'd be lousy at it.

"Just some club soda, please. With lemon, not lime."

He seemed to accept that with just the mildest of once-overs. I looked around.

This room was totally unlike the last room we were in, and yet it seemed vaguely familiar to me. Especially the small bandstand and the tables. I knew I'd never been here before, and still there was that haunting sense of having once seen it, of having experienced it.

The bartender brought my drink.

"Rick's," he said.

"Huh?"

"Rick's."

"Of course! *Casablanca*!"

I must have expressed my realization in an overly high-pitched voice, because everyone around edged away from me, and the bartender wasn't smiling anymore.

"My suggestion is that you drink up quickly and leave," he said quietly.

"Why am I so unpopular all of a sudden?"

"You're out of your league in this club, lady. My friends don't like straight people here. It unrelaxes them."

"Actually . . ." I took a chance, "I'm looking for a friend, and I wonder if he comes in here and you know him."

"No I don't and no one else does either."

"I could show you a picture. . . ."

"Doesn't matter. Whoever he is, whether or not he comes in here, we don't know him and never saw him, get it?"

"Got it. Oh, well. We'll always have Paris."

He walked to the other end of the bar. I smiled hopefully at the few people still remaining alongside me, and they all turned their backs. From not far away, I could see Bushy Mustache approaching. I waved to him, keeping a modest hand on my jacket lapels.

"Just leaving," I said.

I waited outside, ignoring the stares of the few passersby, and Lionel showed up about fifteen minutes later.

"I can't take you anywhere," he said. "You are just so damn straight."

19

By the next morning, Lionel had abandoned his hard-line stand. He promised he would take me out again that evening. But first he stood around and watched while I pricked my finger for testing, and then he made me swear a blood oath that I would be as low profile as possible. As soon as he left, I logged on to the Internet and Google and found out more than I wanted to know about all the Web resources there were for cross-dressers.

There were articles, stories, cartoons, and jokes. There were links to resorts that feature one-on-one fantasy training for transvestites. There were shopping services. There was a store that would beat the lowest prices for breast forms anywhere. There was even a dissertation on Transvestism Through The Ages. There were references to cinema drag, from Fatty Arbuckle in *Miss Fatty's Seaside Lovers* and Harold Lloyd in *Spit-Ball Sadie* to Billy Wilder's *Some Like It Hot* and Hitchcock's *Psycho* and Larry Gelbart's *Tootsie*.

In the midst of all this enlightenment, I had a phone call from Henrik. He was telling me about his case and how it was going, and all the while I was picturing him in a garter belt and red satin bra. For modesty's sake, I added the red power tie.

"Maybe not red," I said. "How about peach?"

"What?"

I shook the image from my mind.

"Sorry, Henrik. I was boning up on cross-dressers. Did I tell you I'm getting some first-hand experience?"

"Did I tell you I miss you?"

"Want some phone sex? What are you wearing?"

"Jockey shorts. Call me, Maggie."

I hung up, smiling. Henrik always knew when to be brief, when to be sensitive, when to be everything. He pushed all the right buttons.

Time to work on the screenplay.

I took out a disc to back it up, and there in my desk drawer I saw it. The Zip I had downloaded from Roger's computer. With all the chaos of the last several days, I had forgotten all about it.

In a few minutes I was looking at Roger's files and his Internet mail. There was a lot of correspondence with residual collection societies, letters to a few studio heads, which lent substance to Monty Cane's contention that he might have been looking for another position, some personal e-mail messages to people with strange-sounding user names, and, blessedly, a personal address file.

Some of the listings I knew from Industry and Union connections. Interestingly enough, the name of Dewey P. Forrestal was among them. There were some others, as well, that might be promising. At least it was worth some investigative phone calls.

I got started on it, identifying myself as a *Vanity Fair* writer, and asking for any information they might have to shed light on Roger's life. Several hours and more than a dozen hang-ups later, along with a recorded political announcement from Forrestal's office, I found out exactly what they wanted me to find out.

Zilch.

I went back to the files and looked them over again. I could understand most of them, or at least they seemed logical, but one file made no sense. It was small, and, other than an address in Imperial, California, it consisted of initials and numbers. Strange. I printed it out and studied it. No connection came to mind.

The initials at the top were R.U. Could have been Roger's initials or could stand for something entirely different, like Redlands University, or Roman Uncial. In case you're wondering, Roman Uncial is a handwriting used in Latin manuscripts of the fourth to the eighth centuries. I found it in my dictionary when, in desperation, I looked up all the R's and U's. Then there were the initials C.D.C., followed by the initial T and a five-digit number. The more I stared at it, the less sense it made. I jotted down a notation in my notebook and left it.

When Lionel came home I was wearing the yellow linen pantsuit, the same outfit as the night before, complete with the Blahnik mules. He sighed when he saw me.

"I was hoping you would forget," he said.

"Are you kidding? Tonight's our night, I can feel it."

"Could you wait until after dinner to feel it?"

"No. We'll stop for a bite."

Later, as we drove north on Laurel Canyon, I asked about the evening's destination.

"We're going to try the Pleasure Palace on Lankershim," he said. "And that's it. Nowhere else."

"I've been doing a lot of research into cross-dressing," I said. "You'll be proud of me."

"I doubt it."

"Hey, I've got a joke for you."

"I don't do knock-knock."

"There's this very wealthy couple and they're going out to a party—"

"Is the punch line 'Jeeves, if I ever catch you wearing my clothes again, you're fired'?"

I sat out the rest of the journey in wounded silence. Lankershim, north of the freeway, is a street of small shops which were closed for the evening. We parked in front of a small store-like establishment with a so discreet as to be almost invisible sign identifying it as the Pleasure Palace. I moved to get out, but Lionel stopped me.

"Here's the game plan," he said. "I'm going inside and you're going to stay in the car and wait for me."

"But, Lionel—"

"No argument, Mag. It's my way or the freeway." He got out. "Now lock the doors."

I nodded reluctant agreement, and sat back, watching him disappear through a nondescript door with graffiti scrawled all over it. The temperature was still in the eighties, even though it was late, and there was some fog creeping in. I could see the halo around the street lamps.

The neighborhood was on the seedy side, probably awaiting reclamation by the NoHo cultural devotees, and there was a homeless person sleeping in a doorway across the street. I thought briefly of opening a window for some air, and decided against it.

After a while my back started to stiffen up, and I saw by my watch that Lionel had been gone almost half an hour. Opening the door, and keeping a wary eye on the sleeper across the street, I got out and stretched a few times, then leaned back against the car and looked up at the sky to see if I could see any stars.

There weren't any.

Maybe if I walked to the corner and back, it would make the time go faster.

It was on my fourth trip that, making the U-turn at the corner, I noticed that the homeless person had disappeared from the doorway. I wondered about that for a moment and then became aware that a woman in spiked heels, wearing a skimpy black halter-top and silver micro-mini shorts, was approaching me.

"Beat it," she said.

"I beg your pardon?"

"This is my corner. Go peddle your sorry ass somewhere else."

"What?"

"Get with it, girl," said Mercedes "She thinks you're a hooker."

"I happen to be waiting for someone," I said.

"Well, so am I, and if anyone shows, he's mine. Now move it."

I was only too happy to oblige without further discussion, but before I could, a rough hand spun me around and a flashlight shone bright in my eyes.

A cop was on the other end of the flashlight.

"Okay, ladies," he said. "You can't hustle here."

"Me? I'm not hustling," I said. "I'm waiting—"

"Go back to your own turf and wait there. Now get moving or I'll run you in."

The woman gave me a one-finger salute and walked away. I decided to make one more stab at redemption.

"Officer, you're making a big mistake—"

"Look, sweetheart, you can either relocate real fast or you can climb in the squad car and spend a night in the tank."

I relocated. Reaching my car, I noticed a black-and-white parked half a block behind. Another policeman was getting out from behind the wheel, and was looking in my direction. Any thoughts I had of remaining there to wait for Lionel were immediately squashed. As I drove off, I could see that the two cops were entering the Pleasure Palace.

I drove home, figuring they must have jotted down my license plate number. There went any prospects I might have for an elective office. I'd have to call Henrik and we'd have a good laugh about this. Maybe even tell Joe. Maybe not.

Lionel came home not long after, limping exaggeratedly and carrying a pair of stiletto-heeled gold sandals that he flung on the floor. He looked like a thundercloud. By then I had taken a shower and washed my hair, and was comfortably ensconced on the couch with a cup of hot herbal tea.

The man detonated right in front of me.

"Goddamn it, Maggie! What the fuck do you mean stranding me like that? Fuck you! I'll never, *never* go out of my way to help you again!" He sat down on a chair, and, grimacing, removed his boots. "I about kill myself tonight while you pretty as you please decide to come home and wash your goddamn hair! Do you know how long it took to find a fucking cab that would pick me up?"

I said, "You're swearing too much and you've got a hole in your sock."

"Never mind that. Answer my question. Why the fuck did you abandon me?"

"You should have called Troy. He would have picked you up."

"And let him know how you humiliated me? Not a chance. Besides, he wasn't home."

Lionel went on for some minutes seething and fuming. He was obviously owed some answers but he didn't draw breath long enough for me to give any. The cats had also relocated and were in hiding. I sipped my tea while the curses and the abuse continued to rain down on my towel-wrapped head.

The storm blew over at last. Lionel disappeared into the kitchen and came out munching on a lamb chop.

"If you're ready to listen to reason," I said, "I'll tell you what happened."

"Go."

"The cops rousted me. They thought I was a hooker."

He stared at me.

"That's right. A hooker. A prostitute. A fucking ho, Lionel."

At that, he laughed so hard he almost choked. Then, still sputtering a bit, he settled down and filled me in on his Pleasure Palace venture. At first he met with the usual lack of progress. One of his acquaintances thought a guy who might have been Roger might have been in a few times, but that was as far as he would go. He was pretty vague about it. Others just shrugged and changed the subject.

Then he stopped at the bar and, taking a tip from me, I couldn't help noting, showed Roger's picture to the bartender. The bartender nodded in the direction of a statuesque blonde, an obvious cross-dresser, sitting alone at a nearby table. He said he didn't know her name but he had seen them together a few times. Her and the guy in the picture.

Lionel sat down at the blonde's table and once more showed the picture, mentioning Roger's name.

"She didn't say she knew him and she didn't say she didn't. But there was definitely a spark of recognition there. And then . . ."

"And then what?"

"Guess what happened next."

He was maddening. But, suddenly, the night's events clicked into place.

"The police came in," I said.

"You got it. The blonde bolted for the back door."

"Why didn't you go after her?"

"I did. I chased her down Lankershim. She turned into an alley, kicked off her shoes, and last I saw of her, she was climbing over a fence at least six feet high. Something I could not and would not emulate. The family jewels were at stake."

"What about the cops? Didn't they come after you?"

"In that area they're only interested in chasing away hos like you."

I stood up. "Good night, Lionel."

"Don't go. I have her shoes," he said, indicating the gold sandals thrown on the floor. They were strappy and encrusted with sparkling crystals. "Size ten and a half, only slightly scuffed, and perhaps just a tad too large for you."

"End of story?"

"End of story. Except, of course, that now you have a lead."

And a pair of great-looking sandals I couldn't even wear. Still, it was a beginning. I planted a kiss on Lionel's cheek.

"Thanks, love. I'm sorry I messed up."

"It's a good thing I don't help you too often," Lionel said as we retreated to our rooms. "It would kill me. Who can run like that?"

By the next morning, my blood sugars were going up and down on a trampoline. I adjusted and gave myself a little more insulin, then ate a big breakfast because of the insulin, and made a call to Roger's Aunt Theodosia. This time I got her in, and, after I introduced myself, she was more than willing for me to come pay her a visit.

Although I didn't invite him, Lionel was adamant about not accompanying me.

"I don't do Pasadena," he said. "It's filled with little old ladies in tennis shoes and Rose Parade leftovers. You can't get in too much trouble there."

"I can try."

"Really, Maggie, this is what comes of your not having any female friends. If you had any friends of your own gender, you could ask them along and you could stop for tea and scones at this captivating little cottage I know of. . . ."

"It's okay, Lionel. I have you. I don't need any other girlfriends."

"That just proves my point. There's something wrong with you if you have me for a friend."

"Lionel . . ."

"Yes?"

"Bye."

There are parts of Pasadena that Angelenos don't ever see. Aside from the Rose Bowl, and Old Town, the shops and restaurants, and maybe a concert venue or a museum or two, they never see the real Pasadena, the authentic hideaway places they don't feature in the guidebooks.

On the last Sunday in April, there is a walking tour of the restored old homes. Roger's aunt lived in one such place. It was a beautiful vintage neighborhood, with California oaks and Chinese elms bordering the sidewalks. None of the streets advanced in a straight line. They curved gently, sinuously, around small pocket parks of green, with Japanese maples shading old iron benches. The homes were well set back, with sloping lawns and a look of very true gentility and very old money.

Aunt Theodosia lived in a California Craftsman bungalow, perhaps a Greene and Greene design, wide and broad, two stories, with a massive veranda studded with rattan easy chairs with printed floral cushions, very faded and lovely, and delicate glass end tables. Gracing the entrance were colorful blossoming plants in multi-sized flowerpots. All my flowerpots are empty, their occupants long since deceased.

Also, there was silence. Only the sound of a distant lawn mower. No harsh gas blowers allowed here.

I parked the RAV on the street and walked up to the front door along a path that meandered through the lawn. It was edged by luxuriant flower beds that showed not a leaf loose on the ground.

The doorbell was a melodic chime that sounded faintly from the recesses of the house. I waited, but heard no suggestion of movement, no foot tread. I rang again, heard nothing, and turned to leave the veranda, prepared to walk around to the rear of the house.

As I reached the foot of the steps, the door behind me opened.

"I'm sorry, but I'm not as fast as I once was," a voice said. A voice as low and musical as a church organ.

I looked up at the woman standing in the doorway. True, I had seen her at the funeral, but this was my first close-up view. She was short and petite, with pale brown hair streaked with gray twisted into a bun at the back of her neck, pale brown eyebrows and eyes, and ivory skin that bore no makeup.

"Please," I said, going up the stairs again. "Don't apologize."

She had on a plain white robe with long full sleeves, gathered at the waist with a gold cord. Once, for a school play, I was an angel, and my mother made me just such a robe out of a cotton sheet. I stared as I passed her going into the house, but she didn't have the wings I wore, made out of bent hangers and aluminum foil.

I expressed my sympathies to her, and she led me down a center hall on whose walls were many framed pictures of Theodosia in a robe such as she was wearing now. Then she ushered me into a large room at the back of the house.

Clearly it was a room well lived in, and I could see why. On three sides were French windows, almost floor to ceiling, overlooking the rear grounds, which were really grounds, not a backyard. Like the pocket parks I drove past on my way here, the terrain was not level, but had gentle swells. Tall and slender willow trees swayed over rock gardens and massive flower beds with lilacs, if you can imagine. Lilacs in Southern California!

That voice asked me if I would like a drink, and I nodded yes to iced tea, no sugar please, which she poured from a frosted crystal pitcher standing on a small marble-topped table.

I perched on the edge of a faded chintz chair and she sat down on the sofa and smiled across at me.

"I've seen you somewhere before, haven't I?" she said.

"Yes, at the funeral, but we didn't actually meet, Mrs. Urban. That is, I wanted to meet . . . but we didn't."

I was stumbling badly, but this woman had me off balance. It wasn't just the musicality of the voice. She had a presence, a center of serenity that was overwhelming, and, furthermore, I think she knew her effect on me. It must happen to everyone in her ambit.

"Please, my friends call me Theo. Roger, of course, insisted on using the full Theodosia, but he was the only one."

There was something I just had to know. "Did you sing professionally?"

"I used to be what nowadays is called an evangelist," she said. "Do you know what that is?"

"Kind of a religious zealot?"

She laughed. "Not exactly. My father was a preacher in

Kansas, like his father before him. They had no real church, they traveled from town to town and set up a tent and had revival meetings. I grew up in those tents, singing and collecting whatever the audience offered. When my family moved to Los Angeles, I followed in my father's footsteps and began preaching."

Wait till Lionel heard that Roger's aunt was a preacher woman!

"In those days there were many wide-open fields along Third Street, east of the old Farmer's Market, and we set up our tent and preached redemption, salvation and redemption."

"Were you on television?" I said. "So many evangelists were."

She smiled, a little sadly I thought. "No, we were never on television. That came after our time. A grateful redeemed sinner deeded us an old building on Alvarado that we converted into a church. Just about that time my father's health gave out, so I took over the church and the congregation and did all my preaching there. Much better than those drafty tents, let me tell you."

She poured more tea.

"Was Roger involved in the church?"

Somehow, that wasn't conceivable to me, so I wasn't surprised when she shook her head no.

"His father, my late husband's brother, was rather ashamed of us, his poor crazy relations from Kansas, so we saw little of him."

This was the opening I had been looking for, and I jumped right in. "Tell me about Roger's family. I know so little about him and nothing at all about his family."

It occurred to me that she might have wondered how come I was so interested in Roger's past, but she seemed to accept it, perhaps as being part of the well-known nosiness of a writer.

"Well, his father was one of those traveling salesmen we used to hear all those jokes about. He worked for a tool company and took orders for their products, all kinds of instruments and hardware. When he was home, he never wanted to go out. He just wanted to lie in his BarcaLounger, watching television, stirring himself every once in a while but only to change channels. His mother kept busy with cooking and cleaning and as long as the family was fed and clothed, she figured her duty had been done."

"This was in Sunland?"

"Yes. Back then and maybe now for all I know, Sunland was a cultural desert. There was nothing there except fast-food restaurants, gas stations, and cheap apartment housing. Hotter than Hades in the summer and no air conditioning. It's no wonder those kids escaped as soon as possible."

"Kids?" It must have come out as a squeak, and I found myself on the edge of my chair. "There was more than just Roger?"

Theodosia just looked at me, and the serenity in her face calmed me down. "A brother," she said. "Roger never mentioned him?"

"Well . . . not to me, anyway."

"He probably never spoke of him to anyone, and it's no wonder. Richard was two years older than Roger and a terror. Well, they both were terrors. But, of course, the older brother always leads the younger, don't you think?"

I nodded, mutely. An older brother! Mentally I was already filling several pages in my spiral notebook.

"They were both talented, bright young boys with, I'm sorry to say, no guidance." She shook her head. "And don't look at me as if I should have stepped in. I tried, but what standing did I have as an aunt?"

I don't think she was expecting an answer. Besides, I had none.

"Do you know I had to bar them from the church? They were stealing from the collection plates. And not just the collection, but the plates as well. Very sad."

I desperately wanted to hear more about this mysterious older brother. "And where is he now, Richard, I mean?"

"He left high school in the eleventh grade and virtually disappeared. His parents never spoke of him again, and I haven't heard from him since."

"How sad for Roger, growing up alone after that."

"Yes, but he was a smart little bugger. Without Richard to scheme with, he earned good grades in school and got that scholarship to UCLA. After that, there was no stopping him. I've been very proud of Roger."

"I'm sure you must be."

"Even though he refused to be saved. But then, salvation comes only when the sinner is ready, and I guess Roger wasn't ready."

Her voice trailed off, and I thought this might be a good time to hit on another topic.

"What about his friends? Do you know if he had any . . . special friend?"

"Oh. Like a girlfriend?"

I didn't exactly know whether I meant girl or boyfriend, but I nodded.

"I thought you might ask me that. Yes, he had many girl-friends. I believe there was one connected with your Union."

"Did she work at the office?"

"You're thinking of Samantha, right?"

"Was it Samantha?" I tried not to sound too excited.

"No. Oh, there was Samantha, of course. . . . But I was thinking of someone else. Someone I met at a premiere Roger invited me to."

She gave it some thought for a moment, then shrugged. "Sorry. I've drawn a blank. Besides, last year, when we were in Paris together, he mentioned that the relationship was over, so I'm afraid I paid little attention."

"Did you travel a lot together?"

"No, just that once, and we weren't traveling together, we had arranged to meet in Paris. He was there on Union busi-ness. I remember we ate at little out-of-the-way cafés that he discovered, did a museum tour, roamed the bookstalls along the Left Bank . . . He came home with so many books he had to purchase another suitcase. We had a lovely time."

A deep sigh of regret and then she rose, my signal that the interview was over.

She said, "It's been so lovely being able to reminisce with you, my dear. Thank you for coming to see me."

It was as charming a dismissal as I had ever received.

Graciously, she escorted me down the long hall to the front door.

"You've been more than kind, Theo," I said. "If you think of the name of Roger's woman friend, would you call me?"

I gave her my card and she took it almost absently, as she stopped in front of one of her framed photos.

"Roger loved show business," she said. "He was the one who suggested that with my voice as lead, the choir and I could make records—there were records then, not CDs—and we would knock 'em dead." She glanced at me. "His words, of course."

I was entranced. "And did you?"

"Yes, my dear, we were a big hit. We recorded hymns and sold many records. Roger helped us set up the deal with the recording company, our retention of rights and other legal gibberish, and we were on our way. We went platinum with our third record."

I finally understood what lay behind the opulence of these surroundings.

"And was Roger part of your success?"

"He felt that his talents deserved a wider field," she said. "Our mission was far too limiting for him, and, truthfully, he lacked the patience and compassion necessary to deal with sinners and to sell salvation. He had far grander ideas."

"Like what?"

"Well, I think he felt he could be a leading figure in Hollywood, a combination of Lew Wasserman and Michael Eisner. Did I say those names right?"

I nodded, smiling.

"Forgive me," she said, patting my hand, "but I imagine your Union was just a stepping-stone for him. The COW you call it, right?" Her laughter was a light ripple. "The COW . . . Roger was very smitten with that name."

Smitten? Well, I guess it was an Aunt Theodosia kind of word.

I ventured a direct question. "Did he indicate he was planning on leaving us and going to a studio?"

"He never spoke of it to me," she said, "but he might very well have thought of it. He was very, very deep."

And very, very ambitious, I confirmed to myself. It fit in with what Monty Cane had told me.

We reached the door and she held it open for me, as we exchanged good-byes.

"You never did tell me why you were asking about Roger," she said. "Did you know my nephew well?"

"No," I said. "I only thought I did."

The door closed. There was a light rain, barely more than a mist, and the smell of lilacs drifted on the breeze. In the dimming afternoon light, the streets radiated loneliness.

I hurried to my car, thinking of what I had learned from Aunt Theodosia, which was worth adding to the mix. I had found out that Roger might or might not have been having an affair with someone who either worked or didn't work at the Union, and that he had a brother. Or, at least, once had a brother.

Okay. Along with the gold sandals, that made three leads.

"Four, if you count both shoes," said Mercedes.

I was already in my car, ready to get moving, when I noticed a flyer tucked under my windshield wiper. Grimacing, I turned on the ignition and started up the wipers. Back and forth they went, clearing the windshield of everything except the flyer.

It was through the glass, my head going back and forth along with the wipers, that I was able to read the crude lettering:

LET THE DEAD REST IN PEACE.

20

I shifted into Park and got out and retrieved it. There was no signature. Just the basic block letters, crudely formed. Looking around, I spotted a figure coming out from around the side of the neighboring house. He appeared to be carrying something long and metallic in his hands, and for a moment I felt a chill of apprehension.

Then, as he came into focus, I could see that he was a gardener, preparing to haul his tools back to the pickup truck parked a little way down the street.

"Hey, you! Can I talk to you?" I caught up with him, waving the piece of paper. "Did you see who might have left this on my car?"

"No, I have not seen anyone." He was an elderly man who stood slightly stooped over and looked up at me from under his grass-stained gardener's hat, not at all curious about the lettering. "I have been working around the back. There was no one to see."

I thanked him and returned to my car slowly, scoping out the neighborhood as I walked. There was no one else in sight and, except for the pickup truck, not another vehicle. I looked over at the house directly across the street, and, on impulse, decided to try it. I rang the bell, and eventually a maid in a starched black uniform opened the door.

She looked at me quizzically. "May I help you?"

Now I really felt foolish. But it was too late to retreat.

"Yes, did you happen to see who put a flyer on my car? It's parked over there." I pointed to the RAV.

"Sorry, no."

As she was about to close the door, a woman approached from the stairway. She wore a pale blue denim blouse and skirt, and had on a necklace of creamy pearls.

"Is something wrong?"

I tried again. "Someone put a flyer on my car while I was visiting across the street, and I was wondering if anyone saw who it was."

"I didn't notice anything."

"Are you sure? I was just visiting Mrs. Urban across the street."

The maid disappeared, and the woman said, "In this neighborhood, we are not in the habit of spying on our neighbors."

My bad luck to have this happen in old Pasadena.

She closed the door and I heard a lock click as I turned away.

I put the piece of paper in my bag, got into the RAV, and drove off. Even though it was warm in the car, my hands had gone very cold and I was shivering. Who would want to threaten me? Someone who knows I'm investigating Roger's murder? Of course. But how would they know I was in Pasadena?

I was just pulling onto the 134 when the revelation hit. Oh my God, I'm being followed! On the freeway, there was little traffic for that hour. The drizzle of rain had stopped, and there hadn't been enough of it to cool things off. Instead the heat had intensified and the air flowing in the windows was like a blast from a hair dryer. But I was too preoccupied to have it matter.

LET THE DEAD REST IN PEACE.

I tried to think it through. Obviously it wasn't a religious message. Someone didn't want me investigating Roger's death. And that someone knew I was at Theodosia's house. Was I being followed now? I drove with my eyes on the rearview mirror but spotted nothing suspicious. I tried a few sudden lane shifts while watching my rear, and still saw nothing out of the ordinary. I even got off at Laurel Canyon, then immediately went back on the on-ramp.

It didn't look as though I was being followed. But how did I know for sure? I must be stepping on someone's toes, but whose?

I drove a circuitous route home, almost getting myself lost in the process. With all my maneuvering, it took twice as long to get back as did the earlier trip out to Pasadena, and I didn't spot a tail. Still and all, the note was a warning, and it unsettled me. I pulled up to the condo and into the underground garage, but remained locked in the car, until I saw the familiar figure of a neighbor drive in. I waited until he exited his car and headed for the elevator, then got out and hurried in after him.

Lionel wasn't home. I fixed dinner for myself and considered what I should do next. The obvious answer, at least for a rational person, would be to call Joe. He was a professional and could advise me.

On the other hand, he would just go ballistic and throw up every roadblock he could in my way. Then the assignment would be kaput and so would the extra money. No, I couldn't tell Joe.

On the other, other hand, the note in my bag was all too real.

I called Joe.

His reaction was to be expected.

"Maggie, this is exactly what I was afraid of. You're messing around in a dangerous situation with dangerous people. You've got to watch your every step."

"What about you? Can't the police do something?"

"We'll look into it. We'll need the note."

"That's it? What about protection?"

"We can't put you under surveillance. We don't have the manpower."

"You mean there's nothing you can do for me?"

"How about . . . I come over and hold your hand."

"Thanks, but I have other people for that job."

"I'll bet you do," he said. "Put the note in an envelope and bring it in. Oh, and leave a set of your prints. It's probably already too late, but try not to handle it too much."

"Sure. Bye."

"And, Maggie?"

"What?"

"Be careful."

I hung up, wishing I hadn't called him. It was nice to know that he was concerned about me, but, still, he wasn't going to do anything about it. Well, what did I want him to do? Rush over and put his arms around me and tell me everything was going to be all right? Lie by my side all night, holding me closer than close, murmuring endearments, promising that he wouldn't let anyone or anything hurt me . . .

What was the matter with me! I was an emotional basket case. And to make matters worse, my cheeks were suspiciously wet. I dabbed at them with the back of my hand.

"Suck it up, girl," said Mercedes.

I sucked it up and went to bed, vowing not to fall asleep until I heard Lionel's key in the lock. But the day had been too much for me. I drifted off.

I awoke to find I had forgotten to set my alarm and it was later than my usual morning launch. Lionel had made coffee and was closeted behind his bedroom door.

"Lionel? You up?"

"Depends who's asking?"

I had an impulse to tell him right then about last night's warning. Somehow in the light of a fresh new day, it didn't seem nearly as scary. Besides, I knew Lionel. If he thought there was anything of substance to the threat, he'd be sitting on me like a mother hen. Maybe I'd tell him later.

"Only me. I'm going out for a walk."

"Fine. I'm taking the day off and Troy's coming over to try on masks with me. We're getting ready for tonight."

Or maybe I just wouldn't tell him at all.

The phone rang. It was U.G. He was trying to sound calm, but I recognized the effort.

"What's wrong, Dad?"

"Nothing's wrong. I just called to ask you to have breakfast with me."

Something was definitely wrong, and I was hoping it didn't involve explosions or cash outlays. We arranged to meet halfway between Santa Monica and his retirement home. There was a small café on the beach that was known for its breakfasts.

I pulled on some sweats and hit the beach, checking behind me a good part of the way.

After my run, I drove down to meet U.G. He was waiting at a table on the sand.

Before I was even seated, he plunged right in. "I talked to Joe this morning." Uh-oh! I knew what was coming.

"Listen, Dad—"

"No, Mag. You listen to me. Joe is worried that your investigating could be putting you in danger and I won't have it."

"Let's not go off half-cocked here. It was just a note tucked under my windshield wiper. That's all. If someone had wanted to confront me, he would have. But he didn't. He settled for an anonymous note. That's the last refuge of cowards, and you know it."

I wished I felt as confident as I sounded.

"Then how about if I go with you while you're investigating? That way you won't be alone."

"Dad, I'll be all right. I've got Lionel watching over me."

"That's worse than being alone. He's useless."

"Dad!"

"You know what I mean. You're not going to eat those bagels, are you?"

I pushed the basket over to him. "I promise you I'll be careful. Didn't I call Joe right away?"

"Yeah."

"So. Not to worry."

"But I do worry. You're all I have left."

The waiter came over with our coffee. I knew U.G. didn't buy my reassurances, but I got him talking about his latest invention that was going to "make us filthy rich," and he appeared to give up on the other topic. Only I knew he probably hadn't.

By the time I got back and made a pit stop in the living room, Lionel and Troy were having a great time sampling an assortment of scary rubber heads.

I said, "What's with the faces? Aren't your God-given ones spooky enough?"

"Ha. Ha. Very funny," Lionel said.

Troy said, "Which do you think I should be?" He held up one, then the other. "Frankenstein's monster or Medusa?"

I clapped my head in pretended sudden enlightenment. "I forgot. Halloween!"

"And the Halloween Gay Pride parade," Lionel said. "Wait till you see my outfit."

"Scheherazade? I saw it already."

"Très passé. I found something better. Want some decaf?" He didn't wait for an answer but poured me some.

"Thanks. What time are the festivities?"

Lionel stopped in mid-pour. "Oh, no you don't. Troy, she's going to want to come with us. Tell her she can't."

"Me?" Troy said.

"Lionel, listen to me. Won't everybody in the local cross-dressing population be at the parade?" This time I didn't wait for the answer. "Maybe Gold Shoes will be there."

"Who's Gold Shoes?" Troy said.

"I can't look for her or him by myself. I never saw her. Or him. But you did. Come on, Lionel, help me out this once."

Troy said, "Who's Gold Shoes?"

"This once? This once? I nearly got killed the other night when I was leaping over fences for you."

Troy said, "I am so impressed, Lionel. I didn't know you could leap over fences."

"Well, I almost did before I thought better of it. She just stranded me there because some witless cops thought she was a hooker."

Troy was ecstatic. "She sounds like a fun date. Let's ask her along."

I put on a pleading face. Lionel and Troy exchanged glances.

"She'll need a costume," Lionel said.

"She'll find something."

"She'll be the only straight person at the parade!"

"Who cares? She'll be our straight person."

I'd about had it with Tweedle Dumb and Tweedle Dumber. "Will you please stop talking about me as though I weren't here!"

"We should be so lucky," Lionel said.

We arranged to meet here, garbed for the parade, at eight o'clock.

"I'm not leaving," Troy said, "until you tell me who Gold Shoes is."

"We're saving that for Trick or Treat," Lionel said, and nudged him out the door.

21

After showering and changing into my writing clothes, another set of sweats, I sat down at the computer and brought up my screenplay.

```
EXT. DARKNESS—(MOVING)

We HEAR the GROGGY SOUNDS of Mercedes re-
gaining consciousness. There's a RUMBLING
coming from all around her as we can HEAR
her totter to her feet and bump into things
as she moves. . . .
```

That could wait, as always. I closed the file, picked up the phone, and, walking with it into the kitchen, dialed Aunt Theodosia's number.

"How are you, my dear?" she said.

"Fine, thank you. I'm sorry to bother you—"

"It's no bother at all. I was just going outside to work in the garden."

"Then I won't keep you. I was just wondering if you knew what street Roger's family used to live on."

"In Sunland?"

"Yes. Where he grew up."

"Let me think now. . . ."

I waited. They say older people can recall things from the distant past more readily than their morning breakfast. But with Aunt Theodosia, one could never be sure. I waited some more.

Then, suddenly: "Tinker, tailor, soldier, sailor."

"What?"

"I think it was an old nursery rhyme . . . or was it when we were little girls, and we used to count the buttons on our dress and chant those words so we could tell whom we were going to marry. Tinker, tailor, soldier, sailor."

"Mrs. Urban . . . Theo . . ."

"In the end I married an optician. We didn't have a chant for that."

I was not only running out of patience, I was losing hope. "Roger's street . . . did you think of where that was?"

"I just told you, my dear. It was Tinker Street, of course."

Of course. I thanked her, went back to the computer, and was on the Board of Education site in no time. I located the high schools in the general area of Tinker Street and made my notes. This was good. I was rolling along. Maybe towards the edge of a cliff, but any forward movement at all was better than none.

While I was hot, I decided to push my luck and go to the Cyber Detective site and log on. I owed money, so I went through the garbage of paying for my next six months use via credit card, trying not to think of how I was going to manage that when the bill came in. After an eternity, I was cleared, and after checking in my notebook, I went to the Reverse Directory for Imperial, California. In a moment the name and phone number that had been in Roger's personal address file popped up. It was a California State Prison.

I signed off and just sat there. What was Roger doing with a San Diego, California, prison address in his files? And what did those R.U. initials stand for? It must have been his brother, Richard Urban. It couldn't have been Roger. He wouldn't have referred to himself by his own initials, would he? But then again, what did I know about Roger Urban?

Back to the telephone. I dialed the number that had popped up.

"Department of Corrections, Centinela State Prison."

It was a recorded mechanical voice. I waited for the inevitable If You Want English Press One, Para Español, Es Numero Dos, and then before the message could go any further, like telling me that if I wanted a porterhouse steak for my last meal, press three, I employed my usual trick of hitting the O button, which immediately connected me with a human person.

"Where can I direct your call?" The bored tone of the voice already told me that directing me to anyone or anything useful was the furthest thing from his mind.

"I'm inquiring about some initials and numbers associated with the prison. Can you help me?"

"Initials and numbers?" Still bored.

"Yes. I'm trying to find out what they mean."

"What they mean?"

My God! I was having a conversation with the prison parrot. "Yes. The initials and numbers. I need to find out what they mean."

"Sorry. Can't help you."

"Wait! Don't hang up! Do you have a Public Information Officer?"

"Information?"

I was ready to scream. "Public Information Officer."

"Just a minute."

I waited several minutes. At least there was no canned music. Excuse the pun.

Another voice, more crisp and authoritative. "Amy Webster. May I help you?"

I explained I was writing an article, making sure to emphasize that the article was about a man who had just died, and was not about the prison. I told her about the mystifying initials and numbers I had found. In written correspondence, I amended, not wanting to divulge that I had been a computer hacker. Who knows how many years she could give me for that.

"And now I'm trying to decipher those initials and numbers," I concluded.

"C.D.C. stands for California Detention Center, and the letter T followed by numbers is a prisoner number. If you would like to locate the prisoner, you can go online to *corr.ca.gov* and click on Inmate Locator. We have thirty-two prisons in the state. This Web site will locate that prisoner for you."

"What if he's no longer in prison? Will it tell me where I can find him now?"

"In that case, it would tell you whether he has been released or paroled."

I thanked her and wasted no time getting to *corr.ca.gov*. I found out that my suspicions were right. The prisoner was Richard Urban, Roger's long-lost brother. He had been paroled five years ago to the Los Angeles County area. The trail came to an end there, unless I could find out the name of his Parole Officer. The Web site did not offer that information.

Still, I felt more than a little satisfied with my morning's work. The next item on my agenda was to deliver the threatening note to Joe at the police station.

I left the house with a flashlight, a heavy one, gripped firmly in my hand. I checked out the garage thoroughly before I made a dash for my car, got in, locked the doors, and floored it out of there. Once again I made some sharp turns, signaling right and turning left several times, driving other drivers crazier than usual, until I finally convinced myself no one was following me.

Neither Joe nor Martin was at the station, so I left the envelope with the officer at the desk. I was directed to another officer who would take my fingerprints. What is there about having your fingerprints taken that makes you feel like a criminal?

A few blocks away from the police station I stopped for a quick bite. Next door was a small general store that featured

Japanese items. There I purchased a mask of a painted geisha face. With the throngs of people sure to be at the parade this evening, I thought it wise not to be readily identifiable.

My next stop was the spy shop on Wilshire Boulevard in Beverly Hills. After an edifying discussion with the salesman, I selected a handy-dandy pepper spray that was guaranteed to stop a three-hundred-pound man dead in his tracks. Or two one-hundred-and-fifty-pound men, whoever came at me first.

While he was dealing with my credit card, my phone rang.

"Good news," Henrik said.

"You won your case?"

"Better than that, court's dark. The opposing attorney has a scheduling conflict. I'm free for the afternoon."

"No, you're not. I'll be right over, and we can make up for lost time."

"Sounds great. I'll pick up lunch."

"Forget the lunch, just set the bed."

I hung up and noticed the salesman grinning at me.

"Here you are," he said, handing me my package and receipt, "and have a *really* nice day."

It was a stellar matinee performance. A much needed respite for both of us. Afterward, while we were lying in each other's arms, Henrik caught me up on how his case was going and I filled him in on how my articles were progressing. I finished by telling him of my conversation with the Public Information Officer at Centinela State Prison. "Only I couldn't find out the name of his Parole Officer."

Henrik said, "I've got an idea."

I glanced at my watch. "Do we have time?"

He laughed. "How about if I get you that info?"

"Would you do that? I'd give anything to know where Richard Urban is now."

"I'll call you when I have something for you."

"In that case," I said, moving down, "I have something for you, and we do have time."

22

By five minutes of eight that evening, I was all set for the Halloween Gay Pride doings in an old kimono, skinny black cotton pants, and flats, no Manolos. And, of course, my mask.

"And who are you supposed to be?" Lionel said.

"Madame Butterfly," I said.

The two of them gave me the once-over.

"She'll do," said Troy.

High praise indeed.

By eight thirty the three of us—Lionel as Cruella De Vil, Troy as the Marquis de Sade—were on Santa Monica Boulevard near the corner of Robertson, but the location was unrecognizable. It was wall-to-wall pandemonium. Think New Orleans Mardi Gras. Think Rio Carnival.

Floats were inching their way down the street, festooned with flowers and greenery, pergolas and birdcages, armchairs and Persian rugs. Revelers in shimmery, glittering costumes and wearing exotic papier-mâché masks were draped all over them. Rainbow-colored balloons were drifting on the air currents and klieg lights were crisscrossing the sky.

All around the floats were surges of people, dancing,

strolling, swinging down the street, dressed as Bedouins and burlesque girls, wrestlers and doctors, ballet dancers and comic book characters, sexy screen stars and orangutans, Queen Elizabeths and Whistler's mothers. Music came from everywhere, all sorts of wonderful discordant sounds blending into the general cacophony.

It was impossible to talk and almost impossible to move. I walked along, clutching one of the gold sandals, Lionel had the other, and I lost myself to being utterly captivated by the scene. It was exciting to be in a crowd of joyous people, and I found the joy contagious.

Before long, with the crowd billowing around me, I had lost sight of both Lionel and Troy. I tried to push myself towards where the curb should be, figuring it would be a better vantage point to look for the guys, but the throng pressed me along towards San Vicente. Streams of confetti covered my shoulders and head, and a conga line grabbed me from the rear and conga-ed me down San Vicente and across and through the parking lot of the Blue Whale. There was no fighting it, so I swung along, screaming with everyone else.

When the line finally let go of my hips, I was back on what should be Santa Monica Boulevard, near a bank, and a group of goofballs on stilts was playing something with a large beach ball and cestas. Miraculously the powdered and beauty-marked face of the Marquis de Sade loomed in front of me and Troy was saying something about Lionel. But the enveloping noise of the crowd made him impossible to understand. I mimed that I couldn't hear, and he proceeded to bellow in my ear.

"Lionel said to meet him on the terrace of Green Gables!"

All but deafened, I nodded, and Troy flitted away.

The Green Gables was a restaurant I knew. As I tried to jostle through the crowd on the sidewalk, I just hoped that it wasn't too far away. Making any progress was futile, but then inspiration struck. I shouldered my way out into the street and grabbed a float gliding by.

Some kind soul hoisted me up onto the float platform and I turned to thank whoever it was.

It was Marilyn Monroe, tall, beautiful, and sexy in the infamous gown from JFK's birthday bash.

"Hey, honey," Marilyn said in dulcet tones. "Where did you get that gorgeous sandal?"

I forgot I was still clutching the stiletto-heeled gold shoe.

I said, "Would you believe I was looking for Cinderella?"

"Call me Cindy. I would positively adore a pair of shoes like that. Where's the other one?"

"A friend has it."

And with that she gave me a shove and pushed me off the float. Fortunately, it wasn't moving fast, and since I have a penchant for landing on my ass, I managed to do it again.

A passing reveler garbed as a policeman helped me to my feet. If ever there was a time I could have used a taxi and told the driver, "Follow that float," this would have been it. I looked around. The float was still in sight, but there was no Marilyn on her.

"Did you see where she went?" I asked my Good Samaritan, who was busy eyeing where I was rubbing. I stopped rubbing.

"Who?"

"Marilyn Monroe."

"Oh, yeah. What a shame she died so young."

But then, blessedly, I caught sight of her. She was hightailing it up Santa Monica towards the Pavilions parking lot as fast as she could sprint, undoubtedly heading for her car.

"Thanks."

Grateful for my flat shoes, I started running.

"Be careful out there, Ma'am," he called after me. And only then did I have an inkling he might be a real cop.

There were fewer people in this area, and the distance began to widen between us. She reached the parking lot driveway. I was lamenting the fact that I had never taken track in high school, or, for that matter, anything else more athletic than dodge ball, when I saw Marilyn plow right into Cruella De Vil. The force of the collision knocked them both down.

Praying it was my Cruella De Vil I picked up the pace, even as Marilyn was scrambling to her feet.

I let out a yell. "Lionel! It's her! Stop her!"

Lionel was still on the ground, but he reached out a hand and somehow was able to clutch at the hem of her gown and hold on. She fought to get away, dragging Lionel a few feet with her, until he lost his hold and let go. But she had been slowed down.

"Get the lead out," said Mercedes.

I put on an extra burst of speed and managed to grab her around the waist. I held on, puffing and panting, and had her in a semi-tackle when Lionel got up from the ground to help me control her.

"Lionel, I think Marilyn here belongs to the gold shoes."

"Goddamn it, let go of me! I'll sue you for aggravated assault! Look what you did to my dress! It's a rental!"

The tones were no longer dulcet. In fact, they sounded familiar. I had heard them before, but where?

Lionel said, "What a shame. And me without my sewing kit."

"We need to talk," I said.

"Are you nuts?" Marilyn was still trying to free herself from our grasp. "Talk about what?"

"About how we adored you in *Some Like It Hot.*"

Between us, we managed to propel her into the far reaches of the Pavilions parking lot, where we pinned her up against a silver-blue SUV.

"All right," Lionel said. "What's your name?"

I was infinitely proud of him. I never knew him to sound so masterful.

"Why the hell should I tell you?" Marilyn said.

"Because my plainclothes partner here is with the LAPD, that's why."

I tried to put on an official-looking face.

"Yeah, that's why," I said.

"I don't believe you. Let me see your I.D."

Reaching into my fanny pack, I pulled out a card case. I was going to flash my COW card, which I figured would look fairly authentic in the dark corner of the lot.

"Oh, screw it," our erstwhile Marilyn said. "I've got to sit down. My feet are killing me." She leaned against the SUV and exhaled heavily. "My name is Madame Merlot. Now what do you creeps want?"

"My partner maybe, but me a creep?" Lionel was doing offended. "And who the hell calls herself Madame Merlot?"

He reached out and grabbed a handful of Marilyn's blond hair, and the wig flew off. Marilyn, surprise, surprise, was a he, with light, thinning hair.

"Christ, give me back my hair. It's cold out here."

"Wait, I know who you are," I said. "Lionel, I've met him somewhere."

"Probably in a lineup," Lionel said. "You cops never forget a face."

I was still struggling to make the connection when the SUV's owner, an overweight guy with glasses, the kind who should never wear plaid shorts but who was wearing plaid shorts, came up to the car, a shopping bag in the crook of each arm.

"Beat it, you creeps."

That made it official. We *were* creeps.

"Come on, we'll go inside for some coffee," I said.

"Nice car," Lionel said to the owner, "for a gas guzzler."

We walked on either side of Marilyn, aka Madame Merlot, into the market café. We found a table, and I left Lionel to keep an eye on our quarry while I fetched the coffee. When I came back with the mugs, Merlot was slumped in his seat looking utterly dejected. I suddenly brightened. The lipstick and the eye shadow had thrown me off, but now I remembered.

I gave them their coffee and sat down.

"Cream?" I asked him. "You do take cream, don't you, Dewey?" He slumped even further. I turned to Lionel.

"Lionel, meet Dewey P. Forrestal," I said. "We bumped into each other at Spago's."

"The head of the Committee on Moral Decency is a certified cross-dresser?" Lionel obviously couldn't believe it. "This is absolutely luscious."

"Keep it down, will you," Marilyn/Merlot/Forrestal said,

glancing around nervously to make sure we weren't being overheard. "What do you guys want?"

"Just some information about one of your transvestite buddies," I said.

He winced. "This is about Roger, right?"

Lionel and I nodded in unison.

"Okay." He planted his wig once more firmly on his head. "Maybe we can do business." He paused and appeared to be thinking.

We waited while the market sounds circulated around us.

"I'll trade you," he finally said. "I'll tell you what I know, but I want your promise that you'll keep my identity secret."

"You got it," Lionel said.

"Wait a minute," I protested. "We don't have to negotiate anything."

Lionel's glare told me to shut the fuck up.

There was a thin sheen of sweat on Forrestal's brow. He dabbed at it with a paper napkin.

"Roger and I were not gay," he said. "We just liked the jolt of dressing as women. I know you can't understand that—"

"I can," I said. "Lionel told me—"

Lionel glared at me again.

"It's a freedom we both love . . . loved," Forrestal said. "In his job, and, naturally, in mine, we could never, never reveal that side of our personality. It was this secret we both shared that brought us together. There's nothing wrong with cross-dressing, you know. It's not a crime."

It is when you excoriate others under the cover of the Committee on Moral Decency, I thought. But I didn't say it. I didn't want to derail him from what he had to offer about Roger.

He was whispering now, and we had to lean forward to hear his words.

"Roger and I met at the Pleasure Palace about two years ago. We sometimes club-hopped, but even at those other places, mostly all we did was just sit and drink at the bar."

I said, "What did you talk about when you were together?"

He shrugged. "How hard it was to keep our secret from

the public. What a conservative world we still have, even in Hollywood. Places we could go where it would be safe to dress as we liked. And, of course, we talked about the sex."

That's the trouble with investigative reporting. Ask someone a question and you're liable to find out more than you want to know.

"Wearing women's clothes makes you give great sex and, believe me, it gets you the same. . . ." His voice trailed off and a blissful look came over his face. "The right panties and you'll never need Viagra."

I was afraid he was going to have an orgasm right there in Pavilions. A first for any supermarket.

"When did you last see Roger?" I said.

"Who?" He snapped out of it. "Oh, yes, Roger. The night before . . . before he was killed. We hoisted a few at the Pleasure Palace and then he left early."

"Did he mention where he was going?"

"No. . . ."

"Did he say anything about meeting someone?"

"I didn't ask."

"You must have talked about something besides sex."

The café was starting to fill up with other Halloween revelers in need of thirst-quenchers. Forrestal was looking increasingly uneasy. He fortified himself with the last of his coffee. "He told me he was having some trouble with a woman."

"A woman? Who?"

He shook his head. "Sorry."

"What was the trouble about?" Lionel said.

"All he told me is that this woman was driving him crazy and he wanted to have it out with her, but he wasn't holding out much hope that talking was going to solve the problem."

We asked more questions but that was the total that Forrestal had to offer. He stood up.

"In case you're wondering," he said, "I was at a committee meeting the night that Roger was killed. I have witnesses."

"All of them Decent, I'm sure," I said.

"Remember," he said. "You promised to leave me out of this."

And with that, Dewey P. Forrestal, chairman of the Committee on Moral Decency, did a hip-swinging Marilyn Monroe walk out of the café.

"Okay, Lionel," I said, "what now?"

"As long as we're in the market," he said, "I could do some shopping. Harpo and Groucho are running low."

That was a switch. Cruella De Vil shopping for cat food.

23

Lionel and I went home afterward, never having run into Troy again, but knowing he'd likely turn up sooner or later with a tale of his Halloween amorous misadventures. Feeling a warm sense of camaraderie with Lionel after our night's escapade, once we were safely back in the apartment, I told him about the note on my car.

I should have known better. He immediately ignited.

"Maggie! You've got to report this! You've got to tell your mouthpiece. He'll know what to do."

"My mouthpiece?"

"Heinrich."

"You mean Henrik and no way. He'll want me to quit my investigation."

"What a great idea! Why didn't I think of that?"

"Lionel, no. Forget it."

"Okay. Then tell that ex-dick of yours."

"I already did."

"And what did he say?"

"He told me to be careful."

"That's it? That's all Sherlock could come up with?"

"Well, what else could he do?"

"He could put you in protective custody. Or—or—in the Witness Protection Program. Wouldn't you like to move to Katmandu?"

"Only if you'd move with me."

"Only if I can sell records to the Sherpas." He hugged me. "You listen to Joe. Be careful."

We hugged again and said good night. My blood sugar was low, probably because of all the exercise I hadn't planned on. I adjusted my insulin and went to bed, still thinking about Forrestal's double life.

In the morning, prompted by a phone call from Fowler, still pleasant, but getting a little more insistent, I went back to work on my screenplay. I had stopped giving him a promised date of delivery, because I had let so many self-imposed deadlines go by.

                    MERCEDES
     Where the hell am I? I am moving but
     where the hell am I? Ow, my head hurts.
     My body hurts. The big bump on top of my
     head . . . that hurts. Wait. . . .

   Mercedes searches through her pockets and
   fumbles with her keys. She drops them on
   the floor.

                    MERCEDES
     Shit.

   She searches the floor in the darkness.

                    MERCEDES
     Keys, where are you, keys?

   We hear a BUMP.

                    MERCEDES
    Ow!

We HEAR her search the floor a little more,
then HEAR the jingle of the KEYS.

                    MERCEDES
    Got you!

She gets to her feet and switches on her KEY
CHAIN FLASHLIGHT. She's amid a large ship-
ment of barrels of oil. As she moves around,
her flashlight's beam illuminates the LIFE-
LESS FACE OF TAYLOR BILLINGS, a BULLET HOLE
in the middle of his forehead.

                    MERCEDES
    Ouch! That's really got to hurt.

Lionel wasn't going to his shop until eleven, so when the
phone rang, and he was passing by, I said, "Lionel, please
get that. Whoever it is, I'm busy."
    I heard him say, "Hello," and then, "I'm sorry. She's
busy. . . . I will. Thank you."

She moves the FLASHLIGHT BEAM around and we
realize we're in the back of a TRACTOR
TRAILER moving at high speed. Mercedes hits
a latch across the back doors. The doors
swing open as the tractor trailer hits a
bump, sending Mercedes sprawling forward
out of the back of the moving vehicle. She
reaches out and grabs the latch on the
swinging door and just saves herself from
hitting the highway.

At that point I took a break and went into the kitchen, where Lionel was packing a lunch for himself.

"Lionel, who was it?"

"Who was who?"

"The phone call."

"Oh." He trimmed the crusts off his sandwich. "Theodosia Urban."

"And you told her I was busy!"

Lionel said, "Woman, why do I even bother."

I called her back and was relieved to find her still there.

"I remembered the name of Roger's friend," she said. "It came to me when I was in the bakery buying some croissants for my breakfast. Roger introduced me to croissants when we were in Paris, and I do so enjoy them laden with butter to go with my morning coffee, don't you?"

I said, "Always." Wishing it were so.

"Let's see now. . . . Where were we?"

"In the bakery."

"Oh, yes. And I was looking at all the cakes and cookies and bread and I spotted the rye bread. And that's how I remembered."

"Her name sounded like bread?"

"Rye. *The Catcher in the Rye.*"

Then it hit me. J. D. Salinger. "Her name was Salinger?" I said. "Dana Salinger?"

"Yes. She was his flame for a while. Oh, dear, do people still use that expression?"

I thanked her profusely and went back into the kitchen and found Lionel getting ready to leave.

"I know who Roger's flame was," I said.

"No time to ask," he said, "but you better tell me when I come home. And don't forget—"

"I'll be careful."

He left, and I went back to my screenplay . . .

EXT. HIGHWAY—DAY—CONTINUOUS

The TRACTOR TRAILER speeds along the high-

way, the back doors swinging freely off the
back . . . Mercedes swinging freely off the
door.

MERCEDES POV

Nothing but ninety-mile-an-hour pavement
below her.

. . . only to put it aside one more time, when the phone
rang. I had to answer it in case it was Henrik. And it was.

"I haven't had time to get that information yet," he said.

"I really need to know the name and phone number of the
Parole Officer. He's the only link I have to Richard Urban
and I have to track him down and talk to him."

"I'll find that out for you as soon as I can."

"Thanks. You're a doll for doing this."

"My pleasure and, remembering yesterday, I mean that
literally."

I smiled.

He said, "If that is what people do when they take time off
from work, I may give up my job altogether."

"And do what?"

"Something less time-consuming. I always wanted to be a
vintner. What do you say? Will you live at my vineyard with
me and stomp the grapes?"

"Only if I'm not in Katmandu."

"What are you doing in Katmandu?"

"Missing you. Listen, I thought you ought to know. . . ." I
told him about the note.

Henrik was very quiet. "Maggie, what are you doing?"

"I'm investigating. You do your lawyer thing. I do my investigating thing."

"This isn't a game you're playing. Leave it to the profes-
sionals."

"You sound just like Joe!"

More silence. Shit! I really put my foot in it this time. In
the Women's Handbook of What Never to Say to a Lover is

Rule Number Two: "Never utter an ex-lover's name in vain."
Rule Number One: "Always observe Rule Number Two."

I started to apologize when Henrik cut in. "I've got to run now. Bye."

"Henrik, I'm really sorry—"

But he was gone.

What in hell was wrong with me? It seems that every relationship I've had with the opposite sex requires that opposite individual to understand and forgive my gaffes. My guess is, a shrink would say those blunders are deliberate. Am I doing that with Henrik? Am I subconsciously trying to get him to quit on me, so that my problem with the triangle of me, Joe, and Henrik would morph into a straight line that leads from me to Joe? I prefer to think I just made an innocent error in the heat of the moment.

But what do I know.

Well, I might as well move my foot. The damage was done. Henrik and I were overdue for a long talk. That is, after I had an even longer discussion with myself.

24

The restless way I felt, it was futile for me to try to get back to my screenplay. I decided to hit the road and follow one of two paths. Dana Salinger? Or Roger's brother? Family won out. Taking the now-usual precautions, I left the house.

The freeway traffic was relatively open and I made it to Sunland in good time. There were three high schools in the neighborhood of Tinker Street, where Roger and his brother had lived. Verdugo Hills High was a few blocks away from Tinker Street and I pulled into the parking lot a little before noon.

There was a guard at the front entrance to the school, and I explained that I was on my way to the Principal's office. No, my name was not on any list. I didn't have an appointment. Whereupon more questions had to be asked and answered and he carefully examined my Driver's License and went through my tote bag. Surprisingly, he only glanced warily at the Swiss Army knife I always carry with me, but reserved a harder look at the spare tampons in the inner pocket. Finally, deciding that a tampon was not a weapon of mass destruction, he directed me to Miss Saunders' office.

"Ms.?" I asked, by way of gentle correction.

"Miss," he said firmly.

Her assistant was very pleasant and explained to me that Miss Saunders—definitely a Miss—was in a classroom but would return very soon. Did I have an appointment? No, I did not, and held out my tote bag for inspection. She disregarded it, invited me to sit down and wait, indicating a scarred wooden bench already inhabited by two sullen teenagers, both girls. One had green spiked hair and dark kohl around her eyes. The other must have been into Heavy Metal, because she had most of it through her nose and eyebrows.

I sat down, looked around me at the counter and the file cabinets and the institutional oak of the furniture, and was instantly transported back to my school years in New York. There were no guards at the entrances then, and I took the subway to school, but the look of my surroundings and the sounds of hallway lockers closing, and the laughter and shouts from outside the office, brought my youth back in a wave of warmth. I smiled at my bench mates.

"I was just remembering my own high school days," I said. "And, in case you were wondering, I didn't go here."

"We weren't wondering," Green Spiked Hair said.

My reverie burst. I retreated to waiting some more.

In a few minutes a handsome-looking African-American woman came in from outside carrying a sheaf of papers. The assistant spoke quietly to her, and nodded in my direction. The woman came over.

"Miss Mars? I'm Miss Saunders," she said. "How can I help?"

"It's about a former student," I said. "I hope you can give me some information I need."

"Possibly," she said. "Please come in."

"Hey," Green Spiked Hair said, "we were here first."

"I know," Miss Saunders said amiably. "But this woman isn't being sent to Detention and you are."

I followed her into her office, and sat down on a hard-backed chair. There was only one comfortably upholstered chair, and that was Miss Saunders'. Visitors to the Principal's office obviously weren't meant to stay long.

I told her as little about Roger's murder as I could reveal, with the red undies understandably omitted. *Vanity Fair* and the article I was writing came in for only a passing mention. Something told me the Principal of Verdugo Hills High would not want to see her school mentioned in a questionable light or, for that matter, any light at all.

"So anything you could tell me about Roger Urban and his brother would be helpful," I concluded.

"I wasn't at this school then," Miss Saunders said, "and the Board of Education has strict rules relating to information about our students."

"Well, they were students quite a while ago, so perhaps the Statute of Limitations has passed?"

She fixed me with a stare that brooked no nonsense.

"That doesn't make a difference. No information about our students, period. Is there anything else I can help you with?"

I thought better of pointing out that she hadn't helped me with anything at all. What I needed was another line of attack. Thinking quickly, I decided to take advantage of my being on the school campus.

"Would you mind if I had lunch in the cafeteria? I'm kind of in a nostalgic mood."

She looked at me rather skeptically, but decided I was harmless if not downright dim for wanting to eat in a school cafeteria.

"If you'd like to wait outside in the office for a minute, I'll see to it that you get a Visitors card."

I thanked her and went outside to sit on the bench again. The girls were still there.

"Long day," I said.

"Who asked you," said Heavy Metal.

Children can be so very cruel.

The assistant was brown-bagging it at her desk. She answered the intercom buzzer and said, "Of course."

She withdrew a card from a drawer, scribbled a signature on it, and held it out.

"Here you are. You may go to the cafeteria."

Both girls stood.

"Not you," the assistant said.

Inside the cafeteria I moved down the line with a tray in my hand. Believe it or not, they were serving Fall Surprise, a spaghetti medley of whatever they had left over from the day before. I ate my spaghetti and drank my iced tea, lost in memories. When I went to the drink dispenser to refill my drink, a student was there getting a Coke. He had a shaved head, chains hanging from his ears, pants hanging low on his slim hips, and pimples covering his chin.

I said, "Pardon me. Do you know where the library is?"

"Of course I do, Madame!" He extended one hand in a grand flourish. "Exit through those doors and turn right. Anon you will see a pair of double doors on your left. Pray, enter there." And then he bowed with a sweep of his arm.

Go figure!

I followed directions and found myself in the school library. What a difference from my days in school. There were study cubicles down the center of the room with computer terminals in each. No more card catalogues. Everything was online. There was no librarian. Maybe she or he was out to lunch, or maybe budget cuts made that a permanent situation. At any rate, there was no one who might look at my Visitors card, which stated plainly it was for the cafeteria.

There was, however, a student librarian sitting on a stool behind the desk. A stick-on tag on her chest announced her position. She was looking at *Glamour* magazine and her eyes were glued to a double-truck page of makeup tips.

"Hi," I said. She didn't look up. "Do you have the school yearbooks here?"

No response.

"The school yearbooks?" A little louder.

She put a shushing finger to her lips, her other arm waved towards the back wall, and the eyes never moved from the page.

I walked to the back shelves. There were the yearbooks for the last thirty years, or, at least, most of them. I found two yearbooks for the years when Roger attended the school and one for Richard.

I looked first for a picture of Richard. His name was listed among his classmates, but there was no photo. He was listed as absent.

Roger, however, had his likeness on several pages. He had been in the Honors group, a member of the Student Government, and the Junior Manager of the Varsity baseball team. Funny. I never thought of Roger as being sports-minded, but there he was, along with the baseball team. The coach was in the picture also and his name was Cliff Sparks. I made notes in my spiral notebook.

Replacing the books I returned to the desk.

"Would you happen to have a local phone book?" Still entranced by the makeup tips, she reached under the desk and produced the desired directory. I turned to the S's and was rewarded with a listing for a Clifford Sparks, which I copied into my notebook.

My next stop was back at the Principal's office, where I returned my Visitors card with thanks, and as soon as I was in my car I called Cliff Sparks.

Twenty minutes later, I was in Mr. Sparks' driveway, shooting hoops with him.

25

He had greeted me at the door holding a basketball and wearing a Verdugo Hills sweatshirt and gym shorts, which exposed his knobby knees. I had barely gotten a "Nice to meet you" out of my lips when he tossed the ball at me and invited me over to the driveway.

"Come on," he said. "We can play a little one-on-one and talk at the same time. Exercise is good for you."

I didn't doubt that, but this was definitely not part of the job description.

"Those Urban kids were something," he said, dribbling around me. "They tell you anything at the school?"

He sunk a basket and handed me the ball. I shook my head no, and made a feeble throw upward in the general direction of the net.

"I'm not surprised. All that privacy crap. Well, let me tell you. . . ." He recovered the ball, which had rolled into some bushes along the side. "They were good-looking kids, kids with promise, but absolutely no guidance at home. Their father was always occupied with his television game shows, leastwise when he wasn't on the road with those screwdrivers and monkey wrenches he was hawking. Their mother tried, but she couldn't handle them. She couldn't tell a lie from the truth, a serious defect in a mother."

He made another basket from way out. "Three points," he said. "That was a three-pointer."

Whatever.

I caught the ball from him, and this time bided my time and took careful aim.

"Richard was older and stronger," he said, "and most folks believed that he led Roger astray."

"But you didn't."

"Nope. He was older, but Roger was smarter. Way smarter. He was always at the head of the class with his grades. Not Richard. It wasn't because he couldn't do the work, but because he wouldn't even try."

"Shoot already," said Mercedes, "before you get traded."

I did. The ball went way wide of the rim.

He said, "You're not very good at this, are you?"

"Nope."

"Come on then, let's sit down."

He led me around to the back patio, and we continued our talk over Diet Cokes, sitting at an umbrella-topped table. There was a rainbird going in the yard, and its rotating swish-swish-swish was mesmerizing.

I said, "I heard that Roger went on to UCLA on a scholarship. What about Richard?"

"Dropped out before he finished school." The coach looked off into the distance. "When Richard was in the eleventh grade, I had arranged for a major-league scout to come see him. He could really throw a baseball, that kid. It was over Richard's objections, because he had been talking it over with Roger, he said, and he wasn't sure he wanted to make a career of it. The night before the scout was due, Richard got himself caught in some penny-ante shoplifting thing, and didn't show up the next day. He never returned to school."

We both stared at the rainbird going round and round.

"You're saying Roger might have led Richard into shoplifting . . . to prevent the scout from seeing him play?"

He shrugged. "Either that or Richard wanted to sabotage his own chances. My money was on Roger."

"Would you know what happened to Richard after that?" I said.

"Not a clue."

"What about any friends I might talk to?"

"They didn't have any friends. They had each other, and that wasn't good for Richard."

I drove home thinking about those two boys. Maybe there was something in that long-ago relationship that wasn't right, had maybe even led to murder. But whatever it was, I seem to have missed it.

The next morning, after bringing my notebook up to date with the interviews of the day before, I decided to tackle Dana Salinger. Her address was on our Board roster, and when I looked it up in my Thomas Guide, I saw that it was on the fringes of Hollywood. There were some gracious old Spanish duplexes there with spacious rooms and high ceilings.

I dialed her number and heard it ring several times before Dana's voice cut in with a peremptory "I'm not home. You know what to do. Do it."

I didn't do it. I took the coward's way out and just hung up.

What I would do, I told myself, was drop in on Samantha at the Union offices and see if she had anything to offer on the promising subject of Roger and Dana. Then, well fortified, I would tackle Dana in person. Driving there, I kept a wary eye out for anyone following me. There was so much stop-and-go traffic on the road that if someone were tailing me, lots of luck.

Samantha's office door was open. She was sitting on the floor, in the midst of several sealed boxes, packing stuff into an open one. I knocked on the doorjamb and went in, smiling to show that I had come in peace.

"You're packing," I said, displaying my acute powers of observation.

She looked up. "Oh, hi. Hand me that clock on the desk, would you."

I picked up the clock and held on to it for a moment, still trying to assess what was going on.

"Don't worry," she said, "it's not the Union's. It's mine."

I gave it to her. "What are you doing, redecorating?"

She shook her head no and put the clock along with a potted green plant into a carton where two other plants and a ceramic owl were already residing.

"You're moving into another office?"

"I'm leaving."

"Leaving?"

"The Union. And before you ask, no, I haven't got a better job offer."

I sat down in her visitor's chair, alongside a stuffed Piglet, and then thought better of it. I said, "You're not packing this chair, are you?"

Her phone rang. She ignored it, something I've never been able to do.

Samantha said, "Dee Dee's taking my messages."

The phone stopped ringing.

"Sam, I don't understand. Where are you going?"

She thought about that for a few seconds, as though debating whether to tell me. Or maybe she just didn't know.

"Las Vegas," she said finally. Then, defensively, "I've always wanted to live there."

"Really? You mean like for more than a weekend?"

She gave me a sharp look. "Why not? Vegas is really booming."

"True, but unless you have a job there"—I waited but she didn't confirm or deny—"you're going to need some funding."

"I've got enough to sustain myself," she said, looking around the room, which by now was fairly well stripped of personal items. "I'll get my accumulated vacation days money, and I've got a little of my own."

"Sounds good." I wondered if she had an additional source of income. I waited, but the information wasn't forthcoming.

"I can't tell you how much I'm looking forward to getting out of L.A.," she said. "I feel like I've been reborn, without having to change my religion."

She looked really happy, and I must have looked really confused. I was still wondering about the source of her fuck-you money. Maybe being a COW staff member paid better than writing. But, then, what occupation didn't. Still, Samantha sounded so confident, it must be that she had some other cash cow grazing in her pasture, and that puzzled me. Did I know her well enough to ask? When had that ever stopped me before?

What did stop me was that Neville Lake came in.

"Dee Dee said you're not answering your phone. Oh, Maggie, hi."

"Sam's leaving," I said.

"I already told him," Samantha said. To Neville, she said, "I'm almost finished here."

"I've been trying to reach Noelle Sears. New York says they don't know where she is."

"Neither do I," Samantha said. "I'm not my Branch Manager's keeper."

Neville looked at me. I shook my head to show that I didn't know where Noelle was either.

"I'm trying to find her to set up an interview with her in New York. For the Search Committee," he said.

"Then she'll find you," I said. "Listen, Neville, as long as you're here, I have a favor to ask. You know Wendy Bassett?"

"The computer girl?"

"She's a woman, not a girl. She's worried about her job and I promised I'd put in a good word for her. She'd like some assurance that you'll keep her on."

"I'll do what I can," Neville said, "but it may not be up to me."

With that, he left the office.

"A real sweetheart, that guy," Samantha said, shaking her head, and went back to her packing.

I tried again. "Sam, c'mon, just between us guys, why are you really leaving?"

"I told you. Greener pastures."

"There must be another reason. Las Vegas? Come on, you know you can level with me."

Obviously she didn't know, because she looked straight at me and said, "If you don't mind, Maggie, I'm really busy." It wasn't exactly a brush-off but it came close enough.

"Well, then, I'll call you to say good-bye, okay?"

"Better make it soon," she said.

I nodded and waved good-bye, still having an uneasy feeling about why she was leaving.

Just as I was getting on the elevator, Bark got off.

"Hey, Maggie," he said. "Where you running?"

"Well . . ." I looked at my watch.

"Come with me," he said, taking my arm.

We went down the hall to his office. Office of the President read the sign on the door, and inside the room was a round, polished mahogany conference table, surrounded by possibly genuine Queen Anne chairs, beautifully covered in a muted striped damask. The sideboard was also antique and the small couch was pale gold velvet. Over the standard office carpeting was a beautiful, faded Chinese rug. Pretty fancy for a Union, especially the chairs and the rug, but somehow it was exactly the right setting for Bark. I figured Althea had chosen the furnishings and he had footed the bill.

He pulled out a chair for me at the conference table, and crossed to the sideboard. Reaching into a lower cabinet, he pulled out two bottles. Scotch and vodka.

"Buy you a drink?"

"Thanks, no."

"A snack, maybe? We can raid the staff kitchen."

"I'm really not hungry."

"What kind of excuse is that?" He poured himself a drink. "You're a writer. You eat because it's there, because you're nervous, and because, with the possible exception of sex, there's nothing more companionable."

I laughed. I had never mentioned anything about my diabetes to Bark. *My* diabetes? Why are we so proprietary about our disorders? I'd gladly have given up my claim. At any rate, I decided to tell him. Bark took it in stride. I mean it wasn't as though I had suddenly disclosed I had three boobs. One on my back for dancing, as some comedienne once said.

At any rate, he wanted to know more about it, and what I did to control it, and he told me an uncle of his had diabetes, but, not to worry, he had died of something else.

"That's a great comfort," I said, almost meaning it.

"Hey, did you know that attention to health is life's greatest hindrance?"

"Shaw?"

"Plato."

"I'm impressed."

"Don't be. Plato was a bore. Nietzsche."

I laughed.

"There's more," he said. "Nietzsche was stupid and abnormal. Tolstoy."

"And did anyone say anything about Tolstoy?"

"Everybody."

Over the rim of his glass, he peered at me searchingly.

"So . . . How are you coming with those articles for *Vanity Fair?*"

As briefly as possible, hitting only the high points, I filled him in. There was so much I wasn't ready to talk about yet.

"You're doing better than the police," he said. "But do you mind a piece of advice?"

He reached over and took my hand.

"As long as you don't tell me to let them handle it."

He let go my hand and got up to refill his glass.

I said, "You were going to tell me that, weren't you?"

"I'm fond of you, Maggie. I wouldn't want anything to happen to you."

"Nothing's going to happen to me." I wondered what he would say if I told him about the note on my windshield.

"You ask the wrong person the wrong questions sometimes, and who knows what you can stir up. Let me tell you about the situation I was in a few years ago when I was doing research for this terrorist movie I was writing—"

I didn't learn what it was, because just then Neville barged in. Again.

"Bark, I still haven't been able to reach Noelle."

"Have you tried her at home?"

I stood up to go. "This where I came in," I said. "Bark, is there anything else?"

"Nope," he said. "Happy Hour's over."

When I came home that evening, my message light was blinking. It was Martin calling to let me know they had nothing to report. No fingerprint match, the paper and ink were of a common variety, and the lab had come up empty. Thanks a lot, I thought. Now Joe communicates with me through Martin. Once more I felt distanced from his life.

Lionel was away at a friend's house for a chamber music gathering, and the evening stretched out ahead of me. It occurred to me then that I still wanted to ask Samantha about Roger and Dana. The news of her abrupt retirement had driven other thoughts from my mind, and she could be leaving town any day now.

I picked up the phone to call her. The number was on the Board list, and so, too, was her home address. Why call, I thought, putting down the phone. It would be much more effective talking face-to-face, so I could push further on why the Las Vegas move.

Samantha lived in Toluca Lake, an area to which I seldom ventured, since it seemed to be populated solely by NBC, the Disney Studios, and off-ramps named for Bob Hope. Lionel had borrowed my Thomas Guide, but eventually I found the street, stopping three times at gas stations to ask directions and filling up at one of them because it was my encore visit.

The address belonged to a modest, faded gray apartment building on a pleasant tree-lined street. I looked up her name on the apartment directory, noting that she lived on the top floor, the third, but before I could buzz, a guy with a dog came out and obligingly held the door open. I never look a gift entrance in the mouth, so I smiled back at the nice man and even at the dog and went on in.

The elevator deposited me practically in front of her door. I rang. No answer. Serves me right, I thought. I should have called. But I pushed the bell again. Then I knocked. And then, I don't know why—I still don't know why—I tried the knob. It turned in my hand and the door swung open.

I remained on the threshold. "Samantha?" I tried again, a little louder. "It's me, Sam, Maggie. . . ."

A woman poked a head full of rollers outside a nearby door. Swell. Now all the neighbors would know. She gave me a cursory glance, then popped back in. I took a few steps inside, into the living room, and closed the door behind me.

"Samantha?"

There was no sound, no answer. Of course, she could have gone out, but she wouldn't leave the door open. I wouldn't. I put my bag down on a side table near the door and looked around. Everything seemed normal, as far as I could tell, except, of course, who knew what was normal when I had never been there before.

Then I saw it. At the far end of the room, the sliding glass doors were open. The balcony, I thought, heading in that direction. It was a warm evening. She could be out on the balcony.

"Sam?"

I went outside and found myself on a narrow balcony. There was just room for a lounge chair and a patio chair with a small table alongside. It was still a pleasant evening, but Samantha wasn't there. I went over to the low wall and looked out at the view. Only, there was no view, unless you consider a courtyard flanked by inner sides of the building and an adjacent alley a picturesque vista. If you looked up you could see a crammed-in patch of sky. And if you looked down—

I looked down, and even from three stories up I could make out the form that lay in a crumpled heap at the bottom. Oh, God, no. No, no, no.

26

Just as I turned away, the balcony door slid closed behind me and I heard the telltale click of the lock. It could have been the wind, but there was no wind. Not even a breeze. I tried to slide the door open by pulling on the recessed handle. It wouldn't open. I tried pushing on the frame, putting all my strength into it, and it wouldn't budge.

Frantic now, common sense deserting me, I banged on it, I pounded on it, screaming frenzied imprecations addressed to the fucking door.

No use. I was locked out. I went to the balcony wall, leaned out, and screamed for help, over and over again. No response. No one in any of the apartments whose windows faced out on the courtyard gave any indication I had been heard. All those rollers in that stupid woman's stupid hair must have deafened her. I tried to remain calm. I had always prided myself on remaining calm. Of course I had never found myself on a narrow balcony before, with a door locked behind me and a body lying below. I looked out over the wall again. She was still there. Hadn't moved. Of course she was still there. What did I expect?

A wave of dizziness swept over me, and I groped my way over to the patio chair and sat down, breathing deeply, deep cleansing breaths. I became dimly aware that it was starting to rain. Terrific. Two days a year it rains in Southern California, and today had to be one of them.

I felt in my pocket for my cell phone. But it was in my bag by the front door. It was obvious that somehow I would have to get that door open—already proven infeasible—or wait out here.

The latter seemed like the preferable option. Surely someone would see me or hear me. Eventually. I berated myself for not having told Lionel where I was going, but then he never asked. That was our arrangement. We were two independent spirits. Maybe from now on it might be a good idea to let Lionel know, just in case I didn't come home—Quickly I got off that track, and held on to the certainty that I would be rescued.

Maybe I could break the glass in the door with something. But what? The aluminum patio chair I was sitting on! I got up, lifted the chair, and realized that it was too light to do any good.

Suddenly, a new and frightening thought occurred to me. Samantha couldn't have just fallen. Someone, the someone who had closed the door and trapped me out here, had pushed her over the balcony, had murdered her!

What if the murderer hadn't gone away? What if the murderer were still on the other side of the door just waiting for the right time to open the door! And there I'd be! I set the chair down and cringed against the wall, as another wave of dizziness came over me.

There was one other option, I told myself, shuddering even as I thought of it. I could climb down to the courtyard.

Fearfully, I turned around and looked over the wall, trying to keep my gaze averted from the crumbled heap at the bottom. I searched for any footholds, anything at all, along the side of the building that I might possibly use to make my way down.

There was nothing. No pipes, no wires, no fire escapes. Whatever happened to fire escapes? They used to be plentiful in New York. Didn't people ever have to escape in Southern California?

Neither was there any handy clothesline nearby, nor any of those bedsheets that teenage girls always used to climb down from their bedrooms. I had never climbed down from my bedroom when I was a teenage girl, but then my family lived in a one-story house.

I went back to the chair. It was getting wet from the rain and when I tried to wipe off the seat, I suddenly became aware that the chair, both chairs, were made of plastic cording. Maybe, I thought, just maybe . . .

If only I had a knife with me to make the first cut. Like the little Swiss Army knife in my bag with my cell phone. Okay, try something else. I turned the chair upside down. A piece of cording near the frame was frayed. I yanked on it, and yanked some more until it came undone.

Before long I was pulling out the rest of the cording. That wasn't too difficult, sort of like pulling out the basting of a hem. But when I had finished stripping the chair, it was apparent that the cord wasn't going to be anywhere near long enough. I turned my attention to the lounge chair.

That proved a little trickier, and it took a little more time. Halfway through I resorted to yelling for help again— keeping a wary eye out for any movement behind the sliding door—and then went back to work.

Finally I was able to tie the two lengths together, and when I dropped it over the balcony wall, checking it for distance, it seemed okay even though it didn't quite reach. It would at least get me to the balcony below me where there might be help. Worst-case scenario, if there weren't and I had to descend all the way, I estimated I'd have about a five-foot jump at the end of it. I could probably manage that. There were worse scenarios than breaking an ankle.

There was the real possibility of that door behind me opening.

The thing was, of course, I'd have to tie one end of it to something on the balcony. I looked around. There was no door handle. Nothing else projected from anywhere. And then I saw it, a drain hole in the middle of the cement floor. A thin stream of water from the rain was already trickling through it.

I double-knotted one end of the cording to the back frame of the stripped-down patio chair, leaving a short length to work with, then poked the free end through the drain hole and kept maneuvering the cord through until the knotted chair began to move with it. I held my breath. The chair jammed against the floor and held there.

Tentatively I climbed over the wall and, with my left hand still on the wall, fumbled for the cord until it was clutched in my right hand. Another deep breath. Okay, Maggie. This is it. Go for it! I let go of the wall and began to rappel down, trying not to look below, remembering what it had been like in gym class when we had to climb the rope, touch the top plate, and then descend, slowly, slowly. . . .

Maybe I couldn't shoot hoops, but Cliff Sparks would be proud of me.

Slowly seemed to take forever. Several times I hit the rough stucco of the building wall and I knew I would be black-and-blue tomorrow. But at least, maybe, there would be a tomorrow. . . . Above me I could hear the chair banging against the drain hole, and I prayed that the double-knot would hold. . . .

Memo to Maggie: Start working out your leg and arm muscles every day.

When I came even with the balcony of the apartment below, I grabbed its wall so I could catch my breath. I yelled at the apartment, but it was dark and appeared uninhabited. With a safe grip on both the railing and the rope, I looked over my shoulder down to the courtyard. Samantha lay motionless, but not far from her . . . a sudden movement caught the corner of my eye. There was something in the shadows near the gate to the alley. Someone was there, silently watching me.

Waiting for me.

Fear propelled me over the wall onto that balcony, still

clutching the rope with a death grip. Backing up out of the ambient light, I pressed my quaking spine against the corner where the sliding glass door met the wall, and tried to get my breathing under control. Minutes crept by.

Mustering up my courage, I looked down at the courtyard again. Once more I saw movement. Then I saw a cat run out of the shadows and dart away.

I was so relieved that my knees gave way, and for a moment I sat there on the wet floor of the balcony, with the rope in my hands and tears of relief in my eyes.

Getting up, I tried to open the door. Locked. I pounded on it. Nothing happened. Nobody home.

Frustration set in. There was nothing to do but get going again. Over the wall, rope in hand. I threw myself away from the building and rappelled down. Finally I reached the end and had to let go and jump.

It was a bigger jump than I had thought, and I landed, not too gracefully, a foot or two away from where Samantha lay. I didn't try to see if she was still breathing. I could tell by her crushed head and the awkward angle of her neck that she wasn't.

I scrambled to my feet, ignoring the twinge in my right ankle, and staggered towards the alley gate. It was locked. You had to enter a combination of numbers into the panel on the wall. That was a dead end.

I noticed another door, one that led into the building from the courtyard. One that proved to be also locked. There was the same panel of numbers requiring the right Open Sesame.

I went through the routine as before of pounding and banging.

"Help! Let me in!"

I repeated the words like a mantra, my voice growing hoarse with desperation and fright. After a few moments, I gave it up and just leaned against the door, my forehead pressed against its coolness. The enormity of what I had just gone through, was still going through, caught up with me. My heart was hammering against my ribs, echoing my violent thumps on the door. I couldn't suck in air fast enough or deep enough.

Then, suddenly the door in front of me was flung open and I stumbled forward into the chest and arms—of the murderer! It had to be! He must have followed me downstairs.

For a moment, I was too paralyzed to move. I mustered the last strains of my voice and let out a raspy croak.

"Get away from me!"

At the same time I kneed him in the crotch and was gratified to hear a groan. The enclosing arms dropped away from me, and I found myself looking at an elderly man who was now bent double, face contorted in agony, holding his nether regions.

This couldn't be the murderer. He looked to be about eighty, and was wearing an old brown bathrobe over Star Wars-patterned pajamas. I must have just gotten him out of bed. Either that, or he was a refugee from an AARP centerfold.

I took my chances and ventured a cautious "Are you all right?"

He said, between moans, "You were hollering you wanted to come in."

"I did. Only I thought you were someone else."

"This is how you say hello?"

He managed painfully to straighten up and I saw he was shorter than I was. Short and skinny. Clearly no threat.

"I was afraid you were . . . someone dangerous."

"Lady, you're the one who's dangerous." He turned to go back inside.

I hurried after him. "Wait! Are you a tenant?"

"Why? Do you want to knee me again?"

"I want to use your phone. I have to call the police!"

His name was Arthur Critchfield, and he lived in Apartment 103, which was on the other side of the hall and didn't face the courtyard. When he heard my end of the phone conversation, he put a hand to his heart and sat down hard. I rummaged in the neat-as-a-pin kitchen, found a bottle of scotch in a cupboard, and brought him some in a glass. As soon as I saw the color return to his face, I went back in and fetched another glass for me, with an inch of scotch in it.

My ankle still throbbed, and my head was fogged in, but the drink seemed to help. I asked Arthur Critchfield if he had heard anything. Seen any strangers. Nothing. No one. He had just come home. Samantha had always been very nice to him. She often brought him invitations to movie previews. He couldn't believe what I was telling him.

That made two of us.

27

The police arrived in less than twenty minutes. It is a well-known fact that they will arrive sooner when a dead body is involved than when a live person needs help.

After that everything became a jumble of action scenes. Like a montage in a Jean-Claude Van Damme movie on MTV. I know one cop went into the courtyard to guard the body, and I know the Crime Scene Unit arrived.

The police swarmed over Samantha's apartment. At first they didn't want me to come in with them, and I was told to wait in the hallway, but the door was open and I could see them searching around. Finally, two detectives arrived, Monahan and O'Toole, and they allowed me in. I had to go over my story again, this time in a show-and-tell mode.

They went out on the balcony and looked down and one of the uniformed cops pointed out my rappelling cord to the detectives. They all glanced at me significantly, even though I had already given them a fairly detailed account of my descent to the courtyard. They also seemed suspicious of the fact that my bag was lying on Samantha's table, and O'Toole went through it.

"I just walked in to talk to her, that's all, just talk," I said, over and over, changing it once to, "I don't even know why I looked out on the balcony, I just did. . . ."

In the end they took me to their station. Monahan said that they needed to ask more questions and an interrogation room was a more comfortable setting. Maybe for him. I asked if I could call Henrik. I was told I didn't need an attorney since I wasn't under arrest. I called him anyway.

Then, thinking I could use all the ammunition I could summon up, I mentioned Joe. I was once a very close friend of a Los Angeles detective. The once close friend, very close friend, of a fellow lawman wouldn't kill someone, would she?

They didn't answer that. They were the ones asking the questions. Monahan and his partner, O'Toole, came up with a lot of questions. I didn't think there were any Irish detectives west of New York. To judge from his arrogance and his impeccable attire, Monahan must have migrated during the potato soufflé famine.

They asked about my writing career, neither of them having seen my movie, which was probably just as well as I am not a fan of self-incrimination, then made small talk until Henrik showed up with a comforting pat on my shoulder and some very lawyer-like phraseology. Monahan, I think, was impressed that a prominent defense attorney would come so quickly to my aid. O'Toole took it as an admission of my guilt, on a slightly lesser scale than if I had called in Gerry Spence.

Again I went through the litany of what had happened, in only slightly incoherent sequence, trying not to relive the terror and let it overtake me. Henrik looked a little tired, but he listened carefully, not saying anything, then turned to the detectives. "You searched the apartment?" he said.

Both men nodded, O'Toole with a gesture of his hand to indicate that it was at best a perfunctory search.

"Find anything?"

"Like what, Counselor?" That was Monahan.

"Yeah. Could you be a little more specific, Counselor?" said O'Toole.

"Oh, I don't know. How about a note of some kind?"

The detectives looked at each other, and then back at Henrik. No hint was forthcoming.

"You mean—like a suicide note?" O'Toole said.

I let out a gasp. "No! Samantha wouldn't commit suicide!"

Monahan said, unsmiling, "Counselor, shouldn't you remind your client she has the right to remain silent?"

"Why? Am I under arrest?" I was exhausted and every part of me ached. Mercedes would have reamed them. I'd had it. "I'll have you know," I said, "that my father is the Chief of Police, and this other detective, I just found out he knocked me up."

O'Toole and Monahan looked at each other.

"What the fuck is she talking about?" O'Toole said.

"Pay no attention to her, fellows," Henrik said. "She's a screenwriter and she's got a lively imagination." He aimed a reproachful look in my direction. "So what have you got?"

"We might or might not have found a suicide note," said O'Toole.

"But we also might or might not have found something else," said Monahan.

Monahan & O'Toole. A vaudeville act.

I opened up my mouth to say something, but never did, because just then Joe came into the room.

If you've never had to introduce your ex-lover to your present lover while hanging out in the interrogation room of a police station, then you must have lived an unimpeachable life. Obviously I hadn't.

Somehow I got out the right words without forgetting either man's name and without any unnecessary elaboration. The two men cordially shook hands and smiled at each other. Suddenly I became uncomfortably aware of my torn pants, broken fingernails, filthy face, and scotch breath.

I said, "Joe, tell these guys I had nothing to do with this, tell them."

Joe said, "Maggie—"

"And tell them she didn't commit suicide."

It was Henrik's turn. "Maggie—"

Joe said, "We'll look into it."

"There's nothing to look into. Somebody pushed her."

"Excuse us a minute." Joe nodded towards the door and O'Toole and Monahan followed him out.

As soon as they were out of the room, Henrik came over and put his arms around me.

He said, "Maggie, the important thing is to get you out of here. The less said right now, the better."

"But she was going away! She was looking forward to it. Why would she kill herself? And who locked me out?"

"Let's hear what they've got first." He kissed my forehead. "Are you okay?"

"No, I'm not okay," I said. And I wasn't. The scotch was wearing off, my ankle was still throbbing, and my arms and legs gave a new definition to pain.

"A warm bath, a good night's sleep, and you'll be fine."

"Will you come home with me?"

"Just long enough to tuck you in bed. I'm pulling another all-nighter."

I barely heard him. A frightening new thought had invaded my mind.

"Henrik, do you think the same person who killed Roger also killed Samantha?"

He took his arms away. "Maggie—"

"Maybe she knew too much."

He shook his head and just then Joe came back in with the Irish Tenors.

Joe said, "Hey, Mag, sounds like you had quite a night."

I said, "It was nothing compared to Samantha's." And thought, Don't call me Mag. Not here.

"Okay, you're free to go, Ms. Mars," Monahan said.

"But not too far," said O'Toole, not to be outdone.

"You'll find out who killed her?" I said, looking at Joe.

But it was O'Toole who said, "She did it herself."

"No," I said.

"There's some evidence in that regard," said Joe.

"I don't care! She didn't do it!"

"Maggie, they found the gun."

Henrik's surprised look matched my own. "Gun?"

"She didn't shoot herself," I said. "I saw the body."

Joe said, "It appears to be the gun that killed Roger."

"Ballistics will check and confirm," Monahan said.

"Her fingerprints were on it," said O'Toole.

My head spun.

Henrik said, "You're saying she shot Roger. And then, what, jumped from the balcony in a fit of remorse?"

"I like it," said Monahan.

"Then why didn't she just shoot herself?" I said. "She had the gun."

"Too messy," said O'Toole.

"And jumping off the balcony is tidy?"

They shrugged in unison. I was too dazed to protest any further.

"I want to take a look at the scene," Joe said. "Your car's there, Maggie?"

I nodded. "In front of her apartment house."

"I'll drive her there and then see that she gets home. Okay?" He was asking Henrik's permission, not mine.

"Fine with me." Henrik looked at me. "All right, Maggie?"

Well, no it wasn't fine with me, but I had no choice. I found myself resenting the fact that they were behaving in such a rational, friendly way towards each other. But then what did I expect? That they would come to blows over me?

"Works for me," said Mercedes.

Henrik said, "Call me tomorrow, Maggie."

"Of course." I kissed him. Kissed him hard. "Thanks for coming."

"Yeah," said O'Toole. "Thanks a lot."

As for Joe, his expression was unreadable.

28

I drove back to Samantha's house with Joe, giving him my first-hand account again, this time with even more embellishment.

"I needed to talk to her about something. Also, she had told me she had come into some money, and I wanted to find out more about it."

"Why?"

"I don't know. I thought it could be important. I rang the bell and I knocked and I called her, and she didn't answer. That's when I saw the door was unlocked, so I went in, and when I saw the balcony door was wide open, I thought she was out there. So I went out there and then . . . and then . . ."

"Take your time," he said.

"Someone was in that apartment," I said. "He—she—they locked me out on the balcony and then got away."

"Those sliding doors sometimes cause problems," he said.

"Meaning what?"

"Meaning it could have closed and locked by itself."

I looked over at him, but he was intent on his driving, his expression unfathomable.

"You don't believe me either."

"I believe you," he said. "I'm just suggesting a different—what do you movie people call it—plot line."

"I hate that—'you movie people'—and keep your different plot lines to yourself."

We had nothing more to say to each other after that until we drove up alongside my car. We both got out and he watched while I beeped open my door.

Joe said, "You okay to drive?"

"I'm fine," I said. "I often drive with a sprained ankle."

"Doesn't look swollen to me. Let me feel it."

"No. And don't beg."

He grinned. "Go ahead. I'll follow you home."

I slid behind the wheel, turned the key, and rolled down my window.

"You said you wanted to take a look at the scene."

"It'll keep till tomorrow."

I thought about the implication of his change of mind, and then decided I had better forget it. So I drove home, this time grateful that I knew someone was following me. Joe's headlights remained close in my rearview mirror.

When we pulled into my parking garage, it was almost one thirty and I was dead on my feet, but Joe announced he would see me into the apartment. Once inside, I noted that Lionel had already gone to bed. Not that it mattered.

I flopped on the couch, put my head back, and closed my eyes. Eyes still closed, I said, "This is so like what happened in my screenplay. The police call it a suicide, but Mercedes is sure that Amanda Peterson was murdered."

"You said it yourself, Maggie. That's just a screenplay. This is real life."

"Then what about that note on my windshield?"

"The note's real, too, and it's still very much on my mind."

"And, by the way," I said, "thanks for setting the land speed record in telling my dad about the note."

"I thought he should know. Sometimes you need to be watched over, by people who care."

I had no answer to that.

Joe went right on. "But with Samantha, there's nothing to suggest anything other than suicide."

"It just feels wrong."

"Then you know what would feel right? How about if I pour us some wine?"

Grateful for the reprieve, I stood. "There should be a bottle of white wine chilling in the refrigerator." It was one of Lionel's pricey favorites, but what the hell. "I'm going to get out of these clothes. They're filthy."

Joe called after me, "Better check your blood sugar while you're at it."

Unbelievably, the reading was okay. Must have been the physical exertion. There was some kind of connection there, but I didn't have time to speculate on it now.

The problem was deciding what to change into. Another pair of jeans? At this hour of the night? A nightgown? Too suggestive. My usual T-shirt and boxer shorts? Much too off-putting. In the end I settled for a quick shower and a terry robe.

When I came out again, Joe was settled on the couch and had opened the wine and poured two glasses. "You took your time," he said, offering me a glass.

"Thanks, but no thanks. I better not."

He said, "You look a hell of a lot better than you did."

I joined him on the couch.

"So," he said, after a while. "Talk to me."

"What about?"

"Oh, I don't know. Tell me about Henrik."

"That's not talking, that's questioning. And I've had enough of that for one night."

"Okay. Would you rather talk about us?"

"There is no us," I said.

He looked down into his glass. "There used to be, didn't there?"

I nodded.

"Maggie, how did it all go wrong?"

I could feel the muscles in my neck tense. We were going where we had never ventured before. We were getting in too deep. I knew it, and yet I was powerless to stop it.

"Shit happens," I said.

He shook his head. "No. It doesn't just happen. We screwed up."

"I guess it couldn't be helped," I said. "It was what was going on in our lives at the time."

"So we're talking no fault, is that what you're saying?"

"Honestly, Joe, I don't know what I'm saying. If you hadn't gone to California . . . Or I hadn't stayed in New York . . . The relationship came undone, that's all, and we can't go back and change that."

"When you can't go back," Joe said, "you go forward. . . ."

With that, he leaned over and kissed me lightly on the lips. At first, lightly, and then, more insistently. I tried to pull away, or I think I did, but I fell into a time warp. The now of tonight had disappeared and there were only all those other nights. . . .

I'm not sure why or how things happened after that. It could have been a delayed reaction to the ordeal I'd been through, it could have been Mr. Critchfield's scotch. It certainly wasn't the terry robe that conveniently seemed to unbelt itself. Somehow, we moved from the couch to my bedroom, and after that the why and the how didn't matter at all.

Sex, by its very nature, should never get to be routine. And yet, here were Joe and myself settling into the old, familiar choreography. He always knew how to turn me on, and I always knew the moves that worked him up just so far and no farther until it was time . . .

I guess it's like what they say about riding a bicycle. Once you do it you never forget how.

My orgasm was pure fireworks . . . Again and again . . . And then Joe came, too, and held me, until in the afterglow there was a sense of deep contentment, of being home again. In the days before good-bye.

Finally he let me go and I waited for whatever postscript

there might be, but there was nothing. He got up and took his clothes into the bathroom and I lay there listening to the running water, trying to settle my churning thoughts. Finally he came out, tucking his shirt into his pants, and just stood by the edge of the bed, looking down at me.

"Feel like talking about Henrik now?" he said.

29

In the morning I had breakfast with Lionel, who surveyed me rather enigmatically but was content to satisfy himself with the pecan waffles he had prepared and I had waved off in favor of toast and orange juice. I told him about Samantha and the night before.

"Oh, my dear," he said. "How perfectly ghastly for you."

"Lionel, do you think she committed suicide?"

"Me? I have no idea. But if I were going to snuff out my life, I certainly wouldn't hurl myself over a balcony. It's much too disorderly. Especially when there was a gun handy. Which is rather disorderly, too, come to think of it. . . . Maybe I'd just take an overdose of Viagra."

"Lionel . . ."

"Well, I agree that it all seems rather peculiar."

I nodded miserably. "She was so upbeat about moving to Las Vegas."

Lionel said, "Maybe she couldn't face listening to Wayne Newton."

I gave him a withering look.

"And anyway, she couldn't have killed Roger," I said. "What reason did she have?"

"You did say his aunt seemed to recall a former girlfriend. Could it have been Samantha?"

I realized I hadn't told him about Dana Salinger. I filled him in.

"Still and all," he said. "That doesn't leave Samantha out of the picture. There could have been other women in Roger's orbit. I told you he was a babe magnet."

"Samantha wasn't a 'babe.' "

"Then, how come she was crying buckets at the funeral? Where there's smoke, there's a smoking gun."

"Okay, you made your point," I said. "Maybe she killed Roger, but she sure didn't kill herself. And, if she killed Roger and someone else killed her, then we're dealing with two murderers. And that's too wild for even me to contemplate."

"Fine, she's a long shot," Lionel said. "Anyone else of the true feminine gender?"

"Noelle Sears?"

"From the New York branch?"

"She was here for the annual meeting."

"Okay, okay. I've had my jollies playing Pin the Tail on the Suspect. Now I better get to work so I'll have some."

He headed for his room.

"Oh, by the way," I said. "We helped ourselves to your wine last night."

"I noticed," he said. "I thought it would be too provincial of me to say anything."

"Sorry. I owe you one."

"Oh, you owe me more than that. Who was it? Henrik?"

I didn't answer.

"No, it wasn't Henrik, the noises were different. It sounded more like *déjà* screw." He regarded me appraisingly. "How do you feel about that?"

"*Déjà* screw you."

He disappeared into his room.

How did I feel about that? Last night it was . . . wonderful. It was like returning home to a well-remembered place, where all my senses came alive. This morning I was conflicted as all hell. My mornings-after with Henrik were never like this, which should have told me something. But what?

I sat down at my laptop, determined to get back to my screenplay, but gave up the pretense even before I could get started, picked up the phone, and called New York. Noelle Sears wasn't there. No, they didn't know where she was or when she'd be back, but they'd be happy to take a message. I wasn't happy to leave one.

I remembered Neville not being able to reach her. Was it possible that she was here in Los Angeles, had been here last night? I thought of calling around to the various major hotels, but that would have been an exercise in pointlessness. She could have used a different name, or stayed at a motel, or lodged with a friend, or even not been here at all.

I tried another tack. I called Dana Salinger again.

This time she was home.

"I'm not feeling well," she said. "I have a cold." She coughed by way of validation. "Besides, I'm trying to finish something I've put off for much too long. You know what that's like."

As a matter of fact, I did. Just ask Fowler Mohr. She hung up on me before I could ask her if I could come over anyway. So that's just what I decided to do.

First, though, I called Wendy Bassett at the COW office. Figuring that it was a good idea to remind her of the favor I had done her before asking for one in return, I told her that I had spoken to Neville and he had promised to do what he could.

"Thank you so much. I knew I could count on you."

"Yes, well, I wonder if you could do something for me. Could you please access Credits and get me a listing of Dana Salinger's directing credits over the past five years?"

"Oh, I couldn't do that. That's not my department."

"Please? I've reached the point in my screenplay where I should be considering directors. It would be a favor not just to me," I said pointedly, "but possibly to Dana as well."

I guess that salved her conscience, if not mine, because in a few minutes she told me that Dana had only a handful of credits in the last five years, just enough to remain in Active membership. While I held on, she made a phone call and reported back that Dana was not directing any project at the present time.

Next I depleted more of my account with Cyber Detective. I soon learned that Dana had only one discoverable bank account and it was in the low four figures.

I wondered how she had been supplementing her non-directing income. Department store sales maybe. Or real estate. Maybe waiting on tables. They say a listing of restaurants can be found in an actor's résumé, so why not a director's?

I drove to Dana's, following the now routine evasive movements: quick turns, speeding up, slowing down, once pulling over and parking in front of an Urgent Care Center. There was no tail.

There were some gracious old Spanish duplexes in Dana's neighborhood, but she didn't happen to live in one. Her address belonged to a nondescript, characterless building that might have started life out as an imposing private home but was now reduced to an upstairs and downstairs, the product of an unfriendly architectural divorce. How like Dana. Faded glory seemed to be her hallmark.

She lived in the upper unit, and I trudged up the exterior stairs to find myself on a porch littered with dying plants and splintered chairs and a rusty table frame. I felt as though I had wandered onto the set of a Tennessee Williams play.

I rang the bell. From inside a dog barked. A big dog, from the sound of it.

"Who is it?"

"Delivery from Creative Artists Union."

The door opened to reveal Dana, swathed in a chenille robe and clutching the collar of a pit bull. I stood there mesmerized by the sight of the panting animal, trying not to think of all the graphic news stories that featured them so prominently.

"Oh, it's you," she said, cordial as ever. "What do you want?"

"Just to talk," I said. "Could I come in?"

She must have relaxed her grip on the collar, because the creature lunged a little towards me. I stepped back.

"I told you I had a cold. What do you need to talk about?"

"Well . . . did you hear about Samantha?"

"Yes, but I don't care to discuss it."

"I just have a few questions. . . ."

"I don't have to answer any of your questions about Samantha, and I don't want to talk about Roger either."

The dog was drooling, straining at her hold on him.

I said, "Why don't I come back when you're feeling better."

I left. All told, it had not been one of my better interviews.

30

Joe's phone call woke me up next morning. Hearing his voice reminded me of my dilemma about him and Henrik. No matter what spin I might choose to put on it, I couldn't lie to myself. I had to face it. My feelings for Joe were not just holdovers from the past. They were new. They were thoroughly disturbing my equilibrium and my relationship with Henrik. How could I sleep with both men?

"It's de rigueur," said Mercedes. *"Didn't you ever watch* Sex and the City*?"*

Well, it's not S.O.P. with me. I'm a one-man woman.

"All you have to do is figure out which one man," said *Mercedes.*

"Hey, Maggie. Are you there?"

"I'm sorry, Joe. My thoughts were wandering. What did you say?"

"Could we have lunch?"

He was quick to suggest a small neighborhood deli a few blocks from the West L.A. Police Station, in case, I suppose, I had any ideas about the Polo Lounge or Pinot Bistro. He hung up before I could ask if there was any news.

I tried not to look forward to it. I even finished two scenes of the screenplay to occupy my mind in other directions.

Well, actually one scene. Okay, *part* of one scene. But I had to write it twice.

```
TIGHT ON MERCEDES

As she struggles to try and catch her foot
onto the trailer as it swings towards the
truck. She just can't reach out that far.
From behind her, we HEAR a HONKING of a
HORN. She looks behind her to see an ATTRAC-
TIVE COWBOY, ten-gallon hat and all, driving
alongside the van in an old convertible
Cadillac.


          COWBOY
     Need some help, Ma'am?


          MERCEDES
     You seem like a bright one.
     Sure, I could use a little.


          COWBOY
     Yes, Ma'am.


          MERCEDES
     Can the Ma'am crap and get your car
     close to me.


The Cowboy maneuvers the convertible along-
side Mercedes and she drops down into the
passenger seat.
```

Joe greeted me perfunctorily, as though the other night had never taken place. What did I expect? Certainly not "Was it good for you?" We were well beyond that. At least *something* to show that we had marked a milestone in our relationship.

Be careful what you wish for. . . . As we sat down, Joe said, "Maggie, about the other night . . ."

He didn't finish, because the waitress had come over and was setting down glasses of water and oversized menus. She waited there, pencil and pad in hand.

We ordered.

"What?" I said, when she finally moved away.

"What what?"

"About the other night?"

"The other night was—well, you know what it was. You were there."

"Right, I was there." But I couldn't reveal my feelings to him because they were a jumble. Had been a jumble ever since the murders brought him back into my life. I felt as awkward as a schoolgirl around him.

He said, "Maggie . . . there's been a development, and I thought you might want to hear it from me."

"Good news or bad news?"

"Depends on whose side you're on."

"I'm on the unpopular side. Mine."

The waitress brought Joe's coffee and my iced herbal tea.

Joe said, "The police have closed the case."

"Samantha . . ."

"A suicide. The gun that killed Roger was in a night table drawer. Ballistics has confirmed it. Her fingerprints were on it."

"What about what happened to me! There was someone in that apartment. I know it!"

"I'm sorry, Maggie."

"Sure. You're sorry. Everybody's sorry. The whole world is sorry. . . . Was there a suicide note?"

"No."

"Doesn't that prove something?"

"All it proves is that she didn't leave a suicide note. Lots of people don't."

"I would."

"You're a writer."

I decided to head down a different road. "What about Karen?"

"Thorstensen?"

"You had her in for questioning. Didn't you get the feeling she's hiding something?"

"Why? When did you talk to her?"

"I asked you first."

"Maggie, forget it. The case is officially closed."

He reached across for my hand. I quickly buried it in my lap.

"Joe, Samantha wouldn't have committed suicide. I saw her in her office. She was all excited. She was moving to Las Vegas, and she was looking forward to it."

Joe said, "The case is closed officially—"

"Yeah, I heard."

"Let me finish. You never let me finish, goddamn it. There's nothing more the police can do—officially. Have you heard anything else from your note writer? Has anyone been following you?"

"No. No notes, no followers that I can see."

"Are you still on assignment?"

"That's what my editor pays me for." I wondered where he was going with this.

"I think, when the papers write about Samantha and say that the police have closed the case, you won't be bothered any longer. You'll still need to be very careful. Just in case." He sipped his coffee, and thought for a moment. "And there's a favor I have to ask of you."

"Aha! Now we're there. What favor?"

"As you do your work, will you keep me informed, every step of the way?"

"Why, if you've closed the case?"

"Because I still have some questions about it. Somehow, things just aren't adding up right. If you stick with your assignment, maybe someone or something will crack open and let us know whether we're right about Samantha or not. I'm not talking about you playing sleuth, that's not your job. If you get any more notes or see anything suspicious, you're to notify me immediately."

"You think there'll be another threat?"

"Who knows. I don't like what happened to you on the balcony."

"I wasn't too crazy about it either."

"And no stepping over the line. If you get caught doing something you shouldn't, you're on your own, until I throw you in jail."

"You would."

"I mean it, Maggie. Keep your nose clean."

"Understood."

I rose to go. Joe got up, leaving some bills on the table, and walked to the door with me.

"One more thing," he said once we were outside, "it's important that you keep whatever you discover confidential. That means no gossip with Lionel or pillow talk with Heinrich."

"It's Henrik."

"Him, too. . . ."

He put his hand on my cheek. "Promise me you'll be careful. Don't go out on any more balconies, and watch your back at all times. I think the threat to you is over, but . . . just in case."

My cheek flamed under his touch. It was time for me to get out of there.

31

Lionel wasn't too surprised to hear that the case had been closed.

"That's what police do," he said. "They need the time to allot to more important things. Like ticketing bicycle riders."

"Lionel! You didn't!"

"The light was definitely green when I entered the intersection. Well, maybe it had turned yellow a little, a nice shade of saffron yellow, but it positively wasn't red!"

I sighed.

"Well, all right," Lionel said. "But you're not going to give up on it, are you?"

"Never have, never will."

"Now what's our next move?"

"Our?"

"I'm here for you if you need me, as long as it doesn't involve anything grubby."

That earned a smile from me. "Thanks, Lionel. But right now I'm going to put on my investigative reporter hard hat, poke around a little more, and see what turns up. I owe that much to Samantha."

"And to Roger," he said.

I nodded, grateful for his understanding. "Sometimes, it's

not so much the facts you dig up as the fact that you're digging. Know what I mean?"

"Haven't a clue."

"Good." I kissed him on the cheek and starting setting the table for dinner. . . .

After dinner I called U.G. and let him know that the police had closed the case.

"I know. Joe told me."

"What is it with you and Joe anyway?"

"What is it with you minding so much that I talk to my buddy? The news is a big relief, Mag."

I didn't want to shake that belief so I mentioned nothing about my doubts, or Joe's for that matter, and left him a happy man.

Retrieving my spiral notebook and pencil from the desk, I began putting down extensive notes for my *Vanity Fair* article. It was all in fragments still, bits and pieces that would somehow have to be fused together into a story. But it was a beginning.

The next morning I headed back to COW and to Samantha's office. As I expected, the office was closed. I knocked, and when no one answered, I went in and shut the door behind me. I wasn't sure what I was searching for, since others must have already looked around. The police, staff members, who knows . . . For now, I just wanted to absorb the surroundings.

It's not like I believe in the supernatural—well, maybe a little, as in, it couldn't hurt. If there was any aura of Samantha around, I wanted to have my antennae up.

There was nothing. The file drawers were locked. The desk drawers held pencils, pens, stationery, paper clips . . . the usual stock of office supplies. But something was shoved in the back of the top drawer, behind a zippered purple cosmetics bag and a plastic box of disc labels. I worked it out. It was an Incoming/Outgoing Call Register book.

You know how sometimes you save what you think are the

best things for last? It's called delayed gratification, and it's not just a sexual thing. Though that's good, too. I put the telephone book aside and opened the makeup bag.

Lipsticks, blush, comb, powder compact . . . the usual. No folded pieces of paper with writing on them. No out-of-the-ordinary devices or gadgets.

I zipped up the bag and was putting it back in the drawer when Dee Dee Russell came in.

"Hi," she said. "I thought I saw you come in here."

"I was just . . . I was just . . ." Just what? "Looking around," I said unconvincingly. "The news about Samantha is so awful."

"I know. We're all devastated."

Her gaze took in the room and stopped unerringly on the Call Register lying in plain sight on the desk.

"Oh. There it is," said Dee Dee.

"There what is?" I said, Ms. Casual.

"Samantha's telephone log. I've been tearing the place up trying to find it, and it's been here all the time."

She picked it up and started to turn the pages.

"Like Poe's Purloined Letter," I said. "Hidden in plain sight."

Dee Dee nodded. She waved a few fingers at me and went out, Register in hand.

Dispirited, I slumped down in a chair. Now what? Probably there was nothing in the book of any consequence, but in a murder case probably was just not good enough. Think, Maggie, think.

Several minutes went by until the nub of an idea presented itself. Immediately, I rejected it as being too risky. But then, as no other scheme presented itself, it took on an aura of cross-your-fingers feasibility. I picked up the phone and called U.G. Fortunately I located him in his room.

"Dad, I need you to do something for me."

"Anything, sweetheart, you only have to ask."

"I need you to—"

"This won't take long, will it? I'm just going down for lunch and the ladies are waiting."

"Not too long. I want you to call this woman for me," I said. "Pretend you're the garage attendant, and tell her she left the lights on in her car."

"Just like a woman. What kind of car is it?"

I gritted my teeth. "It doesn't matter what kind of car it is. Just say her lights are on and it's going to run down the battery."

"I don't know if I can be a garage attendant. Will I have to speak Spanish?"

"No! Give her the message, that's all."

"Wait a minute. Why are we doing this?"

"Not to worry. It's just a practical joke." I gave him Dee Dee's name and extension number.

In a little while I heard the sound of hurrying footsteps and I looked out. Dee Dee was rushing past.

"I left my lights on," she called back.

"Don't you hate when that happens?"

As soon as she was out of sight I headed for her office. The Register was open on her desk. I picked it up.

"Maggie, hi," a voice said.

I looked up and Althea was there in the doorway.

"Oh, hi," I said, hoping I sounded welcoming, but not overly. "If you're looking for Dee Dee, she had to go down to the garage. She left her lights on."

"Don't you hate when that happens?" Althea said, and came all the way in. "Actually, it's you I wanted to talk to. Bark's car is in for service, so I dropped him off in his office and then I had to use the ladies', and someone said you were around here somewhere. What are you reading?"

"Me? I'm not reading. Oh, this." I looked at the Register in my hands. "Just a telephone log."

She reached out an imperious hand, and automatically, I responded by giving it to her. She began to riffle through the pages.

"I was looking for you to ask if you might be available for dinner tonight?" She was still turning pages. "I know it's short notice, but Bark wanted to get the Search Committee together to talk about the New York trip."

"The New York trip?"

"Bark will tell you about it. It's to interview candidates back there. Not very interesting material," she said, putting the Register down on the desk and walking to the door. "Significant others are invited, so please ask your very significant Henrik."

I nodded.

"Eight o'clock. Our place. See you then." She paused on the threshold. "Do you really think Samantha killed Roger?"

"No," I said. "Do you?"

She said, without expression, "Something else we can talk about over dinner."

When the door closed behind her, only too aware that Dee Dee would be returning momentarily, I took a hurried look through the Register. It went back in time some three months or so, and appeared to be just regular office calls with some personal calls sprinkled in . . . doctors, dentists, libraries . . . more than a few to libraries . . . And then I saw it.

The day after Roger's funeral, Samantha had placed a call to the *Société des Auteurs* in Paris. There was no phone number written down or anything to indicate the reason for the call. Obviously Roger knew someone there, because it was one of the organizations in his Zip file, and perhaps Samantha was calling to inform them of Roger's death. It might mean nothing at all, but it was still worth a follow-up. I jotted it down in my notebook and put Samantha's book back on the desk, just as Dee Dee came back in, plainly irritated.

"My car was fine. The attendant said he hadn't called me."

"One of those prank calls, I guess," I said.

"I should have known," she said. "The caller had this weird Spanish accent, obviously a fake."

"Obviously." I left her sitting at her desk.

Althea had said to ask Henrik, so I called him and reined him in for the evening's dinner at Bark and Althea's, and made my way to my car.

Once on the road I got on my cell phone and called Janice Ryder in New York. A good investigative reporter manages to assemble a collection of friends who are not just friends but links to information outlets. Sort of like Personal Search Engines. Janice was my source for telephone data. She worked for a telecommunications corporation, and if anyone could trace a call to the *Société des Auteurs,* it would be Janice.

"Maggie! How are you? Where are you?"

"In traffic," I said. "I'm calling from my car."

"You couldn't be in New York. Nobody drives in New York."

"Still in L.A., but I'll be coming east soon and I'll call you. Listen, Janice, I need a favor. . . ."

We arranged for her to call me back at the apartment, and even as I was letting myself in, the phone was ringing. Janice had retrieved a number for me along with the name of the person to whom Samantha had spoken at the *Société's* offices. Chantal Maupin.

Why do the French have such beautiful names and we Americans have Maggie?

"What time is it in Paris now?" I asked.

"Nine hours later," she said. "They'll probably be closed, but you never know."

"You're right," I said. "You never do. Thanks. You're a doll."

I made the call and I must have been living right that day—it could happen—because Chantal Maupin was working late, probably an overachiever type, and she spoke English.

She was thrilled to be receiving another call from California. That's what she said. "Another call . . ."

"Then you remember speaking to Samantha Winger?"

"Yes. That was the name she gave. I inquired if she might know my cousin who is in California. Perhaps you do. He lives in Burlingame?"

I said I didn't know her cousin.

"She did not know him either, the woman who called me."

"Samantha Winger."

"Yes. I guess it is not, as you say, a small world, after all."

I brought her back to Samantha and their conversation. Chantal was unhappy to learn of her untimely death and we ran up even more of my international telephone charges deploring the unfairness of it all.

Finally, though, she remembered what Samantha had called her about.

"She wanted to know about a book."

"A book? Do you remember its name?"

"One moment please. I will look to see if I perhaps write it down."

I could hear her rustling through papers as the dollar amounts continued to swell in my future billing.

"No," she said. "I regret it."

"And I regret it, too. But thank you, anyway."

I was about to hang up when she said, "Perhaps you will want to know the name of the author?"

I couldn't believe the turn of luck. "You have that?"

"One moment please. I will look to see."

No recourse but to wait.

Finally: "Yes. His name is Alain."

I waited, but nothing more seemed to be forthcoming from the other side of the Atlantic.

"Alain what?"

"*Je ne sais pas.*" I could envision her shrugging. "I only write down Alain because it is the name of my cousin who lives in Burlingame."

We had come full circle, and I was more in the dark than ever. I thanked her once again and gave her my home phone number, just in case anything further occurred to her or if she had any other relatives in Burlingame. As an indication of my disbelief that anything would come of it, I even told her she could call collect.

Then I hung up and plopped on the couch, displacing Harpo and Groucho, and thought about what I had not learned. The name of a French book Samantha had inquired about, and the name of its French author. I pictured myself offering it to Joe as a tangible piece of evidence.

"Okay, Joe, here's proof that Samantha was murdered."

"Let's hear it."

"A book by Alain."

"Alain who?"

"Alain Somebody. I'm still working on that."

"And this Alain Somebody killed Roger as well?"

Forget it. I tried to chase it out of my mind, by getting back to Mercedes and the Cowboy in my screenplay . . .

INT. CADILLAC—CONTINUOUS

She takes a deep breath and smiles at the
Cowboy as they keep pace with the tractor
trailer.

                    MERCEDES
     How old are you?

                    COWBOY
     Nineteen.

                    MERCEDES
     Ouch.
          (beat)
     You wouldn't have a gun on you .   .
     would you?

                    COWBOY
     Ma'am, this is Texas.

The Cowboy reaches under his seat and pulls
out a large .44 MAGNUM and hands it to her.

                    MERCEDES
     You certainly have a big one.

                    COWBOY
     What are you going to do with it?

                          MERCEDES
        Kill me a truck.

    Mercedes leans out the window and EMPTIES
    the CLIP into the tires of the moving truck.

    ON THE TRUCK

    As it swerves, hits the side of the embank-
    ment, and turns over, grinding to a stop on
    the pavement upside down.

    BACK TO THE CADILLAC

    Which has stopped behind the turned-over
    truck. Mercedes is standing in the passenger
    seat, blowing the smoke from the barrel of
    the gun.

                          MERCEDES
        I hope you have good taxidermists here
        in Texas.

. . . but I was still brooding about it when Lionel came home,
the day's mail in hand, and deposited it on the table.

"Lionel, did you ever hear of a French author named
Alain?"

"Alain who?"

"That's what everyone says."

"You don't know?"

"Haven't the foggiest."

"Well, if the rest of Alain is as delectable as his first name,
I'd love to meet him."

He was no help either. I gave him a look that told him so
and went in to get dressed for the Thomases' dinner party.

It was while I was showering that Lionel came into the

bathroom and yelled above the running water that Henrik was on the phone.

"What does he want?"

After about a minute, Lionel reported back. "Says he can't make it tonight. Says something came up and he has to meet with a client."

"Can't it wait until tomorrow?"

Another interval. "No it can't. You should invite me along instead."

I turned off the water.

"Did Henrik say that?"

"No, I did."

"Lionel! Give me a towel."

Lionel threw a towel over the shower door. I wrapped it around myself and came out to reclaim the phone.

32

In the end, Lionel went with me to the dinner, looking very presentable in an unstructured black corduroy jacket, pink shirt, and charcoal slacks, and all atingle at the thought of being among the Union's "glitterati."

I assured him he would be bored out of his gourd. Clark Newman was a Yale Drama School graduate who wrote all the episodes of the hit television drama he had created and was so full of himself there was no room for anyone else in his orbit, Chris Osborne and Ian McConnell were little short of vapid, and Dana Salinger owned a pit bull and wasn't afraid to use him.

Naturally Lionel charmed them beyond belief. Within twenty minutes of our arrival, and my apologies to Althea on behalf of Henrik, Lionel was holding court and fascinating them with his inexhaustible supply of Hollywood scandal morsels. If the Search Committee could have voted right there and then, Lionel would have been selected as the new COW Executive Director and we wouldn't have had to look any further.

The Thomases' home on Loma Vista Drive in Beverly Hills was a showplace. Framed reproductions in the powder room gave testimony to the fact that it had been featured in *House Beautiful, Architectural Digest,* and the *Los Angeles Times* magazine section. The rooms were large and high ceilinged, with walls of glass looking out over a white-bricked patio. The furniture was modular, framed in tubular stainless steel, and the couches and easy chairs were upholstered in cream leather that was as soft as butter.

The one discordant note was the slate flooring, which made the total effect somewhat cold and sterile, antiseptic even. I wondered about that because Bark seemed so multi-hued, a man of warmth and vibrancy. Perhaps, as in his office, the décor was more Althea, but she had changed direction, veering off to a Bauhaus scheme.

During cocktails and hors d'oeuvres in the library, which was strikingly attractive with a hammered copper ceiling, we learned from Bark that the Search Committee would fly into New York on Sunday and the interviews would begin on Monday.

"Bark and I will be going in a few days earlier," Althea said. "We want to catch some shows."

"You know, I think I'll do that, too," I said.

Bark said, "Great. I'll call my agent and he'll arrange for extra tickets."

"I appreciate the offer," I said, "but there are some friends I want to visit and some background stuff I need to look into for my *Vanity Fair* articles."

"Don't tell me you're going to be a bi-coastal snoop," Dana said.

Chris took his nose out of his martini glass. "Our Maggie Mars? A snoop?"

Dana shrugged. "She barged in on me the other day, asking all kinds of nosy things about Samantha and Roger."

The others all looked at me.

"What fun," Ian said. "You'll have to grill me, Maggie. I don't know anything, but I'd love to be quoted."

Just then the uniformed waitress from the catering service came in to announce that dinner was served and we trooped out onto the patio for a five-course dinner highlighted by pistachio nut-encrusted salmon. Lionel should have worn a bib. He practically drooled.

Althea was an accomplished hostess. There were twelve of us, counting Chris' and Clark's wives and Dana and Ian's "significant others," and she had arranged two tables of six beside the pool and overlooking the gardens, with their soft lighting meant to look like moonlight. Centerpieces of pale green orchids touched off the requisite crystal, silver, and china, and one could let oneself believe that everyone lived like this. Or should.

I found myself at a table with Bark on my left and Clark on my right, and Chris' wife, Ian's woman friend, and Dana's date filling out the grouping. I noted with interest that Dana had brought along a not bad-looking guy, Eric Hummel, who was obviously several years younger than she. He had mentioned he was an actor but seemed purposefully vague about the films in which he had appeared. Lionel whispered to me that he was sure he was a porno star, which made me, at least briefly, think of Dana in a respectful new light.

It crossed my mind that maybe that was how she had been supplementing her income. Directing porn films? I put the thought in my mental file cabinet.

Chris' wife, Sheila, was seductively attractive. She sat on the other side of Bark and kept him and Clark the target of her conversational attentions. Ian's lady companion was very quiet and when I later found out she was an associate professor of psychology at California State University, Long Beach, I wondered if she had spent the evening analyzing us.

Inevitably the table talk came around to the subject of Roger's murder. It was at this point that Bark left Sheila Osborne to fend for herself and turned his focus on me.

He said, "Do I get the impression you're not accepting the theory that Sam killed Roger and then herself?"

For a moment his question hung in mid-air and hovered there.

"Why would Samantha kill Roger?" I said. "There's no

motive. And as for Samantha taking her own life, she had no reason to."

"The heart has its reasons that reason knows nothing of," Bark said.

Wouldn't you know that Sheila smiled tenderly at him, as a mother would at a bright child who has just recited well.

"In any event," Sheila said, "it's over. Very sad, of course, but over. I know Chris is bummed out about it, too." She called over to the other table, "Aren't you, Chris?"

"I didn't hear what preceded that, but whatever you say, dear," Chris called back.

"Sam was pushed over the balcony," I said. "There was someone else in her apartment the night I was there."

Clark stopped as he was reaching for another roll. "You were there?"

I realized the others didn't know the whole story of what had happened. I debated whether I should tell them, and then thought why not. This was an opportunity to stir things up and gauge their reactions.

I proceeded to give them my account and relived again the unspeakable terror of looking over the railing and seeing what lay crumpled at the bottom. Afterward there was silence, as though no one knew what to say, or, to put a more kindly interpretation on it, if they knew, maybe they didn't want to upset me further.

Then Bark squeezed my hand and I was inordinately appreciative of the gesture.

"Maggie, as far as I'm concerned, your story does make us all think twice about Samantha." He looked purposefully around the table for corroboration.

There were murmurs of assent, even though the "laypeople," the non-Unionists among us, were not really up on all the details. Surprisingly though, Eric said, "You guys ought to see what you can do about clearing this Samantha's name. It sounds to me like she deserves better."

Hey, porno star or no porno star, good for you, Eric.

Clark Newman said, "My advice is to stay in touch with the police and not go off on your own."

"That's the producer of a cop show speaking," said Bark.

I became aware that Dana was hovering behind Bark, and must have overheard some of the conversation.

Dana said, "I'm sure Joe Camanetti wouldn't want any of us venturing off into anything foolish. Wouldn't you say, Maggie?"

I still wasn't sure how much Dana knew about my relationship with Joe, but nevertheless it irritated me, having her talk about him so familiarly. At any rate, I was spared the necessity of answering because she had already moved back into the house, heading for the powder room.

By the time I said my good nights and thank-yous, Bark and Althea had arranged for the three of us to fly into New York Friday morning and they would pick me up on the way to the airport.

Lionel was in an effervescent mood as we drove home.

"You had a good time," I said.

"The best. I gave Althea my card and she's coming into the shop."

"Did you talk about the murders at your table?"

"Of course. They were all very sympathetic."

"Then you told them what I had gone through."

"No. I told them about what I was going through, having to live with a woman who thinks she's Lara Croft, Tomb Raider."

We compared notes on the evening, but I learned nothing further, other than what I had already suspected: that Dana was an over-ardent subscriber to the police's closed-case theory.

A familiar car was parked in front of our place, and Henrik hopped out just as we pulled into the garage driveway.

I leaned out to talk to him. "What are you doing here?"

"My meeting just ended and I thought I might catch you, see if you wanted to come back to my place."

He gave me a kiss through the open car window.

I should have gone. Turn back the calendar to another

time, another night, and I would have gone. Henrik was always a thoroughly considerate, pleasing partner. But now something had happened. Joe had happened.

I said, "Henrik," and stopped. How do you tell a man, "Not tonight, dear. I have a heartache."

"Got it," he said. "You're tired."

"It's been a long day and a longer evening. Be glad you weren't there."

"Rain check?"

"Rain check."

He kissed me again and went back to his car. I watched him drive off.

"Well," said Lionel, a world of insinuation in the one word. "I hope you didn't not go on account of me. I can crawl into bed all by myself."

"So can I," I said.

But I wasn't feeling all that complacent about it. You only hurt the ones you love, so went the line of an old song. I didn't want to hurt Henrik. He didn't deserve it. Going to bed with Joe was an aberration, just a glitch. It wouldn't happen again.

"Hey, it's no crime to sleep around. It's fun," said Mercedes.

"I'm not sleeping around," I said. "Lots of other women have two men in their lives."

But, deep down, I knew I couldn't handle it. Sooner or later there was bound to be a reckoning.

In the morning, I noticed that yesterday's mail was still on the table where Lionel had left it. I took it in with me and looked it over while I ate breakfast. Spreading an English muffin with sugar-free jam, I scanned through the pile. The usual circulars and bills. Then I stopped. There was an envelope typewritten and addressed to me, without a return address, and, chillingly, without a stamp.

I pounded on Lionel's door, and he flung it open.

"What?"

He tried to look angry, but the effect was spoiled by the globs of shaving cream on his face.

"Where'd this come from?" I waved the envelope under his nose, smudging some of the shaving cream on it.

"How do I know? Was it in your mail? Then it was in the mailbox."

"How did it get there without a stamp?"

"No stamp?" He grabbed the envelope to take a closer look, then immediately dropped it to the floor.

"Oh my God, is it anthrax?"

We both stared down at the envelope.

"I doubt it."

"Your doubting it is not good enough for me."

I picked up the envelope and went into the kitchen. Lionel trailed me, staring down at the floor to make sure I wasn't dribbling any powder. We sat at the kitchen table, the envelope between us.

Finally I said, "Oh, what the hell," got a paring knife out of the drawer, and slit it open.

A page fell out. This time it was a typewritten message, all in caps, and, naturally, unsigned.

"What does it say?" Lionel said.

"Stop messing around in other people's lives."

"Is there an 'or else'?"

I looked at both sides. "Nope. Maybe he couldn't think of one."

He grabbed it away from me, and checked it for himself. "Maggie, this isn't funny."

"I know."

Lionel said, "You've got to call Joe."

"No, I don't got to. But I will. Lionel, go finish shaving, go."

He huffed his way back into the bedroom and closed the door.

I called Joe at the station and left a message for him to call me back.

I tried to think. The front door to the building is supposed to be locked at all times, but this rule, like so many others, is honored in the breach. The reality is that anyone could have walked in and put the envelope in our mailbox. And I think that's mainly what whoever dropped this off was trying to tell me. The message didn't have to be too explicit. The real message was that I was vulnerable. I could be gotten to wherever and whenever.

Still and all, there was a positive spin to this. Sam's death hadn't ended this thing. Maybe I was getting somewhere after all. I just didn't know where.

I put the note in an envelope, stashed it in my bag, and made myself a cup of tea. I'm one of those people who, the more you warn me off, the more I push forward, especially when I'm in the right.

My mother used to say, "Woe be to the one who is right." Woe indeed.

I wondered what my mother would say if she knew about my investigation. She wasn't as worried about me as my dad was my whole life. My mother always believed that I had a head on my shoulders and would use it when I needed to. Not for the first time, I wished she were around so I could talk to her.

As I sipped my tea, my mind churned up the notion that it might be a useful idea to go through Roger's condo and have a look around. I knew the police had been there already, but they might, just might, have overlooked something. What that could be, I didn't have the faintest idea, but the only way to find out was to have a look for myself.

I mentioned it to Lionel when he emerged from his room again. You would have thought that I told him that I killed Elvis. He was appalled.

"You are doing no such thing. Are you out of your mind?"

"There's no danger in it. Either I can talk my way in or I can't. Roger's dead. There's no one lying in wait for me there. No one knows I'm going except you and you won't tell."

"If you do this brainless thing, I'll tell everyone right now. I'll call Joe. I'll even call U.G. My God, someone has threatened you twice now. Have you had a frontal lobotomy when I wasn't looking?"

Then I tried that same argument on him that I used on U.G. The one about anonymous notes being the last refuge of cowards. He wasn't buying it.

"That's patriotism, you fool," he said.

"Patriotism is the last refuge of scoundrels, not cowards, Lionel. What's the problem with going to Roger's place anyway? The police are done with it. They've closed the case. It's harmless enough. All I want to do is soak up the background for my articles."

He considered that. "Well, if you insist on going, okay. But I'm going with you."

"I don't need a chaperone."

"You need a baby-sitter. I can't go now. We'll go tonight after I get back from work."

"Thanks, Lionel, I do love you. We'll go tonight."

Pretending to be busy at my laptop, I waited for him to leave. I don't like to lie to Lionel, or to anyone. Well, not unless I absolutely have to, like with the New Jersey State Police, but sometimes a little white lie is necessary. I wasn't going to hang around for tonight and Lionel. I was going right now.

33

An hour or so later, when I arrived at Roger's condo building, I found myself talking to Earle, the manager, a balding middle-aged man wearing green seersucker shorts and a T-shirt that read: SCREW THE TURTLES. SAVE THE SARDINES. From inside his unit I could hear television sounds, leading me to suspect I had just interrupted his watching a favorite television show.

"The Young and the Restless," he said, confirming my suspicion. "The wife and I try not to miss it."

Good for them. "Look, I'm Mr. Urban's sister, so if you could just let me have the key, I'll take a look around for myself."

"Which one?"

I was confused. "There's more than one key?"

"More than one sister. A few have been here already."

"Oh. Well, we're a large family."

Obviously, the women of Roger's legendary love life must have wasted no time revisiting the scene of his prime. But I was too deep into it now to speculate who they were or what they might have found, or even removed from his condo.

"Wait here."

I waited at the door and during a commercial Earle returned with the key. His glance lingered behind him to the sounds from the living room, where the Young and the Restless were growing younger and more restless.

"There'll be a problem reselling the place," he said, as he led me down a flower- and fountain-bordered path. "The owner murdered like that."

I said, "He wasn't murdered in his condo."

"Makes no difference. He's in the atmosphere. Know what I mean?"

I knew what he meant. As soon as he showed me in, I could sense Roger everywhere. In the white leather furniture and the Lucite tables and the stacks and stacks of blond-oak bookcases, crammed with books and videos in disarrayed order. The question became not so much what to look for but where to look first?

Earle perched in the doorway, obviously determined to keep an eye on me.

I managed something between a sniffle and a sob. "If you don't mind," I said, "I would like to be alone . . . with my memories."

"Sure," he said and remained right where he was.

"While you can be alone with this." And I fished a twenty-dollar bill out of my bag.

He stared at it and raised his eyebrows mockingly. It was apparent that Roger's other "sisters" had been more generous.

It cost me another twenty and he took the money and gave me the key.

"Lock up after you go," he said, "and be careful of the stuff in there. Some aunt or someone is making arrangements. They'll pick up his furniture and personal effects by the end of the week."

He disappeared and I looked around some more. There was an exotically decorated master bedroom, a black tile bathroom, a kitchen—with gleaming stainless steel appliances—and a dining area that I doubted had ever seen a dinner party. Roger had been a notorious restaurant frequenter.

I decided that the police must have looked through all the

more obvious places—the desk, the bedroom drawers, the bathroom cabinets, the bookshelves . . . But still my attention lingered on the shelves and their unappealing clutter. Maybe they had searched behind the books and between the books, but maybe, just maybe, they hadn't gone through all the pages of all the books or possibly not even looked inside the cassette boxes.

The problem with not knowing exactly what you're looking for is, how do you know when you've found it?

It was a job that would faze anyone less demented than I. I started in. . . .

I was sitting on the floor, in the middle of shaking out a third row of books, when, suddenly, I heard a key in the lock. Earle? No! I had his key!

I jumped to my feet and headed for the hall closet. I was halfway there when I remembered I had left my bag on the floor and inside the bag was my pepper spray. I ran back and got the bag and barely made it inside the closet when I heard the door open and someone come in. Whoever it was seemed familiar with the territory, for there were no sounds of anyone going on into the bedroom or kitchen areas.

I was squashed in among some cartons and framed paintings, and a large men's golf umbrella had tilted and was jabbing me in the ribs, but I managed to open my bag and fumble about for the pepper spray. I finally dug it out just as I began to hear other noises, sporadic thumping noises, as though things were being dumped on the floor.

Clutching the pepper spray tightly in my hand, I opened the door a sliver and peered out.

Karen Thorstensen was pulling video boxes out of Roger's bookcase and looking at the cassettes, then stuffing them back so hurriedly that they were falling to the floor.

Finally she evidently found what she had been looking for. She jammed the cassette in her bag and turned to go. That was my cue to step out of the closet, barring her exit. It would have been a smooth-as-silk ambush, except that the umbrella clattered out behind me, smacking me in the ankle.

"Hi," I said, trying not to grimace.

She looked at me uncertainly.

I said, "Are you a member of our large family, too?"

"What?"

"Roger's sister. How much did it cost you to lose Earle?"

And then I realized.

"Of course," I said. "You had your own key. Roger must have given it to you."

She decided to brazen it out, for which I had to give her credit. "And you? What are you snooping around here for?"

I said, "Probably the same thing you are. Only you found it first."

"What's that in your hand?"

I looked down. "Pepper spray. You're lucky I didn't use it on you."

She said, "You've got it backwards."

She was right. I was holding the damn thing with the business end pointed right at me.

"Never mind that," I said. "I'll take the cassette, please."

She clutched her bag closer. "I don't have to give it to you."

"True. You don't. And I don't have to mention it to the police. But I probably will."

She hesitated and I could see the fire go out of her spirit. Then she reached into her bag and handed me the boxed cassette.

"Please don't say anything," she said. "I'll be ruined."

I said, "I think you and I need to do some more talking."

We sat down on the couch and Karen told me about her and Roger, while I tried to make sense of what I was hearing.

It seemed that as the owner of a thriving housecleaning business, Karen had access to many vacant homes, some of them lavish estates, and she and Roger would sometimes use them as love nests. The house where his body was found, that was their favorite one. And yes, she was supposed to meet him there that night. The night he was murdered. My surmise about the reason for the underwear was correct.

So she hadn't exactly been truthful with me before. My

thoughts were spinning. "You mean you were there? You saw it happen?"

She shook her head. "I got there and let myself in . . . and found him that . . . that way. And then I ran."

"Did you see anyone? Hear anything?"

"Nothing. But someone was there. Watching me. I know it."

She shuddered and I put my arm around her, feeling what she was feeling. Remembering what it had been like for me in Samantha's apartment . . .

I said, "Was there any reason that night for that particular house?"

"It belonged to a famous producer," she said. "We used it often, 'cause it turned Roger on. It was like, while he was, you know, fucking me, he was saying, 'Fuck you' to the producer."

And it was the night of the Union's vote on the new contract with management. I smiled inwardly. That was so Roger.

"Please," Karen said. "If you tell the police, if you tell anyone about this, it's the end of my business."

I indicated the cassette. "What about this?"

She winced. "It's me and Roger. He had a camcorder and he made a tape of us. After we'd . . . do it, he liked to watch it. Sometimes he had me do a, you know, a retake."

A porno movie, I thought. It was to my credit that I didn't react. Probably I should let her keep it. For sentimental reasons. But then something else occurred to me.

"By any chance, was this tape made in that house? The same one where they found him?"

She nodded miserably.

I got up to go. I said, "Karen, I'm going to keep this tape for a while."

"I suppose so you can blackmail me."

"What should we demand, free vacuuming for a year?" said Mercedes.

"I'm not into blackmail," I said. "Though I might consider it if my writing income dries up."

"Then promise me you'll destroy it?"

"I'll see. I can't promise."

She nodded. Right now she had no other choice.

She followed me out. "I look terrible in it," she said. "My hair was a mess. . . ."

34

As I drove home, checking my rearview mirror, I reflected that I was back to square one. I had been operating on the general theory that the underwear Roger was wearing was important to the case. Now that I knew that he had expected to meet Karen, it no longer factored in. I could discard the underwear, so to speak.

As soon as I came in, Lionel poked his head out of his bedroom door. "Where have you been? Are we going to Roger's condo or not? I'm ready."

I flinched inwardly. "I've been thinking about it, and I decided we can postpone it for a while. I checked and his aunt hasn't cleared the place out yet, so we have some time."

He nodded and disappeared back into his room. I knew I left him with the impression that I had checked by speaking with Theodosia, but that was all right. I'll have to own up to my lies, but his impressions are not my problem.

My message machine was blinking. Joe had called. Damn it, we were playing telephone tag.

The second message was from Gracie. Did I have a timetable for my first article? The New York papers had picked up the story about Sam's "suicide" that ran in the

L.A. papers. Now I'd have to convince him, too, that Sam wasn't the killer and she hadn't committed suicide. A tall order right now, with nothing to support my theory.

The last call was from U.G. wishing me a good flight to New York. That was up to the airline, I thought. I called him back and we made arrangements to see each other after I returned.

I left the cassette on top of the VCR and went in to take a nice long soak in the tub. I do my best thinking in the tub and this new development with Karen deserved a lot of sudsy meditation.

How did it affect the Samantha situation? Had she known about Roger's kinky lovemaking in bizarre locations? Presumably, as his executive assistant, she might have. And she might have told someone else. I had to believe that, rather than accept she had killed him and then herself.

By the time the water gurgled down the drain, I was no closer to a conclusion. I put on boxer shorts and a T-shirt, which passed for pajamas on a warm night, and decided I had put it off long enough. I had better go inside and look at the tape.

Lionel was sitting on the couch, eyes practically riveted to the taped images on the screen. The cassette box on top of the VCR was open and empty.

I froze. "What are you looking at?"

"I think this delicious tape is one you probably stole from Roger's condo today, when you went without me."

"Lionel, I'm . . ."

"My sweet lying Maggie. Did you really think I would buy that drivel about 'we have some time'? I know you too well, and besides, it's exactly what I would have done."

"Then you're not angry at me?"

"Well, you returned safe and sound and now that I've caught you in a lie, I'll have something to hold over your head should you try something that idiotic in the future. Meanwhile you're interrupting my entertainment."

"Lionel this tape could be important evidence in a murder case!"

"Well, I didn't think you had rented it at Blockbuster's. Karen Thorstensen and the late Roger Urban, if I'm not mistaken."

"Yes." I sat down. "And that's the house where Roger's body was found."

"And a very healthy body it is, too."

I gave him a recap of what Karen told me. He rewound and we watched together. I had never watched a porno tape with Lionel before. It was a strange, unsettling experience. The genders were right, but the affiliations were wrong.

Looking at it closely, I saw for sure that anyone who had ever been in the house could identify it from the background and furnishings that were in the shots. That meant the owner, the real estate agent, the detectives for sure, who knows who else . . . It was a damning piece of film, and Karen was right. It could definitely shut down her business.

Lionel said, "How come our cleaning person doesn't give service like that?"

"For one thing, you are our cleaning person."

"I've been thinking," Lionel said, "maybe we ought to hire a houseboy."

"Lionel, someone had to know that this house was where they got it on."

"Samantha might have."

I said, "I'm talking about the murderer."

"Do the math," Lionel said.

Abruptly I got up, rewound the tape again, and turned off the set. For the first time, my hitherto unshakable faith was being shaken.

It was when I was putting the tape back in the cassette box that the phone rang.

"I don't want to talk to Fowler now. Tell him I'm incommunicado," I said.

"How can you be incommunicado if you've told me to say that?"

Another ring. I motioned to Lionel to wait just a second.

"What?" he said, peevishly, hand hovering over the instrument.

"I don't want to talk to Gracie either."

Dodging phone calls seems to have become my avocation.

Glancing at me with mild disgust, Lionel picked up the phone. "Hello. . . . Oh, I'm sure she won't. That sounds dreadfully expensive. . . . Just a minute." He covered the mouthpiece. "Do you want to take a collect call from Paris?"

I grabbed the phone from him.

"Aha. So there is someone you're willing to talk to," Lionel said.

It was Chantal.

She said, "Remember I think perhaps I write it down?"

I nodded, which, of course, she could not see.

"Well, I do write it down."

I held my breath.

"The name of the book is *L'Homme Qui Rit.*"

"And the author? Alain? Do you have that, too?"

"He is Alain Dubert."

I mimed for Lionel to bring me a paper and pencil. He stared at me blankly.

I said to Chantal, "Do you know where I can get a copy?"

Chantal said, "She asks the same thing. Samantha."

"And?"

"I regret it. It is out of print."

We disconnected on our mutual regrets, and I swung around on Lionel.

"Why didn't you bring me something to write on?"

"Why didn't you ask me?"

Belatedly I remembered that I had never been very good at Charades.

"I think she said something like Lum Key Ree."

Lionel frowned. "She spoke Chinese?"

"French!"

"Something like Lum Key Ree. . . ." He reflected on it a moment. Then: "Of course," Lionel said. "*L'Homme Qui Rit.* The Laughing Man."

"By Alain . . . Doo Bear?"

"Dubert," he said, rolling the r.

"You've heard of him?"

"No."

Join the club.

Early the next morning, all packed and ready to go, I knocked on Lionel's door.

"It's okay, I'm up. *Entrez.*"

Lionel was in bed, reading. I put the envelope with the threatening note on his nightstand.

"Do me a favor," I said. "Drop this off for Joe at the West L.A. Police Station."

"No problem. Fly well and bring me something scrumptious from Dean and DeLuca."

"Done."

I blew him a kiss, and as I reached the door, I said, "Oh, by the way, when you're at the station, give them a set of your fingerprints."

I closed the door behind me, before he could yell at me, but not before I heard something heavy thump against the door from the other side. It sounded suspiciously like the book he had been reading.

The flight to New York was uneventful. The lines were long at the Security Gate and they confiscated my pepper spray. Althea and Bark sat together two rows ahead of me, and never moved out of their seats except to go forward to the john.

Because Bark disliked the chaos of JFK, we flew into Newark, and I have to admit it really is easier than landing in New York. Less of a maze, less of a mass of people conversing in Tower of Babel tongues, and less traffic. Our luggage, however, came in the same old slo-mo time. When we walked out front, the limo was waiting.

No doubt about it. It's good to travel with first-class people.

I could barely look at the New York skyline. Not seeing the familiar silhouette of the World Trade Center was heart-wrenching.

We pulled up to the Rihga Royal a little before six, and Althea informed me that they had made reservations for *Av-*

enue Q, me included, so there was no time to change or even to pee before rushing off to dinner. I really didn't want to be included, but I couldn't think of a graceful way to get out of it. I murmured my thanks and hoped I could hold off the ladies' room visit at least until the restaurant.

Dinner was pleasant enough at one of their favorite spots, Cafe Un Deux Trois in the theater district, and I was allowing myself to relax over an excellent fillet of sole when, apropos of nothing, Althea said, "I heard that Roger was in negotiations to become the new head of production for Dreamworks, and that he definitely wasn't taking Samantha along."

Bark gave her a sharp glance. "Where on earth did you hear that?"

"There are people all over this town who've been talking about him leaving the Union. I know I told you," she said.

"Yeah, but now you're putting the rumor in circulation." He signaled the waiter for coffee.

"Well, I know Maggie believes that Samantha had no motive for killing Roger." She turned to me. "But now you have, Maggie. Do you know how much Samantha could have made as executive assistant to the head of production?"

"Probably not," Bark said for me. "But I'm sure you're going to tell her."

"Try starting at about one hundred and fifty thou, plus all the benefits. And he wasn't going to take her along. People have been killed for a lot less."

"But it's still only gossip," I said.

She smiled. "Well, I happen to have heard it from my hairdresser."

"Oh, for God's sake, that hairdresser again," Bark said. "How the hell would he know?"

"Because he does Ellie Brownleaf's sister's hair, that's how."

I frowned. Thad Brownleaf was the current head of production at Dreamworks. I hadn't heard that he was leaving the job, and, clearly, neither had Bark.

Avenue Q was a Tony Awards multi-winner, it was impossible to get tickets, but the Thomases, of course, had been able to wangle three, and it was uproariously funny. I'm sure I must have laughed and applauded in all the right places, which were many, and yet I couldn't wait to get back to the hotel to check my blood and brush my teeth and brood some more about Roger and Samantha.

Before I went to bed, I sat down with a sheet of hotel stationery and made a list of possible murder suspects. Don't laugh. That's what all great investigators do. Anyway, it was a very short list: Noelle, Dana, Karen, and, all right, Samantha. All women. So I started thinking about men. There was Neville, who maybe wanted Roger's job. And then there was Richard Urban. I don't know why I thought of him, especially since his whereabouts were still unknown. I put a big question mark after his name.

Okay, so now I had a list of sorts, and I was still as baffled as ever.

35

The next morning I awoke feeling sharp and energetic. New York does that to me. I went to the hotel gym and ran on the treadmill for thirty minutes, working my arms at the same time with ten-pound weights.

Later, I made my way over to Fifth and headed downtown to the Library. I keep tons of useless information in my head, just in case I'm ever marooned on a deserted island with a crossword puzzle and two of the clues are the names of the Library Lions, which are "Patience" and "Fortitude." The problem is I can never remember which one is which. Saying hello to the lion on the right, my particular pal, who was either very patient or very full of fortitude, I went to the Special Request desk and inquired about *L'Homme Qui Rit*. After a few minutes, the response was that it was out of print.

Okay. I expected that. I then went to the computer room, filled out the form, and logged on. At ***Booksearch.com*** I requested a search, entered all the info, and used my Internet American Express Blue and my e-mail address, ***Wargod@aol.com.*** The "Wargod," of course, was from my last name, Mars. I can be cute when I want to be.

Anyway, it was now in the lap of the cyber-gods.

Stopping only for a light nibble and a cup of tea, I walked over to Times Square and the offices of *Vanity Fair.* I had to wait while Gracie finished up on the phone, and I looked around at my surroundings with a rush of nostalgia.

The walls boasted a lovely, small pencil drawing by Leonardo da Vinci, owned by Gracie, and a large Lichtenstein and a wonderful Hockney, owned by the magazine. Also, there were framed articles from old issues, signed by Tom Wolfe, Jacqueline Kennedy, Bill Clinton, and the like.

When Gracie hung up and smiled at me, it felt like the sun had come out right there in his office.

Tears welled up in my eyes from nowhere.

Gracie, tactful as always, handed me his handkerchief and said, "Is the left coast as bad as all that?"

I dabbed at my eyes and sniffled.

"Then come home, my darling. We'll welcome you with open arms."

"I'm sorry, Gracie. I don't know what's come over me."

"What's come over you is murder. Murder is very unsettling, even to someone with your professional approach. You're a bulldog of an investigator, but that doesn't mean you don't have feelings."

I nodded. "Everywhere I look, I find a dead end. I can't make any headway and the cops have closed the case. They're calling it a murder-suicide, and I feel in my gut that it's wrong, all wrong."

"So what's the problem? Go with your gut. Remember those dormitory killings in New Hampshire? You stuck with what you believed and eventually uncovered the real murderer. And, by the way, those were great articles. I'm looking for more of the same now."

I had to smile through the tears. How like him to pat me on the back, and give me a push at the same time. But I had to make my confession.

"It's worse than you think."

"It couldn't be. There is nothing worse."

"I don't have any pages for you. All I have are a clutter of notes in search of an article, and a lot of guesswork that's no substitute for legitimate facts."

"Okay, so I'll wait," he said. "You've come through for me many times before and I've got every confidence you'll do it again." He stood. "Just don't make me wait too long. This story has a shelf life, and we can't go past that."

"I know, I know. Actually, there are a few leads I'm following right here in New York, so maybe something will spring loose."

He nodded. "Right." He came around the desk and perched on the corner of it. "Listen, have you run into Joe, may I ask?"

I took a last blow in his handkerchief. "Yes."

"Yes you've run into him or yes I may ask?"

"Both. He's one of the detectives on the case."

"Uh-huh. I see."

"And what's that supposed to mean?"

"Nothing. I just wondered if something else was getting to you, something besides the murder investigation."

"Nope," I said, lying through my teeth, "nothing else is getting to me."

"Good." He went back to the top drawer of his desk, took out a checkbook, and proceeded to write a check with a Mont Blanc pen and real ink.

"Here." He handed it to me.

"What's this for?"

"The first two articles, less your advance."

"But I haven't written them yet."

"This is to insure that you will. Do you need more?"

"Gracie, you're wonderful."

He said, "Tell me something I don't know."

I blew him a kiss and left him doing the usual, picking up the phone.

Those surprise tears had frightened me. It wasn't like me to have a crying jag. Joe used to complain that I was too unemotional, too locked up. So maybe the tears were a good sign. Then again, maybe a very bad sign.

Another bad sign, I realized, was that I had forgotten to return Gracie's handkerchief.

* * *

A walk on Madison Avenue, window-shopping at designer stores where I could never afford even a casual browse inside, lightened my spirits considerably. Then it was back to the hotel to spend the rest of the day going over the job description and the candidates' résumés for the interviews on Monday.

I hadn't ever been on a Search Committee before, and I found I had a lot to learn about the skills and personal qualities required of a Union Executive Director. It made me speculate whether Roger Urban would be hired if he submitted his application today.

Well, maybe not today, but let's say the week before he was murdered.

I thought there might be a call from Althea and Bark inviting me for dinner and a show again that evening, but there was none. I'm sure I would have politely declined, but, still, one does like to keep one's options open. I phoned a few friends left over from my previous New York existence, including Janice Ryder, but short notice brought about the expected fruitless results.

In the end, I ordered my evening meal Chez Room Service, and watched a semi-porno flick on the pay channel. It compared quite unfavorably with Karen and Roger, and besides, the male star wasn't as good-looking as Eric Hummel.

The next day was crisp and cool. The trees in the park were red and orange and yellow, and the streets were full of energetic New York people all hurrying to leave or to get someplace. I took a bus down to Greenwich Village, and wove my way around the streets, browsing in small, overstocked bookstores and making unproductive inquiries about *L'Homme Qui Rit*.

I stopped for a bite, then took another bus uptown and made my way back to the hotel. My room, which was a junior suite, had a port for my laptop, so I didn't have to worry about the foibles of my battery. I was equally captivated by

the bathroom, whose main attraction was the toilet—excuse
me, the commode. There was a sidearm on it containing a
panel of buttons, all of which, when pressed, did amazing
things. Modesty spares me from being any more descriptive.

I made myself comfortable with a diet soda from the
mini-bar and settled down to my screenplay. . . .

INT. JACK'S BEDROOM—NIGHT

Jack Mackenzie, in his tight-fitting briefs,
is spread-eagled, handcuffed to the headboard of the bed. Mercedes stands in front
of him in seductive lingerie.

                    MERCEDES
    This was your fantasy, right?

                    JACK
    Oh, yeah.

                    MERCEDES
    Well, I have a fantasy, too.

                    JACK
    It's only fair.

                    MERCEDES
    Great.   My   fantasy   is   to . . . Is
    to . . . Is to get an apology from your
    sorry ass.

                    JACK
    What? Not a chance. Get me out of these.

                    MERCEDES
    Not until you apologize. You've been
    rude to me.

                    JACK
You deserved being rude to.

                  MERCEDES
You had me arrested.

                    JACK
You broke the law. Trespassing. Interfering in a police investigation. Theft
of a patrol car.

                  MERCEDES
I broke your case wide open.

She picks up a phone.

                    JACK
It would have happened twice as fast
without you. What are you doing?

                  MERCEDES
Calling nine-one-one.
        (into phone)
Officer in trouble.

                    JACK
I'm not in trouble.

                  MERCEDES
Yes, you are. I'm leaving.

Mercedes turns and heads out the door, slam-
ming it shut.

                    JACK
Wait! I'm sorry. You were right. I was
wrong. I'm a bully. I'm sorry.

EXT. JACK'S HOUSE—NIGHT

Mercedes, now wearing a trench coat, walks
down the street as a siren-wailing POLICE
CAR, FIRE TRUCK, and AMBULANCE slide to a
stop in front of the detective's house. Mercedes smiles and walks on.

I typed in FADE OUT, but it was a cheat. I hadn't really
finished my screenplay. What I had done was write the last
scene: one, because the content gave me a perverted sense
of satisfaction, and two, because I would now have a blue-
print of what other scenes I had to write in order to get
there.

By that evening the rest of the Search Committee had arrived and we all had dinner together at Halcyon, the restaurant at our hotel. The room was spacious and elegant with
table settings of beautiful Villeroy and Boch French Garden
plates. The question briefly crossed my mind as to whether
Bark or COW was taking care of the check, but it didn't
lessen my enjoyment of the meal.

We mostly talked about the schedule for the next day's interviews, except for when, during the dessert course, each
selection an absolute work of art with the chef's signature
drizzled on the presentation dish, Althea spoke to me across
the table to ask what I had been up to that day.

"Working," I said. "Meeting with my editor."

"Now I feel guilty for not having entertained you more.
We could have done Bergdorf's."

There was no doubt about it. The woman lived on another
planet.

The next day was spent in the Boardroom of our New
York branch, interviewing those whose résumés had made
the cut. The job was an odd amalgam of abilities. It required
someone who was a savvy Entertainment Industry type, who

understood all the Hollywood labor contracts, who delegated well, who was a canny negotiator and a people person who could deal with creative people and their angst.

Altogether, a difficult package to find in one individual. Especially since, as Clark Newman jokingly said, "Shouldn't we question the sanity of anyone who actually wants this job?"

Noelle Sears' interview wasn't until the following day, but she was there to greet us and make sure we had everything we needed. I didn't think it would be politic of me at that moment to ask where she had been when Neville Lake and I had been trying to reach her, so I didn't.

We allowed about forty-five minutes for each candidate, with a brief interval in between for recording our impressions of each, and were able to finish with three before we broke for lunch. The office staff had prepared a spread for us, but I begged off eating with the others and went out for some air.

It had turned unseasonably warm in New York also, and my clothes were hot and itchy. I stopped at a corner café for a turkey sandwich and an iced decaf, then took a stroll down Fifth, examining the wares displayed on the peddlers' carts. On Forty-ninth I found a cart that had wraparound skirts of an Indian print cotton, so I purchased one for twelve ninety-five. A little farther on, I met up with a T-shirt cart and bought a short-sleeved cotton one for five dollars.

Returning to the office, I carried my packages back to the ladies' room, and when I appeared for the afternoon session I was casually cool and chic and comfortable in my eighteen-dollar investment, with my warm clothes stuffed in my tote.

The afternoon interviews went smoothly, maybe because the committee was unanimous in turning most of them down. One candidate captivated us all, and we put a hold on him, in spite of a few misgivings. E. Preston Masters was a wheelchair-bound attorney with long black hair, a wicked sense of humor, and a morbid turn of phrase. Just right for COW. The problem was that his background was in anti-trust. He had very little knowledge about the entertainment industry and its specialized labor movement.

I left the branch office with Bark at my side still discussing the guy. I was willing to keep E. Preston in the running, because he was smart and could work well with people, both individually and in groups. Bark was more hesitant and judicial, worried that the learning curve might take too long. We parted after I turned down an invitation for dinner.

As I walked down Fifth, my mind still on E. Preston and wondering what the E stood for, someone said, "Maggie Mars. I don't believe it."

I looked up and found myself face-to-face with an old friend, Danny Wilde, grinning broadly. Danny had some kind of mid-level job with CBS News and had been helpful to me in other *Vanity Fair* investigations.

"Are you back from Sodom permanently, or just here for a breath of civilization?"

"Hey there, Wilde man. What's up?"

We air kissed and started walking together down Fifty-seventh, even as I remembered his favorite bar was down the street.

After we were settled, Danny with his Ketel One and me with my Diet Coke, we did a lot of catching-up talk. I told him about the screenplay and about Lionel, whom he knew slightly, and then he said, "What about those Union murders I've been reading about? What's the lowdown?"

"No lowdown. The cases are closed. Finished. Over and done with. Period."

"Then the Assistant did it after all?"

"That's a big question mark, Danny, at least for me."

"So, are you writing it up for *Vanity Fair?*"

"You bet, because I don't buy what the police are selling."

"Speaking of police . . ."

I knew what was coming, and jumped in before he could finish.

"Yes, I've seen Joe, and no, I have nothing to say about him, especially to you, the big mouth of CBS."

We had another drink and talked New York trash talk and I felt right at home. Later, standing on the sidewalk outside the bar, while he was trying to hail a cab, Danny said, "Oh, by the way, I talked to a Union friend of yours a little while ago. Dana Salinger?"

"Dana? I didn't even know you knew her. What was that about?"

"A mutual friend gave her my name. She wanted a recommendation for a job. Something about being a Network Liaison for the Union." A cab had pulled up. "Can I drop you?"

"No, thanks, I'll walk. But tell me, did you do it? Recommend her?"

"Sure. And I copied your Executive Director. Did I do wrong?"

"No . . . of course not. . . ."

"Gotta run. Love you, Maggie."

His cab pulled away and I was left puzzled. Network Liaison? I hadn't heard anything about that. It certainly required further analysis.

There were more interviews in the following days, which yielded only one potential candidate. He had good qualifications, but, to my way of thinking, he asked too many questions about the celebrity quotient involved with his duties. The last appointment of the last day was with Noelle Sears.

She looked very business-like and executive-ish in a black Armani suit and tailored silk shirt set off with a stunning patterned scarf. The résumé she handed us was quite detailed, and I must admit I was impressed. I didn't know she had gone to Oxford and had spent several years working in London.

Bark had cautioned us to question her very delicately, since we would all have to continue to work with her, whether or not she got the job. We already knew of her familiarity with the industry and with the labor end of negotiations.

"Why don't you tell us why you want to move to the west coast, and what you see as your strong points," Bark said.

That was all the opening Noelle needed. She talked about her ideas for opportunities ahead for the Union, about her ability to pull disparate elements together, and, since she had no children, she was free to pull up stakes and go where the real action was.

The back-and-forth progressed smoothly, and it was obvious Noelle had all the necessary experience and qualifications.

By the time it was over, I was sure she would be one of the finalists for the position, and yet something nagged at me about her. Maybe it was because I remembered what Dennis Bird had told me about the argument he had overheard between Noelle and Roger. Maybe it was the negative comments of Wendy Bassett, who had worked for her. Or maybe it was just that there were other questions I had that just couldn't be asked at an interview.

I was the last one to leave, having stayed behind to call the hotel and check on my messages. Noelle's assistant, Laura, offered the use of the phone on her desk, and I was listening to the voice mail for my room when Noelle came out of her office and stood there, obviously waiting for me to finish.

"Are you busy this evening, Maggie?" she said when I hung up.

Unfortunately I was. One of the messages I had received was from an old school friend who was inviting me to dinner at her Riverside Drive apartment. It was something I wanted to do, but I still didn't want to lose out on a chance to get together with Noelle and do a little more probing.

"I have a dinner engagement later," I said. "But I have time for a drink."

"Good. How about the bar in the St. Regis in . . ."—glancing at her Movado watch—"say, half an hour?"

"I'll see you there. Oh, by the way, did I hear you were in Los Angeles a little while ago?"

"When was that?"

"Oh . . . sometime around Halloween, I think it was." That was the best I could do rather than say, bluntly, around the time Samantha was murdered.

"Halloween . . . Let me think. . . . Oh, right. I wasn't in L.A. then. I was home in bed with the flu."

"I'm sorry to hear that." And I was, sorry to hear that she was probably lying to me, and I wondered why.

She left and I called back my friend and arranged to be at her place later.

Laura was leaving just as I was, and we stood in the hallway together, waiting for the elevator. I smiled over at her, and after a reasonable amount of chitchat, I took a spur-of-the-moment plunge, knowing that as Noelle's assistant, she must be aware of her application for the L.A. job.

"So, Laura," I said, "what happens to you if Noelle takes over the west coast office? Will you come out with her?"

Laura looked at me, sizing me up and deciding she didn't know me well enough not to be circumspect.

"I'm really not sure yet. Noelle hasn't spoken to me about it, so I'll just wait and see."

"Obviously you get along very well with her." That wasn't obvious at all, but what the hell, it might lead to something.

"Well . . . she's very tough to work for, very demanding, and . . ." Her voice trailed off just as the elevator arrived.

We stepped in. There was a briefcase-and-suited attorney-type in the car, and Laura nodded a greeting to him, so I knew there would be nothing more in the way of confidences.

We kept each other company walking down to the corner where Laura would catch her bus.

"You know," she said, "I remember you now. You were one of the ones who called to ask where Noelle was."

"Right. I wanted to get in touch with her and I thought she might have been back in Los Angeles."

"If that's where she was, she made her own reservations, and she very rarely does anything like that for herself . . ." Her tone of voice implied the finish to that was . . . not if she can stick someone else with the job.

"Anyway, I found out she was home with the flu."

I looked inquiringly at Laura, wondering if she could verify that.

"Well, if that's what she told you," Laura said, "then she must have been."

Some thirty minutes later, Noelle and I were wedged in at a small table in a smoky bar, she over a martini and me thinking that if I stayed in New York much longer, I would never want to look at another Diet Coke again.

At first I was treated to a continuance of Noelle's interview with the committee, since she was bent on convincing me that she was the right person for the job. After that we veered off into some woman-to-woman chatter, and only then did she get to the point that was probably her real motive for this get-together.

"I hope, whomever the committee chooses," she said, "it won't be Neville."

I said, "Why do you say that? Neville knows the territory, he has a lot of experience, and he gets along well with members."

Noelle shot a look at me that said better than words: "How dumb can you be?" She ordered another drink, but I declined.

"For one thing," she said, "Roger didn't think too highly of him. You knew that."

No, I didn't know that. Maybe I was as dumb as I could be.

"You're talking about what went down between them," I said, figuring that was general enough to serve as a trial balloon.

"Exactly. Roger knew damn well that Neville wasn't doing his job and he spoke to him several times about it."

Bingo. I nodded sagely.

"Neville was out of the office a lot," she said, "calling in sick, neglecting his reports, and Roger was plain fed up. He told me confidentially, not to be repeated, of course"—except to me, of course— "he was getting ready to fire Neville. He had given him a poor performance review last time around."

I wondered, briefly, why Roger would have confided anything to her.

"The committee should certainly take that under advisement," I said.

"And if you're looking for a motive for murder . . ."

The words hung there, and I let them settle for a while before I said, "Well, according to the police they already must have one, since they think that Samantha did it."

"Samantha?" The waiter came over and Noelle exchanged her dead drink for a live one. "I don't believe that"—she held up her martini in a mocking toast—"and neither do you."

We talked some more, mostly Union business and when our group would be flying back to the coast. Then I reached for the check, over Noelle's protests, and signaled the waiter.

"I hope I'll be hearing from you," she said, as we came out of the St. Regis into the busy street.

"I'm sure you will," I said. One way or another.

My flight home was made to order. They had one empty seat in first class and I got bumped up. The reward for arriving late and having my original confirmed seat taken.

My seat companion was none other than Faye Dunaway. She couldn't have been more charming. We bonded because our drinks of choice were herbal teas, and we gabbed our way across country.

Over the Rockies I could feel Lionel's spirit goading me on. "*Chinatown* is one of my all-time favorite films," I said. "How did you like working with Robert Towne and Jack Nicholson?"

"They were the most fun," she said. "They are very bad boys."

She fluttered those eyes at me, and I enjoyed very bad visions of the very bad boys.

"Jack is the most wonderful actor and a very good friend. And Robert just works magic with the same twenty-six letters we all use, but somehow, he puts them together in such a unique fashion. The difficult one was, of course, John. . . ."

And despite my best efforts to get back to Jack Nicholson, she talked about John Huston all the rest of the way.

It was close to midnight by the time I got home. Harpo greeted me at the front door by raising his back up and hissing at me. Cats have no memory at all. Lionel's door was closed, but I could see a crack of light from underneath and hear television voices.

I dropped my suitcases by the couch. "Lionel? Are you up?"

"I am now."

"Your light was on and I can hear the television."

"Then why did you bother asking? Come on in."

I opened the door. Lionel was propped up like a sultan on an assortment of fluffy pillows. His right leg was in a cast.

36

He said, "For your information, I dropped off the note and I bitched plenty about the messy fingerprints. How was New York?"

I gaped at him. "Never mind New York. What happened to you?"

"In a word, some hit-and-run son-of-a-bitch prick side-swiped my bike. It's demolished completely."

"Are you okay?"

"Do I look okay? Good thing I was wearing a helmet, or my head would be in a cast."

I sat down on the bed, obviously disturbing his leg enough that he winced.

"Sorry." I got up. He winced again. "Did you at least get a license?"

"I was a poor, pathetic mound in the middle of the street. I made a police report, but I couldn't even see the kind of car she was driving. The old bat."

"She? I thought you said it was a prick."

"What are you? The Anatomical Police?"

I looked around the room. It appeared neat and orderly. There were a pair or crutches within Lionel's reach and a water pitcher and glass on Lionel's bedside table. The drapes were drawn and the spread neatly folded at the foot of the bed.

I said, "Who's been taking care of you?"

"Troy. He's been driving me back and forth from work. I refer to it as his community service."

"You should have called me."

"What for? You were on vacation."

"Vacation? This was strictly business. I was working every day."

"Then I certainly wasn't going to call you."

"Good night, Lionel. Your leg may be broken, but not your spirit."

" 'Night. I'm glad you're home."

I closed the door and headed for my room.

"Maggie?"

I stopped, waited.

"Your ex called. Three times."

"He's not my ex. Didn't you tell him I was out of town?"

"No. I said you didn't want to talk to him and not to call here ever again, on pain of castration. Of course I told him you were away, but he kept calling anyway. Wants to see you at the station first thing tomorrow morning."

"But it's Sunday. Why would he want to see me on a Sunday?"

"What do you expect, he's just your typical flatfoot."

"The word," I said to the closed door, "is dick."

"That, too. Good night."

I was too energized to go to sleep, but not quite energized enough to want to unpack, or to open my laptop and get back to the screenplay. Or even to speculate about Joe's phone call. What I did was undress, wrap myself in a terry robe, and settle down on the couch with a cup of herbal tea and my spiral notebook.

Harpo and Groucho padded over and looked up at me with soulful eyes. At least I think they were soulful. Who knows with cats?

"What is it, guys? You feel sorry for Lionel?"

Not even one meow of agreement.

"Well, I feel sorry for Lionel, too. And, if you don't mind, I'm also feeling sorry for myself." I took a sip of tea. Too hot. "You know I've been working on Roger's murder, right?"

And, suddenly, there they were, both of them, up on the couch with me, ears perked towards me. I thought of the cat hairs that I'd have to vacuum up in the morning, but I didn't shoo them off.

"Anyhow, I've got suspects coming out of the wazoo, with motives to match, and the more I find out, the less I'm really sure of."

Groucho looked away. Harpo curled up in my lap and remained attentive. I took heart from that and went on.

"There's Karen Thorstensen, and Dana Salinger, and Noelle Sears . . . and maybe I should consider some other women as well . . . maybe even Wendy Bassett. Though Wendy is so pissed with Roger for being dead, it's highly improbable she would have caused him to get that way."

Harpo's whiskers twitched. I guess that didn't make too much sense to him either.

"Also, there was Samantha Winger. Note the past tense, because Samantha was killed. I was there when it happened, guys. Well, anyway, right after it happened." I decided not to go into detail about that. Even cats could be squeamish. "The police said it was suicide and that Sam had killed Roger. But I don't believe it. She was planning on going away and starting a new life. She was excited about it. So why would she commit suicide, right?"

Groucho gave a little cough. Either he shared my opinion, or it was a hairball.

"Then there's a brother in the picture. A long-lost brother. I learned, too, that Roger was looking to fire Neville Lake, so there's another motive to explore. But meanwhile, guess what? I've been getting some threatening notes."

I looked for one or the other of them to hiss or spit. No hissing. No spitting. I guess you can't expect loyalty from a cat. If I wanted loyalty, I should have made Lionel get a dog.

"Now Joe wants me to keep him informed if anything looks odd, but it all looks odd. Joe's an old, well, let's call him an old boyfriend. He's the detective handling the case. He thinks he's handling me, too, but he's wrong. So... what do you think?"

For answer, there was a lot of licking of paws and assorted body parts. And then it hit me.

"Oh my God," I said. "I'm actually sitting here and talking to cats."

"Yes," said Mercedes. "And you're boring them out of eight of their lives."

I scattered them off the couch and went to bed.

The next morning I called Joe and was put through to Martin.

After a few weather-related comments were exchanged, he said, "Joe would like you to come down to the station."

"I just got back from New York and I've got kind of a busy day. Can't I speak to him now?"

"Okay, just a second."

He put me on hold. There was no music to keep me entertained. There weren't even any police bulletins. Just the kind of silence that makes you wonder if you're still on hold or if you've been cut off.

"Listen, Maggie," Martin was back, "Joe would really appreciate it if—"

"Fuck the appreciation!" It was Joe, cutting in. "Get your ass down here!"

I bridled. "What is that, an order? 'Cause if it's an order, I'll be damned if I show up. You want to see me, you ask me nice and politely, and I'll check my schedule."

There was no confusion about this silence. I was definitely talking to a hung-up line.

I got my ass down there. Not to show up would let him know that he still had the power to infuriate me. Whereas, if I showed up because *I* chose to do so, well, that would prove

I was still master of my fate, captain of my soul, and kidder of no one. Most of all myself.

I called Henrik from my car and told him I was heading for the station to see Joe. Command performance.

"Do you want me to meet you there? I've got to finish a brief which will take about an hour, and then I can join you."

"No, no, I'll be fine. Nothing's going to happen. I just wanted you to know."

"Call me later, okay, Maggie? Welcome back, and don't confess to anything."

"What?"

"Only kidding."

That made me worry. Henrik never kids.

37

As I walked into the station, I saw Martin at the coffee machine. I greeted him warily.

"How's the weather over there?" I said, indicating Joe at his desk.

"Want some coffee first?"

He hadn't answered my question, and yet, of course, he had. I shook my head no and went over to see Joe.

He didn't rise. He just sat there, behind the grim fortress of his desk.

"What in hell do you think you're doing?"

"No hello? No nice to see you?"

"Hello nice to see you what in hell do you think you're doing?"

"That's better. Nice to see you, too."

Joe got up and confronted me nose to nose. Too close. Much too close.

"Can the bullshit, Maggie. I thought we had a deal."

Martin had followed me over and was standing in the corner, his face absolutely blank, drinking his coffee, probably waiting for the bell to ring at the end of Round One so he could call in the cut man.

"We do. Lionel dropped the note off, didn't he?"

"I'm not talking about the note. We'll get to that later. I'm talking about how you lied to get into Roger's place and you stole a videocassette, thereby contaminating evidence. You left fingerprints—and you tainted whatever fingerprints were already there. You mangled at least a dozen laws, breaking and entering, petty theft, tampering with evidence, interfering with police business, and furthermore . . ."

The list of my offenses went on and on like a hardened criminal's rap sheet. I hardly heard him, thinking as I watched his lips move that it hadn't been so long ago those same lips had been exploring every curve and crevice of my body.

"—You never know when to stop, Maggie. You just never know when enough is enough!"

His face was getting redder, the veins standing out in his neck, as he enunciated every syllable. I was in real trouble. First, because he was so very angry, and, second, because he was right. I backed away from him a bit, his closeness more and more unsettling.

"You didn't see anything wrong with my continuing to investigate for my articles. You asked to be kept informed, so what are you howling about now?" I kept my voice down, glancing over at Martin, not sure whether Joe had taken him into his confidence.

"I also told you to keep your nose clean!"

He had no compunction about speaking loud enough so that not only Martin could hear, but everyone in the police station.

"Joe, calm down." I glanced over at Martin but he was still staying out of it. "Technically you're right."

"Technically? Technically? What the fuck are you talking about? The law is the law!"

"It was for my articles. I wanted to see Roger's place so I could kind of paint a backdrop for him, set him in his own surroundings. It helps with making him come alive for the reader—sorry, unfortunate phrase that. It makes him a more colorful character, that's what I mean."

Martin said, quietly, "Maggie, what you're doing is very dangerous."

"I'll handle this, thank you," Joe said, glowering at Martin. "Maggie, just trust me for once, will you?"

Uh-oh. Here comes the Good Cop.

"I knew you were going to investigate for your articles and that no one on earth could stop you. But, as always, you go too far. . . ."

"Who made you the authority on when I go too far?" I still kept my voice low but insistent.

"You have to stay out of situations that could be dangerous. I'm not always going to be around to protect you."

That did it.

"Protect me? You haven't been around for years! Where do you get off, protect me! I don't need your protection. I don't want it!"

The Bad Cop again. "You are not going to mess up my case. You are not going around breaking and entering." His audience was rapt. Everyone in the station was listening.

"I didn't break and enter. The manager let me in. If you want to throw me in jail for impersonating a relative of a dead man, fine. My *Vanity Fair* readers will love it."

"All right, you two," Martin said. "That's enough."

He stepped in front of me and pushed me into a chair, then gave a significant look to Joe. Joe took a long, deep breath and sat down behind the desk.

"Let's have the cassette," he said.

I dug it out of my bag and placed it on the desk.

"I was going to give this to you as soon as I found out what it was."

"Uh-huh."

I managed to restrain myself. "It explains what Karen was hiding. I guess she told you about it?"

He didn't respond except to take the cassette and stash it in a drawer. I waited some more.

"Can I go now," I said, "or are you going to read me my rights?"

He said, "I'll walk you out."

I decided to take the hint, but just as we reached the door, I turned to him.

"Joe, I am going to continue to investigate and do everything I can to insure that my articles are the very best. I owe that to myself."

His answer was no answer.

"Just try to stay out of trouble, will you? That second note ratchets up the danger considerably and I don't want to be worrying about you."

The anger was gone. Maybe. It was my cue to be a little more reasonable, as well.

"I was out of line," I said. "It won't happen again."

He grabbed me by the shoulders and kissed me hard and fast on the lips. We stared at each other for a second and then he went back to his desk.

I left the station house with my stomach in a knot. Walking out into the sunshine, I bumped right into Henrik.

"I got here as soon as I could," he said. "Are you all right?"

Was I all right? No, I wasn't. There was that kiss. I wondered if it showed on my face.

"I'm out on bail," I said, grabbing his arm and steering him towards my car. "Come, buy me breakfast."

We drove to IHOP, on Santa Monica Boulevard, and settled into German apple pancakes and coffee. Henrik knew the sugar was a slight indulgence for me and he eyed me warily as we began to eat.

"What's up, Maggie? What were you caught doing?"

"Nothing. Not a thing. Well, maybe just a little thing. Nothing to get excited about. Joe's got some kind of bug up his ass about my investigation."

He was silent.

"What?"

"I didn't say anything."

"I know you, Henrik. You're thinking something."

He shook his head.

"Okay." I lifted another forkful of pancake, decided I'd transgressed enough, and put it down.

Henrik said, "Joe's back in your life, isn't he?"

"Well, that's a no-brainer. You just saw for yourself. Or

would have seen, if you'd arrived five minutes earlier. It's strictly police stuff."

"Is it?"

I kept my eyes down at my plate.

"The connection's still there, isn't it, Maggie?"

"What is this, a cross-examination?"

"Tell me he doesn't matter anymore."

What could I say? Did Joe matter to me anymore? I didn't know the answer to that. I thought it was long over between us, but he could still make my heart go wild, my knees go wobbly, and my mouth go dry. And what significance was there to that kiss? Intellectually, I knew he was out of my life, but my emotions were signaling just the opposite.

I looked up and found Henrik silently staring at me.

"I think it's just the strangeness of us working on the same case at the same time," I said. "That's all it is. It's perplexing the hell out of me."

"I thought he closed the case." Here is where I had better tread carefully. I couldn't reveal to him that Joe was still working on it, unofficially.

"He has, but I haven't. So we're bound to lock horns over it every now and then, right?" I smiled, relieved at having sorted it all out. "That's why I need a good lawyer to stick round."

I reached out for his hand and briefly considered making a suggestion that I collect on that rain check. But I didn't. Some other time, I thought. When there wouldn't be three of us in bed together.

38

I needed to reload on pepper spray, and, this time, I went to the spy shop across from Gelson's on Van Nuys Boulevard. I was tempted by a camera/recorder the size of a credit card because it was so cool, but passed on it and just bought the pepper spray.

That evening Lionel sensed my mood and seemed content to hobble around the house and keep out of my way. I actually broiled some fish and threw together a chopped salad for dinner and I knew he wanted to complain about its ordinariness, but didn't.

As a reward, I brought him up-to-date on the little I had learned in New York. I told him about my book search, and about Dana Salinger and about my conversation with Noelle Sears.

"I still haven't been able to find out if she was in town at the time of Samantha's murder. I'm thinking of calling a few different hotels, but if Noelle was here to kill Samantha, she wouldn't stay at a hotel where she was known."

Lionel said, "Let me ask around. I've got better sources."

A little before eleven, with Lionel safely tucked in bed, I decided it was the perfect hour to catch Dana at home. Of course, if Dana was home, so was the pit bull. I put the pepper spray in my bag.

I pulled on a black leather jacket over my jeans and turtleneck, grabbed my bag, and drove over to her place.

While driving, I noticed that my black jeans were covered with cat hair. Nothing makes you feel more incompetent than being covered with cat hair, but, for the time being, I took a few desultory swipes and vowed to talk to Lionel about using a depilatory on his felines.

Stopping at an all-night convenience store, I bought a box of dog biscuits as a sop to the pit bull.

The clerk said, "You've got hair all over you."

"Must be a full moon," I said.

At this time of night, I was relieved to find a parking spot right in front of Dana's building. When I looked up, I saw that her lights were still on. It would have been better to wake her up. Maybe she wouldn't function on all cylinders when abruptly roused from sleep. But you make do with what you get. The bigger issue was whether the pit bull was awake. I put my pepper spray in my hand, and the biscuits in my pocket.

When Dana answered the door, I don't know who was more startled. Dana to see me, at eleven o'clock, all in black and covered with hair, or me to see Dana, at eleven o'clock, in a filmy peignoir, trimmed honest-to-God with some white furry stuff, and high-heeled red satin mules. The fact that she hadn't asked, "Who is it?" when I rang, spoke volumes. She was expecting someone and I didn't fit the description.

She said, "Not you again."

"I guess you couldn't sleep either, huh? May I come in?"

She was just a second too late trying to block me. I pushed my way through, and tried to look casually around. There was neither sign nor sound of the canine. Maybe she had knocked him out for the night, given that she and her peignoir were going to be otherwise engaged.

"I'm calling the police right now if you don't get out."

She moved towards the phone. I plunked myself down on the couch.

"Go right ahead."

Dana picked up the receiver, and then hesitated. "I forgot. You have connections."

She gave up on the phone and sat down next to me.

"Just say what you have to say, and leave."

I knew I had her. "Okay. Let me tell you a story. It's about an older woman trying to hold on to her youth for as long as she can. She has a younger boyfriend who holds a very prominent industry position. They have an affair. It's secret because it's against the policy of his company, but she doesn't care. She thinks he's in love with her and she actually expects to marry the guy. Only he dumps her. Not only is he not going to marry her, he is just about to land a really big job with a studio. A major, front-office kind of job. She would have liked to be on his arm at all those black-tie affairs. She could have connected with some very influential people that way."

"Maybe she's the one who broke it off," Dana said. "Maybe he was too immature for her."

I ignored that. I was too caught up in the story I was spinning. "Then, the final straw. A job comes up which this woman wants. Network Liaison. She wants it badly. She goes to her ex-lover and asks him to get her the job. He refuses. They argue. He turns up dead. Fade Out. What do you think of it?"

"I think you're a lousy writer with a trashy imagination." She stared into the distance and seemed to come to some kind of inward resolution.

"Okay, we were lovers," she said. "You're right about that. And you're right about my trying to hold on to my youth. You don't know what life is like in this town when you're past your prime. But you'll learn."

"So why did you break it off?"

"He was getting squirrelly, acting so strange it made me nervous. I knew we weren't going anywhere. I knew we weren't going to marry. No matter what else you think of me, you can bet I wasn't nuts enough to have believed that."

"What about the Network Liaison job?"

"He didn't want to give it to me at first. But then he calmed down and relented. He promised to recommend me. For auld lang syne, he said." A faint smile of reminiscence, and then, "But the truth was he probably wanted to get rid of me." She shrugged. "He was my lifeline to that job. Why would I kill him? It makes no sense."

She was right. It made no sense. If she was telling the truth. Big if.

The funny thing was that I believed her.

Just then the front door opened, and a man stood there, key in hand.

"Oh, hi," Eric Hummel said.

"Hi," I said. "Nice to see you again."

"Right. We met at some kind of dinner, didn't we?"

Dana said, "She was just leaving."

I handed Eric the dog biscuits. "Here," I said. "You may need these."

I left. The last I saw of Dana she was furiously brushing cat hair off the couch.

There was heavier traffic than usual on the San Diego Freeway as I made my way to Manhattan Beach the next morning. In hot weather everyone goes to the beach, and it seems they all drive the 405. I knew they couldn't all have been tailing me. Traffic was bumper to bumper all the way, with two stalled cars in my lane thrown in for good measure.

When I got to the Pacific Sunset Village, I parked in one of the guest slots and went into the lobby. Usually it's a trip to go into that lobby. U.G. once told me, "When you get to know retirement homes, you learn never to come on a Sunday." Thankfully I hadn't. On a Sunday, there would be people everywhere, sons and daughters and grandchildren visiting their loved ones. A great many of the retirees are somewhat hard of hearing, so the level of noise was akin to sitting in the first row at the Indianapolis Speedway during the 500 race.

This morning was blissfully quiet and I took a nice, appreciative look around the lobby with its plants and cheerful print-cushioned chairs before taking the elevator up to U.G.'s floor.

When I came in, U.G. put his arms around me and gave me a big welcoming hug. His apartment, one large room actually, was typical of him. The bed was a single bed, pushed into the corner against the wall, with a lamp to read by attached to the headboard. Books, magazines, and papers were piled on the floor next to the bed. There were bookcases filled to overflowing with more books, manuals, and odd items like mortars, pestles, and assorted glass beakers.

Against another wall was a long, maybe six-foot bench, which served him as a worktable. It was covered with even more scientific-looking papers and manuals, along with metal cylinders, hollow wooden blocks, and a variety of tools. There were several very functional-looking lamps hanging over the table.

"Let me give you an idea what I'm doing," U.G. said. He was really like a child, so excited over his current project and wanting to show it off.

He motioned to me to come over and look at something on his worktable.

"What am I looking at, U.G.?"

"I think I have the right formula for my gas sensor device. Now I'm working on packaging it so it's portable." He pointed with pride to several cylinders of varying sizes. "I'm trying to fit the sensor into a small, durable case, so it can be carried easily from place to place. The problem is, of course, that while it's being carried, the movement can't upset the sensor, or the unit is worthless. Understand?"

I thought I did. I nodded. Then I noticed a small cylinder off to one side, with a red X marked on it. It was about the size of a champagne split.

"What's that one, Dad?"

"That's one I've got to get rid of," he said. "I don't need those gasses anymore, and I'm trying to figure out how and where to dispose of it. Not here, of course."

"Thank you for that," I said, wondering if it was the cylinder that had caused the evacuation, but thinking it more diplomatic not to mention it. "How about if I take it and drop it off at the Fire Department on my way home? They'll know what to do with it."

"Good idea. Just tell them that it contains glycerol and potassium permanganate and don't let it get wet." He picked up his keys.

"I'm starving. Where are we going?"

"We're going to a place on the Redondo Beach pier where they have a fantastic seafood brunch."

"I love it already."

It was only when we were in the elevator that he said, "I've invited some friends to join us. They've been wanting to meet you."

The friends turned out to be two elderly women, residents of the retirement home, who were thoroughly entranced by U.G. Each was vying with the other for his attention and, after greeting me and saying hello, never looked at me again. So much for them wanting to meet me.

We ate outside, watching the fishermen and the seagulls and enjoying the sun. How pleasurable for U.G., I thought, and was more determined than ever to help him go on living there.

I left to go back to town, putting the cylinder on the floor in the back of my car. It was my intention to take it to the Fire Station on Sunset, but a radio traffic advisory informed me that the Sunset off-ramp was closed because of a fish-tailed truck. I got off at Wilshire instead and drove home from there.

When I got in, there was a message from Fowler. Please call. I sometimes feel that the invention of the answering machine was a big step backwards for a writer's autonomy.

I called him back.

"I've been thinking about who should play Mercedes," he said. "I'm sending you a list of my top five choices."

"I'm hoping Lisa Kudrow will be one of them," I said, and then qualified it. "With dark hair."

"Just as long as it isn't one of those bimbos from Bay-watch," said Mercedes.

"Listen, Fowler. The screenplay is coming along great. I can smell finish."

"Wonderful. Anything I can do to speed things along?"

Just stop calling me, I thought. What I said was, "Nope. I've got it all worked out."

As soon as I hung up, another call came through. It was Dee Dee, reminding me that Bark had called a Search Committee meeting at four. I had almost forgotten about that. The investigation was weighing heavily on my mind, and so was Joe. I hadn't heard from him since I dropped off the cassette. I put him out of my thoughts. What was more important right now was that this afternoon I would have another chance to get into Samantha's files.

I thought about those files and about felony breaking and entering. I didn't know if the cops were more lenient if you were a first timer or not. I qualified since my entry into Roger's place was not B and E.

Would anyone let me see those files? I didn't have a con-federate on COW's staff, so it was up to me. Somehow I would have to get in and out of those files. I would have to pick the lock. If my old metal nail file didn't do it, it was much too late to take Lockpicking 101.

39

On my way to the Union offices, I passed a small Mom-and-Pop bookstore, Carousel Books. A sign in the window announced that they specialized in antiquarian books and they had a Book Finding Service. I was suddenly reminded of Alain Dubert and his Laughing Man book, whatever that could possibly have to do with anything. On a hunch, I made a right turn at the next corner, came around again, and found a parking place only a few doors down. A good omen, I thought.

Wrong.

As I was turning off the ignition, I saw in my rearview mirror a car coming fast round the corner, and then slowing. I dug out the pepper spray from my bag, crouched down behind the wheel, and waited. There were sounds of another vehicle stopping alongside me, and the next thing I knew, Martin Wu was peering in my driver's side window. I straightened up and glared at him.

He had the gall to smile back, until he saw the spray in my hand. I lowered the window.

"Put that away, Maggie. That stuff stings like hell."

I peered out past him and saw that he had been driving the plain-Jane car used by the LAPD for their undercover work.

"You were following me, weren't you?"

"Ummm, yes, I had you under surveillance."

"I can't believe it. Don't you guys have anything better to do than chase me? There must be some real criminals around for you to find."

"It was protective surveillance."

"Really? On whose orders?"

I heard the radio squawking in his car.

"Okay," he said, "I'll let you off with a warning."

With that he smiled, climbed back in his car, and drove off.

Fine, so Martin Wu had a sense of humor, but what was that tailing all about? It looked as though Joe and Martin were keeping an eye on me. I didn't know whether to be happy that I was safer out on the street, or whether to be disturbed that now they would know my every move.

The more I analyzed it, the more it defied analysis. I gave up and went on into the bookstore.

Inside I met with the same disheartening report. No, they didn't have the book. It was out of print.

"I know it's out of print," I told the clerk, a dumpling of a woman wearing thick glasses. She must be Mom, and she must do a lot of sampling of the wares. "Can you get it for me?"

"We don't do that sort of thing," she said, somehow making the act of book finding sound like an illicit sexual practice.

"But your sign says—"

"It doesn't apply to out-of-print books."

I thought about stopping at some other bookstores along the way, but a glance at my watch told me I was already running late. Besides, I was sure the results would be more of the same. My last remaining hope was that Booksearch might still come through for me.

Once at the Union offices, I went quickly past the meeting room and headed for Samantha's office, ready to tackle the files again. The office door was open and, cautiously, I looked in. There were no files. They were gone. And Dee Dee was sitting behind the desk.

"Hi," I said. "I see you've moved in."

"For the time being anyway. Neville's out of the building. Did you want something, Maggie?"

"No. Just wondering what happened to Samantha's stuff?"

"Her stuff?"

"You know, her files, her pictures . . . I remember she had this stuffed Piglet sitting on a chair."

I threw in the pictures and Piglet to draw attention away from the files.

"Oh, yeah," Dee Dee said. "Everything got moved into the storeroom. Do you like my Paddington bear?"

She pointed to a fuzzy little fellow in a yellow rain hat and slicker now occupying the chair.

"Love it," I said. "The storeroom on the first floor?"

"No, the one up here, next to the ladies."

"Oh, yeah. Thanks, Dee Dee."

I patted Paddington Bear on his rain cap and escaped to the meeting.

But not before Dee Dee had called after me, "I'll tell Neville you were here."

By the time I joined the Search Committee, a discussion was already in progress. Bark and Chris were solidly in favor of Neville, while Ian was holding out for Noelle, Clark liked E. Preston Masters, and Dana felt strongly that we should place some ads and interview more people. Maybe tap our professional headhunter for additional suggestions. For once I agreed with Dana, and I said so.

Anyway, we came up with the names of several other possibilities, and it was agreed that Bark would call them and invite them to submit an application. I paid lukewarm attention. All I could think of was getting into that storeroom to look at Samantha's files and whatever else was in there.

What I expected to find, I didn't know. But it was something to do. Not just sit around and listen to—

"Maggie!"

I blinked.

"You still with us?" Bark said.

"Sorry. You were saying?"

"I was saying we'll meet again next Thursday and we'll have two more interviews. That okay for you?"

"Fine."

I made a big show out of writing the next meeting date on my pad.

He stopped me as I was leaving. "You sure you're okay, Maggie? You were a million miles away."

"I'm sorry. I just lost my concentration for a minute. I've had a lot of things on my mind."

"I can tell. Want to talk about it? We could stop somewhere for a bite."

"Love to, but I can't. I'm expecting some results from an Internet inquiry."

"Research?"

I said, "It's for my article and it's very very iffy right now, so I don't want to jinx it. And, anyway, I've got to take care of a roommate with a broken leg."

"You're lucky," he said. "All I've got to take care of is Althea."

I looked at him, and he was smiling, so there was no way of telling how he meant it. When we reached the elevator and the car arrived, I hung back.

"I better make a pit stop first," I said. "Good night."

" 'Night, Maggie."

The doors closed behind him, and I made good on my declaration. I went straight to the ladies' room and I stayed there. Before long I could hear the building's closing-hour noises, but I remained where I was, parked in one of the cubicles. I waited there. It was a luxury I don't often have in the third-floor ladies' room. It's only a two-seater, and usually it's so packed that it's standing room only.

When I thought it was safe, about an hour, two flushes, and three hand washes later, I peeked out. It was dark and quiet. By feeling along the wall, I inched my way to the storeroom next door.

The door was locked. Again, Joe's caveats ran through my mind, but I had gone through a lot of machinations to get as far as this locked door, and I wasn't going to back away now.

I tried the nail file. The only thing that happened was that I broke the tip of the file. Now what? A credit card, right? In movies and on TV it works all the time.

I consulted my wallet. Did it matter which card? Were some thinner than others?

"The only thing that's thin is your credit line," said Mercedes.

On the third try a video rental card actually worked. I opened the door and took out the roll of Scotch tape I carried with me, ever since reading about Watergate. I put a piece of it over the lock so it wouldn't lock behind me, then closed the door carefully and turned on the light.

Fortunately the storeroom wasn't jammed full. I spotted Samantha's file drawers in the far corner and went to work on them. It was all Union stuff, business as usual, nothing marked Personal, nothing about Alain Dubert or his mysterious book. But one drawer held files behind a tab reading Confidential, and it was there that I found something halfway rewarding. Neville Lake's file was there among a half dozen other employee files.

I leaned against some piled cartons and went through its contents. Noelle was right. Roger had given him a poor performance review. He had been taking too much time off, not focusing on his work, not showing enough initiative . . . There was no question that Roger must have been preparing to fire him.

I was still looking through the file when I learned the hard way that the trouble with the door not locking behind you is that anyone can walk in. And not just anyone.

Neville Lake.

40

Incongruously the familiar Mae West line ran across my mind. "Is that a gun in your pocket or are you just glad to see me?" Except that the gun wasn't in Neville's pocket, it was in his hand. And in no way was he glad to see me. Nor, for that matter, was I positively thrilled to see him.

He said, "Dee Dee told me you were asking about the storeroom. Looking for anything in particular?"

"Just snooping around," I said.

"How'd you get in?"

"The door was open," I said.

"Sure, and the tape was there over the lock, right?" Neville wasn't buying my story.

"I was trying to find out if Dana was being considered for a Network Liaison job."

"Why? Do you want it?"

"No, I don't want it. I was just wondering about Dana."

Still keeping the gun unwaveringly on me, Neville looked at the file in my hand.

"Lake, Neville," he said, reading the tab. "Did you get that confused with Salinger, Dana?"

"If you'd just put down the armament, maybe we could talk about this."

"Roger got himself killed," he said. "How do I know you didn't do it?"

"The police think that Samantha—"

He gave a short laugh. "Saying that the police think anything is a contradiction in terms. What were you doing looking in my file?"

I took a deep breath. "I know that Roger was about to fire you."

"So?"

"So maybe you killed him."

He waved the gun wildly. "You don't know what you're talking about!"

How I wished I had done some research on the Internet about How to Disarm a Possibly Deranged Assistant Executive Director. Or even How to Get Your Pepper Spray When It's in Your Bag Across the Room. One thing was for certain. The way he was wigwagging that gun around, it could go off any minute and take me or him with it.

Him preferably.

He put out his hand. "Give me my file."

So—I gave it to him.

I took the file and chopped down on his gun hand. The gun clattered to the floor. I picked it up while he was still rubbing his hand.

Immediately he turned contrite. "I wasn't really going to shoot you. I heard some noises in here and I thought it was an intruder."

"I'm supposed to believe that?"

I looked at the gun. The safety was on.

"There are no bullets in it either," he said. "Look, it's true that Roger would have fired me, but I didn't kill him. I was quitting anyway. I've already put out a few feelers. I've even been out on a few interviews."

"You were being considered for Roger's job," I said, feeling it unnecessary for me to add that he could damn well forget about that now.

"I don't want Roger's job. I hope you hire Noelle, because

she has the job I really want. My kids and my ex live in New York, and I'd like to be close to them."

"I see. . . ."

At least I thought I saw. If Neville was telling the truth, then Noelle's insinuations were way off base. But how did I know he was telling the truth? At least Noelle hadn't held a gun on me.

I put the file back, put the gun in the drawer, and locked it.

"Now supposing we just leave," I said.

"Oh by the way, Maggie, I spoke to Wendy and told her that far as I was concerned, her job was safe."

"I'm sure she was grateful."

"So grateful, in fact, that she gave me two weeks notice. She announced that she's leaving. She's had a better job offer."

I winced. Once again, a good deed had backfired. I swear I don't know how the Boy Scouts do it.

"And as for Dana," Neville said, "she wasn't going to get that position."

"Network Liaison?"

"Roger was not going to recommend her for it."

"How do you know?"

"Because he told me. If I had given you the chance to poke around those files some more, you'd have seen his memo."

I shrugged. "You can't blame a girl for trying."

"You know something?" he said. "You're pathetic as an investigator."

"Bite me," said Mercedes.

I thought about it on the way home. Not, of course, that I was pathetic as an investigator. There were times I had told myself the same thing. But Dana could now be tagged with two solid reasons for having killed Roger, no matter how forcefully she denied them. One, she was the proverbial woman scorned, and two, he had not recommended her for the Network Liaison job. I could settle for either motive, along with possibly none of the above. But had she killed Samantha also?

One thing I knew for certain. Joe wasn't going to buy any of it.

There was good news waiting for me on the Internet. Booksearch had located a copy of *L'Homme Qui Rit*. The price was a little over three hundred dollars. Was that satisfactory? No, it wasn't. It was a shock to my credit card balance, but I was in this too deep now to climb out. I replied with my card number authorization and told them to send it.

For someone who was making progress on several different fronts, why was I still feeling so fogged in? Maybe it wasn't all mental. Maybe it was part physical. It was time I checked my blood.

I was right. My insulin level was low. Lower than usual. I checked it again to be sure. The same reading. I injected the indicated amount and went back to my laptop to work on my article.

I was still there when Jack Nicholson came in from my bedroom and put his arms around me and kissed the nape of my neck. I had a meltdown. It was all the bliss I thought it would be.

"Jack, what were you doing in my bedroom?"

"You ought to know, babe. You were there."

"I was?"

I turned around to see him, but he was moving away, drifting towards the front door. I tried to get up from the computer, but my feet were leaden, they wouldn't move.

"Jack, no! Don't leave me . . . don't go . . . please don't go. . . .

41

"Come back," I said. "Please come back. . . ."

I seemed to be swimming up from levels of black-on-black darkness into pale light. I opened my eyes. I was no longer at the computer. I was in some kind of bed. And it wasn't Jack Nicholson in the room there with me. It was Lionel. Sitting in a wheelchair.

"I'm not going anywhere," he said. "They made me use this baby buggy so I wouldn't break my other leg." He reached out for my hand. "I'm right here, Maggie."

Where? Where was here? I looked around, trying to focus on something familiar. Nothing.

"You're in the hospital," Lionel said.

"What?" I tried to sit up.

"Lie still. You're going to be all right."

As compared to what? Only I didn't say it. My voice wasn't keeping up with my thoughts.

A woman in a white dress came into the room. If Lionel was telling me the truth and I was in the hospital, she must be a nurse. And she did all the nurse-like things. Stuck a thermometer in my mouth. Wrapped something tight around my arm. Scanned some kind of a line reading that was affixed to the wall.

"Welcome back." She patted my hand and went out again.

"Lionel, what happened?"

"Nothing. Well, maybe something. Just a little something. You overdosed." He got up from the wheelchair and took up his crutches.

"Don't be an idiot! I don't do drugs."

"Insulin, darling."

There was a sudden clamor of voices outside, and then U.G. came bursting in and rushed over to wrap me in a big hug.

"Are you okay, sweetheart?"

"She's fine," Lionel said.

"Was I talking to you?" U.G. said.

"I'm fine, really, Dad. What day is it?"

"It's Wednesday," U.G. said.

"You've been on an out-of-town trip for a little while," Lionel said.

I tried to make sense of that. "Then—Jack Nicholson wasn't real?"

"Oh, he's real, all right," Lionel said. "But we can both dream, can't we?"

"Forgive me, baby," said U.G. "I would have been here sooner, but the Jag is in the shop and I couldn't get a ride."

"Not even a loaner?" Lionel said.

U.G. glared at him. "Yes, but it took me a while. The people who would lend me a car don't drive, and the ones who do drive wouldn't lend me a car."

Joe appeared in the doorway. "Hey, you're awake."

"She's fine," Lionel said.

"Why do you keep butting in?" U.G. said. "He wasn't talking to you."

Joe came in, stood by the bed, and gave me a light kiss on the cheek. U.G. practically beamed.

"Are you up to telling me about it?" Joe said.

I said, "I can't. Lionel tells me I was out of it."

Joe nodded. "A good thing he found you in time."

"Yeah," said U.G. "We've got to give Twinkletoes credit for that."

"It was more than a good thing, it was a fucking miracle," Lionel said. "Ordinarily I would be much later coming home from work, but Troy picked me up early."

I turned my head towards him and managed a weak smile. "Thanks, Lionel. I owe you."

"It might turn out that I've already been paid back. Depends on if he calls me or not."

"Who—"

"The paramedic. The tall blond one with the great buns, remember? Oh, why am I asking you." He made his way to the door. "Listen, I'm going downstairs for some coffee. Joe?"

"No, thanks."

"Ugh?"

"Lionel, I told you," I said.

"Excuuuuse me! Ulysses, some coffee?"

"Much as I'd love to join you, Rumpelstiltskin, I have to get the car back."

U.G. came over to me, gave me a big kiss, shook hands with Joe, said, "Good to see you, big guy," and left.

Joe waited for Lionel to leave, then took a chair, turned it back to front, and straddled it.

"Okay, now talk."

"There's nothing to talk about. Lionel says I overdosed. It could have been an accident, but I don't see how. I'm always very careful."

"Uh-huh."

"What do you mean uh-huh?"

"Just that. You're always very careful. Only this time you weren't."

And then it hit me. "You think I tried to kill myself?"

It sounded so absurd, so unworthy an accusation, that I knew he would deny it forcefully.

What he said was, "Not on purpose, of course."

"No!" I said. "No!"

"You've been under a great deal of stress. It could happen."

"But it didn't."

"All I'm saying is, it was a subconscious attempt. Psychiatrists will tell you that a lot of people who have accidents have a subliminal desire to inflict harm on themselves."

"You're full of shit," I said, just as the nurse came into the room.

"Not me. It's the bedpans I lug around," she said.

She made a big show of plumping my pillow and refilling my water glass.

"Need anything else?"

"Yes, but my HMO doesn't offer it."

She left.

I said, "Joe, someone tried to kill me."

"It's a strong possibility," he said, "and if that's the case, you're out of it. No more investigating. No articles, no nothing!"

I passed on that. I was too tired to argue.

Joe left, Lionel stayed away for a while, and I was free to lie back and try to orchestrate my discordant thoughts. The overdose was no accident. I would have to check my testing kit, and if the reading was incorrect, that could only mean one thing.

Someone had monkeyed around with the testing strips. Someone had tried to kill me.

42

By the afternoon of the next day, I was allowed more visitors, even though the roster of people and their timetable of arrivals and departures were kind of a blur. I know that Henrik stopped in, all too briefly, in between courtroom appearances, and Bark and Althea . . . or did Bark come by himself, and again later with Althea on their way to a dinner date? Even Karen came to see me, surprisingly, and Neville, even more surprisingly. Dee Dee tagged along with him, bearing a huge plant and well wishes from the Union staff. There was a bouquet of flowers from Fowler. Probably charged them to the movie for which I hadn't even finished the script.

I have a still-foggy notion that Dana dropped by, too, most likely hoping that the rumors of my survival had been grossly exaggerated.

Lionel, of course, was a steady presence, running in and out . . . well, not exactly running, since he was on crutches, but he and Troy were there more often than the doctor or nurse. U.G. was there until late in the afternoon, when he finally, and reluctantly, took off for home. But of course he had to get in a parting shot when he shook hands with Lionel.

"Take good care of her, Nurse Nancy," he said.

The only one who didn't come back to see me was Joe. The nurse did tell me there was a detective hanging around the hallway, but she didn't ask for a name and she couldn't say what he looked like. I guess, to nurses, no one was identifiable above the waist.

I remember that at one point, after he had left, Henrik called me from the courthouse.

"Good news. I found out the name of that Parole Officer," he told me.

Why was that good news? What Parole Officer? My memory was still mushy. And then I remembered.

"Roger's brother," I said. "How can I find him?"

I gestured for something to write on, and someone handed me a pen and a piece of paper.

"Okay," I said to Henrik.

"His name is Abel Stinson, and here is his number." Henrik gave it to me and I jotted it down.

"I'm glad you're in the hospital," Henrik said.

"You're glad?"

"Yeah. I don't have to worry about you running around stumbling over dead bodies."

"One dead body and all of a sudden I'm Jessica Fletcher?"

"Take care. Remember I love you."

Well, he hadn't ever mentioned that before. It was something I'd have to sort out later. Maybe after everyone had left. But once I was alone, and the nurse had come and gone with my afternoon snack on a bed tray, my thoughts focused on Roger's brother. As soon as I was out of the hospital, I would try to track him down. In fact, I could start right now by calling his Parole Officer's number.

I consulted the piece of paper and dialed on the bedside phone. There was only a taped "please leave a message" message. I said I would call back, and didn't leave my phone number.

It could have been the result of my medication, but my heart lifted for the first time in many days. Things were starting to break open. It seemed to me that investigations always follow a certain rhythm, at least mine do. There is a lot of chaos as the facts get known and categorized. The characters shift, like elusive shadows. I get the feeling that I'll never work it out. Then, there comes a moment when, suddenly, there is a light at the end of the tunnel.

Okay, I know. Probably an oncoming train. But more usually than not, it turns out that the clues are arranging and rearranging themselves into their logical places in the whole scheme of things.

Someone felt threatened enough to try to kill me. That was scary. Scary as hell. But it was gratifying to know that I was getting close.

Towards evening, a late shift of visitors returned, maybe the same ones again, maybe some new faces, a few of the Board members, I think. Henrik was there, straight from court.

It had been a wearisome day and I wasn't up to much talking, and, fortunately, Lionel was there to take over the chore. He was in a positively cheerful mood. The police had apprehended the hit-and-run driver, and an insurance settlement was in the offing. He also had welcome news for me.

"A package arrived from Booksearch," he said. "Must be that French book you ordered, *L'Homme Qui Rit*."

I didn't realize others had been listening until Henrik said, "Those people are good. They can find law books that have been out of print for decades."

Bark said, "That research you told me you were doing, Maggie, must have paid off."

"Maybe now you won't have to do so much undercover work." That was Neville of course.

"Tell me," said Dana.

"We all know how much pressure you've been under."

Who was that? I'm still not sure. But it was the closest anyone came to referring to my overdose. My overdose . . . It had now taken its place in the inventory of my personal belongings alongside my diabetes.

I closed my eyes and became immersed in their voices.

"Is that book in French?"

"Can she read French?"

"Doesn't matter. She can go to a French Literature chat room and get on their bulletin board."

"Sure. And get hundreds of replies from all over the country."

"Is this Internet talk? That stuff mystifies me."

"You're way behind the times. All Maggie has to do is request someone in her area."

I opened my eyes. "Internet talk," I said in a sleepy echo.

The nurse came in to check whatever they check, and the voices and their owners went away.

They discharged me the next day. Troy picked me up, and Lionel sat beside me in the back, firing directives.

"Don't go so fast!"

"Watch out for that speed bump!"

"Can't you find a street with a few less potholes?"

He treated me as though I were a piece of rare porcelain. And I loved it.

"Troy has to get me back to the shop," Lionel announced, once I was ensconced on the sofa with a blanket, a cup of hot tea, and three pieces of zwieback. Zwieback, would you believe it!

"Now you stay put," he said. "I'll be checking up on you and you can call me if you need me."

I said, "Lionel, I love you."

"I know. So behave."

They left, and I briefly behaved. But then I had to know. I had to satisfy myself. I went into the bathroom and retrieved my kit and did a blood sugar check. Before I was allowed to leave the hospital, the nurse had done a reading, and I knew what it last was. The reading now would tell me if my current glucose level was approximately close.

There was no approximate about it. The reading was way off.

If it were to be believed, I would need a heavy dose of insulin this time. And I knew for sure I didn't.

43

I called Joe. He wasn't there and I left a message for him, saying it was urgent.

Lionel had left my book package on one of the living room chairs. It was heavily sealed, and I had to get a knife from the kitchen to cut through the tape. Then there it was. *L'Homme Qui Rit* by Alain Dubert. It was a slim volume, much too slim for the money I paid for it. It probably cost about two dollars a page.

I sat down and opened it. It was all in French. Painstakingly I went through it, trying to see if I could decipher even a few words. But it was hopeless. My high school French had deserted me. Nothing. Not one noun, feminine or masculine, not one verb, regular or irregular, translated itself to my mind.

After a while I gave up, put the book aside, and was heading for the kitchen to replace the knife when there was a knock on the door. I took a detour and opened it and Joe was there.

He said, "What's so urgent?"

I said, "Hi. I thought you'd call."

"How come you opened the door without asking who it was?"

"I recognized the knock. I knew it was you."

"No, you didn't. You just said you were expecting me to call."

"The only thing I ever expect of you is to do the unexpected."

"Obviously you're still delirious," he said, and he came in. "And what are you doing with that knife in your hand?"

I looked at it blankly. "It was for just in case it wasn't you."

He took it from me.

"You're not going to need that. You're not getting involved in this case anymore. No way. No how. No nothing."

He could be so exasperating! "Could we just go back to where you asked me why I called you?"

"Okay," he said, "tell me."

As best as I could explain to a layperson, no pun intended, I told him about the blood glucose testing kit and gave him a brief lesson on how it worked.

"It was definitely no accident, Joe. Someone must have come in the house and put in a different strip code."

He had been listening very intently.

"I know," he said. "That's one reason I'm here, to pick up your testing kit and have the lab guys look it over."

"I thought it was because I called you."

"That's the other reason."

"Well, at least we know it wasn't Samantha. She didn't come back from the dead to tamper with my fucking machine!"

"That would mean," he said, "one, that someone tried to kill you."

"That's what I've been trying to tell you. I was getting too close to the real killer."

"And two, that you corrupted whatever prints were on the kit and got your damn fingerprints all over it again!"

I wasn't to be browbeaten this time. "Like the person who did it didn't wear gloves?"

For the next half hour or so I filled him in on everything I had learned, well, almost everything, complete with all my doubts and suspicions. I held back on the French book and on Roger's brother. Right now they were nothing but X factors in the case.

"The only thing is," he said, "if someone came into your condo, how did they get in?"

"I don't know. You're the detective. Did you spot anyone hanging around the premises?"

"Huh?"

"When you were following me."

He didn't even have the balls to look guilty.

"Even if we were following you," he said, "and I'm not saying we were, no matter what Martin may have told you, we didn't have a stakeout on your home."

He went to the front door. I followed and saw that he was looking closely at the locks.

"Well?"

"No sign of a break-in."

"That doesn't mean anything. The murderer could have known how to pick a lock. That's what I did."

"When did you do that?"

"Uh-oh," said Mercedes.

"Research for my screenplay," I said.

"Tell you what, Maggie. I'll make a deal with you."

"Another one? I don't like it already. But you could start by giving me back my knife."

He did. "The deal is you have to promise me something."

"What?"

"Now that your investigation seems to be pushing someone's buttons, you'll quit. No more research, no more investigation. Cease and desist."

"My articles aren't finished."

"Wrong. They're finished. Promise me, Maggie."

So I promised him. What the hell, it didn't cost me anything. "Okay," I said, "but what do I get out of the deal?"

"I won't put a twenty-four/seven watch on you to make sure you keep your promise."

"I thought you didn't have the manpower."

"Try me."

I gave him my testing kit, after assuring him I had another

one to use in the meantime, one that was still in pristine shrink-wrapped condition.

Then I locked the door after him, put the knife back in the kitchen, and sat down at my laptop computer. Now what? I didn't feel energetic enough to tackle my screenplay. *L'Homme Qui Rit* was a dead end because it was in French. The Laughing Man was laughing at me.

It was then that something emerged from the dim recesses of my memory. The voices in the hospital room. Something about a French Literature chat room. On the Internet, I Googled French Translators. Selecting one site that seemed general enough for my purposes, I went on its bulletin board and requested someone who could translate the book for me.

The next morning, I managed to abstain from looking at the bulletin board until after I had satisfied Lionel that yes, I was feeling fine and no, he didn't have to stay home with me to play nurse. Or guardian. As soon as Troy picked him up and they left for the shop, I checked the bulletin board and saw that a flood of responses had come in from all over the world. I thought about it and amended my request to cover my local area.

I called Henrik. He called back within ten minutes. "What's happening, Maggie?"

"Henrik. I think you and I have lots to say to each other . . . and maybe do to each other?"

There was a heavy pause at the other end. I plunged ahead. "But, right now, I need a favor."

"I'm not doing you any favor that might put you in danger." More and more he sounded like Joe. But that comment would never again escape my lips.

"It's just a phone call."

"What's the favor?"

"You have clients on parole, don't you?"

"I don't like where this is going."

"Between you and your partners, maybe one of your clients has the same Parole Officer as Richard Urban and maybe your client would do you a favor and talk to the P.O. for me."

After an overlong silence, Henrik said, "Here's what I will do. You tell me what you want to know and I'll see if I can get you the information you need."

"First of all I need to know where Urban is now, and—"

"Hold it. That would mean you'd go looking for him and that's not a smart thing to do. On second thought, scratch what I said before. You'll have to trust that I know how to ask questions and get answers probably better than you."

"Then you're doing my work for me."

"It's take it or leave it, Maggie."

"I suppose now you'll want a credit in *Vanity Fair,* but okay."

"I'll call you when I get something helpful. Bye."

I was holding a dead phone.

To atone for past sins, while I was waiting for his return call, I went back to work on my screenplay, but first I wanted to read over what I had already done and fix a few typos. I began to review my script.

Within the hour, Henrik called back. He told me that the P.O. hadn't seen Richard Urban for five years. That he couldn't release any information about the reasons for Urban being jailed. As far as he knew, Urban had been a model prisoner and was never in trouble. And that was about it.

After thanking Henrik, I dug out the P.O.'s number and called him.

I got the message machine, and said, "I'm calling for Henrik Hudson and—"

Before I finished the message, the phone was picked up.

"This is Abel Stinson. What can I do for you?"

"Mr. Stinson, I'm Mr. Hudson's assistant. You just spoke to him."

"Yes."

"Mr. Hudson feels so foolish, but he wrote down the address of a Mr. Richard Urban, and finds he's mislaid it. May I have that address again so I can give it to him?"

I was gambling that Henrik would have asked that question and gotten an answer, even though he hadn't divulged it to me.

"Yes, here's his last known address, but as I told Mr. Hudson, the address was from five years ago and could be no good by now."

I jotted it down and hung up. Mission accomplished.

I dressed hurriedly, pepper spray in my bag, Yahooed for a map and driving directions, and took off. I was hoping to get there and back before Lionel or U.G. checked up on me again. As I headed up the freeway on-ramp, I noticed there was smoke coming out of my tailpipe. I thought I remembered that white smoke was good and black smoke was bad. Or was that for a new Pope? If my RAV were the Vatican, there'd be a new driver, because this smoke was white.

But it was bad, too, because it was while I was checking the smoke in my rearview mirror that I noticed a car a few cars back following my every move. It switched lanes when I did, and slowed down when I did. I couldn't see the driver clearly but I didn't need to. The car looked familiar, the same kind of plain-Jane car Martin had used. Chances were Joe had him following me again.

Looking at the driving directions, I turned onto a street that was clearly a commercial area, although small and run-down.

Martin followed me around the corner, and idled there, evidently waiting to see where I was going. I pulled to the curb near where the address I was trying to find should be located, and parked in front of a small cinder-block building with the word PLASTICS in large letters on a sign over the door. The door was gated and shut.

A man was loading sheets of something onto a flatbed truck in the driveway. He was staring at me but trying not to be obvious about it.

Next to the Plastics building was a small, old house with peeling yellow paint, cardboard windows, and no address numbers. There was a fallen chain-link fence enclosing a dirt yard. My guess was that the owner didn't have a green thumb. What he or she did have was a sign nailed to the front door.

I went up the steps, walking gingerly along the side of the steps, because the wood was rotten and they looked like they could fall in any minute. The sign read: DANGER!! NO ENTRY!!

"Hey, lady! Don't go in there!"

I turned. The truck driver in the Plastics driveway was waving at me.

I shouted back, "I'm looking for 2306."

"You're standing on it."

I was afraid of that. "Is anybody living here?"

"You mean, besides the rats? Lady, all kinds of creatures could be living in there. It's scheduled for demolition."

He got into the truck, closed the door, and leaned out the window. "I'd get out of here if I were you. It can get ugly real fast in this neighborhood."

He pulled out, giving a honk on his horn as he drove past me.

I looked at the door and then I looked down the street. Martin's car was still at the end of the block. I couldn't see him but I knew he was there. I gave the front door a shove and it opened partway. Staring at the empty street again, I realized that with Martin out there, my back was covered. No harm in looking around, just in case Richard Urban was still on the premises.

I squeezed through the door into a dark, dank hall with an overpowering smell. It was the smell of mildew, and mold, and alcohol and urine, very heavy on the urine.

"Anybody here?" I called.

Scurrying, rustling sounds answered me. Probably the rats. Maybe this wasn't such a terrific idea after all. There was a door leading to a room off the hall, and I decided to try it and then leave. In the room, the stench was even worse and

I had to breathe through my mouth to keep from gagging. I turned to go and tripped over a pile of rags.

"What the fuck?" a gravelly voice said. The pile moved and stood, revealing himself to be a red-eyed, bony derelict who had evidently been living in the condemned building.

"Sorry. I'm so sorry. I'm looking for someone who used to live here." I discovered you couldn't breathe through your mouth and talk at the same time, so I had to endure the disgusting reek. "I can see he doesn't live here now."

I started to back away from him, and let out a small scream as I felt something behind me. I swiveled. There were two more homeless vagrants standing there.

Rag Pile said, "Hey, sweetheart, come on over here." He started to stumble towards me and I saw that his torn pants were open and his penis was out.

Swell.

I don't know if he had a broken zipper, or no zipper, or I interrupted him when he was playing solitaire, and I didn't care. I backed up farther into the other two guys. Immediately, one of them grabbed my arm and snatched my bag.

Miserably, I remembered the fortune cookie message from my Dim Sum lunch with Henrik. "You will be given the chance to take part in an exciting adventure." Why couldn't I have gotten one that said, "You will lead a long and happy life"?

"I'm not alone here, you know," I said loudly. "There's a cop right outside." I yelled, "Martin!"

"You don't need no cop," said the guy with my bag. When he opened his mouth, his breath was so rank, I almost threw up on the spot.

"Martin!" I yelled again. "He's right here," I said, "so I'll be going now."

Fetid Mouth opened my bag to look inside, and while he was fumbling around in it, I saw my one and only chance. I gave him a swift kick in the nuts and grabbed my bag back. Reaching inside, I took out the pepper spray.

Fetid Mouth lay writhing on the ground, moaning. I was

admiring my handiwork when Rag Pile and the other guy came at me. I helped them both to a dose of pepper spray.

They howled and dropped to the ground, eyes streaming with tears.

"Martin! Get your ass in here!"

Fetid Mouth staggered to his feet. I ran to the front door with him in frenzied pursuit. Reaching it, I prayed I could get through the narrow opening again when, suddenly, the door was pushed all the way open and Royal Underhill burst in.

"Okay, what's going on!"

Huh? Royal Underhill? What was he doing here? I was speechless.

"Nothin', Officer," said Fetid Mouth. "We don't mean no trouble. We was just welcomin' the pretty lady to our home sweet home. And she took what you might call umbrage."

Royal grabbed hold of my arm and pulled me out the door. "Let's get out of here. These guys don't seem too rational to me."

We stumbled down the steps together, with him still clutching my arm, and headed for my car.

"Royal, I don't understand. What in hell are you doing here?"

"For heaven's sake, Maggie! Move!"

He pulled me to the curb and over to the Plastics building, where I leaned against my car, taking in great gulps of smoggy air, clearing the stench from my nose and mouth. Finally, when I'd breathed in enough smog to put a normal person into Cedars, I looked around for Martin. But there was no Martin.

I turned to Royal. "Where's Martin?"

"Who's Martin?"

"He's a detective, a friend of mine. He followed me here. You can see his car down at the end of the street."

He followed my gaze. "That's my car."

I shook my head to clear it. "You're the one who followed me here?"

Royal nodded.

"You mean my back wasn't covered? I was alone in that house?"

"Seems to me you did pretty good on your own."

He moved around me to reach over to my windshield.

What was he doing? I still didn't get it. I didn't get it until I saw the piece of paper in his hand.

"Royal, give me that."

"It's nothing, just a flyer, forget it."

"Royal, hand it over!"

He was looking sheepish. I put my hand out and he gave it to me.

I didn't even need to read it. I could see the type was the same, the same capital letters forming a single sentence:

KEEP YOUR NOSE OUT OF THIS!

Royal started to walk towards his car.

"Hold it! You're not going anywhere."

I got right in his face and waved the paper in front of him.

"I don't believe it. You're the one who's been threatening me? Maybe I'd have been better off with those other perverts."

"I'm sorry, Maggie, I really am," he said.

"Sorry's just not good enough. Royal, what's going on?"

"I'll explain everything, Maggie, but not here. It's not safe."

The big question was whether I was safe with him anywhere. But I desperately needed to talk to him. I remembered passing a McDonald's a few blocks back.

"We'll go to McDonald's and get some coffee."

"Good. I'll follow you."

"No," I said. "This time I'll follow you."

In McDonald's we settled into a booth with coffee and just sat. I stared at him. He didn't look like a killer, with his bow tie and glasses. But I'd been wrong before. Anyway, the restaurant was crowded, so I wasn't really afraid.

Royal seemed to be having trouble getting started, so after a while I prompted him.

"Well? Are you going to tell me why you killed Roger and Samantha?"

I was thinking I could frame the title for my lead article in *Vanity Fair:* "Killer comes McClean in McDonald's."

"It wasn't me, Maggie. I didn't kill them."

"Then why were you trying to stop me from finding out who did it?"

He stared into his cup as though the answer were there.

"Why?" I said again.

"I didn't want you to find me. I didn't want anyone to find me."

The balls were going *ca-ching, ca-ching, ca-ching* and falling into place.

"Royal Underhill. R.U. You changed your name," I said. "You're Richard Urban, Roger's brother."

He nodded. "That's my real name, the name I was born and grew up with. I changed it a few years ago."

Whoa. I sure hadn't seen this coming.

"Roger is—was younger than me," he said. "He was the smart one. He was the good-looking one. I wasn't exactly a model kid. I wasn't a brilliant student, except I did like math. But I was a great athlete. Roger couldn't compete with me in that arena."

I said, "Royal, this is interesting and probably therapeutic for you, but what's it got to do—"

He cut me off. "Let me tell it my way, and you'll see." He stirred his coffee. "I was always getting into trouble, but it was Roger leading the way."

I gave him a skeptical look.

"For example, one day Roger suggested that we steal some beer from the 7–Eleven. He said, 'You go down the aisle and grab some beer. I'll keep the cashier busy.' Well, I did what Roger told me and heisted a few bottles. When I turned to leave I could see Roger wasn't even in the store. The cashier must have signaled the manager, and there he was, coming at me brandishing a rifle. Next thing I knew . . . Juvey!"

I couldn't believe this pathetic rationalization. "Are you saying Roger led you into a life of crime? What are you? A guy with oatmeal for brains?"

Royal reached across the table and gripped my wrist. "Hear me out. Of course he didn't lead me into crime. I found that life for myself. I'm only saying that Roger wasn't such a squeaky-clean guy when he was young. He did plenty. Only it was always me that got caught. He had a great talent for keeping his skirts clean. Up to the very end."

Probably there wasn't any intentional humor to that remark about "skirts," but I'd like to think so. I shook my wrist free of his grasp.

He drank the last of his coffee. "When I was inside, I took classes and discovered statistics. When I got out, I was an ex-con, and no one would give me a job, not one using stats. Eventually I called Roger at the Union, and he gave me a staff job on one condition."

"That you not tell anyone you were his brother. That's why you changed your name. Right?"

"Right. He was going places in this town, that's a quote, and he didn't want me throwing up a roadblock. A brother who was an ex-con. So I took the job and the condition. It wasn't hard for me. I didn't want anyone knowing he was my brother, either, he was such a prick."

We got up and started to walk out, Royal thinking his thoughts, me trying to collate all the facts.

"So the police . . . ?"

"I never told the cops. They'd have made me their ideal suspect. An ex-con. A jealous brother. They wouldn't look any further, and the real killer would get away with it."

"And the notes?"

"I knew something about you. I knew you were a good investigator, and if you kept at it, you'd find out about me. So I tried to stop you by scaring you off. But you don't scare so easy."

"You tried to kill me!"

"Are you crazy? What do you mean, tried to kill you? How? When?"

"My blood glucose tester. You changed it so I would take an overdose of insulin." I wasn't so sure I believed that, but I had to try it on for size.

Royal looked astonished. "What are you talking about? Someone did that?" He paused and then nodded. "Oh, I see. That's why you were in the hospital."

"Yes."

"I cop to the notes, Maggie, and that's it."

"And to following me."

"I followed you out to my aunt's, because I was afraid she would give you one hint too many. But I didn't start out to follow you today. You know the Staples store two blocks from where you live?"

I glanced at him accusingly, and he had the grace to look shamefaced.

"Yeah, I know where you live. I left the second note there. Anyway, I was on my way to buy something at Staples today when I saw you come out of your garage and head for the freeway. I followed you and then I saw you were headed for East L.A., and I figured you had discovered my old address. That made me determined to scare you off. You were getting too close. You know the rest."

I knew the rest. What I didn't know was whether I believed him.

44

I came back into the house just as the phone was ringing. I sprinted for it.

"Lionel, I've been home all day."

"This isn't Lionel, and, no, you haven't."

Joe. He, too, was checking up on me.

"I was probably in the bathroom."

"I'm holding you to your promise, Maggie."

"Do you guys still intend to follow me?"

"Why, should we?"

"I'm really busy," I said. "Good-bye."

I went in the kitchen and took a slice of turkey to munch on. The phone rang again. I grabbed it.

"Joe, you don't have to keep calling me! Cut it out!"

There was a foreboding silence. I said, "Isn't this Joe?"

"It's Henrik. Just wanted to make sure you were okay."

I gulped. "I'm fine. Honestly. How's your trial going?"

We chatted for a few minutes, all the while I was feeling miserable about having blown it with him. He was a wonderful man. Every time I asked a favor of him, he came through for me. He didn't deserve the added complication of Joe in our relationship.

"Listen," I said, "about having thought you were Joe . . ."

"You don't have to explain."

"I want to. You know that Joe and I were once very close. You also know that it ended years ago."

"I don't need or want the recap, Mag."

"Joe is also very much a cop."

"I repeat, I don't need—"

"I know you don't need, Henrik. But I need to explain to you."

I chose my words with care.

"The combination of past closeness, his job, and my work for *Vanity Fair* has proved to be a combustible mixture. I'm having trouble dealing with it, and I hope you don't push me into resolving anything now—it's way too premature."

"The best defense is a great offense," said Mercedes.

"I'm not pushing, Maggie. I'm reserving my options."

We left it at that. I took off my shoes and flopped onto the couch.

The phone rang again.

"Who is it this time!"

"Is that any way to talk to your father? How come you haven't called me back? I left three messages."

I noticed the message light was blinking and there was a 3 in the little window.

"I was in the bathroom. And I'm fine, truly. Listen, Dad. I solved the mystery of those threatening notes."

"Who were they from?"

Briefly, I gave him the salient facts.

"That's a real compliment to your detective work. Nice going, Sherlock."

"Now you can stop worrying about me."

"I will, sweetheart, if you take care of yourself and keep in touch."

"Will do."

I sat down at my laptop and checked the bulletin board again. This time I found several responses, three of which were most interesting:

**Graduate French student. Fluent in the language.
North County, San Diego. Resume on request. Contact
Rrockingham@studynet.com.**

San Diego wasn't exactly geographically desirable, but it
could work.

**Retired CSUN Professor. Specialist in 19th-century
French novels. Available immediately to translate.
Reside in Northridge. Contact *Olddog34@msn.com*.**

Now *that* sounded promising.

**Former UN translator. Everything from books to
poetry to French postcards. Can start the 10th of next
month. Contact *Multilang@earthlink.net*.**

Well, Multilang had a sense of humor but it couldn't wait
until the tenth of next month. Not when Olddog was so ac-
cessible. Let's try Olddog.

**Thanks for your reply. When can we meet to discuss
the job? *Wargod@aol.com***

I sprawled on the couch, going over the entries in my
notebook. They didn't give any more illumination than they
had when I wrote them down. Maybe I should call the Parole
Officer and check out the parts of Royal's story that were
checkable.
I dialed the number but hung up before it rang a second
time. I wasn't sure yet about Royal, but I didn't think I
wanted to raise any possibly unfounded suspicions with his
former P.O.
I sat down with my notebook again. Okay, threatening
notes were no longer a mystery, but I couldn't write an article
about that. Somebody had murdered Roger. Somebody had
killed Samantha and made it look like a suicide. And somebody had sure tried to kill me and had come damn close.

But who?

Lionel wasn't home yet, so I undressed, checked my blood with my new tester, and went to the computer.

Olddog34 had replied.

Sooner the better. Have other jobs waiting. Tomorrow evening good for me. How about you?
Olddog34@msn.com

Where? I live in West Hollywood. *Wargod@aol.com*

Someplace halfway. What about Valley Inn in Sherman Oaks? *Olddog34@msn.com*

No, someplace a little more open, I thought. A deli would be safe. And it should be my choice, not his.

Prefer the deli in shopping center on Beverly Glen and Mulholland. Good corned beef sandwiches.
Wargod@aol.com

Not that I had ever had one of them myself.

Olddog34 sent an okay and we agreed to get together the next evening at seven P.M.

When Lionel came in, I first had to hear all about the ballet he and Troy had gone to, and who was there, and I really must go with them next time, it would do wonders for my unsophisticated, unrefined tastes, and I would certainly enjoy, as they had, the too-tight tights, and then, finally, he got round to asking me how my evening went.

I said, "Lionel, you're not going to believe this."

I told him what had happened with Royal, including the homeless guys. His jaw dropped a little as I got into my story, and by the time I was finished, he was fully agape.

"I don't believe this," he said. "And you were supposed to be home resting. Tell me again what Royal said."

I repeated my story and he listened even more intently.

"So what do you think?"

"I think you never should have gone to that dreadful part of town all by yourself!"

"Lionel! Is Royal telling the truth?"

"A good question. And, anyway, what is truth?"

"Don't get existential on me."

"Okay," Lionel said. "It sounds very plausible that Royal did not commit those murders."

"Plausible, yes. Clear-cut, unambiguous, no."

"Listen to the words of Cicero. 'Nature has planted in our minds an insatiable longing to see the truth.' And in the words of Lionel, trust yourself."

"Trust myself? What's that supposed to mean?"

"It means you should go to bed, sleep on it, and in the morning all will be revealed."

In the morning, the only thing that was revealed was that I was still in the throes of doubt. I wanted to talk it over with someone knowledgeable. I wanted to talk to Joe. But I couldn't. Cops have a different view about suspects. They look for indications of guilt, not suggestions of innocence. And if Royal was telling the truth, I didn't want it to become public.

In the end I called Henrik and I met him at his favorite diner in Los Feliz.

"Henrik, how do you know when someone is telling you the truth?"

"I never have to wonder about that. My client is always telling the truth and the prosecution is always lying. In my work, that's how it goes."

He saw my crestfallen look and took pity.

"Okay, tell me about it, but make it quick. I have to go to the office for a few hours."

I made it quick. I figured that Henrik would keep the confidentiality of an attorney-client privilege, even though I wasn't exactly his client.

At the end of my account, as Henrik was paying the

check, he said, "You have to go with your gut reaction on this."

Inwardly I sighed. "You mean, trust myself."

"Exactly."

"Lionel says that means I should go to bed and sleep on it. I've already been to bed but I couldn't sleep. Unless you—"

The words were barely out of my mouth when I regretted them. But he had no reaction. I guess it would take a while for him to get Joe out of his system. Henrik and me both.

The question was, did I want Joe out of my system? Did I want to push him back where I once resolved to place him, in the rearview mirror of my life? I honestly didn't know.

At home I reviewed my small list of possible suspects, adding Royal's name, and then crossing it off. Right now I still liked Dana for the murders. She had the most going for her. She had an affair with Roger and he dumped her. She didn't get the job he promised her. I put a star next to her name and then put Royal back on the list.

Well, the meeting tonight would put an end to my speculation about the book. Or not. It could all be a waste of time. At any rate, I'd get to enjoy a nice salad.

That out of the way, I tried to work on my *Vanity Fair* piece. Lionel had been at the shop taking inventory, but by the time Troy drove him home that evening, I was no further along in my article than I was in my conjectures about suspects and whether Royal should be on or off the list.

"How goes it?" Lionel wanted to know.

"Fine. I met with Henrik and he gave me the same advice you did."

"Smart man."

"Well, at least I found somebody on the Internet who can translate the book."

"You didn't tell me that."

"Sorry. I guess I forgot."

"You never tell me anything." Then he relented. "I once met this real cute guy on the Internet, but it didn't work out. He wasn't into classical music and I wasn't into whips and chains."

I laughed, my mood brightening, and headed for my bedroom to change for the meeting.

Lionel called after me. "Troy and I are going to a movie tonight, so you'll have to make do with leftovers in the refrigerator."

In the bedroom I was kicking off my sneakers. "I ate the leftovers, but it's no problem! I won't be home anyway!"

Lionel came hobbling into the bedroom as I was pulling my sweatshirt over my head.

"You're going out? Where? To do what?"

"Why? Do you need a ride?"

"No. Troy's taking me. Answer me. Where are you going?"

"I'm meeting the guy who's doing the translation."

"Where? Where are you meeting him?"

"In a deli," I said. "Where it's perfectly safe." I pulled a sweater from a jumbled dresser drawer.

"A guy you only know from the Internet?"

"Well, he didn't say anything about being into whips and chains."

"Are you crazy! Somebody's after you! They already tried once. You want to give them a reprise? You're not going!"

"Of course I'm going," I said with as much authority as I could muster, standing there in my sweater and cotton panties.

"Then I'm going with you."

"With your broken leg? Lionel, hand me my jeans, and be reasonable. Go to the movie and stop worrying about me."

"Goddamn it, Maggie! You're not going and that's final!"

"That's final? Who the hell are you to tell me what I can and can't do!"

"I'm the guy who found you half dead and schlepped you to the hospital, that's the hell who!"

"So what do you want? A medal? A citation for valor? How about a Most Valuable Roommate Trophy?" I picked up my jeans myself and stepped into them. "Stop interfering."

Lionel turned and limped out. I zipped up, collected my bag and the book, and went out to the living room. He wasn't there.

"See you later," I said to the closed door of his room.

No answer.

"You blew it again," said Mercedes.

And I had.

What was wrong with me that I seem to be failing at all my emotional interactions? Joe, Henrik, and now, Lionel. If ever there was a misbegotten Midas, that was me. Everything I touched turned to shit.

45

It took me a little longer than it might have to get to the shopping center deli, due to the fact that Beverly Glen, south of the center, was closed to through traffic because of construction. I was heading north, but it was rush hour and the going was still slow and snail-like.

The heat was still holding, the air heavy and still, despite the early evening hour, and the tables outside were empty. I went inside, spied a table in the back corner, and beelined for it, beating out a biker chick with a skin-gallery of tattoos and purple-rimmed eyes. Pretending not to notice her glower, I scanned the menu, ordered a veggie salad, so much for their renowned corned beef, and a bottle of designer water, and settled in to wait for my Internet professor.

I kept one eye on the entrance as I ate, and that's how I caught sight of an exiting customer holding open the door for someone who was on crutches.

Someone who looked altogether too much like Lionel to be anyone other than Lionel!

He briefly surveyed the room, spotted me, and made his way over to the table. I couldn't believe it, and yet I might have known.

"Oh, hi," he said. "Fancy meeting me here."

"You sent me that e-mail?"

Carefully propping his crutches against the wall, he managed to deposit himself in the seat across from mine.

"I did not," he said. "But now that you mention it, it would have been a yummy idea."

"Then what are you doing here?" I answered my own question. "You followed me."

"Followed you indeed. How plebeian." He picked up a menu. "Let's see. What looks good here?"

"Not you. Go home."

"I can't. Troy dropped me off. I told him if he doesn't hear from me in the next twenty-four hours, he can have my no-stick crepe pan."

The waitress came over to the table with a setting for Lionel and waited there, pencil poised over her pad.

He said, "What's the specialty of the house?"

"Everything," she said.

"Good. I'll have an omelet."

"Cheese? Mushroom? Onion? Spinach? Spanish? Western?"

"Surprise me."

The waitress shrugged and went off with his menu.

"Lionel, the truth now, how did you find me?"

"It was a no-brainer. I opened up your e-mail."

"You couldn't have! How did you know my password?"

"You are such an amateur. I've known it ever since you moved in. Just in case you ever did something foolhardy like arrange to meet someone you only knew from the Internet. And now that I'm here"—he picked up a roll and buttered it—"there's no way you can get rid of me."

"Wrong," I said. "I can call for a taxi."

I picked up my cell phone and just at that moment it rang. I looked around to see if the sound of the William Tell Overture had disturbed anyone, and discovered that half the people in the deli were busy talking on their own cell phones.

Joe was yelling at me even before I could say hello.

"Why aren't you at home? Where are you?"

"In a deli near Beverly Glen."

"Get out of there, Maggie!"

"I can't. I'm meeting someone."

"Who?"

I didn't say anything.

"Okay, never mind who. Just get out of there. It's too dangerous."

I said, "It's perfectly safe. It's a very public place, lots of people around."

"I swear you must have a death wish. Maggie, you are in danger. Someone is trying to kill you. You told me that yourself."

"What did the lab results on my glucose tester show?"

"I'll tell you when you get home. Leave now, okay?"

"Joe, lighten up. You don't have to be so concerned." I glanced over at Lionel, who was busy buttering another roll. "And besides," I said, "Lionel is here to protect me."

Lionel smirked at me. "See? I come in handy."

I said into the phone, "Of course he'd be of use. . . . No, he is not a miserable, inadequate excuse for a—"

"Let me have that!"

Lionel reached across the table and grabbed the phone from me.

"See here, Joe, what makes you think—" He looked at the phone, then at me. "The line is dead."

"I know. Joe hung up right after I told him to lighten up."

He gave me back the phone and glared icicles at me, but he didn't dare say anything, not with the threat of the taxi still looming. Besides, the waitress had returned and was placing his omelet in front of him.

He poked at it with his fork. "It's chicken livers," he said. "I hate chicken livers."

The waitress said, "Surprise."

After that we ate in silence. Every time someone new entered the deli, my head bounced up like it was on a spring wire. By the time I had ordered and finished a bowl of sugar-free strawberry ice cream, all but demanding a notarized statement from the waitress that it was indeed sugar-free, and Lionel had devoured the last crumb of his Death by Chocolate flourless cake, it was almost eight, and I finally realized that I had been stood up.

"Might as well go," I said. "He's not coming."

Lionel said, "Good," and reached for the check. I let him.

He retrieved his crutches and paid at the cash register and we walked out into the still-oppressive heat.

Pulling out of the parking lot driveway, I coasted up to the red light at the corner and turned right.

Lionel said, "You're back to square one, aren't you?"

"I'll just go back to the bulletin board and try another one. I had several responses."

"Fuck that! It's just not safe," said Lionel. "Why don't you try UCLA. They teach French there. They must have a translator."

Before I could answer I saw the red cones ahead and re-membered the construction on the southbound lane.

Lionel said, "You can't go that way. They've got it blocked off."

"I *know* that."

More widening, more pipe work, more paving work, more inconvenience, more, more, more.

Lionel said, "We'll have to go by way of Mulholland."

"Thank you, Rand McNally."

I U-turned the RAV and headed back up to Mulholland, then made a right going east. The heat made the lights of the Valley sparkle like a million gems, more like four million. It was a huge, twinkling, beautiful stretch of stars, but I was in no mood to admire its resplendence.

However, after a minute or so, I began to feel a little more cheerful about the situation. Maybe I hadn't been stood up. Maybe something came up, and, after all, the pro-fessor had no way of reaching me to tell me why he couldn't make it. I was even a little glad that I had company on the ride home, although, of course, I would never tell Li-onel that.

He must have read my thoughts. "Isn't this pleasant," he said. "We so rarely go for a scenic drive like this."

It was at that moment that the cannon went off in the back of my car.

46

"What in hell was that?" said Lionel, taking the words right out of my suddenly dry mouth.

Automatically, my foot jammed on the brake, and the car began to swerve wildly, bolting to the cliff, towards the left. From somewhere deep in the recesses of my brain, I remembered you weren't supposed to brake in this kind of emergency, so I took my foot off the pedal, wrestled the wheel back to the right, and glanced in the rearview mirror.

What I saw in the mirror all but paralyzed me. There was a pair of headlights practically on top of my rear end.

"Lionel, someone's behind us! The sonofabitch is trying to run us off the road!"

Lionel said, "I'm calling Joe." He dug in my bag for the phone. "This whole thing was a booby trap, and you're the booby."

"Tell me something I don't know."

"Is Joe on your speed dial?"

"No. Why should he be?"

"Honestly, Maggie, this is not the time for—"

"Press one. It'll connect you with nine-one-one."

"Yes, this is an emergency," Lionel was saying into the

phone. "We're on Mulholland Drive and someone is trying to—"

The cannon went off again.

"Did you hear that? They're ramming us from behind! Hello! Hello!"

My mind had immediately gone into overdrive and again I wrenched the wheel to the right. As I somehow succeeded in getting the car headed away from the cliff, towards the road, and stepped on the gas, I saw that the lights behind me were once more pulling closer to ram me again.

"What'd they say?"

"I lost the connection. That's the trouble with these cell phones. I swear that's how the companies make their money. They make you call again and—"

"Lionel! Hang up and shut up!"

In front of me were the remains of a partially cleared stand of eucalyptus trees.

I said, "Just hold on!"

Clenching the wheel as tightly as I could, I deliberately slammed into one of the trees head-on.

The explosion of the driver's air bag, echoing in the car like a bomb blast, shut out all other sound.

My heart was beating so hard it felt as though it would burst in my chest. The air bag was smothering me. Frightened, adrenaline pumping, I unhooked my seat belt and struggled to get out from under the bag. The doors on the driver side had popped open. I rolled out and away from the car, gasping for breath.

When I came to a stop, something was under my back. It was the cylinder I'd taken from U.G. and forgotten to drop off at the Fire Department. As I stood up, I grabbed it. It was solid, and I gripped it tightly, knowing somehow that I might just need something in my hand.

The silence was thundering. Fear clutched my throat. I saw the car behind me pull off across the road and stop in a dark, bushy recess. The headlights went out.

It was only then that I remembered Lionel. He was not in

sight. He must still be inside the car, unable to move because of his broken leg.

I got on my feet and tore around to the other side of the car. I had to move fast because someone was getting out of that darkened car and coming across the road towards me.

Fortunately, the RAV was vintage enough not to have a passenger side air bag, and I could see Lionel still in his seat, struggling to get out of his seat belt. The door must have jammed against it. I tried to open it from the outside, straining to turn the handle, but it wouldn't budge.

It was then that the first bullet hit. It kicked up dirt from right behind the car. We were both sitting ducks, especially Lionel, who was immobilized.

Somehow I had to lead the killer away from Lionel.

"Wait here!" I tried to yell to him, only no sounds seemed to emerge from my throat. But I had no time to conjecture about that, because, just then, the second bullet hit the back tire. I took off.

Mulholland Drive was deserted. There were only the high fences and gates that protected the privacy of the privileged few who lived above it. I could sense more than see the person running after me as I raced to get away. Farther down the road and across from me I could see a driveway.

Crossing over would mean I would be out in the open, but I had to chance it. I veered off course to head for the driveway. Immediately, chips of asphalt were flying alongside of me. The killer was still shooting at me!

I was running out of gas, tiring rapidly and regretting all those mornings I had skipped my exercise, when I plunged into some kind of high wire fence. Stumbling alongside it for a few feet, I finally reached the driveway which I now saw led to a pair of big, wrought-iron gates.

Big, closed wrought-iron gates.

The sprinklers must have just turned off, because there were large puddles all along the ground and on the cement. The call box was embedded in a gatepost of the fence. Frantically I pushed all the buttons, screaming for help.

At least I think I screamed. I still couldn't hear myself. I couldn't hear anything. I wondered how many bullets were left in that gun when, all at once, searing pain flamed through my right shoulder. I fell to the ground in agony. The cylinder dropped from my hand and rolled away.

I tried screaming some more, with no better result. My whole right side was numb, completely deadened. I put my hand to my shoulder and it came away wet with blood. I struggled to get my feet under me so I could stand. Suddenly this hooded figure was on top of me, shoving me back down.

I couldn't get loose. We tumbled around on the driveway, rolling over and over together through puddles of water and cement ridges. I had never been in a knockdown, drag-out fight before, but I sure as hell was in one now. Every inch of me was being battered, and my right hand was useless.

At least I knew now that there were no more bullets, because surely the killer would have shot at me again by now. Small comfort. The blood loss was making me weaker by the minute. I had to get away, but what could I do?

The pain was excruciating, but I managed to reach up and grab on to a hunk of material. It was the hood shielding my assailant's face. I yanked as hard as I could and found myself staring up at . . .

Althea!!!

For a moment she was disconcerted, but only for a moment. She began to strike me some more when, all of a sudden, a bank of security lights turned on, illuminating the whole area in a blaze of brighter-than-day whiteness.

Althea raised her hand to shield her eyes from the blinding glare. This was my chance! I pushed her off me, willed myself up to my feet, and stumbled away. I knew I had to move fast, but I was too exhausted, too hurting. From over my shoulder, I could see her coming after me.

I looked around for a weapon, a stick, a stone, anything. And then I spotted the cylinder. I picked it up with my good hand, and, turning, I flung it at her. It fell to the ground in a large puddle of water at her feet.

Shit! I missed!

Suddenly, a wave of intense heat rose from the puddle where the cylinder had broken open. Heat so intense you could see it as it rose all around Althea. I was rooted to the spot, watching her fall to the ground and thrash about in torment.

I leaned back against the gates, my breath ragged, and my thoughts a jumble. Althea was on the ground, curled up in a fetal position with her face in the roiling puddle. I was still laboring to sort it all out when the gates behind me swung open and I collapsed to the ground. Then someone behind me lifted me to my feet and grinned that grin at me.

It was Jack Nicholson, with a golf club in his hands.

I knew I must be delirious again. I let go of all feeling and sank into welcoming darkness. . . .

47

I opened my eyes and attempted to focus. On a table alongside a window was a large floral arrangement, all yellow roses and baby's breath and lemon leaves. I stared at it while my vision cleared. A guy in a white coat came into view. He was writing something in a chart.

He looked down at me and smiled approvingly.

"You're back. Good."

Then he left.

I tried to sit up to call him back, but my right arm and shoulder weren't working.

"Maggie? Can you hear me?"

It was Lionel's voice. I looked to my other side and there he was, balanced on his crutches.

"Hi there," another voice said. It was a little weak and croaky, but I recognized it as mine.

"Can you hear me?"

I nodded.

"What did I just say?"

"You asked if I could hear you. Of course I can hear you."

"Wonderful. Your ears are working again," said U.G. from the foot of my bed. He was holding two roses, yellow, wrapped in foil.

"What's that supposed to mean?"

"You were deaf as a doornail," said Lionel.

"You're thinking of dead as a doornail."

"Well, we're certainly glad you're not that."

"Why can't I move my right arm?" And then I saw. "Oh, it's bandaged."

"You've been shot, darling," U.G. said.

I strained to remember. "I tried to scream. Did I scream?"

"Loud and clear," said Lionel.

"Nothing came out."

"There was something wrong with the air bag in that stupid car of yours and it deployed with the mother of all explosions. That's what temporarily deafened you."

"It's not a stupid car."

"No matter," said U.G. "The front end's all stove in and the back end's no better, and you'll be getting a new one."

It was all too much for me to compute. I let it go and closed my eyes.

"And don't worry, I'm fine," Lionel said.

"What?" My eyes flew open again.

"Just in case you were wondering."

More and more pieces of memory were fitting into the jigsaw puzzle.

"Your leg," I said. "You were trapped in the car."

"Thank you."

"How long have I been, you know, not with it?"

"Only a few hours this time," U.G. said. "You're definitely improving."

"Maybe the next time she's taken to Emergency she'll only be in a coma for a measly five minutes," said Lionel.

"I thought I saw Jack Nicholson with a golf club. I must have been hallucinating."

"No way," Lionel said. "That was Nicholson's driveway and that was his call box you screamed into."

"It really was Jack Nicholson?"

"You betcha. He and his security guys were running to save you, but you'd already creamed Althea."

"Oh, no! That was not the way I planned to meet him. What must he think of me?"

"See that huge teddy bear sitting on the windowsill?" U.G. said.

I peered around, painfully. In between two vases of yellow roses, there was a large, brown teddy bear seated on the windowsill, holding a miniature putter in one paw. I had to laugh. Everything Nicholson does is pure Jack.

"And all the flowers?"

Lionel said, "One vase of yellow roses is from Fowler Mohr. The other vase of yellow roses is from Griffin Grace. The ostentatious arrangement of yellow roses on the table is from Heinrich."

I didn't bother correcting him. I was thinking the florists must have had a run on yellow roses.

"Did the police ever get there?"

"Who? Oh, if you mean Joe—" Lionel said.

"Of course she means Joe," said U.G. "He and Martin and a couple of West L.A. squad cars came in for the cleanup. You missed all the fun."

"Then it was Althea all the time." I half sat up, then fell back again, the effort a little too much. My head was beginning to ache. "Something in that French book was worth killing over."

"*Très bien, cherie.*" Lionel took a wet washrag from the basin on the table and placed it over my forehead. Its coolness felt good.

I said, "What was it? Something to do with Bark, I guess."

"Right on the nose. Bark lifted that Laughing Man story wholesale and turned it into a screenplay and then a play and then a musical. His entire career was based on a plagiarized book."

I was starting to feel a little drowsy. "And Roger and Samantha knew about the plagiarism?"

"More than knew. Roger came across a copy of the book and was blackmailing Bark. Althea killed him. And with Roger out of the picture, foolish Samantha picked up on it and tried some blackmail of her own. Althea again stepped in to protect the only things she cared about. Bark's career and her very posh lifestyle."

"My Maggie was next on her list," U.G. said.

"Of course," said Lionel. "It must have been Althea who broke into our house and got her hands on the testing kit."

"But how did she arrange for the meet with Maggie?"

"The Internet," said Lionel. "Althea was posing as the translator. When she visited Maggie in the hospital, she must have overheard the suggestion that Maggie go to a French chat room. I tried to tell your daughter that people on the Web are not what they appear to be, but she wouldn't listen. Surprise. Surprise."

U.G. nodded. "That's okay. She doesn't listen to me either."

The orderly came back into the room. "Time for our pill," he said.

"Not yet, just a sec." There was still something I had to know. "Dad, what was in that cylinder? What happened to Althea?"

"Remember I told you not to get it wet? When those gasses get wet, they release a tremendous wave of heat. That's what happened to Althea."

The orderly said, "The pill?"

"One more sec. Dad, is she . . ."

"Unfortunately not. She's in a room down the hall, with a police guard in front."

"And I've got you and your invention to thank for saving my Maggie," Lionel said. "U.G., I love you!"

And he proceeded to plant a big fat juicy kiss on U.G.'s mouth.

"Wow," said the orderly.

"Purely platonic," U.G. said. He thrust the two foil-wrapped roses in my hand and rushed out of the room, rubbing away at his lips.

I put U.G.'s roses on my bed table and took the pill and waited for the fog to roll in.

"Before you nod off," Lionel said, "here's an appetizing little tidbit. Gleaned from my New York contacts. Three guesses."

"Lionel . . ."

"Okay, you're probably not up to counting to three, anyway. Remember Noelle Sears' mysterious disappearance when nobody had an inkling where she was?"

"She was in Los Angeles all the time?"

"Close, but no cigar, as Clinton told his other paramours. Noelle was in Ojai at a fat farm. And here's the most delicious part. She was kicked out for gaining weight! She was considered a bad influence on the other people there."

No doubt about it. That made my day.

"I think I've got my article now, Lionel. Could you please bring me my . . . you know, my . . ."

I was thinking "my laptop . . ." but I couldn't get it out.

I must have fallen asleep on the words, because when I stirred again and opened my eyes, Joe was perched on the end of my bed holding a bouquet of yellow roses, also wrapped in foil.

"Baby," he said, "you scared the hell out of me."

I put my fingers up to my ears and shook my head from side to side, pretending that I was still deafened.

"Don't give me that. You can hear me."

I shook my head some more.

"I ran into Lionel outside. He told me your hearing was back to normal."

Lionel always had to blab everything!

I shook my head and indicated my ears. "You'll have to talk louder. I can't hear you anymore. I must be having a relapse."

He looked at me, somewhat suspiciously, but raised his voice a little.

"I knew that when you left the deli, that's when you'd be most at risk. Martin and I drove Beverly Glen from Pico north scouring the area for a deli."

I liked that. The picture of them covering the Glen looking for me.

"Finally we found it and you had already left. At Mulholland, we turned right figuring you'd gone that way towards home. Soon as we saw the car wreck, we called for backup and the troops arrived."

"The what? The snoops?"

"Troops! You know! The cops." He made a loud wailing noise like a police siren.

A nurse stuck her head in. Joe waved her off.

"Here. I brought you these flowers. Maybe the nurse can put them in a vase."

He laid the yellow roses on the bedside table next to U.G.'s yellow roses. I glanced at what he and U.G. had brought, both offerings wrapped in foil and not the usual green florist tissue, and something prompted me to glance at the table near the window. The arrangement Henrik had sent me was now reduced to just baby's breath and lemon leaves. Gone were the yellow roses. Well, not exactly gone. . . .

How like them! U.G. and Joe, soul mates in chicanery.

"To be continued," Joe said. "You go back to sleep and get some rest."

He leaned over and kissed me on the lips. I tried not to betray any reaction to that. I'm not sure I succeeded.

As he neared the door, he said, softly, "See you in the morning."

"I'll be here," I said.

Oops.

Joe fixed me with a knowing glance, waved, and was gone.

I smiled, then closed my eyes and drifted off. There was so much I had to think about. . . .

Not just Althea and Bark . . .

But the article I was going to write for *Vanity Fair* . . .

And my screenplay I could once more turn my attention to and finish. . . .

I wondered what was going on between Joe and me. . . .

I wondered what were my true feelings about Henrik, and how he fit into my future . . . how they both fit into my future.

I even entertained myself with the farfetched notion that perhaps Althea would ask Henrik to defend her. . . .

"Wouldn't that frost your ass," said Mercedes Pell.

Turn the page for a preview of

a few good Murders

(0-7653-1365-0)

by cady kalian

• • •

Available in August 2007 from Forge

1

Carpe diem.

Seize the Day.

Whoever first said that back in ancient Rome would certainly never have *carped* this *diem*. If one could have gotten out of bed in the morning and known what this particular Monday held in store, and the murders it would later lead to, one would never have—

Okay, enough with the impersonal "one." It's the personal me I'm talking about. Me. Maggie Mars. Transplanted New Yorker. Former investigative reporter. And current screenwriter for however long it lasts.

I would have stayed in bed, cowering under the covers, and never would have washed my face, brushed my hair, put on my lip gloss, and driven to the Malibu set where they were shooting my movie.

My movie. *Murder Becomes Her*. Written by Maggie Mars. "Written by Maggie Mars . . ." The most beautiful four words in the English language. Until murder became a reality off-screen as well as on.

As it was, all unknowing, I backed my studio-loaned car out of the garage and thought again of how nice it would be to have a limo come by and pick me up. But executive transportation isn't for writers. Directors maybe, producers probably, and, of course, stars. Stars like Allegra Cort, who had been cast in the role of my heroine, Mercedes Pell.

"Blecccch," said Mercedes Pell.

" 'Blecccch'? What's that supposed to mean?"

"It's a euphemism for 'what a bitch'!"

Well, that's Mercedes for you. My alter ego. The free spirit who says all the stuff I think of but can never get past my Politically Correct lips.

"What dumbass was responsible for having her play me?" Mercedes said. "She doesn't look like me at all. She's got two whole cup sizes to go!"

Now that wasn't exactly true, but I didn't say so aloud. There's only so much talking to myself I can do in Los Angeles traffic.

Besides, whether Allegra Cort looked like Mercedes was not the issue. At least not with me. From the first day we met in Fowler Mohr's office, Allegra and I were not on the same page. Hell, we weren't even on the same planet.

"I love the script," she said to me. "I positively adore the script," she said to Fowler, who beamed. That was sweet music to any producer's ears, as well as to the writer who wrote it.

"I can hardly wait," she then said, "until I can give Maggie my ideas for rewrites."

Which she did. Starting on Page One. Every day she asked for more changes in her lines, which meant more rewrites, and sometimes whole new scenes. At first I sought a Rodney King why-can't-we-all-get-along approach.

"Why not first try the lines as written," I said.

Even the director was in favor of that. "Sounds like a plan," Buzz Harding said. "We can always change them later."

"Not later, now," Allegra said. "It's just not happening for me. F'rinstance . . ."

Allegra Cort could f'rinstance you to death. She'd riffle through the script pages, and tap a glossily enameled fingernail on one or more lines of dialogue.

Last Friday the line was in the jail scene. " 'I've got this dickhead detective torn between trying to get in my pants and arresting me . . .' " she said, reading. And then, looking up, " 'Dickhead detective . . .' I would never say that kind of language."

"You're not saying that," I said. "Mercedes is."

That was my failing. I was being reasonable.

"There's your trouble, right there," Allegra said. "Mercedes needs to be a little more feminine . . . a little more Scarlett O'Hara . . ."

"Well, fiddle-dee-dee," said Mercedes. "That friggin' feminine enough for you?"

"Allegra," I said. "You don't want to soften Mercedes' character. Her attitude is what makes her so special and different. It sets her apart from your usual run-of-the-screen heroines. Reese, Keira, Charlize—"

She cut me off with a dismissive wave. "Spare me the laundry list." A dramatic pause, and then, "I'll think about it," she said.

Blecccch, I thought.

And, as usual, she swept off to her trailer dressing room, trailed by her pallid mouse of an assistant, Lisa Lindsey, and didn't reappear for hours. Production ground to a halt. Cast and crew sat around, waiting, earning good Minimum Basic Agreement wages for not doing anything.

"For God's sake, Maggie," Buzz Harding said. "Help me out here."

"But the lines are okay as they are. You said so."

"They're just words. It's not neurosurgery."

"Brain surgery," I said.

"Whatever. They're not carved in cement."

And Buzz was on *my* side. At least that's what he claimed when he took me out to dinner at Doug Arango's. The first of several evening meetings—I guess you could call them dates—during pre-production. Buzz and I were both members of the Creative Artists Union—the one known as CAU—and our friendship had risen several notches above the traditional writer-director antipathy. Nothing, of course, for Joe Camanetti to feel alarmed about. But then, who knows with Joe.

That's the price I pay for being in a relationship with a detective. Ever since we had picked up on the West Coast where we had left off on the East Coast, Joe had been more adept than ever at playing Good Lover, Bad Lover.

My own producer, Fowler Mohr, who had attempted to nurse me through every comma, colon, and question mark of the script, came down on Allegra's side.

"A little bit of honey goes a long way," he said.

"I may barf," said Mercedes.

Me, too, but I was the one who had to knock on Allegra's dressing room door and agree to make a few changes. The latest of many changes, with no end in sight and a writer slowly being driven mad. Little did I know I wasn't the only one being driven mad . . . There was someone who would act on it.